Aramaya

Other Avon Eos Books by
Jane Routley

FIRE ANGELS
MAGE HEART

Aramaya

JANE ROUTLEY

AVON · EOS

AVON BOOKS, INC.
1350 Avenue of the Americas
New York, New York 10019

Copyright © 1999 by B. J. Routley
Cover art by Donato
Published by arrangement with the author
Library of Congress Catalog Card Number: 99-94757
ISBN: 0-380-79428-4
www.avonbooks.com/eos

First Avon Eos Trade Printing: June 1999

AVON EOS TRADEMARK REG. U.S. PAT. OFF. AND IN OTHER COUNTRIES, MARCA REGISTRADA, HECHO EN U.S.A.

Printed in the U.S.A.

OPM 10 9 8 7 6 5 4 3 2 1

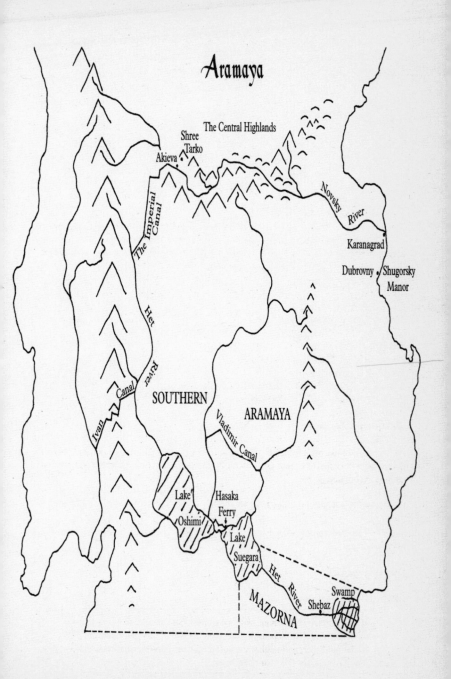

Aramaya

IN A COUPLE of days we would be in Aramaya. I leaned against the rail of the ship looking down into the dark grey sea. I should have been excited about seeing the center of the world, but instead my mood matched the color of the water.

"Thinking of Ruinac again?" asked Kitten, appearing at the rail by my side. She put her arm around my shoulders.

I smiled ruefully at her.

"For once no," I said. "I was thinking of my mother. She took the attitude that men were a temporary part of a woman's life. Once upon a time I thought she was mistaken. I really thought Shad and I would last forever."

My mother, my effortlessly fertile mother, would also have said it was children who were your lasting joy, but I was not going down that path yet again.

"Perhaps she was right, perhaps not," said Kitten squeezing me. "But even if men are temporary, friendship lasts. When we get home to Ishtak, perhaps you will come and live near me. We shall have a lot of fun together."

There was a shout from the foredeck.

"Come on. We need to get below," said Kitten pulling me away from the rail.

3

I looked up at the sky. A huge bank of black clouds was rolling over the horizon. That had come up quickly. No wonder the sea was so dark.

I groaned. By now I well and truly regretted pushing the others into shipping for Aramaya at this time of year. I had wanted to end my inactivity onshore but I had merely exchanged it for the inactivity of shipboard life with the "delightful" extra ingredient of seasickness.

They don't call it Storm Season for nothing," said Kitten. "The captain wants us battened down below decks as usual. Come on."

The two of us shared a little dark cabin on the upper deck. It was small but luxurious compared with the cramped communal room the other ten passengers shared. A communal room is less than pleasant when everyone is seasick during a storm. After the first storm I, in my role as healer, had distributed little magic pills to cure seasickness, but my supply of these pills had run out several days ago due to the sheer number of storms we had gone through since we had left Ishtak.

Our ship, the *Eagle,* was the last ship to risk the thirty-day journey across the Western Ocean to Aramaya before the two-month-long Storm Season made the crossing impossible. Now I could see why. The captain told us that this was a particularly rough year, but he always saw plenty of early storms on this crossing.

So, while Kitten and I dreaded yet more nauseating, lurching hours spent below deck, we did not feel any special anxiety. We had learned early that it was pointless to leave a candle lit, so we lay on our bunks in the dark talking—in Aramayan to give me practice—until the howling of the wind and the crashing of waves made it impossible to hear each other. Then we lay alone in the darkness with our thoughts.

I tried to think about Dally and what sort of actions I would take when I reached the coast of Aramaya, but as usual I thought of Shad. I remembered the last time I had seen him. We had been fighting as usual. I was furious at him about something. I can't remember what exactly. I think it was just everything. Anyway to punish him I had suddenly refused to go to the yearly Gathering in Ernundra.

When I saw how much my refusal hurt him I felt horrible and guilty and this just made me more angry. How could he make me go? The Klementari were not my people but his and now every one of them would know that I was barren, because Edaine would have told them and they would all know my failure and they would look at me with humiliating pity.

How could he put me through that, I shouted. He was supposed to love me, but I hadn't seen much love lately.

"You know they won't care about that," he said trying to sound reasonable but not really succeeding. "Please Dion, won't you do it for me? You know how much it means to me."

"Well then go without me," I said, wanting him to beg, wanting him to suffer as I had suffered.

He was silent for a moment.

"If you would not mind it, I will," he said. His voice sounded tentative, nervous. Why? What was he nervous about? Was he guilty? He wanted to go without me, didn't he? I knew it! I had known it all along. He wanted to be rid of me. Who could blame him? Edaine would take him gladly. Maybe he wanted me out of the way so he could go to her. She'd be able to give him children. My heart felt like it had turned to a stone fist.

"You do that," I said bitterly

"You do mind, don't you?" he said.

"Why should I care? Do what you want. I don't give a damn."

"Dion, I really need to go. The Gathering gives me so much strength and it's been a hard year. For both of us, I know. Please. Stay home if you want, but don't ask me not to go."

He was planning to leave me. I could tell. I had known this would happen. I had known he would leave me from the moment I had lost his child. The inevitability was like a grim march to execution.

"Oh Dion," he said softly. He came up behind me and touched my shoulder. "Don't be like this. I'm sorry. I'm sorry we fight so much. Sometimes I wonder. . . . Maybe it's better I go alone. Time apart. It might cool things down between us."

He *was* going to leave me. Anger stormed into my head. A violent red mist clouded my eyes. How I hated him in that moment. I wanted to break him. I spun round and slapped him hard across the face.

"Get out," I screamed at him. "Get out. Go get yourself a nice new wife, damn you."

He staggered back clutching his cheek.

"I hate you," I shouted. "I never want to see you again. Go on. Go to your Gathering. And go to hell." I picked up a china jug and threw it at him.

His face set into bitter lines.

"Damn you," he shouted. "If that's what you want then I will go."

He stormed from the room, leaving me to kick the furniture and weep enraged tears. I did not stop till I heard his horse outside, trotting away down the road. At that sound I was suddenly overwhelmed with terrible shame and sorrow. I knew I had treated him badly. I ran to the window and shouted his name once, twice. He didn't even slow. Probably he couldn't hear me. After two calls, my pride came back. Accursed pride. Damn him! Let him go! Let him do his worst! I didn't care anymore.

I dried my eyes, went back to my tasks and swallowed my disappointment, for I had wanted to go to the Gathering. The Klemantari in their green homeland were kind and wise and talking with my old friends and participating in the rituals of the Gathering brought me tremendous peace.

I missed Shad from the very first night but I began to see that he had been right. Time apart made me think of him more kindly than I had done for a long time. It was unreasonable for me to blame him for our childlessness. We did not know it was his fault. I knew I had acted badly to him. I had the uneasy feeling that I had gone too far this time and maybe really hurt him.

But I never, never expected him to actually leave me. I never expected that just a few days later, a messenger would come bearing his wedding ring—an act which constituted a request for divorce under Klementari law—and a short, terse letter confirming this.

That moment when I first read that letter. . . . Why must the mind grind over old wounds like that? Though I screwed up my eyes against the pain still the tears leaked out.

Suddenly the ship pitched violently sideways. I found myself, sprawled against the cabin wall clinging to the sloping bunk, all memory forgotten, trying to stop the mattress from falling on top of me. There was a thudding crump of water hitting the deck above us. For a moment it seemed as if the ship was going topple over and then it gave an almighty lurch the opposite way that threw me onto the other side of my bunk and had me scrabbling not to be thrown to the floor. There was another crashing thud of water on the roof and the ship lurched and pitched again. The timbers around us creaked and groaned with effort. There was water running down the side of the cabin. My God, when had the storm got this violent!

Quickly I brought a magelight to mind. Dazzling white light filled the cabin. The floor was covered in inky black water, a miniature sea with waves that splashed around to the violent lurching of the ship.

In that moment as I began to use my power, I was suddenly horribly aware of another power all around us, the power of the sea smashing at the tiny ship—a monstrous power, cold, dark, and very, very deep. Frightened, I pressed my hand against the wall of the cabin and pushed a spell of binding into it and down into the timbers of the ship.

"I'd best see if I can go and help," I cried, sliding gingerly off my bunk and into that inky water. It was ankle deep. When I'd signed on for the journey, I'd signed on using my old name, Dion Michaeline, healer. I did not want to travel as Dion Holyhands, Lady of Ruinac. It was too much baggage for what I hoped would be a discreet journey. Had the ship's crew known who I really was, they might well have already asked me to help them. I knew nothing about the sea and ships, but I knew all about the use of magic as a brute force. I had fought demons.

Kitten shouted something back at me as she jumped down beside me. Together we heaved open the door.

Captain Simonetti, Kitten's servant, was out in the corridor of the ship, hanging onto swaying walls as he came splashing and slipping down the corridor toward us. His wife Suza clutched the frame of their cabin door looking uncharacteristically anxious. In the brief lull between the crashing waves I could hear others in the communal cabins, crying, praying, and being sick. The last made me glad I was a mage and could at least keep my dinner down. Suddenly it seemed stupid for a mage to be walking in water like this. I waved my hand and spoke the words and the water streamed out from under the cabin doorways, back up the corridor and out through the cracks in the hatchway. Kitten turned and gave me a sign of approval.

Just then the ship rolled and dumped all three of us on the floor. There was a roar and a thump and water gushed through the gaps in the hatchway again, soaking us as we struggled to our feet.

Suza Simonetti helped Kitten and me get up and together the four of us staggered to the hatchway. The force of the waves had cracked it. Drenched by the streams of water that flowed through the crack, the four of us pushed the heavy cover open. In a moment Kitten and I were out on the lurching, bucking deck.

The deck was covered in torn rigging and broken spars. The sky above was black with thunderous clouds. It was almost as dark as night. Sheets of rain swept into our eyes, driven by the savage wind. Huge waves rose above us. It was as if the ship was flinging itself over mountains. I clung to a nearby rail while Kitten leaned unsteadily over the hatchway, shouting at the Simonettis to stay below. Using magic I pushed the hatch cover shut over them.

Suddenly, a huge black mass of water rose up and up over the side of the boat. Screaming, I snatched Kitten round the waist and flung the two of us against the mast, binding us to it in a panic of strong magic. There was an awful moment as we stared up at the huge wave and then the force of the water came crashing down on us like a blow. Water, water, endless rushing water. I clung to Kitten and the mast and still there was a heavy blanket of rushing water pushing the air out of my lungs. Even through the calming power of magic it was like being buried alive. The mast was shuddering under me. My lungs were bursting. I fought upward through the tons of water.

Then suddenly it was gone and there was air. Gasping I let go of the magical binding and simply clung to the mast like a bit of discarded seaweed. I must get Kitten below where it was safe. But Kitten was already away gripping the ship's rail, slipping and staggering down the heaving, watery deck with surprising speed. I set off after her as fast as I could, leaning into the roaring wind and stumbling over the rubbish on the deck, but by the time I reached her, we were already at the stairs that led up to the bridge.

"Get below!" I shouted, gesturing as best I could without releasing the rail. She either couldn't or wouldn't make out what I was saying and even as we shouted hopelessly at one another in the inferno of roaring wind, another wave broke over the deck covering us waist deep in powerfully dragging black water.

I contented myself with hanging onto Kitten and keeping her magically warm. Together we crawled up the stairs.

The wheel of the *Eagle* was on the open deck, but wardings surrounded it, designed to protect the helmsman from the fury of such storms. The force of the waves must have been too strong for them this time, for there was the nerve-jangling feeling of broken magic everywhere. Two sailors and the cabin boy were streaming with water as they struggled with the wheel. A fourth was tied by his waist to the mast behind, drooping with unconsciousness or death, blood running down his face. I staggered over to him, letting magic hold me to the deck. It was the captain, unconscious from a blow to the head. He was terribly cold. I stopped the bleeding in his head and set a spell to warm him.

Behind me Kitten was shouting furiously at one of the

struggling sailors who was obviously refusing something, probably our help. I could help them despite themselves. There was no way I could replace the wardings under these conditions, but clinging to the mast I muttered the spells to build a warm bubble of protection around us. Suddenly it was almost as if we were in an invisible cabin. Rain and wind battered against empty air as if it was a roof and the noise of the storm was shut out.

" . . . the Demonslayer of Gallia, you stupid man," Kitten shouted in the sudden quiet.

He wasn't listening.

"Look out!" he screamed, pulling Kitten against him. A huge wall of tumbling white foam was charging down the ship toward us. It smashed itself like a rock into the protection spell. The spell held, but I felt the waves' force like a winding blow to the chest—felt too the weight of the water on the ship's deck pushing it down.

"Away! Away!" I cried to the wild waters. Using all the force I could I threw myself on the deck and pushed my being into the ship's straining, creaking, almost breaking timbers, willing the ship to lift its head, willing it to pull itself over the next wave. Up and up. I was the ship, feeling the poetry of its beautifully crafted timbers—feeling those timbers screaming and cracking under the pounding water. I made myself light—felt myself rising and suddenly I was at the top of the wave in the screaming wind and below was a huge glassy sided black drop. I felt the ship begin to topple. I turned us, righted us, and held us back as we went sliding down that incredible watery slope, the sound of sailors' voices screaming in our ears.

And then another monstrous mound of water loomed above us cutting out all light and leaning over to fall down upon us again.

Oh, the power of the sea! It was too mighty for even the remotest chance of stilling the storm. I had never felt anything as powerful, not even when I had fought Bedazzer the demon back when I was seventeen. The sea wasn't hungry or even angry. It was just raw, mindless power thundering out of control, smashing and smashing. The ship and I were a tiny wooden cocoon that struggled on and on, dragging ourselves up through each terrifying wave and sliding down each vertiginous drop, teeth clenched, muscles and timbers straining in the pound, pound, pounding of the waves. Magic is power singing in your veins, but here it was merely a whimper trying to keep the ship and me from foundering under the weight of the mighty waters. Through that endless weary time we managed to ride the waves, but sometimes that was impossible and then with a teeth clenching effort of will we managed to stay afloat in an act akin to swimming.

The world had changed from black to grey.

"Dion! Dion!" Kitten was kneeling beside me shaking me. As I looked up, startled to see her, she cried "Praise Aumaz!" and hugged me.

What was I doing here lying on the wheel deck? My arms and legs were buried in the wood. They were wood. I had become one with the ship and fought the waves with it. For how long?

Slowly I pulled myself out of the deck. Coming back hurt. The numbness in my limbs changed unpleasantly to pins and needles. I was sopping wet. I ached all over as if it was I who had been battered by the waves. As in fact I had been. I rubbed my eyes and looked around. Little squalls of rain were still splattering against the protection barrier, but the sky had lightened from thunderous black to heavy grey. Though the waves were still big they no longer threatened to swamp the ship. Through my changing hands I could feel that the ship no longer needed holding together. Somehow even though I had been wood I had retained enough of my own mind to know that it was time to change back to my original form.

It could be dangerous to change shape thoughtlessly. Once I had lost consciousness in the shape of a stone and if it had not been for the voice of someone I loved calling me back, I might still be a stone.

It had been Shad's voice that had called me back then. God and Angels, all my thoughts still led back to him.

"My lady," said the cabin boy. He was offering me a

steaming cup. I took it and put my cold hands gratefully around it. It was water and rum. The water was brackish and the rum was rough medicinal stuff, but it was blessedly hot. I felt as cold and damp as waterlogged wood.

"Thank you my lady," said the boy, blushing and bobbing. He scurried away quickly.

"What was that for?" I said.

"You silly thing, you just saved all our skins," cried Kitten "Those waves. . . . My God we would certainly have sunk without you."

Had I been fighting for all our lives or simply instinctively for my own? So often in this last month I had wondered if there was anything still worth living for. Yet it seemed that part of me wanted to live despite that.

Even though the deck was still heaving in the big waves, there were sailors moving about. They were cutting ruined rigging from the masts and hauling up a couple of sails. They had opened the hatchways too, and the green-faced passengers were poking their heads out, risking the frequent rain squalls for the sake of some air. Suza Simonetti waved at us. Twilight was falling over a metal-grey world. The ship rocked over the waves like a galloping horse.

The rain battered against my protection barrier and ran down it as if it were glass. We were nice and warm behind it with the brazier and our hot rum drinks. Everyone's clothes began to steam.

"My God, that was one hell of an experience," said Kitten, walking up and down the deck with remarkable steadiness. "Like riding a horse, only much bigger. Coming down those huge waves. It would have been great if I hadn't been so scared."

The man at the wheel rolled his eyes, but good humoredly. He did not seem the least worried that Kitten had earlier called him a stupid man. The cabin boy and the other sailor looked at Kitten with frank admiration. Who could blame them? Her blue eyes glowed with vitality and her fine skin was luminous in that grey light. Her hair, disheveled by the sea, fell in a charming golden tangle around her face. She had once been the most famous courtesan on the Oesteradd

Peninsula and the Duke of Gallia's favorite mistress. Now she was simply a beautiful and wealthy actress returning to her homeland of Aramaya. Past glories did not hang heavy upon her. Unlike me, she had too much zest for life to regret yesterday.

"Land ho," shouted a voice from above.

"By Aumaz's mighty finger, it'll be the coast of Aramaya," exclaimed the man at the wheel whom I had discovered was the first mate. "We must be very close to see it in this weather. Two days early. This wind has been a kind of blessing. It's blowed us ahead of ourselves."

"So when will we make port, Mr. Mate?" asked Kitten.

"I don't rightly know ma'am. It's possible we've been blown off course. We're likely something south of Karana-grad now.

"The capt'n'd know," said the other sailor regretfully. "He's the man what knows this coastline—the rest of us only bin on this route once before. Best we find a sheltered place to heave to for the night and in the morning we can go ashore and ask."

"Light," shouted a voice from above. "I can see lights."

"Get the chart, Gianni," shouted the first mate.

Shortly afterward even we could see two little lights shining through the gathering dusk. The shore was quite close. I could see a hint of cliffs in the darkness.

The cabin boy returned with a parchment chart and the first and second mates pored over it.

"This light'll be some warning of rocks, maybe these here Ursus rocks," explained the mate. "What we are doing is heading so that we get the lights lined up and then we know we're past them. But what we really need is somewhere quiet to drop anchor. Maybe . . ."

Suddenly there was a sickening tearing crash and the whole ship shuddered, tipped over on its side, and stopped moving. I fell onto the deck and lay there momentarily winded. I could feel the ship's timbers shuddering and tearing under me, hear them screaming as the next wave pushed us forward.

Feet pounded on the deck. "Rocks! Reef!" shouted voices all around. "Lower the boats."

Summoning magic I pushed myself back down into the ship and suddenly knew the rocks that were tearing into its belly and the pressure of the waves that were grinding it further and further onto the jagged shelf. There was a craggy lump of rock embedded in its side timbers. It was the only thing preventing the water from rushing in. I pushed a protection barrier over the hole, letting myself flow through the timbers. There were no more holes yet, but the waves were powerful and they were pushing us slowly forward and grinding the sharp rocks further and further along the side of the ship. I must lift it off the rock and get it somewhere safe. But where? It was so dark. Another wave foamed over the rock shelf around us and the ship shuddered forward again. Timbers ripped open against another jagged lump of rock.

Could I lift the ship? Could I carry it far enough? I could see nothing but rocks all around. I lit a light and suddenly the whole world was illuminated in a blinding white light. I strained magically to see. . . . I could see white water, surf, a shore, a beach, people on the beach.

Could I bring it there? Would it be safe? I had to try. I could feel the rhythm of the waves pounding over the rocks, could feel the next one coming. I held the ship steady and then as the wave broke, I lifted. I felt the strain of carrying it for a moment and then suddenly the wave took hold of us and we shot forward and were off the rocks and lumbering through the shallow water. I let it go, feeling relief from the strain but I held the protection over the hole in its side.

The ship moved forward evenly with the waves and wind for a few minutes. Then it came to another shuddering halt. Sand this time. I gave a push of power and the ship and I, battered by the power of the thundering waves, dragged ourselves slowly up onto the sandy beach until at last the surf was no more than breakers lapping round our bows.

At last I relaxed and slid out of the ship. I found myself lying face down on the sand before it, my stomach feeling as if it had been scraped raw. I rolled over and rubbed it, briefly deafened by the water in my ears. Behind me the *Eagle* was a dark bulk leaning heavily to one side.

Bang! A sudden blast of magic burst against the side of the ship. I felt a sudden horrible frisson of necromancy and struggled to my feet as fast as I could, bringing magical defenses to mind. My eyes were dazzled by fire and flares of white light. Magelight! Sweet Tanza! People were everywhere, shouting and fighting. Two men rushed at me. The leading one held a sword ready to strike.

"No!" I shouted. I threw out a heavy blow of magic at them which sent several people hurtling through the air in a blast of sand and power. There was a screech and a crackle of light as my power hit other power. Strong other power. One of the hurtling figures stopped in midair, turned itself upright and dropped softly to its knees on the sand. As he hit the ground his defenses were already up. I could feel them. Power like a great rock. Oh, God, I thought. Another mage, a strong one. Using his own magic, not necromancy. I was tired. Could I hold out against him long enough?

Kitten was at my side and Simonetti too, with a drawn sword. There were sailors with drawn cutlasses everywhere and more of them were clambering down ropes from the ship. Beyond the light and the huge fire burning nearby, people were fighting but no one was attacking us. It amazed me.

The mage had gone, but I could sense him out there in the darkness. He was calling to others. He was knocking someone over. He was fending off a blow. I felt the great strength of the power he was using to let himself see in the dark and was glad that, for the moment at least, it was not turned against me. As we huddled in a silent group, ready to fight, blasts of magic illuminated struggling bodies. There were other mages out there, not so strong as the first but many of them. Most of them were not using necromancy, but we couldn't be sure that meant they were benign.

"What's happened?" I said.

"Wreckers," said Kitten. "It was a false signal. They lured us onto that reef so we might be wrecked and our cargo taken."

And at least one of them had been using necromancy, although I could feel no sign of it now. At that moment there was a final blast of power and then a momentary silence.

Suddenly white magelight flared over the beach. A group of five, no, six mages stood in formation. They wore long black robes. They stood simply, hands at their sides. Bodies were sprawled all around them and a couple of bound figures knelt before them. I could feel the presence of other mages beyond the circle of light and even see a dark robed figure in the shadows tying something around the wrists of a prone body. The strong mage, however, had to be the tall, dark-skinned man standing in the center of the formation. He was the one making the magelight. Almost as if acknowledging my recognition, he bowed his head politely in my direction and spoke in passable Ishtaki, the dialect of the city we had sailed from on the Peninsula.

"Ladies and Gentlemen. I welcome you to Aramaya and apologize for your noisy reception and the unfortunate damage to your ship. We have now subdued the wreckers and may proceed upon a more civilized level. I am Prince Nikoli Terzu of the Third Regiment of the Imperial Demon Hunters. At your service."

I WOKE UP. It was dark. I was lying on the ground wrapped in a blanket near a big fire. The air smelled of sea salt; in the sky above me ragged dark clouds blew across a full moon. It took a moment or two for me to work out where I was.

The beach. The mages.

The moment I had introduced myself as Dion Holyhands they had known who I was. They never for a moment questioned that I was telling the truth. But then Prince Terzu had had a taste of my power when I had flung him and one of the wreckers back across the beach.

"The Demonslayer of Gallia," the prince had said, bowing comprehensively. "This is an immense honor." Though his words were overly fulsome, he seemed quite serious.

There had been a kind of fluttering among his companions that had made me look at them more closely, and I saw then that they were not mages or at least not grown-up mages but all young men in their teens.

I smiled as I lay there by the fire now, thinking of them and the enthusiastic way they had gathered around me, wanting to shake my hand and ask me about Ruinac and the demons I had fought. Fine young lads despite the occasional spotty face and sweaty palm. Apart from the servants who awaited the party on the clifftop and welcomed us mariners with blankets and warm drinks, the only other member of the prince's party over twenty was his nephew Count Alexi Ivanka.

It seemed we had suddenly become part of a school excursion. Every summer Prince Terzu retired from the capital Akieva to his estates on this coast and it was his habit to invite young mages from his and allied families to come and train with him. Looking for necromancy in the Bowl of Seeing was an obvious part of that training. It was while doing this that they spotted our ship out at sea.

"Your progress over the ocean held us enthralled all afternoon," said Prince Terzu in his cool languid way. "When we saw how close you were coming we set out immediately to greet you. With most felicitous results I am glad to say, since it gave us the opportunity to be of service to you."

I suspected there was more to his story than that, but I did not press him. I doubted their discovery of the wreckers was just good fortune. And his original intentions toward me could well have been less hospitable. A powerful mage heading for your coastline at great speed is not always a blessing. A conscientious public official like a demon hunter might well find it necessary to investigate and even stop such a journey.

As I lay there drowsily in the firelight, I could hear considerable movement away to my left.

"What's going on?" I mumbled at Kitten, who was crouching nearby staring into the fire.

"Oh, hello. Welcome back to the land of the living."

I sat up and rubbed the sleep out of my eyes. Although my magic had not been exhausted, the struggle with the sea had left me physically tired and I had fallen into a deep sleep the moment I had lain down by the fire.

"What time is it?"

"It's after midnight, but dawn is still a way off. You can lie there for a bit longer. The prince has sent for carts to take us to his estate, but they haven't arrived yet."

"So what's all the noise?"

"The mages are getting ready to go off and find this necromancer."

I was suddenly wide awake.

"Necromancer? They didn't say anything about a necromancer."

"Apparently the wreckers are the henchmen of a necromancer who lives further up the coast. It was he who gave them the necromantic power they were using. Now that they've arrested the wreckers, the mages are worried that their master will be warned and escape before reinforcements can come. Count Alexi and Prince Nikoli have been arguing about it for some time, but it seems they have now decided to go."

"Go! Take on a necromancer with just a pack of boys! What does the prince say?"

"Seems to me he is very reluctant to go, but would you let a necromancer slip through your fingers?"

Mages hated necromancy. Necromancers were rogue mages who used the pain and death of other beings to cement their pacts with demons and thus fuel their spells. The most powerful fodder for such magic was, of course, the life force of humans. It was a cruel, violent magic, and naturally most ordinary mages were dedicated to wiping it out. But to take on a necromancer with inexperienced boys. . . . That was terribly dangerous!

"Kitten, do you think the prince would be offended if I offered him my help?"

She grinned wryly. "I think he would be very relieved. In Aramaya it is considered ill-bred to trouble a sleeping guest, but his party has been taking a long time to get ready and making a remarkable amount of noise in doing so. I've been wondering if I should be helpful and wake you myself."

I stood up, brushed myself off and peered round in the darkness. It was hard to make out the shapes after the brightness of the fire.

"So where is he?"

"Come, I'll take you to him."

She gathered a blanket around her shoulders and moved

off easily with her usual quick, sure movements. I stumbled over the tussocks of grass after her, past the bound and guarded wreckers who sat or lay in a huddle near the fire. The staff that had stored the necromantic power they had used on the beach had already been burnt in the fire. Had we been a party of ordinary mariners, the staff and the brute force of the wreckers would have overcome us.

Servants were packing bundles and walking horses around in the grass nearby. I saw immediately what Kitten meant about unnecessary noise and confusion. The night seemed to be full of restless impatient boys nagging servants over their slowness.

However the prince, when we came upon him, was not at all impatient. In fact the air of unhurried calm with which he was sitting cross-legged by a fire drinking kesh out of an exquisite little silver cup and saucer was remarkable. It was a calm not shared by his nephew Alexi, who stood nearby, tapping his riding crop against the top of his boots and sighing. By the look of the long-necked kesh pot on the fire, Prince Nikoli had been there some time and might well be there longer.

Prince Nikoli Terzu was a remarkable looking man. His skin was brown and his hair was as black as night. In his black robes and cap the effect was very somber. Although he was tall, he was gracefully slim and light-boned. His face was smooth and soft-looking as if his cheeks had never been troubled by the roughness of a beard and he had the most beautiful dark eyes. Yet despite his delicate looks, he seemed very much in command. There was the suggestion of a strong will in the set of his finely chiselled lips, and when I came to know him better I discovered that a cynical twinkle was seldom out of his eyes.

"Lady Dion," he said, putting aside his cup, rising, and bowing low. "How are you? May I offer you some kesh?"

"Yes," I said, for kesh was exactly what my sluggish and aching body needed at this moment. But I was not about to be deflected from my aim by someone who I could already see was a master in the art of people management.

"My friend the countess tells me you are planning to try

and arrest a necromancer. Would you be interested in
my. . . . May I offer you my services in this?"

Count Alexi and Prince Terzu looked startled. Kitten
turned her head away from them and winked at me which
reassured me that I had not committed a serious social blun-
der. Later she told me that no Aramayan would have come
to the point of the conversation so quickly and without a
proper exchange of niceties.

The prince smiled as he poured steaming kesh into a cup
held out for him by a servant.

"I would be more than delighted, my lady." After handing
me the cup, he ushered me gently onto one of the folding
stools that the servants had set out for Kitten and myself.
"But do you feel yourself strong enough? You fought the
storm all yesterday. Are you not tired and at a low ebb in
your magic?"

I remembered then that Aramayans liked all things polite
and so I tried to phrase my answer with this in mind.

"Thanks to your kind hospitality, I am feeling much refreshed in body. As for my magic, I cannot with certainty
say, but I do not feel myself very close to being drained. I
beg of you to allow me to come."

"Lady Dion has always been remarkably strong and quick
to recover her magic," said Kitten. "You need not have any
fears on her account, Prince."

"Then I would be honored to accept your company," said
the prince. He dropped his voice. "In fact you have taken
a great load off my mind. Many of my companions are very
gifted, but they none of them have any practical
experience."

He turned suddenly and clapped his hands.

"Yuri! What is taking you all so long?" he cried "Get
those boys to their horses. We have no time to waste. And
you, Alexi my dear boy, why are you standing about like
this? Can't you see we are in a hurry?"

Count Alexi bowed and disappeared into the darkness
with a grin that showed he suddenly understood his uncle's
procrastination. It made him seem terribly young. Oh dear!
I hoped Prince Nikoli and myself would be enough. Though

somehow I never doubted that the prince knew what he was doing.

The prince's servants offered me food and water while the prince strode about giving orders, suddenly all action. He set some servants to take care of the imprisoned wreckers and see that they were handed over to the proper authorities, and organized a guard for our ship.

In a few minutes saddled horses were waiting for Kitten and me to mount.

"You are coming?" I said to Kitten.

"What? Stay here and miss all the fun? Certainly I am coming. Who will see you don't tire yourself out if I don't come? The Simonettis will see to our bags."

This was just like Kitten and there would be no arguing with her. If I had had some of the experiences she had had with necromancers I would have been too scared to go anywhere near them. But for Kitten fear would be the thing that was driving her to come now. For her, fear was a thing to head directly toward and conquer.

As we mounted up there was a muffled cheering from the young men, and several of them bobbed their heads at me as they walked their horses past to form into a column behind us. They did seem very pleased with me. And I had done nothing particular to deserve it.

"You are a celebrity here," said Kitten. "Count Alexi and I were talking when you were asleep. All these boys have studied a report of your activities that was made for the emperor by that mage Rosinsky. I remember you writing to me about him."

"Oh," I said uncomfortably. "Yes, an extremely flattering report. But they don't even know me. Why, they can't even be sure I am who I say I am!"

"Come now. Who else could you be? 'A beautiful young woman fair of skin and hair with powers as mighty as a demon's' as they say in the report. Such things do not grow in every cabbage patch. You forget the prince felt the measure of your power on the beach. He told me he had begun to wonder if you were the Demonslayer even before you gave your name." She poked me in the side with her finger.

"Evidently he knows 'a beautiful young woman' when he sees one."

I pulled a face at her. I knew full well that "beautiful" was no more than the illuminating effect of fame on a face and figure that were perfectly ordinary.

A couple of serving men were also mounted up and carrying torches to light our way. It is a sensible precaution not to use magic when trying to take any kind of mage by surprise.

At a shouted command from Count Alexi, the column moved off.

We took a path that led across the tussocky heathland along the clifftop. I could hear the crashing of surf and from horseback I could just make out the bulk of the *Eagle*, that gallant ship, lying on the beach below. A chill wind blew around us, making our shadows dance and sway in the flickering torchlight. I was glad I had brought one of the blankets to wrap around my shoulders.

I had begun to wonder if Aramayans and Morians fought necromancers in the same way, but I need not have worried. Immediately after we started the prince brought his horse up beside mine and we began to discuss tactics. To my relief they were not very different from what I was used to. This was not so surprising. Four hundred years ago the Peninsula I came from had been conquered by people from Aramaya who had brought with them the discipline of magic that I had studied. In effect Aramaya was still the center of the Peninsula's intellectual and magical world.

"I would not even consider this expedition were it not for various things that lead me to believe that our opponent is not very dangerous," said Prince Nikoli. "For a start, his operating so close to the estate of a known demon hunter smacks of both carelessness and inexperience. One of the stronger boys picked up traces of him quite easily in the Bowl of Seeing. We were actually looking for him again when we came across you. That is why we set out to meet you with such speed."

"For which I thank you," I said.

"Not at all. It was a pleasure to be of some small service.

To continue with the necromancer, my mind search of the leader of the wreckers led me to believe that he has been using the victims of wrecks to prolong his own life. It is a type of necromancy I have often seen. A mage who has been law abiding most of his life is tempted into the lower levels of necromancy by a fear of death. Such men are never very powerful or they would not need to draw on demon power to gain what they seek."

"You make it sound easy and common," I exclaimed, surprised by his calm. "On the Peninsula nothing could be more difficult. The whole of the countryside is constantly watched for signs of necromancy. This is not so in Aramaya, is it?"

"No, though I wish it were. It would please me to have no work. But though the emperor commands all his subjects' loyalty, the nobles are yet very jealous of their freedoms. Except for a few days' ride around Akieva and a couple of the other big cities, there is no systematic watch for necromancy in Aramaya. Communities fend for themselves. Fortunately they often do so quite well. And then we demon hunters do what we can informally. For instance, the fact that I always bring my young mages down here in summer has been enough to discourage necromancy in these parts for many years."

"I would have thought the freedom to commit necromancy was not one worth respecting," I said, shocked at the shortsightedness of it all.

The prince looked startled.

"I beg your pardon. I have been rude," I said, realizing that no one likes to hear criticism of their countrymen.

Prince Nikoli inclined his head. "Not at all. It is I who should beg your pardon for my ill-bred surprise. If you will pardon my saying so, it is simply that you speak your mind more openly than I am used to."

"I must beg your pardon again, Prince. I have yet to accustom myself to the Aramayan way," I said.

"Not at all. It was not a criticism, merely an observation. And I beg you will not change your manner. It seems a remarkably sensible way of going along. I shall try it myself if you do not think you will be offended. As for necromancy, I entirely agree with you. It is a vile, vile practice, but sadly the hatred of it is not as strong among most Aramayans as they say it is among the Peninsula folk."

I was surprised, though shocked might have been a better word, to think this might be true so close to the intellectual center of magery.

The prince must have read my face for he said, "Yes you will think it very decadent and perhaps it is, but you see things are seldom black and white to an Aramayan. In general many Aramayans, or at least those of our class, would ask first what is the quality of the lives being sacrificed to necromancy and why?"

"Quality of lives?" I echoed. "What on earth do you mean?"

"Many would find the sacrifice of animals quite acceptable to necromancy. Such a point can be logically defended. We kill animals to eat them, such people would say. What is wrong with sacrificing them to demons to fuel small useful spells. More sinisterly, there are others who would regard the lives of foreign barbarians as perfectly legitimate fuel for the pursuit of greater power. Or the lives of criminals who must be killed anyway. There are even those who regard their peasants as no better than animals."

"But to fuel a necromantic spell beings are usually tortured to death. What do such people say to that?"

He sighed. "I can imagine all kinds of excuses that might be made, but I will begin to find myself defending the practice if I keep on in this vein and I have no wish to do so. I am only trying to explain what must seem to you a shocking tolerance. You must understand what lies at the root of it. While my countrymen fear powerful rulers, paradoxically they also admire powerful men. And necromancy is about power. Any Aramayan will tell you that a powerful emperor brings effective and orderly rule and that is to be desired. The method of rule is regarded as secondary. To perform evil acts for a good end is seen as perfectly acceptable. Perhaps you can see how this might reflect on how people regard necromancy."

"I can," I said briefly. Many people who knew nothing of necromancy asked if it could not be used to do good things. But the power was always tainted by the cunning demons it was bought from. They could read the thoughts of the humans they colluded with and manipulated necromancers on to worse and worse crimes. It was just such happenings that had led my ancestors to migrate to the Peninsula. Such attitudes to necromancy might conceivably benefit those at the top of a society, but those further down had little to gain.

"Unfortunately, in such an atmosphere necromancy is very hard to completely root out," continued the prince. "I am glad to say that the last three emperors have been enemies of the secret colleges of necromancy and the demon hunters have flourished. But there have been times when the demon hunters have been discouraged, starved of funds, and denied any legal power. The secret colleges have found footholds even in the highest families. Even the imperial family. There have been times when only the prohibition against an emperor being a mage has prevented us from being actually ruled by a necromancer."

He turned and smiled at me.

"I must tell you how grateful we demon hunters are for your work, Lady Dion. The Rosinsky report on your activities is set reading for young mages. Inspiring reading. When the report of your cleansing of Ruinac was first published here in Aramaya, recruits to the demon hunters increased fivefold. And your discovery of just how deceptive demons can be has made the secret colleges of necromancy look like a pack of gullible fools. Which can only be a bad thing for them."

I inclined my head politely, though I actually felt very embarrassed. Rosinsky had come to Ruinac to interview me on behalf of the Emperor of Aramaya. He was looking to be impressed and had gone away and written things that made me seem like a visionary hero.

Shad had said it was a very fair report and he'd chided me for not giving myself enough credit, but I knew better. I had always had very ambivalent feelings about the title of

Demonslayer. What most people did not know was that it was a series of acts of foolishness that led to my confrontation with the demon Bedazzer. Even in my later dealings with Smazor and the other demons I had made mistakes and only really escaped through luck.

"It is a very flattering report," I said.

"I am sure not," said the prince politely. We were back to politeness, a state of being I could see that the prince was more comfortable with.

Dawn had broken by now, a chill grey dawn that was echoed in the chill grey seas below us. Birds began to call, both out over the sea and in the tussocky grass we rode through. Strange to think that only the previous morning I had been out on that sea thinking of Shad. Shortly after dawn we turned inland and rode along a rocky trail through heath and prickly gorse bushes.

After a while of riding through some low hillocks, the prince called a halt. He sent a couple of the boys off on foot and came riding back to us.

"I've sent the boys to reconnoiter. If things are as straightforward as I hope, I suggest that we divide into two groups. You and I shall go carefully in at the front of the house and try to catch the necromancer unaware. Count Alexi and the boys will stay at the back wall and capture anyone who tries to escape."

I doubted that the boys would be happy with this rather pallid role in things, but it was by far the safest plan for them. Prince Nikoli and I would bear the brunt of any fighting.

It would have been useful for us to do some magic together in order to see how we harmonized, but it would have given our presence away to any vigilant mage so we talked more of tactics and power. The prince asked me if I wished to take the lead, but my experience was more with fighting demons than human opponents so I suggested that he should lead the attack and I should defend. I discovered now that Aramayan mages had a far greater awareness of the extent of their own powers than Peninsular mages. On the Peninsula competition between mages was frowned upon. Only your teacher knew the full extent of your abilities.

Here in Aramaya, the Imperial court and the White Colleges held trials for young mages and rated them. The prince was the most powerful mage in the Southern Provinces and one of the ten most powerful in Aramaya. Having felt his power on the beach I could well believe this. If I managed to follow his moves properly, the two of us would be a formidable combination.

Count Alexi came up leading a grubby looking man in a sheepskin coat who was rubbing the sleep from his eyes. The prince questioned him in a language I had never heard before. I looked at Kitten inquiringly.

"It's a southern dialect of peasant Aramayan," she whispered in my ear. The grubby man, who seemed to be a shepherd of some sort, was at first reluctant to answer any questions. However when the prince threatened him with a mindsearch, he became suddenly cooperative and began to talk quickly and urgently. Finally he was taken away and tied up.

"He doesn't know much about the necromancer, but he did know the layout of the manor. He says there are dangerous dogs that walk upright. Sounds like blood beasts."

By this time the two other boys had returned with news of the layout of the house and grounds. After we had examined this, the prince called everyone around him and outlined his plan for them. As I expected there were disappointed looks all round, but no one questioned the prince's judgment or authority. What control he had over these lads! Kitten and the serving men were to stay behind the hill with the horses and the prisoner.

"What will happen to the man?" I asked the prince as the rest of us scrambled up the hill keeping in cover.

"Once we've arrested his master, we'll probably set him free. Serfs are not blamed for their master's sins in this country."

What was a serf? Well, there was no time for questions now for we were at the top of the hill.

Below us was a small wooded valley with a little creek

bubbling down the center. Farther up the valley we could see the stone wall of the manor house with the treetops of an overgrown garden behind it. The wall looked very new and very high. Usually there are people tending fields even this early in the morning, but there was no one in the neglected-looking fields nearby. Prince Nikoli sent the others off around the back of the house. Then a few minutes later the two of us made our way up the gully and along the wall till we found a rough place to get over. Prince Nikoli, who was very tall, climbed the wall with remarkable nimbleness and helped me up after him. A tree branch and a stand of overgrown grey-leaved bushes helped us to climb down the other side of the wall.

The garden was full of gnarled old trees hung about with long strands of moss. The ground beneath was covered in shaggy bushes. It was a storybook scene from a tale of evil magic. As we crept through the undergrowth I caught a scent of sulphur and rot.

"Demons!" I cried, just as two shapes came crashing out of the undergrowth to our right.

Blood beasts. Strong human bodies covered in hair and with the faces of vicious dogs. I threw out a bolt of power. There was a flash of light as the prince did the same. We both hit the closest beast. There was a yelp and stench of sulphur and a mass of burning fur thudded to the ground, just as the prince dodged the claws of the other beast.

"Look out," I shouted and thrust out a blast of power, which knocked the beast back through the air. The prince threw another bolt of power which hit it midflight. For a moment it hung there in the air struggling and shrieking, its skin and hair crackling in the flame, before it too crashed to the ground. Blood beasts are made of human flesh and the bones of a dog mixed with necromantic magic. Being magical creatures, they are very susceptible to magical attack.

The prince turned and shook my hand. "Well saved!" he said as if we were good fellows out shooting ducks together.

"In future, you take the left and I'll take the right," I said.

"Good idea. We'd better go. He knows we're here now."

A few moments of stumbling brought us to the front of

the house. It was a two-story building covered in ivy and greying whitewash and surrounded by a wide, sagging verandah. I could sense quite clearly that someone was awake in that building—awake and using magic.

Without hesitation, the prince dashed toward the front door. I raced after him. He threw out a short blast of power and the door burst open. We plunged through into the front hallway.

The prince stopped short in the middle of the hall.

"Keep watch," he said.

He began muttering the words of a finding spell.

"There's a mage upstairs to the left," I told him, to save time. I could feel the mage's strong magic with its edgy feeling of necromancy. It had to be someone pretty powerful for me to feel him so strongly. I thought nervously about those schoolboys waiting at the back wall. We must try and stop this person before he made a run for it.

The prince held up three fingers on his hand while continuing with the focusing spell. Three. Did he mean there were three necromancers? Now I could feel a second person up there but . . . For a brief moment I felt a very weak trace of a third.

Three? Three necromancers. God and Angels!

Suddenly there was shouting and then a terrible shriek.

Woomph!

A huge fireball came roaring down the stairs.

I yelped and spread a protection spell over the prince and myself. Not a moment too soon. We were engulfed in a world of roaring flame.

In the tiny peace inside the fireball the prince opened his eyes. He grinned at me, lifted one eyebrow questioningly and pointed his finger up toward the ceiling.

"Yes!" I cried exhilarated by our strength and power. Together we lifted our hands above our heads and turning them to fists of stone leaped upward out of the fire.

Crash! The wooden ceiling and upper floor burst apart as we smashed up through it. The prince disappeared in the clouds of rotting timber and swirling dust. There were several flashes of power. I leaped backward out of the dust-cloud, all senses at the ready just in time to see something like blue lightning disappear out of one of the windows.

I darted toward the lightning, tripped over something lying on the floor and fell headlong. Scrambling up, I threw myself at the window. A ball of blue fire was shrieking away through the air. An inexpert fireball exploded close by it. The boys! For a moment I thought of flinging myself after that blue fire, but to do so would draw me a long way away. A room-shaking blast from behind me made up my mind. The prince was shooting blasts of power at a fresh-faced young man. The necromancer was defending himself and sending out bursts of fire, but not at the prince. He was throwing fire all over the room—trying to burn the house down! That was reason enough for me to stop him. I thrust out my power and began extinguishing the flames as fast as I could go. It was not easy. The rotting wood walls and shabby tapestries caught fire easily and beneath us the fireball had turned the ground hallway into an inferno. Sometime during my frenzied extinguishing of the fire, the prince must have bested the other mage for suddenly I found him working beside me.

Shortly afterward we stood together in the smoking hallway surveying the wreckage. Though it had been a tough fight we were smiling. Using magic is exhilarating.

"Where's the mage?" I asked him.

The smile went off the prince's face.

"When I bested him, he turned his power on himself. Poor young fool."

The stairs were unusable so we jumped back up through the ceiling again. The floor in the upper room was sagging alarmingly and together we moved broken pieces of wood around to shore it up.

Two charred bodies lay on the floor of that upper room. With a faint sense of revulsion I saw a footprint in the ashy flesh of one of them and realized that it must have been this that I fell over while racing to the window. I remembered the terrible scream that I had heard just as the fire ball had come rolling out of that upper doorway. It must have rolled right over him.

"The way I interpret this scene is that these fellows have some evidence they wanted to hide," said the prince. He was searching the bodies. "And they would have succeeded too, if you hadn't been here and been so quick thinking as to put out those fires. But see . . . this one here was probably the weakest of them and the other two killed him, so that he wouldn't be mindsearched. There's no honor among necromancers." He pulled something away from the burned corpse's finger. "Ah, yes this is good. A signet ring. We may well find that this is the lord of the manor. Anyway, to continue, then the other young man stayed behind to destroy the manor, letting his master get away. It was probably always intended that he give up his life. Even among necromancers there are those who have the knack of inspiring such slavish devotion. And misusing it. I almost feel sorry that this poor young fellow died for nothing."

He smiled up at me. "However now we shall find out the secret they were hiding. Some new necromantic technique I hope. Necromancers are endlessly inventive."

He came over, took my hand and bowed over it. Since it was covered in ash and dirt I was relieved he did not kiss it.

"I cannot thank you enough for coming with us," he said. "Things could have gone very badly for us without you. I think it was the two of us who scared the strongest one away."

"It was my duty to come and help you. Nothing else," I said.

His dark eyes twinkled at me.

"If all mages did their duty, there would be no demon hunters. By the way, I must compliment you on your sense for magic. You are very sharp. It was a pleasure working with you."

I tried not to blush at his appreciation. We were professionals here.

"Now, let us get the boys, and see what it was these fellows were hiding," he said.

A short time later I cast the Bowl of Seeing in the water barrel in the back stableyard. Using the Bowl together with the pack of foretelling cards which all mages carry lets you see quite precisely what type of magic is being used in what location. And even when the magic is no longer being used you can usually see some traces of where it has been for a few hours afterward.

"Look," said Count Alexi. "This place here glows with necromancy. He looked at the foretelling cards. "Here to the right of the house. It must be some kind of secret cellar. There's something in one of the attic rooms too. Can anyone see anything else?"

"There's something in that lower room," said the chubby young man who was standing beside me holding my stack of cards.

"Very good, Sergi," said Prince Nikoli. "Now you lads can do the house and Lady Dion and Alexi and Sergi and I will do the cellar."

There was a disappointed groan from the others which the Prince received with a good natured twinkle.

"I assure you there will be plenty for you to observe," he said. "And I shall give you all the opportunity to impress me with your careful reports later."

Once again this serious attack on necromancy had turned into a school excursion. Personally my first urge was to send these boys as far away from the manor house as possible, till it was safe for them to come back, but perhaps the prince was right. Student mages needed to gain experience somehow. We had seen the dire results of inexperience on the Peninsula. There, very few people ever came into contact with necromancy and they had trouble recognizing it when they did.

The prince was still very cautious. While the boys swarmed over the manor house, he carefully followed them through the rooms, keeping an eye on them.

As well as the large number of graves in the back garden and the stinking place in the stable where the blood beasts had been kennelled, there was a golem—a clay man covered in runic symbols—slouched in the kitchen. It was inert now, for its master was either dead or very far away. No doubt the necromancers used it as a kind of servant, for there were no human servants anywhere in the house.

In the attic rooms, however, we found two young women in peasant dress lying on their backs on two narrow little beds. They did not react when we entered and at first I thought they must be dead. But their open eyes moved and blinked.

"They have been fed on by demons," said one of the boys. I nodded. It seemed the logical conclusion, and yet something about the girls puzzled me. For a start they were uninjured. Demons feed on the life force of living beings and those forces are enhanced, made more delectable to them, by strong emotions. Though the emotion can be pleasure, necromancers usually use pain in order to extract the most nourishment from their victims. After all, pain is much easier to cause.

If the victims of demon feeding recover from the torture they are still diminished. They usually sleep the sleep of deep exhaustion, waking only for a couple of hours a day to struggle from their beds to see to bodily functions. These girls were neither injured nor exhausted. They reminded me of nothing so much as the golem that lay downstairs—it was as if some essential animating element was simply missing.

"I think I will have my healer look at these two," said Prince Terzu, and I saw that he too was puzzled by the girls.

This painstaking search irritated me, even though I knew that it was important to make sure the house was safe. I was edgy and keen to get into the secret cellar where the real necromantic business would have taken place. What if people were imprisoned there or lying wounded?

At last we found ourselves in the basement of the house. Although we knew there was a secret cellar somewhere nearby, Sergi and Alexi had had no luck finding its entrance; even with all fifteen of us looking we could find nothing. At last Prince Nikoli suggested that we break through the wall and a couple of the boys used magic to pull several bricks out of it. We discovered a large dark space behind one of the walls. A foul stench of sulphur and carrion came from the space. With Prince Nikoli's help, Count Alexi changed himself into a snake and slithered through the small hole in the wall. Shortly afterward magelight shone out of the hole. We could hear the count making gagging sounds and then with a grinding grating noise a portion of the wall directly behind us slid open. As the terrible smell flooded into the room the young men drew back without having to be told.

The prince calmly took a little pot of ointment from his pouch, rubbed a small amount under his nose and passed it around. It was some kind of strong, sharp-smelling unguent, and when I rubbed it under my nose I could smell nothing else.

With magic at the ready and sleeves held before our noses, Prince Nikoli, Sergi, and I stepped through the door. Beyond, a green-faced Count Alexi waited, a magelight burning white in his hand.

Prince Nikoli grinned at him wryly and offered him the pot of ointment.

"Enjoying yourself dear boy?"

"Uncle dear. How could I not enjoy your company and in such appropriate surroundings too?"

The prince bowed ironically as if acknowledging a compliment.

"Please feel free to lead on at your leisure, dear boy."

The count bowed mockingly in return and led the way down a long corridor to where a large cellar opened up. The source of the stench was easy to see. Several bodies lay huddled in a corner of the room. On a large stone table in the middle lay the body of a young woman. The whole of her middle was shattered as if it had burst. Small pieces of entrail, flesh, and bone were spattered all over the walls behind. The sight set me gagging. Sergi leaned in a corner and vomited.

The prince was made of sterner stuff, however. With only the faintest hesitation, he moved forward and began to examine the body.

"Been here most of the night, I would say from the dryness of the blood and other things," he said calmly. He turned away from the table and examined the other bodies.

"This is what happened to the servants then," he sighed.

"Poor souls. Used as fodder." He reached up and pulled at a piece of the wall, which I now saw was a large black curtain. Behind it was a huge mirror. Runes were painted on it in blood.

"Lady Dion, perhaps you could give me your opinion of this."

I read the runes to myself but not aloud. Runes are a language all their own, a language linked with magic. They made out a summoning spell.

"Look, there is the gateway rune," I said. "They were constructing a gateway. To bring a demon through, I suppose, and use it as a bound servant. Though these three people and the girl would not have been much of a sacrifice for such a big spell."

"Perhaps they were used to simply put the gateway rune in place," said the prince.

"Possibly. If that's so, it seems we have come just in time. Though this is not like other gateways I have seen—the runes are in the wrong order and I don't think they are all there. And what were they going to use for fodder when they opened the gate?"

"Perhaps the people from your ship," he said. "Though I agree it doesn't seem enough."

I understood his doubt. The last demon I knew who had come through a gateway into our world had required to be fed the life force of 450 people.

"Strange wounds, this girl," said Count Alexi. "Surely blowing the poor creature open like this would have been too quick for a sacrifice."

I looked more carefully at the runes. I had learned a great deal about them after I had married Shad. His people, the Klementari, used runes much more than normal mages.

"Look at this one," I said. "That's the rune for enclosure. Surely that is not usual in a gateway spell."

"So that's what that is. I've never seen anything like it before. This can only be some kind of new experiment, but unfortunately with the fellows upstairs dead, I'm not sure we'll ever know what they were up to."

He turned and looked at the woman on the table. From here we could only see her face, blank with death.

"Poor woman," he said, echoing my thoughts.

He sent Sergi back upstairs for pen and paper so that we could copy out the runes. While he was gone we examined the rest of the cellar.

Another wooden table in a corner showed signs of recent use. Prince Nikoli noted, with a certain satisfaction, that it had the youth runes carved in it.

"This is the table he would have been using to prolong his life," he said.

A large empty cage stood in a nearby corner. The sight of this chilled me. This horrible fate might have awaited Kitten and me—locked down here in the darkness watching your fellows killed one by one. All Kitten's charm and all my skill at magic, all the things which made us special and our lives unique, made irrelevant by the fact that these monsters needed our life force to power their spells.

Though we spent the rest of the morning searching and scanning the manor and its grounds, it was clear that nothing else was alive there. At this point a party of Peninsula witchfinders would have declared themselves finished. They would probably have burned the house to the ground and left. The Aramayans had no intentions of leaving so precipitately.

First the Prince set Alexi to taking extensive notes on all aspects of the secret cellar while he examined the dead woman's body in gruesome detail. Interestingly enough there were a series of enclosure runes scratched into her back. I wrote them down and named them for him. Then I helped him wrap the body in a linen cloth and remove it for burial. Magic can be very welcome at such moments.

After the autopsy, Prince Nikoli took me and several of the older boys along the rutted cart track to the nearby peasant village. Our arrival at the settlement took on some of the qualities of a raid. The young men rounded up everyone they could find and herded them into the muddy clearing around the village well. The prince addressed the serfs in the same strange dialect of Aramayan he had used with the shepherd. I was astonished by this language. Like all educated Peninsula folk I had learned Aramayan as a child and I could speak it easily with Prince Nikoli, but I could barely understand a word of this peasant dialect.

I was so fascinated at my first glimpses of Aramayan life that my attention quickly wandered from the prince's incomprehensible words. Fascinated but repelled. What a moldy and sagging little village it was. How poor the people looked, all thin and dressed in dirty rags. Some of them were covered in sores and several of the half-naked children had the bloated bellies of those who did not get enough of the right food.

When the prince had finished speaking, a wizened old headman led us up to a great barn. At this time of the year after the harvest the bins were full of grain, apples and vegetables and the loft was stuffed with hay. There was room for a table and chairs to be set up in the middle of the floor however. One of the young men now sat at the table and took notes while the prince proceeded to question everybody in the village. Unable to understand the questions, I read the student's notes over his shoulder. As I had suspected, the prince was questioning the people in great detail on the activities at the manor house. Even though he mindsearched several of them, he seemed to be learning very little that was really useful. They were able to identify the twisted signet ring the prince had taken from the body as that of their lord, Igor Shugorsky, but they had no knowledge of the wreckers.

Rumors of Lord Shugorsky's dark activities had abounded in the village for some time. The two strangers had arrived only a week ago and since then nobody had seen the manor servants. A couple of days before seven girls had been taken from the village to the manor. It was the first time anyone had been taken from the village.

It sounded as if the resident necromancer had invited or been coerced into inviting two other necromancers to his house, but why was not clear. Some revolting experimentation? Had any villages on the Peninsula known so much about necromantic activities at their lord's house without informing their local mage, they would have been severely punished.

"Why did they not send for someone if they suspected all this," I asked one of the boys.

All he said in answer was, "They are serfs my lady."

This explained nothing to me but he gave me such a pitying look for having asked such an obvious question, I did not press him further. Nobody is as good as a youngster at making you feel pitifully foolish.

The prince took the peasants' testimonies without a word of reproof and afterward he gave each person a sack of grain and a bag of vegetables and apples.

"The prince is a soft-hearted fellow," said one of the boys nearby in a low voice. "These people are like the useless sweepings of a stable. They would probably be much better for a taste of the whip."

"Yes it is odd," said Sergi. "It's his one vice, this foolish softness. He's notorious for it. Still he is very successful at finding out information. It is not impossible there is some connection."

And they had seemed such nice young men too, I thought, a bit chilled by the whispered exchange. Later I was to realize that they were just repeating the commonplace thoughts of most Aramayan nobles.

I helped the prince by relieving the pain of the mindsearch victims, but I was very glad when Kitten arrived with the servants. I wanted to do something about all the sick people in this village. They seemed so fearful I did not like to leap on them and just heal them without having someone to translate for me.

"How can this lord have done nothing for them?" I said to Kitten later as we went from house to house, examining the villagers and using healing magic where it was applicable. "They do not even have a village healer. They could not have been very productive workers. It's like the worst excesses of the Revolution of Souls!"

"He would hardly have wanted an educated and independent person in the place," said Kitten.

I picked up a little toddler holding a doll plaited out of

straw. The child clung to me in a way which made my heart ache. Alinya would have been this child's age now had she lived. The thought upset me. I had avoided small children for the last two and a half years for just this reason.

"Oh, look at this child. Its bones are not growing right," I exclaimed. "Tell this woman that her children must have more milk."

"Dion, don't you think these people would give their children milk if they could?"

I dropped my eyes in shame. I had been insensitive. They were obviously too poor to afford milk. I put the child down and tried to forget how empty my arms felt.

"They are serfs," continued Kitten. "They must look to their lord for their well-being."

"What are serfs?"

"They are bound to the land and they belong to the lord in the same way that it does," said Kitten.

"You mean they are slaves!" I cried.

"Not exactly in law, but in fact yes, they are."

"God and Angels, how can this go on!"

"Actually it is like this all over Aramaya. It's the way the country is organized."

No wonder these people were so passive and cowed. No wonder they had not sent for the demon hunters. My God. How awful. All my life people had been telling me things were done better in Aramaya and I, like all peninsula folk, had believed them. No one had ever mentioned the fact that most of the population lived in a state of semi-slavery. They say travel broadens the mind. It certainly opens the eyes.

Kitten and I spent the rest of the day healing people as best we could. Although it was a very short-term solution to the problem, it was better than nothing. Much later as we were helping an old blind woman with her cataracts, I looked up and saw Prince Nikoli standing in the doorway. The old woman's daughter fluttered anxiously to the door and bowed low to him.

If he had come earlier I really think I would have scolded him for the shameless and shocking institution of serfdom, but I had had time to recover my temper and to realize it was not personally his fault.

"Are we going?" I said, a little shortly.

"I was just about to ask if you would mind spending the night here. I have a few more people to question and then we shall be through, but the boys are tired and I imagine you must be too. You seem to have found much to occupy yourself."

"I had to do something about the condition of these people," I said bluntly.

"Yes," said the prince. He leaned against the door frame. "You are angry about something?"

"I am shocked by the state of these people. Shocked!" I cried. "And now the countess tells me that they are virtual slaves of this necromancer. And you said. . . . Do they have no recourse? Is there nothing to be done? At least in Moria people can take to the roads if they are unhappy. Yet here the countess tells me stories of hunting dogs and prison for runaways. . . . It is not what I expected to find at the center of the world."

"Ah, yes" said the prince. "It seems I must again apologize for my countrymen. It is not a system I personally support and with every generation there are more of us against it. We are in hopes that this new emperor will be one of us, but it is too early to tell. No doubt the state of the Morian peasantry is much superior."

That remark took the wind out of my sails. Perhaps it had been intended to. There were plenty of Morian peasants who could not afford to buy their children milk. Many of them had come to Ruinac to seek their fortunes in the new lands we were opening up there and had brought tales of starvation and cruel landlords with them.

"Is there no way that these children can get enough milk to help them grow properly?" I said, perceiving that there was no point arguing with someone who agreed with me.

"Lord Shugorsky had several cows. I can buy a couple of them from his bailiff and give them to the village."

"But will the milk be fairly distributed?"

"These villages operate as units. They must. Usually you

can rely on the village elders, who are also serfs, to see that everybody gets a share. Come. We shall see what can be done."

Nobody wanted to spend the night in the manor house. The tithe barn was the next biggest and cleanest building in the area, so we all spent the night there. An area was partitioned off with blankets for Kitten and me, and comfortable beds of straw were made for us. It must have been all the little children I had handled that day or perhaps I was so tired that for once I did not need magic to put myself to sleep. Anyway, that night I dreamed about my miscarriage.

They say all mothers feel the child in their womb, but a mage feels it even more strongly. From the moment Shad's seed joined with mine, I was aware of the life force of our child within me. For five months I felt intense joy as she grew inside me. And then one terrible day, I felt that spark of life begin to struggle. Though I tried to keep it going, willing my own life force into my womb, still it failed. And was suddenly gone. And it stayed gone. A day later I gave birth to a small dead fetus. In dreams I still saw its tiny hands and feet.

Shad and I called her Alinya and buried her in a small grave in our garden.

"We will have other children," he said. But we did not.

Oh, that terrible moment when the life flickered and I could do nothing. That terrible moment when I realized she had died inside me. Why, oh why had she died?

I awoke and lay there in the darkness and wept silently as I had so many times before. It had been two and half years since Alinya had died, but at such moments the pain was sharp. And the release that tears gave was small. When the tears had gone I lay awake, my eyes open and sore from weeping, a kind of black emptiness pressing down on me. I tried the various relaxation rituals, but the depression was too strong for them to work. The only other option was to put myself back to sleep with magic, but I could see the light of dawn already coming in through the window. Suddenly I wanted to get away from the dark soak of misery I lay in.

Quickly I pulled on my clothes and went out of the barn. It was still quite dark. Though birds were twittering in the trees, there was no movement among the shabby little huts. I walked along the muddy, smelly track through the village and out toward the sea which I could hear and smell a short way away.

I forgot the monstrous waves I had fought (was it already a day ago) in my delight in the sea as it was now. How magnificent the waves were breaking on the wide wet sands. When Shad and I had first lived together at Ruinac, sometimes we would make the long half-day journey to the nearby coast to just such a beach. Though the land around Ruinac was grey and sterile after being laid waste by a demon, the seashore had recovered. The sand dunes were covered in spiky sea grasses and little shrubs, and seagulls nested in the nearby cliffs and swirled and dipped over the waves.

A day at the sea had always refreshed us for the long days of magic and digging that we needed to bring the land around Ruinac back to fruitful life. When it was too cold to swim we would ride our horses through the waves or run along the shore chasing each other and throwing lumps of seaweed. We had been so happy. . . .

I found myself rubbing my ring finger. There was no ring there any longer. I had been too shocked to take my ring off when I first received Shad's ring and letter. It had taken me over a month to bring myself to do it and to send it to Shad at Ruinac, thus granting him the divorce he had asked for.

I had done so the night before Kitten and I had embarked to cross the Western Ocean and find Dally. Anything might happen to me on this journey. It was best to have all my affairs in order before I went. At least this way Shad would be free to get on with his life and with the family that would hopefully inherit Ruinac from him. For myself there was nothing about freedom I wanted.

All kinds of bitter reproaches had filled my mind but when it came time to pen the letter accompanying my ring, I simply wrote telling him how much I regretted that things had not turned out well between us and wishing him happiness for the future. Anything else just seemed too petty.

Now, standing here on the seashore and remembering how happy we had once been, I bitterly regretted sending back that ring. It was so horribly final. I should have hung on. I should have gone back and tried to talk with him. Now there was no hope. But no. There had never been any hope. I could not give him children and he had wanted children. All men did.

Naturally he had turned to Edaine. Edaine, the young Klementari woman who had come to teach my students runework and who had decided it was her role to rescue my husband from the disastrous consequences of marrying a non-Klementari. I could still remember Edaine shouting at me.

"You are selfish keeping Shad with you when everyone knows that you are barren. Why can't you do the decent thing and let him go to find someone who can give him a child?"

Shad had been furious when I told him. He had called Edaine to my office and told her in front of me that there was no longer any place in his house for one who said such things to his wife.

Yet they had been friends and on some level he must have agreed with her, for five months later came the ring and that letter telling me he was going to start a new life with her. Edaine, who was younger than me and more beautiful, who was probably fertile and whose spirit was not blackened and twisted by grief over her childlessness. She had never liked me. I felt petty bitterness at her triumph now. As for Shad, I might rage at his decision but I could not really blame him for it. Not when I thought of our last time together and all the other times like it.

If Alinya had survived I would have had something of Shad to remember him by, just as I had been a souvenir of my mother's love for my father. But if Alinya had lived Shad would never have left. I wanted to weep again for my lost husband and all the promise that had simply disappeared, but I had no tears left. That part of my life, the husband and family part, was over now and I must just learn to accept it.

THE INVESTIGATION OF Lord Shugorsky's manor house was completed that morning. The prince and I destroyed the secret cellar and with great delight the boys burned down the house with the bodies of the golem and the blood beasts inside it. The bodies of the two necromancers and their victims had been removed to be given proper burial. The prince placed one of his servants in control of Lord Shugorsky's land and serfs until it could be decided who their new owner was. The property would be forfeited to the emperor, unless Shugorsky's heirs had special influence at court.

I was impressed by the quiet way Prince Nikoli wielded authority. It was on his sole responsibility that a whole manor house had been destroyed. I had had unpleasant experiences with witchfinders on the Peninsula that had made me wary of those who sought to stand in judgment on their peers. Even when they were not being used by the Government to persecute innocent mages, witchfinders tended to be self-righteous and judgmental men. Yet the prince seemed remarkably easygoing and very kindly to those of lesser rank. And there was always a twinkle in his eye. There must have

been steel behind his velvet exterior however, for even his
students seldom questioned his orders.

With a column of smoke rising behind us, we headed back
south toward Dubrovny, the prince's estate. With us came
a cart carrying all the evidence from the investigation and
the two young women from the attic room. Their heads
turned slightly to stare back at the column of smoke above
the manor house but otherwise they were motionless, not
even moving to brush the flies from their faces.

"What will happen to them?" I asked the prince as we
rode.

"The emperor has a hospital in Akieva for the survivors
of necromancy. There will be great interest in them, for their
case is unusual."

Poor young women. To spend the rest of their lives as
scientific curiosities.

"Then there is no cure for the sickness caused by demons
in Aramaya either?" I asked.

"None," he replied. "For all the clever tricks we have, we
have still found no way to replace life force taken by
demons. Unless the person concerned is a mage and recovers his life force by himself. As you know."

As I indeed knew from my own experience. Of all the
people who lost their life force to demons, mages recovered
the best, though even they never recovered fully. How
strange that with all this wonderful power flowing through
me, I still could not manage to achieve the simple things
ordinary women achieved, such as a husband and a child.
Perhaps it was wrong of me to expect to have everything.

"You sighed?" asked the prince politely. "Are you tired?"

"A little," I said.

"I am not surprised. You set quite a pace, Lady Dion.
There will be time to rest when you reach Dubrovny. It is
a jewel of peace and comfort. My favorite house. You must
promise me that you will let my servants pamper you."

"I will struggle to submit myself to their ministrations," I
said wryly, which made him laugh.

"So mages are able to own property in Aramaya," I said
to Kitten when I was riding beside her later. In Moria mages

were generally not allowed to own more land than it took for a cottage to sit on. My ownership of Ruinac was an exception, and even that was not really ownership but a kind of stewardship. I could have passed it to my children as long as they did not have magical powers. If I had had children.

"In Aramaya a person is an aristocrat first and a mage second," said Kitten. "The aristocracy are jealous of their privileges and since Aramaya is so big that the Emperor cannot rule without them, he is forced to concede to them sometimes. It is a balance. Even here people do not want mages to become too powerful. There are still some limits. The prince will be forced to wear an iron necklace in the presence of the emperor to render him harmless. A mage has never sat upon the Aramayan throne and I expect never will."

"Is he connected with the Imperial Family that his title is prince?" I asked her, interested now in the topic of the prince for its own sake. For he seemed an interesting man. Though he was obviously wealthy, still he worked for the public good.

She laughed. "My dear this is Aramaya. Everything is bigger here, even the titles. Especially the titles. The Terzus came with the Night Emperor from these Southern Provinces. They have a long and distinguished history of Imperial service. And who should serve an emperor but a prince?"

"So he's not actually an Aramayan?" I had wondered about that. My experience of Aramayans had led me to believe them a fair-skinned round-eyed people like Kitten or short dark-haired people like those of the Peninsula folk who had Aramayan ancestry, and yet the young men in the prince's train had a enormous variety of skin colorings and facial features.

She pursed her lips. "The prince would say he is one. Aramaya is a very big place. Over the centuries it has expanded out of its heartlands and absorbed other nations and peoples, all different tribes of people meeting, fighting, and intermarrying. They are all Aramayans. And the Emperor takes all his four wives from different parts of the country so that no physical type has a higher status than any other.

It is true that certain physical types dominate certain regions, but in fact the most typical place in Aramaya is Akieva where you see all physical types and all combinations of physical types and none really dominates."

The prince was right about Dubrovny. It was a jewel of peace and tranquility. As we traveled along the coast toward it, the towering coastal cliffs became smaller and smaller until, around Dubrovny, they simply became rocky headlands and sand dunes. Behind the foreshore the land was rolling plain and heath with an occasional tree-filled valley containing a creek that flowed into the sea. Dubrovny sat in one of these valleys. It was not a manor house. Instead a series of small single-storied guest houses with wide verandahs clustered together around a larger double-storied building that had the most delightful white onion-shaped dome at the center.

The twelve other passengers of the ship were already comfortably settled in the guest houses. Several of them came out to welcome us as our party rode up. Both the spice merchants were there wanting to know if there was any news about the ship's well-being. The rest, who were pilgrims bound for Karanagrad, contented themselves with asking after our quest. They all looked well rested and cared for and the more humble ones were wide-eyed with the luxurious situation they found themselves in.

"This prince is a wonderful host," a middle-aged woman pilgrim told me. "The food and drink is of the finest. And the servants. . . ."

I quickly discovered about the servants. That very night I had a tussle with the chambermaid over which of us was going to do up the laces on my underwear. I was used to having servants help me lace my best dress, but having someone lace up your underwear and tie your shoelaces for you was ridiculous. I wondered if a servant tied the prince's shoelaces. Odd. He had seemed like a man capable of managing such complex tasks for himself.

The ship's crew had already set out for Karanagrad with one of the prince's agents and a couple of the other merchants, but they had left the injured captain and the cabin boy behind. The captain had indeed received a head injury from a falling spar and he had a serious chill from the storm. Though he would recover, it would take several days before he was fit enough to travel. Our first night in Dubrovny the prince suggested that Kitten and I wait until the captain was better and then all of us could travel to Karanagrad together.

"I always return to the capital at this time of year and would be glad of the company," he said.

Kitten and the Simonettis were very happy to take up his suggestion, but personally I dreaded staying at Dubrovny. When I am unhappy, I fear inactivity. I did not insist on our going on, however. Fearing inactivity had made me drive the others into taking a ship across the Western Ocean at the beginning of Storm Season when it would have been more sensible to have waited two months until it was over. It had been a horrible crossing which might have killed all of us. I was ashamed to have been the cause of it and apologized to Kitten as we sat upon the verandah of our guest house the following morning eating a delicious breakfast.

She laughed.

"I cannot say I did not curse you, especially all those nasty times I lost my dinner, but really, my love, if we had had an ordinary peaceful crossing would we be staying in this charming place now?"

That was Kitten exactly. She did not bother worrying about what might have happened. We had been friends since I was seventeen and had been hired to be her magical body-guard. Though I felt that I had failed her, for I had been betrayed and we had both been captured by her enemy, she did not. She seemed to look upon the terrible torture she had endured at his hands as little more than a wrong turning in the path that led to his death and to her being freed from the years of fear she had endured. She had forgiven me for my failure long before I had forgiven myself and seemed to have an immense gratitude and affection for me. I could not understand it, but I was tremendously glad of it. Against all the odds she had remained my best friend.

When she had insisted on coming with me to Aramaya to

find Dally, I thought at first that it was just another example of her generosity, for she had been outlawed there. I had protested strenuously. To my astonishment she then revealed that she had sucessfully applied for a pardon almost three years earlier.

"I always thought I might like to return to Aramaya and now that you are going here is the perfect opportunity."

"Are you sure you want to? Will it not be difficult for you?" I asked. Kitten had an aristocratic family in Aramaya who bore her no love. She had been a barren wife set aside by her husband, but she had refused to retire properly to a convent and be forgotten. Instead she had become a courtesan in Akieva. When her protector had hatched a treasonous plot to overthrow the emperor, she had been implicated and forced to flee the country. I could imagine all kinds of unpleasant situations arising if she returned there.

"Oh pooh to the Deserovs," she said, correctly guessing my reason for being doubtful. "I have been thinking for a long time that it would be nice to see Aramaya again and now I shall. With you."

The life of a courtesan is full of snubs from people who consider themselves your moral superiors. I could understand why she had waited to return until she had a companion to lend her emotional support. What surprised me was that she regarded me as the right companion. A damp-eyed woman who had lost husband and child could be expected to be as much support as a particularly feeble blade of grass. The responsibility put me on my best behavior. I was determined not to let her down again.

Kitten regarded all the young with tenderheartedness which was probably why she had initially taken me under her wing. During the few days we had been with the prince, most of his young students had become completely devoted to her. Now as we sat on the verandah two of them came around the side of the guest house carrying large bunches of wildflowers.

"Ah," cried Kitten, "Speaking of charming (which we had not been, actually), here are Leonid and Sergi Golitsyn.

Good morning gentlemen. I hope you are coming for a long visit."

Both of them blushed at this greeting, but they enjoyed this attention from a beautiful older woman. Lucky fellows. Kitten was a past master at making you feel like the most attractive person in the world; a skill which the boys, especially Leonid, who was at that awkward age, blossomed under. Although she had retired from being a courtesan and now took few lovers, Kitten was such an accomplished flirt that it was almost second nature. In the hands of such a master, flirtation is a delight.

Sergi—almost eighteen and thus quite the man of the world—recovered from his embarrassment first. He bowed and said,

"Prince Nikoli wondered if Lady Dion would care to come and view his library and he charged Leonid and myself to keep you amused, Countess Katerina. Would you care to ride or take a walk to view the hothouses? The late roses are very beautiful, though I venture to say that you may well eclipse them, Countess."

"Why Sergi, what a charming thing to say. But I feel sure you are a flatterer. I think we shall ride, if you gentlemen are willing. I'll see you later, Dion." She turned and winked at me. "Go on. Have some fun. I dare you to."

I was looking forward to seeing the prince's library. We had talked of it on the way home and it seemed he had a number of books on magery that I had never seen. When the servant showed me in, however, the prince was not reading but tinkering with something on a table. For a moment I could only stare. He was wearing a magnificent silk robe of crimson patterned with black shapes and embroidered in gold thread with golden birds. The effect of the silk against his dark skin was very attractive.

Now this is Aramaya! I thought to myself. It was an outfit that even the Duke of Gallia would have saved for state occasions and yet Prince Nikoli Terzu wore it while lounging informally in his library.

"Ah Lady Dion. You are looking well," he said. "I trust my people have been taking care of you. I hope you will

forgive me, but you find me at a delicate moment in the
proceedings and I must finish."

"What are you working on?" I asked, peering at the apparatus. There was a headpiece and wires running to a crystal.
The prince was touching each small connection with the tip
of his long fingers.

"Something quite fascinating. This is an apparatus for
making Arkady Illusions. Perhaps you are familiar with
them."

I was indeed familiar with them. In fact an Arkady Illusion
was responsible for my presence in Aramaya. They were a
new thing, even here where they had been invented. An
Aramayan mage, Count Fedor Arkady, had recently combined magic and science so that a mage's experience or
memory of an event could be copied out of his head, using
a modified form of mindsearch, and stored using runes in a
special kind of crystal. With the application of a minimal
amount of magic, the mage's memories could be played back
as a three-dimensional illusion.

Ishtak, the merchant city where Kitten lived back home,
was the place where all things Aramayan first arrived on the
Peninsula. Just after I came to stay with Kitten, The Great
Zotov—the first traveling Arkady Illusionist—disembarked
there. Of course Kitten, always in the forefront of any new
development, had hired him to entertain her guests at a soi-
ree. The illusion he showed us was of the recent coronation
of the new Aramayan Emperor Zamarton the Fifth, a long
and gorgeous ritual.

If Kitten had hoped the illusion might distract me from
my sadness, she succeeded beyond her wildest dreams.
Rumor had it that many nobles in the audience at the coronation had paid Count Arkady to look at them during the
ceremony so that their faces would appear on the illusion
he made from his memory. As I glumly watched the illusion's focus move from one gorgeously clad figure to another, I saw something which suddenly kindled me to life.

A face. A face in the crowd. The face of my niece Syndal
Holyhands, otherwise known as Dally. I had believed, indeed
I had almost hoped, that she was dead. But it was Dally

Holyhands right enough. I recognized her even though her face had lost its adolescent roundness and gained what the craft of beauty could add. When I had last seen her, five years before, the Great Cathedral at Sanctuary was collapsing around us and it had been clear that she was being nurtured by a demon and well down the path to necromancy. Though I had thought she had died under the rubble, I had always suspected the demon, my old enemy Bedazzer, would not let such a willing tool die so easily. It seemed I had been right. So what was she doing at the Imperial court where all magery of any kind was forbidden? Had she been drawn into necromancy, or had she somehow managed to escape the honey trap of power? I had to know.

I had always felt that I had let Dally down badly. After all, I brought Bedazzer into her vicinity. He was the demon I had fought in Gallia and for years afterward he had sought to gain my attention and to persuade me to give myself over to him. If I had acted as Dally's mentor myself, if I had been less afraid of her blunt passionate nature, if I had simply paid more attention, she would never have fallen into Bedazzer's clutches. She had been a lonely, vengeful child, ignorant of magic and on the verge of developing her own power, a perfect victim for Bedazzer to lure into necromancy. Even if I had been a happily married woman with a horde of children at my knee, I would have felt obliged to try and find her.

But it was not Dally I was thinking of in the Prince's Library that day when he told me he was working with Arkady Illusions. The emperor had given Count Arkady the sole right to create Arkady Illusions, and the trick of making them was still a deep secret.

"Arkady Illusions!" I cried. "Do you know how to make them then?"

"I can channel the memories through the crystal and I've even worked out a way to enhance their clarity, but I can't for the life of me work out how to store them in the crystal." He looked at me hopefully. "Is it possible you would be interested in looking at what I've done?"

"Indeed I would," I said, with an enthusiasm that made him smile.

For the rest of the day we tinkered with the Arkady apparatus. We tried different runes and different spells and different ways of connecting the wires. We experimented with Prince Nikoli's memories and with those of various boys who happened to pass through the library. I was fascinated by the cunning interplay of spells, runes, and material objects.

Neither of us noticed the passing of time until Nikoli's majordomo appeared and reminded him that it was time to dress for dinner. By that time Nikoli and I had dropped the titles and were working on first name terms.

Spending time with a mage discussing work was a new experience for me. On the Peninsula I had few people I could refer to as colleagues. I was one of the only women on the Peninsula trained in magecraft and I had been privately educated by a man who, for the sake of my virtue, had carefully isolated me from other mages. Peninsula magic was a very male world where the prevailing opinion had always been that women were too flighty to be taught magic. Male mages were usually uncomfortable with me and a few of them still actively set out to prove that what everyone believed about women was true.

This situation might have improved over time. However, during the Morian War of Liberation, most of the Morian White College of Mages had colluded with many members of the Gallian White College to have me arrested on a politically motivated charge of necromancy. This had led to a serious estrangement between us all. I would have been prepared to forgive them had they asked, but instead they simply avoided me. I had never been discontented. I was very busy at Ruinac and I had been used to spending my time with nonmages. But now that I could talk to Nikoli Terzu about magery all day, I thoroughly enjoyed it.

We had a great deal in common. Not only did we both have a professional interest in demon magic, but we were both educators of young mages. For the last five years I had been teaching magic to a small group of young women at

Ruinac. I had even hired Edaine to help me do so. But I was not going to think about that anymore.

I sat up late at night talking magery to Nikoli and went with him and the boys when they rode out to the practice range to practice manipulating objects and fighting with magic. I admired the way he taught them. By the time they sat their final exams, Nikoli's students would have far more practical experience of magic than Peninsula mages ever had. I discovered all sorts of new things I could do with my girls when, and if, I ever taught mages again.

I tried to show Nikoli and his students how to perform magic without using the focusing mechanism of spells. They were impressed with my ability, but I did not have much luck with passing the technique on. It must have been something to do with the way I had learned magic or with my raw power.

I had a lot more sucess teaching Nikoli to do nature magic. Magic can either be powered by your own innate ability as it is by most mages and healers in the Western tradition, or by drawing power from outside yourself as necromancers drew on demon power. Shad's people, the Klementari, had tapped into a powerful kind of magic that drew upon the very life force of the natural world. After studying with Klementari mages I had learned to recognize this power and was even able to lift small objects with it. It was a very poor effort compared to the great feats of magic Klementari mages easily performed, but once again early training—or this time the lack of it—seemed to be the cause of this. The Klementari had a profound belief that a spirit ran through all living things and that all life was thus somehow divine. Though I thought this was a wonderful idea, I knew I did not really believe it to my very soul and I was certain this was at the bottom of my problem.

Nikoli was fascinated by the Klementari. There were a number of cults in the border lands, most notably the Marzornite River Cult, who also practiced nature magic, but I was the first person Nikoli had ever met who had real experience with it. He insisted I try and teach him, and so we spent a blustery autumn day sitting cross-legged in a small grove of trees (since nature magic naturally works best among nature) trying to lift small stones. By the end of the day he was managing to make them move around on the ground.

Finally he stood up, let out a deep groan, spread out his arms and, speaking an illusion spell, turned all the trees bright blue and made little stars drop from their branches. I laughed. I remembered doing things like that myself after a day struggling to lift a coin using nature magic.

He laughed too.

"Praise Aumaz! I am still a mage," he said. "I was beginning to wonder."

The stars falling from the trees turned into big wet fish. One of them fell with a plop into my lap. He was a master illusionist. It even smelled fishy. Using magic I picked it up and sent it spinning in his direction. Still laughing he changed it into a flight of pigeons which flew away over his head. Subtly using a new technique which Nikoli had showed me, I bespelled the tree behind him. It reached one of its branches out and tapped him on the shoulder, making him jump in a very satisfactory manner.

"Interfering with my trees? The cheek of you!" he cried in mock outrage.

Suddenly a huge cloud of flowers came streaming down from above burying me completely so that I could see nothing but flowers. The scent of them was wonderful—the sweet fresh smell of lilies and daphne. I breathed in with a sigh.

"They are so beautiful Nikoli. Mmm, how do you get the scent so right?"

A illusory hand seemed to push the flowers away from my face.

"Are you ever going to come out of there?"

"Is there any need too? It's delightful in this illusion."

"But I have refreshment prepared for you and should be most offended if you did not take some."

A couple of servants in livery and white gloves were laying out elegant food and drink on a picnic blanket. Bless Nikoli. He was such a luxury-loving man. Trust him to have servants and food and drink hovering nearby. With a snap the illusion was gone, flowers, blue trees, everything. He pulled me up from the ground and passed me a crystal goblet of sparkling white wine.

"I hardly dare drink it. Is it real or another one of your illusions?" I teased him, knowing full well that since I could touch it, it was real.

He smiled like a pleased cat. "You are a shameless flatterer."

He led me over to the picnic blanket and cast himself down beside me. He was not wearing a robe that day, but a sober brown riding costume of jacket over breeches and tall riding boots. He stretched his long slim legs out with a sigh.

"Now will you have quail or partridge?"

As we ate he created more illusions—a long red dragon that snaked in and out of the tree trunks and a ball of light which grew legs and arms and danced one of the old folk dances of his people. Then he made all kinds of creatures come out of the wood and dance. He was wonderfully imaginative. He made blue rabbits and green fawns and weird mixtures of several different creatures. Finally he created a white horse with a single long horn that he called a unicorn.

He persuaded me to make one of my own and together we made the two beasts race around the grove, rearing and pawing the air with their sparkling white hooves and finally having a sword fight with their horns. The illusion left me breathless and laughing and even the servants, normally models of impassivity, could not help smiling. There must be definite consolations in working for a mage.

"You are a pleasure to picnic with, Nikoli," I told him when we had finished with illusions and were left with a blustery grey day and a slight drizzle falling outside the covering of Nikoli's magic.

"We study to please," he said with a polite gesture of his hand. "But this reminds me of something I must warn you about. The captain recovers well now and soon we shall be setting out for Akieva. We have been very informal here in

Dubrovny but it is not considered proper for unrelated ladies and gentlemen to address each other by their first names. If we are to continue with this Nikoli and Dion, we must do so only in private. I thought I should mention it because I do not wish to lead you into impropriety."

I thanked him for his warning but in fact it made me a little uncomfortable. It reminded me that he was not just a friendly person, but a man and a good-looking one at that. It was not something I wanted to think about. I had been happy in his company. During the day I was able to forget Alinya and Shad and the mess I had made of my private life and remember only that I was a mage and did have talent at that profession. I was extremely grateful to Nikoli Terzu for that reminder.

But though I found diversion and satisfaction at Dubrovny, I had not forgotten the reason we had come to Aramaya in the first place. If anything, Dally was more in my mind now that I was in the same country as her. Several times Kitten suggested that I enlist Nikoli's help in finding her.

"He is a very capable man and he has contacts," she said. "I'm sure he could find out all about her in half the time it will take us."

"How can I enlist his help? He is a demon hunter," I said. "His duty is to seek out and arrest necromancers. And who knows what Dally has been up to these last five years. I am not going to find her just to bring about her execution."

"And if she has been a full blown necromancer?" said Kitten.

This would very likely mean she was responsible for a series of brutal murders. Though you could fuel necromancy with the life force of animals, you could not fuel anything very impressive that way and demons preferred human fuel.

"But maybe she has not been. Perhaps she simply dabbled for a short time and let it be. After all, she cannot be practicing necromancy at the Imperial court. I need time to ascertain how much wrong she has done before I expose her to the attentions of the authorities."

"I hope you realize that compromise is the name of the road you are going down, Dion," said Kitten seriously.

I nodded. There should be no compromise with necromancy. Dally would likely have been burned at the stake in Moria for the amount of necromancy she had practiced before she disappeared and there was a time when I would have seen that as right. But she was my niece. And she had not killed anyone in Moria. In fact she had saved my life and helped me destroy a powerful necromancer. She was a hero, and yet to protect her I had had to hide her role from the report writers.

"You need not be afraid of the prince in this," said Kitten. "This is Aramaya, land of compromise. Do you think that when the emperor or the powerful families catch their relatives dabbling in necromancy they burn them at the stake? The rules are seldom hard and fast here and the prince is intelligent enough to apply them with a reference to circumstances."

"I think it is too dangerous," I told her. "We cannot assume that Prince Nikoli will compromise his integrity and I don't want to put him in that position. Please. Let's not risk it."

So we said nothing to Prince Nikoli. I did not even try to glean information about Dally from him. Those lazily laughing eyes of his were so very perceptive. I was certain that they would see through any ruse I could devise.

At Dubrovny Kitten, the Simonettis, and I shared one of the small guest houses together. The house had a sitting room with three large mirrors. For many years I had avoided mirrors. They formed a gateway between this plane and the demon plane and in certain circumstances, demons could use them to look into this world. Though they had difficulty perceiving and being perceived by ordinary folk, they could see mages, especially those they had had dealings with. For years I had lived in fear that Bedazzer would come to me in the night and call me from the mirror. I dreaded it even more because part of me felt the temptation that he symbolized so strongly. Even after Shad had helped me get over this fear of Bedazzer, I had still avoided mirrors. It is never very pleasant to look up or, worse still, to awake and see a toothy snout leering in at you as if through a window and to know some cunning predator has its eye upon you. Even if Bedazzer had abandoned me for Dally—and there was no way of knowing if he really had—there were several other demons I had offended.

So when I saw the mirrors in the sitting room my first impulse was to call for Simonetti to take them out of the room for me. I did not even want to touch them. Then mid-call, I had a second thought. I carried one of those mirrors into my room and put it near my bed where I could see it. The thought of what I might see when I woke from sleep made me sweat and yet—if Bedazzer did come, if I saw him in this mirror, I might have some chance of finding out what was happening with Dally or of making a connection. It was a slim chance, for even from his own world on the other side of the mirror, Bedazzer could read my mind. He was unlikely to be cooperative. Still there was a possibility that I might find out something. I warned Kitten of what I was doing. Although she feared Bedazzer, she told me to leave the mirrors where they were. It was unlikely that she would be visible to him or he to her. It is the presence of magic that usually makes us attractive and visible to demons.

The first couple of days I jumped every time I saw the mirror. I was forced to use magic to put myself to sleep. I knew whatever happened would be a shock no matter how much I prepared for it. Demons hunger for strong emotions so they like to frighten you.

The fifth night after I had moved the mirror, I was reading late in the prince's library. I had lost track of the time and it was past midnight when the prince came and reminded me how late it was. He insisted on walking me back to my guest house, a typically Aramayan courtesy. When we reached the guest house I invited him to come into the sitting room to continue our discussion over some wine. The servants always left a little oil lamp burning in the sitting room of the guest house and when I pushed open the glass doors, the room was full of shadows leaping in the flickering of the light. The windows beyond were holes of black night. I was reaching for the wine glasses when suddenly the prince exclaimed,

"What . . . ?"

Turning I saw that what I had absentmindedly mistaken as windows were not windows. They were the mirrors—no longer reflecting light but filled with a swirling blackness. There was a sound coming from them, a rustling scratching sound like bristles against glass. My spine froze cold. For a moment we both stood staring as the blackness pressed against the other side of the mirror as if searching for an entrance.

"What the hell is that?" said the prince, breaking my paralysis.

He mustn't. . . . As a mage he would be visible to whatever it was in the mirror.

"Quickly," I cried. "Get out."

I pushed him to the door and out through it.

"Wait," he said turning in my grasp,

"No. If it sees you it will always come back to you. You'll never be free of it. Stay there."

To my surprise he did as he was told.

I went over to the mirror. The blackness looked strangely hairy. It seemed to move and swirl, but at the same time it was hard like part of the body of a creature far far bigger then the mirror.

"Bedazzer?" I called softly. There was no answer. Just a sound like a huge animal pressing itself against a window, steadily testing it for weaknesses.

"Bedazzer?" I called again. There was responsive movement within the blackness, something I could not make out. But no other sound. He was toying with me no doubt. As was his way. There was definitely something alive in that blackness.

Magic might get me a reaction. I lit a magelight on the end of my fingers.

The effect was instantaneous.

Suddenly the blackness in the mirror flung itself against the glass with all its strength. The mirror shuddered under the blow and teetered. I caught it and pushed it back with my body and as I did a repulsive sucking sound came from the other side of the glass. The horror of it overcame me. Without thinking I spoke the words of dispelling. There was a kind of sticky ripping and suddenly the glass showed only golden candlelight and my scared face. And Prince Nikoli rushing in through the doorway behind me.

"What was that? Was it a demon?"

He hurried across to the mirror and peered into it.

"I suppose I should be grateful to you for getting me out of the room so fast but I'm not. I've never seen a demon."

I found my voice.

"I'm not sure that was one. I've never seen anything like it before. The demons I know have a form. They talk to you. This thing just seemed like a formless hungry . . . thing."

Great mindless blackness moving across the face of our world. Overwhelmed by gnawing hungers. Smazor's words came back to me. Describing demons who could not control their hunger enough to collude with humans.

"I would have liked to see it up closer," said Nikoli regretfully. "I know they are evil but I cannot help finding them fascinating."

"Yes. I felt that way once too. But believe me, seeing demons is an experience which palls quickly. And once they know you they will come back for you again and again. They hunger so for our world and our life force and we are the only avenue to what they want. And they are frightening. They read your mind. They know how to tempt your darkness and play on your fears. The first time I saw Bedazzer in a mirror, even though he was safely in his own world he could still exert a force which drew me to the mirror."

"Was that thing the demon you fought in Gallia? Bedazzer, is that what you called him?"

I should not have named him. Even the common names of demons, when used with magic, can bring them to your mirror. If you know their secret names, they will be your slaves.

"If it was a demon, it was not one I knew. It must have been some random entity from the demon plane."

"A random entity? But that doesn't make sense. I mean you have a link with this Bedazzer. That is why you would expect to see him. But any other entity. I am a mage too and I am not without power and demonic entities do not just appear in my mirrors."

"Yes. I'm as mystified as you are."

"It scared you, didn't it?"

"They always scare me. They have so much power and so much cunning and all they want to do is consume you."

"And yet you have fought more of them than any other mage living."

"Circumstances made it necessary to do so. I never sought them out."

I rubbed my face. My palms were sweaty.

"I think we should have that drink, Dion."

Nikoli turned and lit some candles. The shadows in the room receded. While he was pouring wine, I covered the mirrors with blankets from my bedroom. However I did not cover the one in the bedroom, nor did I carry it out.

The break in the conversation gave me the opportunity to think up some good lies. I could tell the prince was bubbling with questions.

"You dread seeing this Bedazzer again don't you? So why have you left these mirrors in the room?" he asked, as we sat on chairs drawn up before the open glass doors enjoying the soft breeze and the sound of the nearby sea. With the candles lit the room seemed too homey to have been the haunt of demon creatures a few moments before.

I was quite pleased with my lie.

"It was an experiment. I wanted to see if he had forgotten about me. It is a nuisance to always avoid mirrors. The experiment has failed. I will ask the servants to remove the mirrors in the morning."

I had a feeling he knew I was lying. I thought guiltily of the other mirror in my bedroom. Surely a man with such a big house didn't know all the mirrors in it. Nikoli did not say anything, however. He simply sat there swirling the wine in his glass.

"I've been curious for some time to know what brings the

Demonslayer of Gallia to Aramaya," he said finally. "Is it impolite of me to ask?"

"I have come to Aramaya to accompany my friend, Countess Katerina. I have always wanted to see the center of the world. What Peninsula person has not? So when my friend asked me to come here with her, I jumped at the chance."

It was a very useful lie because it had the virtue of being almost true.

"The Countess Katerina Ardynne. Now there is an interesting person," he said thoughtfully, speaking Kitten's pseudonym with a certain deliberation.

I tensed myself to fend off questions about Kitten's past. She said that most Aramayans would recognize her as the ex-courtesan who had once been the mistress of the Duke of Gallia and that I shouldn't lie on her account, but I wasn't about to be the one to tell people either.

But Nikoli simply said, "You are a very good friend. Does it not bother you to leave your great work in Ruinac? Restoring a land laid waste by a demon must be a lifetime's work."

"Yes, it is," I said. "Though there are others who can do it now. And the work is no longer so urgent. Many people died during the Revolution of Souls and much of the land we have recovered is lying fallow as it is. I felt it could wait while I took this journey. It was such an opportunity. I did not want to miss it."

"And the Lord of Ruinac? He did not wish to come."

I froze. Here was a subject I did not want to discuss. I had no convenient lies here. I did my best.

"He is not of Aramayan blood so Aramaya did not mean as much to him. In truth he is not overly fond of traveling."

Actually Shad loved to see new places. I thought about him every time I saw something new.

"But he cannot wish to be separated from his wife for so long," said the prince. "A wife such as you. I should not like it."

I did not know what to say to this. Such a remark and with this casual compliment in its wake. I wanted to see the expression on Nikoli's face as he spoke, but I did not dare look him in the eye. I struggled with my emotions for a moment. A shrug was the best I could do.

"He . . . he will manage. I have his permission to come. And now I think I am tired. If you will pardon me, I shall retire to bed."

The whole exchange told him much more than I would have liked. Yet if he was curious for more satisfactory answers, he did not give any sign of it in the next few days. We discussed the demon in the mirror again and pottered about in his workroom as before. Nor did he compliment me again during the time I was at Dubrovny.

As for myself, that night I felt so churned up over Shad I did not think about the implications of what I had seen in the mirror. More and more as I lay awake long into each night, I felt that I should have tried to talk to him instead of just giving up as I did. On the other hand, there had seemed and still seemed no point. All that fighting. For over a year we had hardly spoken a civil word to each other and for months we had not even made love. If only I had not been so angry at him when we had been together. If only I had not blamed him so for our childlessness! What a fool I was to have expected his love to last under such conditions. Had there been anything to salvage? I was beginning to feel that Shad had made the right decision. Yet I missed him terribly. I still loved him.

The mirror remained in my room. Twice before I left Dubrovny I was woken from sleep in the early hours of the morning by the sound of something brushing against glass again, and in the flickering candle light I saw that great shapeless thing pressed against the other side of the mirror. I called to Bedazzer and once even to Smazor, the demon that Darmen Stalker, the necromancer, had used in the Revolution of Souls. There was no answer, just a great swirling blackness that did not seem to be made of feathers or fur or skin, but was still a physical being pressing itself against the inside of the glass like a big animal.

Great mindless blackness. Smazor's words seemed to describe the thing in my mirror perfectly. But what was it doing in my mirror? Both Bedazzer and Smazor had minds. Or had Bedazzer changed in some way? Had the other demons somehow deprived him of his powers in vengeance for helping me? Was such a thing possible? I had no idea.

AFTER ABOUT SEVEN days the captain was well enough to travel by carriage and the party, including Prince Nikoli, Count Alexi, and several of the boys, set out on the six-day journey north to Karanagrad. Here Kitten and I would catch a riverboat for the long trek up the Novsky river to the capital Akieva.

When Kitten had said everything was bigger in Aramaya, I had not really comprehended her meaning. Once we left the coast behind I understood. Aramaya was huge. For day after day we traveled across a great flat landscape under a huge sky. The wheat harvest was over and great fields of stubble stretched out to the horizon. The only variation was the occasional potato field where peasants were still harvesting. All this tremendous empty space was intimidating for those of us used to the rolling hills and compact horizons of the Oesterrad Peninsula.

The landscape was not wholly monotonous, however. There were great houses, monasteries, copses of trees, dusty little villages and towns, and an occasional dip in the road where a creek or river had cut a small gully.

The other thing that impressed me about Aramaya was

its shabbiness. Of course, the time after the harvest is a shabby time of year, but Aramaya was more so. The road, for instance, was sometimes very well kept but more often neglected and badly rutted. When it rained, as it did several times on our journey, the carriage became bogged again and again and Nikoli and I had to pull it out. Goodness knew how those who traveled without mages fared.

Twice we came upon travelers who had been set upon and robbed. Now I understood why Nikoli had been keen that we travel in a large group. I was a little shocked by this sign of lawlessness. Somehow I had expected things to work better at the center of the world. I asked Nikoli why the road varied so and he said it was the responsibility of whoever owned the land round about. Many landowners lived all year round in Akieva and rarely visited these out-of-the-way areas, and so some things became neglected.

Wherever we went the serfs lived in wretched little shacks built of rough-hewn logs and mud. Each miserable little group of cabins had its horde of half-naked, barefoot, runny-nosed children who looked as if they did not get enough food. These peasant shacks did not look like they could survive very heavy falls of snow, so I was glad to learn that the climate was fairly mild on this coastal plain. It was inland in the country around Akieva that the famous long freezing winters of Aramaya occurred.

As a resident of the Peninsula I had never questioned my countrymen's assumption that everything was done better in Aramaya. Of course we did not want to live there. The Peninsula had a nicer climate and freedom from necromancy. But everyone knew that Aramaya was less provincial, more civilized. It was the place all new ideas came from. Now that I was here, I discovered with some surprise the rather obvious fact that some things were actually more civilized on the Peninsula. We did not have such widespread poverty with its attendant ills of hunger and lawlessness. Nor did we have serfdom. How horrifying that someone could have so much power over you. Surely I misunderstood the situation and the amount of power the aristocrats had.

Yet the fact that Nikoli could free his serfs and turn them

into paid laborers and paying tenants without any reference
to the government of the country suggested that the Imperial
government took little interest in them. I remembered how
well clothed and fed Nikoli's peasants had been and ven-
tured to compliment him on this.

Evidently this was too forthright of me, for he looked a little
embarrassed, waved his hand vaguely, and said modestly,

"It is the fashion in Akieva at the moment to worry about
the welfare of the peasants. I do not like to be behind the
times."

If it was mere fashion that prompted him to be a good
landlord, then there were hell of a lot of unfashionable nobles in Aramaya.

We made a large party, what with the two merchants and
the pilgrims. I did not much like the merchants, who had
been haughty when they thought I was just a healer and
overly fulsome when they discovered I was the Demonslayer.
Back on the ship, one of them had offered Kitten a ducat
for a tumble in the sail closet which made me furious, although Kitten was more insulted by the size of the fee offered than the implication that an actress was available for
sexual hire to anybody. We both much preferred the company
of the pilgrims, especially a well-meaning elderly couple who
rode in the carriage with the captain. Despite their reli-
giousness they treated Kitten with the same kindliness as
everyone else and sometimes she rode in the carriage with
them.

For myself, I continued to spend most of my time in
Prince Nikoli's company. We found so much to say to each
other. He was a good host, attentive to pilgrims and merchants alike, but on the road the two of us usually rode
together. Not that there was anything wrong with that. We
were colleagues and I thought we had become friends. And
yet sometimes I wondered. . . . He showed a tendency to
pay me playful compliments at the beginning of the journey,
but his dark eyes quickly perceived that I was uneasy with
this.

Since living with Kitten, I had been in the company of
many charming men, but I was inclined to warily avoid

them. I knew there was a part of me that craved male attention. I longed to have someone find me attractive with a longing that was almost a need. I was ashamed at what seemed to me just wounded pride. I wanted proof I was still lovable even if Shad had stopped loving me, that was all. Such a craving made it difficult for me to tell the difference between mere friendship and more tender feelings and could only lead to disaster.

Shad would have loved seeing this exciting new country. I thought of him and Alinya often, but the thoughts were not as oppressive as they had been on the sea crossing. In fact it would have been a very pleasant journey had it not been for the fact that two days from Karanagrad my women's bleeding started. That changed everything.

In the first year after I had lost Alinya I had gone into mourning every time my bleeding had shown I had not conceived again. But over time as I became more and more hopeless of ever conceiving, this depression had been gradually replaced by the most terrible anger. It was at this time that Shad and I began to have our worst arguments. I had asked the Klementari's chief mage Beg about this once and she had told me that my womb was reminding me that it was unhappy about being empty.

"You should fill it with the child it wants so badly," she said. "As if I have a choice in the matter," I had retorted, at which she snorted and told me I was a mage and should change my mind. Beg could be a mean old cow sometimes.

She was probably right in that it was the death of Alinya that caused these feelings. I had never had any trouble with my bleeding cycle before I conceived a child, but now every month the mild ache of my belly at bleeding time was a constant reminder of Alinya's final struggle for life and that terrible moment of absence. And of my failure. Even the smallest things would fill me with the most dreadful fury. Black depression was my only relief. Then I could do nothing but lie in bed and weep.

In Aramaya as always I did my best to conceal the screaming fury inside me by being as silent and withdrawn as possible, but it did not help any more than it had before. The rubbing of the saddle on my leg, the snorting of the horses, even the jingle of their bits set my teeth on edge. When we stopped at midday, the tumult of voices inside the inn made me want to scream and break things. I went outside to wander around the dusty outhouses and resisted with difficulty the urge to stamp on the chickens that swarmed around my feet.

Then, as ill-luck would have it, I came upon a woman feeding her baby. The soft little creature was curled tenderly against its mother's breast, its tiny fingers grasping softly at her dress. The woman was rocking and humming. The two of them were in a happy dreaming world together. . . . I wanted to step up close and touch the baby's soft skin. My arms felt so achingly empty.

How hungrily I must have looked at them. The mother looked up and her eyes met mine. By some instinct she turned her body away from me as if to protect her child.

She said something to me in peasant Aramayan. Something like "Who are you?" or "What do you want?" I saw fear in her face. The babe, feeling her fear, dropped the breast and began to cry.

"I'm sorry," I mumbled to her in Morian. I turned and stumbled away, my eyes full of unshed tears. I would not cry about this. I had cried enough and it did no good. But the grief was like an unbearable weight. In a silent hay shed, I threw myself down on the hay bales and wept and wept. I could not stop. The tears seemed to feed on themselves.

At some point in this haze of weeping Kitten came in and patiently sat down beside me, rubbing my back. She had seen me like this before. I did not have to tell her what was wrong.

"Oh, Dion, and you were doing so well," she said.

Her words went to my brain like a hot needle. I turned on her.

"Doing well," I shrieked at her. "At what? At getting over it? Well I'm never going to get over it, damn you. Nothing will ever be any good. Nothing will ever console me. A childless woman might as well be dead. How can her life have any meaning?"

Kitten's kind eyes snapped to anger. She jumped up.

"I see. Well I have no children, damn you, and can have none. Do you think *me* better dead?"

She turned on her heel and walked out.

I sat up on the hay bale, sobs choked back by shock. She had never done anything like that before.

As a young married woman, Kitten had had a riding accident and had lost her first child. Her husband had divorced her when it had been proved that she was too badly damaged to have more children. I had always known this, but somehow I had forgotten it or . . . Sweet Tanza what had I said? A woman's life has no meaning without children. But I didn't mean her. I meant me. She couldn't think I meant her, could she? She was one of the finest people I knew. Every day of her life was a celebration of living. And yet I had said a childless woman might as well be dead. Oh God, how those words must have cut her.

I tried to tell myself it served her right for telling me I would learn to live with it. I would never get over losing Alinya and now that Shad was gone my life was destroyed. But the screaming anger of my bleeding had abandoned me, leaving me with a guilt which robbed my thoughts of their conviction. I had let my pain make me hurt my friend. And she had only been trying to help me. What was the justification for such a thing?

Perhaps Kitten did not feel her loss as much I did. But I knew this was untrue. She had lost her child and the love of her husband all at once and been sent to the country to live in seclusion and shame for the rest of her life. At least Shad had not left me the moment I lost Alinya. At least he had kept on trying.

This whole incident echoed the past too closely. Shad too had been the soul of patience at first. Then I had said something which had cut him and we had wound up screaming at each other. Even though we later apologized things had been said which could not be unsaid. He had become less and less patient, probably because my grief had been a reproach to him. We had fought more often until eventually my fury during bleeding time had become simply a small peak in the endless time of anger.

Was this cycle now going to begin with Kitten? I must try and stop it.

"Dion?" said a voice at the doorway. Nikoli Terzu was peering into the dark shed.

"Is anything wrong?" he said tentatively.

I jumped up from the hay bale, glad that it was dim in the shed. My face must have been covered in dust and tear stains.

"No. No. Nothing is wrong. I just wanted to be alone for a little."

He bowed slightly. "Then I must beg your pardon for intruding. The food is almost ready. I have hired a room for you ladies to wash up in."

"Thank you," I said. I went quickly to the door, but as I passed him he caught my arm and said hesitantly, "You are unwell?"

I did not look at him for fear he would guess that I had been crying.

"A small headache," I said. "Nothing more. Thank you." I brushed past him and went quickly out into the sunlight.

Thank God for Aramayan formality, I thought as I ran into the inn. I had no wish to explain my personal griefs to Nikoli, and being an Aramayan it was unlikely that he would ask.

Most of the women in our party had already washed up, but Suza Simonetti was still in the room digging around in her bag. Behind her sat Kitten looking out of the window. Had they been talking about me? Suza too was childless and yet she and Simonetti seemed really happy together. Would she be angry at me as well? It seemed not. When I came into the room, Suza came over and kindly asked me if I was well and offered to get me some hot water for washing. The moment she left the room Kitten got up from the window and came over.

"I'm sorry that I lost my temper," she said.

"No. No. I'm sorry. It's my fault. I shouldn't have said what I did."

We squeezed each other's hands with anxious smiles.

"I didn't mean to say that your life was meaningless," I said. "It's not."

"I know you didn't. I never seriously thought you did," said Kitten.

Yet I could see she had been weeping too.

"You never thought your life was a failure without children, did you?" I said tentatively.

"Oh, often I have." She sat down and looked out of the window and sighed again.

"Sometimes I think of what might have been. Sometimes I wonder about being old and alone with no family about me."

Her words chilled me to the bone. Was there no hope?

She turned.

"Oh, dear. We two are a bad combination at the moment. You are grieving and I am anxious about returning to Akieva and it makes me short-tempered."

"I have not been a good friend to you," I said, overcome by regret. "I have hardly noticed. It must be very hard for you."

She drew me down on the windowseat beside her and we put our arms around each other.

"Are you worried about your family?" I asked.

"Yes. They will be furious at my return. Ah Dion, why do we regret not having children? Is family life anything to long for? At least with no family I can choose my friends and not worry about my children plotting after my money. Can you imagine me as a terrible bossy old woman with smelly little dogs, false teeth, and a bright orange wig? Tyrannizing over my children and forcing them to marry men with bad breath and pot bellies? I think they've had a narrow escape not being born, don't you?"

This unlikely portrait made me laugh.

"You wouldn't be such a woman. You would be one of those terrible old women who worry your family sick by insisting on hunting at the age of eighty, threatening to publish memoirs of a misspent youth, and scandalizing everyone by marrying a forty year old."

She threw back her head and laughed. "Forty year old. Hah! That will be too ancient for me. I've already decided that the mission of my old age is to seduce schoolboys." She leaped up, twirled, and waggled her hips. "They have much more energy and. . . ." She winked. "They're always so grateful."

"So the sun is out again," said Suza, coming in with a bucket of hot water. "Come on you two slow coaches. Let's wash up and get some food. I'm starved."

I cannot say it is the ideal way to achieve this, but at least my argument with Kitten had released something inside me. The midday meal was almost pleasant. I managed to have a conversation with the two merchants in our party without biting either of their heads off and though I felt an almost physical sense of lowness for the rest of our journey to Karanagrad, I no longer felt like killing anybody. Which was a great relief.

Two days later we reached the city of Karanagrad where we were to catch the riverboat up to Akieva. Karanagrad, or Karana's city as it would have translated into Morian, was supposedly built upon the place where Tanza's mother Karana had lived her final years and died. Her body was entombed in the great Cathedral of the Holy Mother. It was a point of pilgrimage for people all over the Aumazite world.

The city streets were crowded with worshippers clad in sun yellow robes and wearing garlands of yellow and orange flowers and ribbons. In theory you could hear many of the Peninsula dialects spoken in Karanagrad because of the large number of pilgrims who crossed the Western Ocean to come here every year, but I could make out nothing through the hubbub of merchants, hawkers, street performers, and religious processions. Toward midday the bells of all the many churches began to add to this clamor as they welcomed the Triumph of the Sun.

I could see why they called Karanagrad the Sunburst City. Over all this noise shone the serene golden domes of the

Cathedral of Holy Mother Karana, topped with the sunburst of Aumaz which caught the sun's rays like a great beacon. It was a breathtakingly beautiful building. Our whole party stopped and stared at it for some time as if to print it on our memories. The cathedral and the enormous monastery that attended it looked like a city all their own. The great soaring white walls and golden domes reached up so high, they seemed as if they would scrape the very blue from the sky.

Karanagrad was enormous, for as well as being a pilgrimage city, the Novsky river was so wide and deep here that oceangoing vessels could come the several miles upriver from the coast to its ports. Their cargoes and passengers could then be transferred to the riverboats that made the long journey up the Novsky to Aramaya's imperial capital at Akieva.

It took us most of the morning to travel from our lodging on the outskirts of the city to the river port where our traveling party broke up to go its separate ways—the pilgrims to various hostels and monasteries and the merchants to their lodgings at the counting house of their business associates.

Kitten, the Simonettis, and I stayed with Nikoli's party, for he had invited us to be guests at his Aunt Euphemia's house overnight before we took the morning boat for Akieva. We crossed the river by ferry and for another hour traveled through a maze of small streets and wide crowded thoroughfares before we began to ascend into the steep hills beneath the cathedral. In all this traveling not once did we leave the city, nor did the number of people and houses thin out to suburbs. How did so many people live in the same place without falling into chaos?

"Is Akieva as big as this?" I asked Count Alexi and he laughed and said that it was twice as big. I was not sure I liked the idea of it. It didn't seem healthy for all these people to live like this—breathing each other's stale air and never seeing any greenery. When I got back to Ruinac I must do something about establishing parks and gardens inside the city itself. But then would I ever be returning to Ruinac?

Once we got out onto the hillside, the city began to be less crowded. We were in the richest quarter now, and instead of houses crammed together, there were great mansions surrounded with high walls behind which I could glimpse gardens full of trees and flowers.

Prince Nikoli's aunt was a very devout Aumazite, which was why she lived in this great white house so close to the wall of the Cathedral. She and her husband welcomed me with great enthusiasm. We were served a huge midday meal in her sunny garden seated at a table set with pure white linen and glass goblets surrounded by liveried serfs with fans to chase away flies. There was none of the sparse simplicity that would have marked the life of a devout Aumazite back home. Or at least that was what I thought at the time. Later I realized that Nikoli's aunt considered herself, and was considered by her peers, to be leading a very simple holy life.

The hills were very steep this close to the Cathedral walls, which meant that we were far enough above the neighboring houses to have a wonderful view of the river valley below us. After eating luncheon, everyone sat upon the stone benches against the garden wall, drinking kesh, talking lazily, and watching all the traffic, tiny at this distance, moving up and down the crowded river. We could see down to the forest of high masts and sails that marked the seaport. It was like being in the front row of an exciting play, and yet we were so far above all the noise and traffic that we could hear the little birds chirping in the trees around us.

"What will you do in Akieva?" asked Nikoli lazily. He had changed out of his riding clothes and was wearing a simple white linen robe open at the throat. He looked very relaxed and handsome.

"See the sights, visit the scenes of Kitten's youth."

"And her relatives no doubt," he said, with just the faintest twitch of his lips.

"No doubt," I said. I knew full well that if Kitten's relatives wanted to see her it could only mean ill and I suspected he did too. However one does not say such things in Aramaya.

"I shall be following you to Akieva in a couple of days. Perhaps you would permit me to escort you around the city and introduce you to friends who are working on interesting experiments. I would be extremely pleased if our association could continue."

"So would I," I said, without thinking of any of the implications of what I said. The beautiful place had made me relaxed and lighthearted. "I have very much enjoyed your company Prince Nikoli."

"I . . ."

"We are all going in," said Kitten. "Lady Euphemia has some paintings she wishes to show me. No, no. Do not feel obliged to come in."

"Do you think anyone would mind if I did stay out here?" I asked Nikoli.

"Not at all. I shall stay with you if you will allow it," he replied with mock gallantry. "Think if the sun were to beat down too roughly upon you or some impertinent fly were to bother you. I must not leave you unprotected."

"No indeed. I feel sure I would faint right away if such dreadful things were to happen. I am only a poor frail female after all."

"A mere Demonslayer," he laughed.

A flock of tiny finches with golden wings and bright red beaks suddenly swirled past us.

"Oh Nikoli," I cried with delight. "What are they called?"

"They are Holy Finches. My aunt puts out seed for them. Their visit is supposed to bring Karana's blessing."

"What a charming conceit!"

"You like birds and animals, don't you?" he said suddenly. "If you come with me now, I shall show you something you shall really enjoy. Quickly now before the sun goes down."

He called a servant to bring us cloaks and then led me out of his aunt's garden and up the long winding road to the monastery. Just before the monastery gates, we turned left. Along the high white walls was a winding little path that led up, along and finally over the hill. It was a long climb to the top and the path was quiet. There was no one else out here in the late afternoon shadows. As we crested the hill the sun was gilding the world with a last golden glow, and the faint wisps of cloud in the deepening blue sky were turning pale pink with the coming sunset. On the hilltop the most wonderful view stretched out before us. The tree-covered land was heaped like a rumpled blanket into wooded hills and craggy mountains. Directly below us the river, curving between one hill and the next, had spread out into a great lazy curve of water and seeped out of its banks to form a marshy lake. A great flock of white birds was feeding noisily in the meadows at the lake side. There must have been hundreds of them.

"Egrets," said Nikoli. "Are they not wonderful? And soon they will be more wonderful. Conditions are just right." He opened the cloak he had seized from the servant and spread it under a tree.

"All the land below belongs to the monastery and so it is not drained and put under cultivation but left as it was when Karana saw it. Now I beg the honored lady to take her seat beneath this unworthy tree upon this humble cloak, so. . . . Perhaps she would like a sugar plum."

With a flourish he produced a box from his pocket and offered it to me.

"You are the perfect host, Nikoli," I said.

"One does one's very humble best," he smiled.

Suddenly the noise of the birds grew and a cloud of them took off into the sky. They swirled and whirled around the valley below in a great white cloud like spring blossom in a wind.

Then suddenly they came streaming up toward us and swept over the hill past us on either side of our tree—dozens and dozens of them. It was like being in the middle of a powerful foam-crested wave. The egrets were so beautiful, with their huge fast-beating white wings, plumed crests, and long dark legs splayed out behind them and as each of them reached the hilltop the setting sun turned its breast feathers rosy pink.

"Oh how wonderful," I cried as they came, and when they had finished passing I found that I was clutching Nikoli's hand in mine.

"That was perfect," I said, as exhilarated as if I had been swimming in a wild surf.

"Oh, Dion, you are the most extraordinary woman," he said and suddenly he put his arms around me and kissed me hard upon the mouth.

The moment, the feel of his lips on mine—it was all intoxicating. I was carried away by it and kissed him back before I remembered everything.

I pulled away from him. We stared at each other.

"Oh Nikoli. I'm sorry. I didn't mean . . ."

He seemed quite calm.

"I know you did not. Your heart is too full of sadness at the moment." He took my hand. "You do not wear a wedding ring. All is not well between you and the Lord of Ruinac, is it?"

Damn. How horribly perceptive he was. I should have brought another ring. In the Aumazite church the only acceptable reason for divorce was barrenness and that carried a terrible stigma for a woman.

I stared at our hands.

"No," I said unhappily.

"I have distressed you," he said ruefully. "Please do not be. It was my intention to comfort you." He kissed my hand. "I was carried away by the moment." He turned my hand over and kissed the palm. "Let me help you forget him," he said softly.

"I . . . I'm not ready to do that," I stammered.

He turned away and looked out over the darkening landscape.

"I am a foolish man," he sighed. "I have made my move much too early and now I have spoiled everything." He stood up and held out his hand. "I hope you will forgive me and still look upon me as a friend."

"I would like that. I hope you will forgive me."

"There is nothing to forgive," he said. He shook out the cloak and put it gently around my shoulders. He was silent throughout our walk back to his aunt's house, but that evening at dinner he sat beside me and behaved so entirely as if nothing had happened that I almost wondered if anything had.

When I told Kitten about this interlude she looked extremely pleased.

"Excellent!" she cried.

"I'm glad you're pleased. We both found it very embarrassing."

"Of course you did. Still don't you think it's nice that you have an admirer? I do. And such an attractive one at that. See. It just proves that your husband was a fool."

"Oh, Kitten, be serious."

She pinched my cheek.

"You know the best place to forget one love is in the arms of another."

"Aumaz! I wish I'd never told you."

She subsided. "I'm sorry," she said. "But I am just so pleased for you. Tell me then what is it that troubles you about it."

It was hard to answer that. I felt guilty in case I hurt Nikoli and guilty in case I had unwittingly led him on and worried that the pleasant friendship I had had with him was destroyed. I liked him. But I did not feel like reviving that part of my life. I wanted to be quiet and safe and talk about magic and other nonpersonal matters with friendly people who did not get too close.

"Do you think Nikoli will get offended and make trouble?"

"You can never say in these situations," said Kitten. "But he seems like an honorable man."

"Maybe I should get another wedding ring. It's just that I'd feel such a hypocrite."

"Ah yes. Perhaps that would be wise. You should go out and get one tomorrow before we leave. This is Aramaya. People prefer certain kinds of deception to the truth. They rarely confront each other." She tweaked my cheek again. "Unless it is in moments of extreme passion."

"You are the end," I said, but actually her teasing made everything less serious. Underneath my anxiety, I was actually very flattered by Nikoli's interest. Flattered but not enough so to lose my head.

"Dion, you're not rejecting the prince out of some misguided loyalty to Shad are you?" said Kitten. "Because really you need feel none. He left you."

"Of course not," I said. But I was not sure how truly I spoke. I still thought of Shad as my husband no matter how much I tried not to.

Had Kitten and I been traveling by ourselves, it would have been difficult for us to find a place on a riverboat going up to Akieva. At this time of year everyone of any breeding was returning to Akieva for the winter social season. However, Prince Nikoli's agents had already booked a place for us on the morning riverboat. Not just any boat either, but the Imperial River Cruiser that had been set up to facilitate the carrying of documents and officials between Akieva and Karanagrad. Ordinarily no amount of money would have enabled us to board this spacious and luxurious official boat, but as a high-ranking demon hunter and hence a court official, Prince Nikoli was able to book us passage.

Extraordinarily enough the Cruiser was powered by teams of four mages who kept it speeding upriver so that it reached Akieva in seven days instead of the usual twelve.

"It must be ferociously expensive to run," I said to Nikoli, who had come with us to the boat. He was just as easy and pleasant as he had been before we had gone to see the egrets the previous night. I found myself forgetting and being as comfortable with him as before.

"It is not at all expensive. Many of the mages powering the boat have been born into serfdom. Such peasant mages automatically belong to the emperor no matter whose estate they have been born on. Even though they receive no wages, Imperial Serfs, especially magely ones, have almost as great a status as free merchants. Their wives and children are all made free. Only when the children are born with magical powers must they remain in serfdom."

I found the idea of mages being born into serfdom even more distasteful than actual serfdom and so I changed the subject. It seemed pointless to beat Nikoli's ear over the whole basis of Aramayan society, especially when he had no taste for serfdom himself.

"Thank you for everything," I said. Somehow thanks seemed inadequate after all the happiness I had had in Nikoli's company. I wanted to ask him to come and visit me in Akieva, but I did not like to lead him on any more than I already had.

"It was entirely my pleasure Lady Dion," he said. He took my hand and kissed it. "Until we meet again in Akieva."

In Moria I had assumed that I would slip into Akieva in my plain brown healer's robes and discreetly find my niece. There was not much chance of that now. Prince Nikoli's agent had booked me onto the riverboat as Lady Dion Holyhands of Ruinac and thanks to Rosinsky's report on me, every mage on the boat knew that I was the Demonslayer of Gallia. Before we were even settled in our cabin a servant came from the boat's team of travel mages asking us to take a meal with them. Though it embarrassed me that they made much of me during the journey, it would be sheer whining to say I did not enjoy it. The travel mages were not at all as cowed as the other serfs I had met, and every night I sat up late talking magic with them.

Aramayan mages seemed to be more used to talking to women about serious matters. None of them tried to patronize me or to trap me into making foolish remarks. I had such a pleasant journey that sometimes I hardly thought about Shad and my lost baby for hours on end. I have always suspected I am a shallow kind of person, easily consoled by trivia.

"My dear if this keeps up my nose shall be thoroughly out of joint," twinkled Kitten. "Here am I one of the Peninsula's great courtesans and all these men are seeking me out simply so that they can talk about you. Humph."

"Isn't it fun. I haven't had a moment to be bored."

"I'm glad," she said. "You know, watching all these fellows fawning over you makes me realize I haven't treated you with enough respect all these years. You really are an amazing person."

"I've been meaning to talk to you about that," I said lightly. "What someone of my amazingness really requires is more people giving me nice presents and coming into my room every morning on their knees bringing fresh strawberries and cream for breakfast. And a team of people following me about all day telling me how terrific I am. So how about organizing something, hmm?"

"Your wish is my command oh Mighty One." She bowed mockingly. "But seriously Dion, how can you feel yourself a failure when you have done such wonderful things in your life? How can you think it's all meaningless when you have made such a difference to everyone?"

"How can *you* say that of all people?" I said in astonishment. "Bedazzer betrayed me because I was stupid and he injured you horribly once he got to you. That was my fault."

She shrugged. "I survived and Norval did not. You killed him. You freed me. Why can you not focus on the good things you have done instead of what you have not managed to do?"

"Is it so great to be a powerful mage when you cannot even do the most simple ordinary things any woman can do? Have a child and a home?"

"You're hopeless," said Kitten ruefully. "What am I going to do with you?"

She turned and went away down the deck shaking her head.

The landscape along the river was magnificent. All along it were great towns with mighty golden cathedrals in their centers. Even the villages along the way were very prosperous looking. Sometimes as we passed, boats came out from them to bring us fresh milk and fish.

We passed through a series of towering canyons and through several mountain ranges. Then two days out of Akieva we came to another great plain. It was just like the plain we had traveled over with Prince Nikoli, a horizon stretching out endlessly. On the coastal plain it had still been early autumn, however. Here the trees had lost their leaves completely and the fields were fallow, their rich chocolate soil plowed ready for next spring's planting. The sky was often overcast and a chill wind and frequent rainstorms made me reluctant to walk on deck. It was like the depths of winter on the Peninsula. The mages, however, talked of fine autumn weather in a way which made me fear the coming winter.

As we got closer and closer to Akieva, Kitten became more and more subdued. I did my best to get her to talk about what was troubling her and tried to spend as much time as possible keeping her company, but sometimes she made it clear that she wanted to be alone. She told me she was simply nervous about returning to the capital and that only time and experience could deal with such emotions, but I could not help remembering that once in Akieva she had been a happy young bride and it had ended very suddenly for her. Such memories must bring sadness with them.

If Karanagrad had seemed huge, Akieva was enormous. It took almost two hours for the fast boat to go from the city's muddy outskirts to its glittering center. I stood on the deck for an hour expecting the port around every corner until one of the mages kindly explained that we still had an hour's journey to go and coaxed me to join him on a comfortable bench in the prow. From here he and another mage pointed out the sights. How many there were! The river was lined with palatial mansions painted in colorful reds, pinks, blues, and yellows and stuccoed with curlicues of white plaster along the roof lines and around the glittering windows. So much glass. . . .

We passed the Naval Academy, marked by a glittering golden spike that towered up into the sky, and the Headquarters of the Army where an enormous black marble arch celebrating the glorious dead graced a huge grass parade ground. And everywhere there were churches and cathedrals and more churches. Each had an onion-domed tower but some glittered with mosaics, some with white marble and some with gold. It was just as it should be at the center of the world, only more magnificent.

Our speed was slowed considerably by the traffic on the river. Produce boats and barges carrying wood or cattle or refuse plowed through the waters. Between them slid all manner of little boats containing passengers or fishermen or market goods. The air was filled with the shouting of the boatmen and the sound of their horns and trumpets.

Finally the Imperial Winter Palace came into view. It was a mighty building with a huge dome on top and a colonnade of white marble around a great red-tiled square. The roof glittered with more gold than I had seen anywhere in this country of golden roofs. A flight of white marble stairs led down from the Palace to a white marble landing platform. Yet despite its size there was a sense of grace about the whole building. The shimmering water caught its reflection so that the river's surface was covered with flecks of gold and white light. Here the river traffic had cleared, or at least was sticking in a subdued manner to the opposite bank.

"Is it not beautiful," said the mage at my side. "The dome is its crowning glory. Vladimir the Tenth built it seventy years ago. Of course such a dome is terribly impractical in our climate. If left to itself the weight of the winter snow would collapse it. A whole regiment of mages works to prevent this happening. But we Akievans love it. It shows that our emperor is even mightier than the weather."

A odd thing for a devoutly Aumazite emperor to aim for, since power over the elements is held to be Aumaz's exclusive province, but I said nothing to the mage, whose face was currently shining with pride.

At that moment Kitten arrived with the captain and Head Travel Mage in tow. She seized my arm and dragged me from my chair.

"Dion, the Head Mage tells me that he sent ahead to tell the Magic College that you are coming and he has just received a message saying that there is a ceremonial greeting party awaiting you at the dock. Quickly, you must tidy your hair and put something decent on. You can't appear to all these people in that old robe."

Suza Simonetti was waiting in my cabin with my second best blue silk mage's robes. I had only brought them because it was the law in many places that a mage show himself by his dress and I had thought that at some time I might be forced to wear them. Now Kitten and Suza laced me into them and unplaited, brushed, and replaited my hair in feverish haste.

"Oh Aumaz!" I groaned "I don't want this. Curse that Head Mage."

"I just wish the silly man had thought to tell us earlier."

"Busy nose. He is just using you to give himself airs," muttered Suza dourly. "Now how will you find your niece quietly? That's what I want to know."

How indeed?

Even as they fussed over me I felt the boat slowing down. By the time I returned to the deck, we were pulling up to a dock. The dock was bristling with people—mages and demon hunters most of them.

"Leave the luggage and the rest to Simonetti and me," said Suza in my ear. "You just enjoy yourself."

Enjoyment was not the first thing on my mind as I surveyed the expectant faces crowded at the dock's edge. The whole of the Akievan White College of Magic must be here, including the students. Oh dear! The Head Mage had also found time to change his robes. He caught my arm.

"Look," he said. "It's Count Igor Strugatsky, the Dean of the White College of Akieva and Prince Dimitri Gagarin, the Master of Students. We *are* being honored."

He took my elbow and ushered me down the gangplank and across the dock to where two mages, resplendent in blue silk robes sprinkled with golden embroidered stars, were standing on a dais.

Akieva

I MUST HAVE met every mage in Akieva by the time that day was over. After the official welcome at the river dock, Kitten and I were loaded into a carriage and driven through the broad streets to the White College of Aramaya. The White College was the organization that trained and regulated the activities of mages in each country. Like most of these organizations, the Aramayan White College was housed in a white stone building, in this case made of shining white marble. It was, of course, like everything in Aramaya, huge, a great barracks of a building.

The carriages drove through enormous white-painted gates into a large courtyard. All around the courtyard the walls of the buildings shimmered with the illusion of constantly falling water. The courtyard was lined with trees. The trees were real enough but their bare winter branches had been clothed in illusions. Some were covered in sparkling lights or glowing fruits, while others had leaves shimmering with different colors. One was even decorated with dozens of brilliantly colored exotic birds who chattered and preened their long glorious tails exactly as if they had been real. In the middle of the courtyard a great blue magical ball floated above a pedestal, and within it a huge golden star slowly turned.

I was led around the courtyard to inspect these wonderful displays. Except for the ball, which was a permanent illusion and had rosters of mages to keep it going, all of these illusions were put on by the ranks of students assembled under the trees. The students bowed as I passed. Representatives of every group came forward to present me with bouquets of flowers and after I had admired each illusion and passed on, it disappeared.

I was overwhelmingly touched by this wonderful reception and the excited faces of the boys and young men who stared up at me as I passed. When I mounted the dais with my arms full of flowers, it became clear that I was being called upon to make a speech. I could think of nothing more than to say that I had no words adequate to thank them for this wonderful reception. Fortunately they seemed to like this example of Morian plain speaking and cheered enthusiastically.

Afterward came a ceremonial banquet which finished with a huge cake coated in chocolate and made in the shape of a demon. I was led forward to ceremonially cut the head off with a huge sword. The concept both amused and shocked me. On the Peninsula we would never have treated demons so lightly and yet there was something very pleasing about the idea of our eating up a demon with our own little teeth.

Once again I was called upon to give a speech but this time I was able to acquit myself better; Kitten and I had managed to put some suitable words together in between the other speeches given in my honor. It was not an easy experience for me and afterward I was so tired all I really wanted to do was go home. My speech was followed by several rounds of plum wine and kesh, however, and it was a couple of hours before Kitten said we might politely leave.

I was offered accommodation at the College but we had already arranged to stay with some friends of Kitten's. I was very glad of this. Though everybody I met was very kind, staying at the White College and living up to everyone's expectations of a Demonslayer would have been like being a caged bird. I could have got nothing done without being seen.

Although we had arrived in Akieva in the early afternoon, it was not until late that night that our hired carriage finally turned off the brightly lit boulevard filled with theaters and shops into a much smaller street. It was a much less grand quarter of town than the one around the White College, but the tall thin house was a very respectable size. There were still lights on in the upper rooms and as we got out of the carriage we could hear music and voices.

A maid opened the door and as she ushered us into the front hallway of a tall thin house, a voice from above called, "That you Katty?"

It was a wonderful voice, deep and rich and mellow, a sound that somehow made me think of golden honey. I looked up and saw its owner leaning over the stairs, an immensely tall woman with a red silk gown cut low over her magnificent bosom and skin as black as coal.

"Peppa!" said Kitten and ran up the stairs into her arms.

The magnificent woman's full name was Pepita Sandorez. I blinked a bit at the Sandorez; it was an Ishtaki name and I'd never heard of anyone from the Peninsula that looked like Pepita. Her husband Wilbert Sandorez, a short little man with huge spaniel eyes, might at a pinch have come from the Peninsula except that his accent was all wrong.

Later Kitten explained the whole thing to me. Pepita was an actor (what better profession for her wonderful voice?) and her husband was a theatrical producer. They were Soprians, which was surprising when you considered that Sopria and Aramaya were traditional enemies, although their perennial tension rarely escalated into war. This was why Pepita and Wilby masqueraded in a very casual and unconvincing way as Ishtakis. Such masquerades were common among the large Soprian colony who had for various reasons settled in Akieva, and by all reports much the same masquerade was taking place among the Aramayans living in the Soprian capital, Habib. As long as nobody was too open about where they really came from, Soprian actors were celebrated in Aramaya and Soprian playhouses were always full. I suspect that the fact that the Soprian colony had had the good taste to leave "disgusting" Habib and settle in "wonderful" Akieva was what really made Aramayans sympathetic to this whole crazy ruse.

"Of course, we have to put up with having a Prekazy informer among our servants," said Pepita.

"Prekazy?" I asked.

"The Prekazy are the organization that collects intelligence for the emperor and protects Aramaya from foreigners and traitors," said Kitten. "It is supposed to be secret, but everybody knows it exists even though the emperor regularly denies it."

"And there is an informer in this house?" I asked. How on earth was I going to get to Dally if this was so?

"Don't worry," said Kitten as she followed me up the stairs. "Peppa knows who the informer is so he will be easy enough to get around." She lowered her voice. "Even if we set up on our own, we would have trouble with the Prekazy. They keep a watch on all foreigners. Better to stay with Pepita."

Pepita had invited a number of people over to celebrate Kitten's return to Akieva and they were all making merry in her upper sitting room. The moment the door opened however, Kitten was enveloped by a cloud of attractive, brightly dressed people of all nationalities, who showered her excited face with butterfly kisses. Although they were friendly and interested in me, she was the center of attention. This was a great relief. I was full of food and drink and exhausted by all the attention I had had that day and my eyes kept wanting to close. I sat quietly in a comfortable chair as Kitten held court, describing in marvelous detail our reception at the White College.

"Peppa my dear," cried Wilby Sandorez, interrupting Kitten's story. "You must send out for supplies tomorrow. I foresee that we shall have droves of these mage fellows—a positive plague of them—calling upon us."

"Dozens of mages calling upon us," said Pepita thoughtfully. A twinkle came into her eyes. "And you say many of them are from very good families. Tell me Wilby dear, do you think mages have any money to invest?"

But the following morning, before Pepita and Wilby had risen, we had a much more surprising and unwelcome visitor.

I had gone out to take what passed in Akieva for some fresh air. I went along Pepita's street and found myself on a kind of open square. Wilby Sandorez's playhouse was here, along with taverns, a cockfighting rink, a building where people played bowls, and a number of closed-up looking houses that I suspected to be brothels. The servants had said there was a park but before I found it, I heard my name called and turned to see Captain Simonetti running toward me.

"Quickly Madame. You must come home," he cried. "Pyotr Deserov has come calling on the countess."

Kitten's cousin Pyotr was also her ex-husband's brother. I had met him when I worked for her in Gallia. He was a cunning, vindictive man who had done his best to get her assassinated before he slipped on his own cleverness and had been sent home to Aramaya in disgrace. I hitched up my skirts and raced back to the house after Simonetti. Inside we found Suza with her ear to a door and her hand clasping the hilt of a knife. I had never seen Suza with a weapon before, but somehow I did not doubt her effectiveness with it. Behind the door people were shouting.

"Thank God," she breathed when she saw us rushing up the stairs. "I can't know how far that Deserov would go, but he'll watch his manners with you around, Madame." She put the knife neatly back inside her blouse and picked up a tray of tea things from a nearby table.

"Come on," she said. She pushed the door open with her foot and went in before me.

Kitten and Pyotr Deserov stood on opposite sides of the room as if the tension between them was too strong to allow them to stand closer. The moment I entered, however, fists unclenched and mouths snapped shut. Silence fell like a brick.

Prince Deserov did not look at all pleased to see me, but he recovered quickly enough. He came over and with the blandest of smiles bowed over my hand.

"Lady Dion. How delightful to see you. Again."

This was a blurring of the truth—the last time he had seen me he had called me a witch. I suspected that this time he had waited till I was out of the house before paying his call. Kitten's eyes sparkled with fury. Perhaps it would be Deserov who needed protection. Would I bother to protect him, I wondered, or would I put in a few blows on my own account?

"My cousin has just been telling me how delighted my family is that I have returned to Akieva," said Kitten with heavy sarcasm. She began to pace around the room.

Suza finished laying out the tea things and left. I sat down and began to pour the tea. I kept my eye on Deserov, though I doubted he would try anything violent. Open hostility was not his way.

"I'm not surprised they are delighted at your return," I said. "You have been so sensitive and discreet about it. Who could complain? Will you have a slice of lemon with your tea? Please Ambassador, do not feel obliged to leave because we are eating. Sit down and have tea with us."

"Ah tea!" said Pyotr evenly, sitting down. "A charming Peninsula custom. So pleasant early in the morning."

"Alas, all my discretion has been in vain," said Kitten tersely. "Apparently someone recognized me at the river dock yesterday and the news is now all over town. My cousin's son was on the point of contracting a very favorable alliance which will be completely overthrown by my presence here. Apparently, I am to be the ruination of all Deserov hopes."

"My goodness," I said. "Could such a small thing be the ruination of a mighty family like the Deserovs? I'm afraid I must ask myself what other things you have been up to Ambassador. Oh, how am I to address you? Is it still Ambassador?"

I rather enjoyed reminding Deserov that his time in Gallia

had ended in disgrace. Unfortunately he did not gratify me by gnashing his teeth.

"It is plain *Prince* now," he said calmly.

"My cousin has become a very important man in the Prekazy," said Kitten.

Suddenly I stopped enjoying myself, though I think I managed to hide this from Deserov. If he was indeed in the Prekazy he had too much of the wrong kind of power.

"I congratulate you," I said.

"I don't know why you care so much, Pyotr," snapped Kitten. "Surely I might be allowed to visit my old home without being ordered back to Moria by you. I am the Countess Katerina Ardynne, widow of the Count of Ardynne and now an actress. If anyone suggests otherwise to me I shall immediately correct them. How could an actress like myself be related to the mighty Deserov family?"

"How indeed?" said Desorov softly. He stirred his tea thoughtfully.

"After all, Akieva is a big place," I said. "Surely it is big enough for all of us. And it is not as if either of us aspire to move in respectable circles."

"Indeed, Lady Dion. It was my impression you were very much enjoying your fame here."

"Of course it is enjoyable," I said. "But I did not come seeking it. I am Lady of Ruinac, and a close friend of Queen Julia of Moria. That is enough fame for me. If nobody had noticed me I would have been just as content. Even without fame Akieva is a splendid city."

"My dear Dion," said Kitten. "How kind of you to say so." She stopped pacing round, sat down beside me, and took up her teacup. "Is it not kind of her, Pyotr?"

"So you have no intention of staying here?" said Deserov.

"Of course not," said Kitten, though the question was addressed oddly enough to me. "My intention is simply to visit old friends and see old sights and in a few months return home to Ishtak. So in fact your real reason for coming here in this tiresome manner is that you want to know when we are leaving. Do I have things right?"

"Ah, Katya. I am sure I have chided you before on your

crudeness. May not a cousin inquire about such matters without it meaning anything unmannerly?" He clinked his spoon on his teacup. "Nonetheless I am glad to hear that neither of you plan to set up house here. You would find it sadly foreign, Lady Dion, and you would find it is not the city you think it is . . . my dear, dear Katya. And now I must take my leave. It has been very pleasant to speak with you."

He smiled the oily smile of a man who knows he has all the best cards in his hand.

"The pleasure has been all mine," said Kitten. "So nice to see you again, Pyotr. Give my love to Vassily. And his family."

"Of course," he bowed and turned to me.

"And very pleasant to see you, Mademoiselle Micheline or . . . I'm wrong am I not. You are a married woman now I believe?"

"Yes," I said making sure he could see the wedding ring on my hand. I wondered if he believed in it.

"Please convey my best wishes to your husband then. I was sorry not to meet him."

"That snake," said Kitten as the door closed on him. "The cheek of him. How dare he come here ordering me to leave Aramaya. I've a mind to settle here just to spite him."

Pepita came in wearing a purple silk dressing gown.

"That wasn't Prince Pyotr Deserov I saw going out just now, was it?" she asked.

"I'm afraid so," said Kitten. "We've been the most fortunate recipients of a morning call."

"Well, well," said Pepita. Her clever eyes took in the whole story at a glance. "I'm sorry I missed him. Do you know he trains the most marvelous servants? The one we have is a wonderful worker and he asked for less money just so that he would get the job. I wonder if I should run down and ask him to send us some more?"

"But why should he care so much?" I asked Kitten when we were talking over Deserov's visit later. "What I said is true. We will not move in the same circles. He need never meet you again and his wife certainly never shall."

"There will be whispers and the odd slighting remark, though I imagine that would happen whether I lived here or not. But it is strange that he cares. Though it is not out of keeping with his nature. He was always determined to have his own way as a boy."

"And now he is one of the heads of the Prekazy. This worries me. Are we in danger of being cast into some secret jail?"

"Oh you need have no fear of that. You are the darling of the White College. He will not dare disappear us now. But I am sorry I brought the Prekazy's interest down on you like this. Pepita did not know Pyotr was a member of it till very recently or she would have told me." She sighed. "Aramaya is full of secret organizations like the Prekazy. But don't worry, we should still be able to make contact with your niece. I would wager our Simonettis to outsmart any Prekazy man born."

I had a sudden thought.

"Is it some problem with Shree Tarko that makes him want you to leave so badly? Perhaps they resent your having it back."

"I don't have it back."

I was surprised. Shree Tarko was Kitten's old family estate, the place where she had grown up. She loved it dearly. It had passed to the wardenship of the Deserovs when she was exiled.

"But I thought the estate was legally yours."

"It is, but why should I take it back from the Deserovs? They have taken good care of it from all reports and when I die, I plan to leave it to Vassily's son anyway. But there is something in what you say. I should write to them and tell them what I intend. Perhaps that will settle them down. I wonder if they would let me visit it in return. Oh I don't know. They're mean people. They'd probably say no."

I stared at Kitten, stunned by her words. I could not understand how she could give Shree Tarko up so easily.

"You would leave it to Vassily's son? But Vassily divorced you."

She smiled at me. "Ah Dion you forget. I too am an Aramayan. The idea of family was drummed into me from my youngest days. I still want Shree Tarko to stay in the Deserov family even though I dislike the current members of it. It was the first family estate."

"But surely you could insist on being allowed to use it in your own lifetime. That is your right as owner."

"But I am not the owner, or at least not clearly so. You see, under Aramayan law when a woman is pronounced barren and divorced, all her lands pass to her ex-husband."

"But how does she live?" I cried.

"Oh, in most cases her family will settle a small income on her. Unfortunately my parents were very poor so I didn't get much. A barren woman's life is hardly very valuable. No one would care if she starved."

This seemed to me a system wide open to abuse. How many women had lost their lands on trumped up charges of infertility?

"So Shree Tarko isn't really yours."

"It's complex. I didn't have any property to pass to Vassily when he divorced me because my father was still alive. He died years later after I was exiled and he willed Shree Tarko to me, though he left it under Vassily's wardenship. You probably don't realize how astonishing this was. I could produce no heirs to the property and would still be free to will it out of the family and thus out of the Deserov patrimony. There is no legal precedent for it. I have written to several lawyers on the subject and they all give different answers. It was a stunningly irresponsible thing for my father to do. And just like him, dear man. He wanted to make some provision for me and he put that before family pride. He was a truly original thinker my father—he was the one who taught me that people could be happy slipping between the rules."

She was silent for a moment, smiling into space.

"And your mother?" I asked curiously. "She's still alive isn't she?"

"Yes. But she would never want to see me. She's religious, you see, and I'm sure she is happy in her convent now."

"My goodness, why on earth did your parents marry?"

"It wasn't their choice. Most of the nobility have marriages arranged for them at eighteen. They rubbed along well enough. My mother was very dutiful. It went with her idea of faith."

It sounded horrible.

"Vassily and I were unusual in that ours was a love match. Or it was supposed to be a love match. Often I've wondered."

She picked up a brush from the dressing table and absently began to brush her hair. I settled myself on the edge of the bed.

"You see Vassily's was the younger branch of the family, but they had all the money which they made from trade. My father was very poor although he was the head of the family and inherited the family estate. Vassily's family had bought much bigger estates, but they were not the family estate. People feel very deeply about that sort of thing in Aramaya. Perhaps he had it half in his mind to marry me when he visited Shree Tarko. I had no other material advantage to offer. I was a terrible tomboy in those days, but men already found me attractive. It filled my mother with despair. Then Vassily came and offered for me—supposedly he had fallen madly in love with me. I thought he was wonderful and my mother was very relieved. More than that—she was actually proud of me for the first time.

"It was a long engagement. First I was schooled in the arts of polite society by Vassily's mother, who was a fascinating woman. I was to be married after my presentation at court, but that was delayed when the empress herself asked for me as a lady in waiting. It was only after I became the empress's favorite that Vassily and I were married, and even then I continued to live at court for most of the time."

"What does being the empress's favorite mean?" I asked, remembering something Kitten had once said.

"Empress Tatiana had the taste for young girls," said Kitten. "I liked her and I wanted to serve my empress. I felt sorry for her really. She was a lonely woman, miserable in the formality of the court. Oh, don't get me wrong. I did not suffer much. She was an expert in the arts of pleasure. But as I've told you before, I am not particularly attracted to women. And I was in love with Vassily. I was idealistic in those days; I believed in the importance of virginity and fidelity. The empress assured me that our lovemaking would not interfere with either of those things, but . . . I think you will agree with me that innocence does not rest in the fact that nothing has ever penetrated your woman's parts."

"Yes," I agreed, remembering my own experiences on that subject. With Bedazzer. "And Vassily knew about this?"

"Oh, yes, he encouraged me. He told me that the empress's favor would make our fortunes. Even then I began to wonder if he really loved me. This worrying threesome with my doing favors that I did not really want to do for the empress. This cynical asking for things in return for sex. But I was only eighteen. For a while I accepted it, though Vassily had to lecture me and coach me to ask for things. But when I became pregnant a year later, that focused my mind. My child was not going to have a mother who was little more than a prostitute and a father who had let his ambition blind him to right and wrong. I decided to save all three of us.

"I told the empress that I must leave her to have my child and I tried to make it clear to her that I wished to leave her service. Then I went to Shree Tarko. Vassily followed me and I told him I was not going back to the empress and that if she ordered me back I would refuse to go. He was furious. I told myself he would thank me in the long run for saving him from so sinister a course, but still we argued. I was angry. I went riding—there was an accident—I lost the child. That's the whole sum of my marriage. It ended when he discovered I was barren. I doubt that he loved me since he put me aside so easily, but I have no idea when he stopped loving me, or if he ever did love me. So much of what he did is a complete mystery. Ah well. I was well rid of him and he of me. He married a very wealthy heiress after that."

"How lucky for him!" I said wryly.

"It was, wasn't it," she said, with twinkling eyes. I was

glad to see she had no regrets. Not that anyone in their right mind would have regretted Vassily Deserov, but the heart is an illogical beast.

"I don't think you owe those Deserovs any favors," I said. "Why don't you try and get Shree Tarko back out of spite? It would be just as they deserve."

The smile went out of her eyes and the sadness came back.

"Oh Dion, you don't know what you are suggesting. To go to court in Aramaya I'd need to have more than spite— it would cost a fortune. The case would have to go before the Imperial Court and they would have to decide if Vassily as my ex-husband was entitled to property I inherited after we were divorced or if I am entitled to have it back now that I am pardoned. All kinds of horrible secrets would be dragged out, my fitness to inherit would have to be proved; my pardon would be questioned; I might have to pay Vassily back for all his improvements; I would probably have to undergo another humiliating examination to prove my barrenness again. After all that the courts would probably decide in Vassily's favor just to stick with the principles of patrimony. Even if I won, could I live out there in the country like that again? And I would still leave the estate to Vassily's son. I am enough of an Aramayan for that. So what would be achieved? It is better to leave it as it is. The only thing I would really like is a chance to see Shree Tarko again. She sighed. "I really doubt they will allow that."

A servant interrupted us then to tell us there was another morning caller. Pepita was right; the mages of the White College came calling on me in droves and a number of them brought their friends. And Kitten too had callers, for she had been an actress for many years in Sopria and so had many theatrical friends. Theatrical folk and mages made an interesting, and sometimes very sucessful, mix. All that day we had at least five callers in the drawing room with us and the hours sped past in sprightly conversation. By the time the last caller had gone, it was time to dress for dinner and the theater.

But despite the exciting day, I remembered Pyotr Deserov's visit. Before we went down to dinner that night I insisted on putting wardings all round Kitten's room. They could not be wardings against intruders because that was very difficult to maintain in a house with busy servants. Instead I put up wardings against violence and made them as sensitive as I could. The wardings would reveal anyone who even entered Kitten's room with violent thoughts.

Kitten laughed when I told her what I was doing, but she let me go ahead with it.

"We have no idea how far Pyotr Deserov will go," I said. "Remember all the things he got up to back on the Peninsula."

"You are entirely right," she said and kissed me on the cheek. "Thank you, Dion. I know I make light of it, but I think I will sleep better for knowing these things are here."

Despite all these concerns we had not forgotten our real reason for coming to Akieva. We only had one clue to help us find the whereabouts of Dally, but it was a useful one. Back in Ishtak the Arkady illusionist, Zotov, had recognized her and told us that her name was Lady Natasha Korosov. It was an interesting choice of name, for Dally's beloved mother's name had been Tasha.

"The Korosovs are close relatives of the Imperial family," said Kitten. "Korosov women have been among the emperor's wives for the last three reigns. One of their number should not be hard to track down. I shall make inquiries."

One of the reasons I had been glad that Kitten had come with me was her marvelous ability to find things out. Sure enough within a couple of days, she knew most of what there was to know about Lady Natasha.

"She is the adopted daughter (the adopted is significant, don't you think?) of Count Taras Korosov. Speculation is that she is his bastard child. Count Taras is one of the emperor's mother's cousins. Not the nicest man, so reports say, and indeed I think I remember him as being unpleasant. The last emperor sent him to be viceroy of Marzorna. A punishment post, probably a sign that Korosov had misbehaved. They say there was some scandal about selling military commissions. But a new reign usually begins with a lot of pardons and so Taras was allowed to come back to Akieva. He brought Lady Natasha with him."

Lady Natasha Korosov had taken Akieva by storm during the last spring Season. The Emperor Zamarton was a keen follower of the New Learning and loved all kinds of new inventions. His special passion was clockwork. He had the biggest collection of clocks and clockwork machines in the known world. Lady Natasha was very well educated for a woman and by a lucky "coincidence" a very keen watchmaker. She and the emperor had thoroughly enjoyed designing a set of clockwork instruments that predicted the movements of the sun and the planets.

"My, my, such debauchery," said Kitten. "This new emperor sounds rather a dear but not even his best friend would call him exciting. Still, don't you think Taras is remarkably fortunate in his ward? Apparently they are laying odds in the army mess halls that he will make her the first of his wives. After all, he does not need to marry all four for policy.

"Count Strezleki, the emperor's chief adviser, is no friend of the lady however. It's whispered that under his advice the emperor did not invite Lady Natasha to visit his estates with him this summer. Strezleki has been a very good guardian to Zamarton and continues to show excellent sense."

"You think it's some kind of plot, don't you?" I said.

"Well it's remarkably coincidental, isn't it? Families are always throwing suitable young girls at the ruler in the hope that she shall win favor. And normally I would say more power to her. But the possibility that Dally may be a necromancer makes me really uneasy. Are you still determined not to bring Prince Terzu into this?"

"I don't think there's any immediate reason to worry. Even if Dally has dabbled in demon magic, how can it touch the emperor here in Akieva? He's well guarded against all forms of magic, much better than the courts on the Peninsula. A bound demon like Bedazzer might have been able to live at the Gallian court, but that could never happen here in Akieva. They check all the courtiers reguarly to make sure they are not demons."

She shrugged. "I know and yet there are all these mages. Korosov is a mage even though his powers are very weak. More to the point, Dally's governess, Madame Bezra Haziz is a mage and reputed to be a very strong one. Nobody likes her much at all."

"Do they think she's a necromancer?"

"Well to be fair I think nobody likes her because she's a Marzornite. Marzornites are very unpopular here because of their inexplicable unwillingness to join the great Aramayan empire. But if a plot is taking place I expect that this Haziz must be the brains behind it; the Taras Korosov I remember is none too bright."

"And Lady Natasha is a mage?" I asked.

"Oh yes. They cannot disguise that. But like every other mage, she is forced to wear an iron necklace whenever she is at court and it is locked on so that she cannot remove it herself. I suppose with all the mages within striking distance disabled, the emperor is not likely to be in any danger from magic. I just feel uneasy."

So did I. Three mages, at least one of whom might be a necromancer. Mages could be dangerous no matter what precautions you took against them. Should I go to Nikoli Terzu? Both Kitten and I felt inclined to trust the demon hunter. But what if Dally had fallen into necromancy and what if we were wrong about Nikoli and he arrested her? Such an arrest was a death sentence in Moria. I would have felt more certain of the proper course had I been able to make some kind of contact with Bedazzer. But there had only been that strange hungry darkness in my mirror which left me mystified.

"In Aramaya it is not so cut-and-dried," said Kitten. "Friends and relatives can save an aristocrat from such a fate."

"I cannot play this friends and relatives game. I'm an outsider."

"None the less, I think Prince Terzu is disposed to be your friend."

"Humph," I said. "Let us wait and see. How can we meet this Lady Natasha anyway?"

"At the moment we can't. She and her foster father have not yet arrived in town for the winter Season. But the emperor's party is believed to be imminent and I imagine the Korosovs will not be long after. I have set Captain Simonetti to find out everything he can about the Korosov house. Beyond that all we can do is simply submit to the terrible fate of enjoying ourselves."

This was not difficult. Akieva was the most fascinating of cities, a complete contrast to the poor and disorganized countryside. Of course there were shabby parts of the city, but the areas where the nobles and the intellectuals lived were the most magnificent I had ever seen. The broad paved streets were filled with fine carriages, carrying people dressed more sumptuously than Peninsula folk could ever dream to be dressed past magnificent public buildings and enormous shops full of exotic things.

I visited the famous sights: the museums, the Akieva Menagerie and the Igor the First Library of Magecraft, the most famous magical library in the known world. Akievan intellectual and scientific life was in a ferment. People were wild for new inventions and techniques and the wealthy competed with each other to patronize them. I was invited to scientific meetings, to watch a demonstration of a new weapon known as a cannon being pitted against a fighting phalanx of mages, and to all kinds of parties. I was also invited to address meetings of a number of magely organizations. Although the speeches themselves were a trial, I thoroughly enjoyed talking to the mages afterward.

I even addressed the Women's College of Magic. It was exciting for me to meet so many women mages and I would have liked to get to know some of them better, but since such noble and respectable women could not properly visit me at the home of an actress this proved difficult. Even though women were taught magic in Aramaya—which was an improvement on Moria—they were still hedged about by ideas of respectability. There was no work for these young women once they finished their training, either. They were destined entirely for marriage and motherhood.

Although there were one or two people who treated me as some kind of fake, most Aramayans seemed to regard me as a cross between a hero and a wise woman. They paid me flattering compliments and hung on every word I said. The news sheets—large sheets of paper hung up on several notice boards around the city that informed the populace of events—gave very flattering descriptions of my appearance and my achievements. They also described my companion the Countess Ardynne in glowing terms and hinted that she had once been the beloved of a foreign ruler.

In the evenings Kitten and I usually attended the theater. The plays were more sophisticated and lavish than anything I had ever seen. Though Kitten and I went alone, there always seemed to be someone calling at our box in the interval and often we were invited backstage after the performance as well.

Is there anybody in the world who does not enjoy such attention? The only real blot on all these wonderful happenings was that Shad was not here to enjoy them with me. I knew I must forget him, but it was not easy.

It was at a balloon ascension, held a couple of weeks after I had arrived in Akieva, that I saw Nikoli Terzu again. It was a raw overcast day that would have been midwinter in Moria but was considered fine autumn weather here.

Prince Gagarin's invitation to see the ascension had included Kitten, and Pepita and Wilby decided to attend it too. It might have been my fame that drew people to our party, but it was Kitten and Pepita's liveliness and charm that kept them there. The two open carriages in which we sat soon became the busiest in the whole viewing enclosure. I did not mind them stealing my audience. I had had my fill of meeting new people and preferred to improve my friendship with those I really liked. I was chatting over the side of the carriage to a stout and cheerful gentleman, Count Boris Dzigan, who for a change was not a mage, when

Prince Nikoli and Count Alexi appeared beside us. Nikoli was looking extremely elegant in dark blue mage's robes.

Count Dzigan was comically dismayed to see him.

"Good God, Nickie! You don't mean to say you already know our Demonslayer? Oh shame on you. I was hoping to impress you for once."

"I apologize profoundly for so displeasing you, Dizzy, but we met down south," said Nikoli. "Hunting necromancers. Lady Dion was invaluable help in dealing with Lord Shugorsky. Count Boris is my cousin, though I call him Uncle," he explained to me.

"Shugorsky! Tsk! Tsk! a bad business. So . . ."

"And I say you are a saucy old devil," said a rich voice nearby.

Startled the three of us turned just in time to see Pepita Sandorez smack Prince Dmitiri Gagarin on the arm with her fan. The elderly mage smirked at her.

"My my," said Nikoli. "If I'd known old Gagarin was a "saucy old devil" I should never have been so afraid of him when I was at school. Tell me, who is the lady?"

"That's Pepita Sandorez, the actress. A charming lady," said Count Boris. "Lady Dion and the countess are staying at her house. I wonder if you would be prepared to let me get into the carriage with you, Lady Dion. I feel sure I should rescue her from old Gargarin. The fellow is obviously a blot."

"An excellent idea Dizzy. Cut him out with your superior manners. Revenge me for all those canings he gave me at school. In the meantime perhaps Lady Dion would care to come for a stroll with me."

"I think these are both excellent ideas," I said.

I climbed out of the carriage and the count climbed into my place. He quickly suceeded in drawing Pepita away from Prince Gagarin. He was a very wealthy man and a known admirer of the theater.

Chatting about all the things I had done in Akieva since I had last seen him, Nikoli and I strolled down to the balloon enclosure. It was good to talk to him again, and I was glad he bore me no ill feeling over that incident at Karanagrad.

Interestingly enough this particular balloon ascension was completely mechanical. The balloon was to be powered for the first time simply with hot air generated by a large burner and with no help from magic. Of course, there were a number of mages in attendance just in case there was an accident. A group of them were having a spirited discussion nearby as to whether it was sensible and even possible to achieve a balloon ascension without magic. We eavesdropped and watched appreciatively as a group of student mages jumped off the roof of a nearby building and performed convoluted aerobatical feats on their way to the ground. Suddenly I noticed something white in the air. For a moment I thought it was ash.

"Is something burning?" I said looking around in alarm. "Oh no. It's . . . is that snow?"

A few little white flakes were drifting downward.

"Yes," said Nikoli. "What, have you never seen snow before?"

"I've seen it lying on the ground, but I've never seen it falling before. How pretty it is. But I suppose we'd better get under cover."

"Not at all. We Aramayans don't panic at the sight of a little snow. Look they're going ahead with the ascension."

I made a face at him.

"You wait till the snow starts," he said. "The winters are long and hard here. There will be days when you will want to stay inside because the air is too full of snow. In winter Akieva becomes like a glowing ember in a plain of freezing white."

"How poetic," I said. "You chill me to the soul."

He laughed. "You shall enjoy it. I promise you. The snow is so beautiful. Perhaps you will allow me to take you sleighing when it comes."

"Slaying?" I laughed. "It sounds gruesome. I hope it's not a blood sport. Oh Nikoli—I mean Prince. Who is that gentleman over there? The one with Prince Deserov."

"That's his brother Vassily. They are an effective team, the Deserov brothers."

So that was the devious Vassily Deserov. He was a tall man with a very handsome face and just a touch of distinguished grey at his temples. No wonder Kitten had lost her heart to him.

"Handsome, isn't he?" said Nikoli. "So you've met Prince Pyotr, have you?"

"I met him back in Gallia when he was Ambassador there," I said.

"Have they been . . . unfriendly?" inquired Nikoli. I looked at him and saw that he was perfectly aware of their relationship to Kitten. I was determined not to involve Nikoli in my quest for Dally, but I had wondered whether to seek his help over Kitten and the Deserovs. If I was going to, now was the time.

"Tell me, Prince Nikoli, is it possible to launch a magical attack on someone in Akieva without being detected?"

"No," said Nikoli. "If I was worried about being attacked, I would guard against more physical methods. And I would hope that my opponent was not Prince Pyotr Deserov, one of the heads of the Prekazy."

"Oh," I said.

He leaned over to me. "Do you think the countess is in danger from him?"

"They are very annoyed to see her back," I said. "They have never liked her. I am anxious, though she will not worry."

Nikoli took my hand. "Is there any way I could help?"

"I feel able to protect the countess myself," I said. "I have done so in the past. But I wish I knew just how hostile— how far the Deserovs would go in their dislike of her. Surely all they need do is ignore her. She is making no particular scandal in just being here."

"It seems the wisest course and the one I would follow. But I could make inquiries if you wish. It would be an honor to serve you."

"I would be very glad of that," I said, squeezing his hand gratefully and smiling into his warm eyes.

* * *

I did wonder if I was being a little overcautious, but a couple of days later we were served at breakfast by a completely new servant, a tall, well-built man with a distinguished air.

"He's new, isn't he?" said Kitten to Pepita after he left the room.

"Yes, Yuri's father was sick and he had to go home, but he offered this fellow to fill in for him. He's called Misha."

"He looks a bit young and fit for a majordomo."

"He says he was a soldier. Got a pretty nice body on him, don't he though? A real meaty sweetie."

The two women laughed. Wilby looked up from the manuscript he was reading and said primly, "I'm not sure my wife should be looking at other men's bodies," which made them laugh even more.

"He's Prekazy, isn't he?" said Kitten.

"Almost certainly." She pinched Kitten's cheek. "Two informers just for you, Katty dear, and the second obviously one of their finest. You should be honored."

She was right. If Misha was Prekazy, he looked a cut above the other Prekazy informer, a rat-faced little man who worked in the kitchen. Was this Misha more than just an informer and if so, what was he? I resolved to double the wardings in Kitten's room.

Despite the busy days, I woke often at night thinking about Shad and my dead child. I had come to Akieva to find Dally, but now that I was here I decided to visit the Imperial College of Healing. I had seen a number of healers, both Morians and those from among Shad's people, who had told me that there was no visible reason why I could not have a child. They said the same about Shad. I knew that my constant wondering which of us was responsible for our childless state had caused a lot of the tension between Shad and me.

Akievan medicine was known to be the best in the world. Surely they would be able to tell once and for all why we couldn't seem to conceive a child. Even though my fertility was hardly relevant now that I was alone, I had to know whose fault it was.

This feeling drove me on to make an appointment with the chief healer specializing in women's medicine. I did not tell Kitten about the appointment. She had enough to worry about.

At the College of Healing I was examined by a kindly faced elderly woman called Madame Irina Vsevolska. Afterward she called for herbal tea and we talked about my magery and my miscarriage and such things.

"You are not barren," she pronounced, "but your womb will not take your husband's seed because you are too afraid of another miscarriage."

I could only stare in astonishment.

"Perhaps you are aware that a mage such as yourself can prevent herself from conceiving when she does not want to," she continued.

"But I want to have a child. I want it desperately," I cried.

"This is not an uncommon problem for a woman mage. You want a child very badly, but you also fear terribly having another miscarriage. Magic listens to your secret heart not your reason. The problem can sometimes be overcome if a woman mates with a more powerful mage than herself. His magic can force the womb to accept his seed. You have been very unfortunate to be so powerful and to have married a man with no power. The simplest solution for you is to overcome your secret fear."

"Sweet Tanza!" I cried. "Is that all?"

She went on to talk about other methods they had been experimenting with—holding the woman mage unconscious while her husband mated with her or using various potions containing ingredients like hazia to put the woman's unconscious to sleep while the seed took hold in her womb. I hardly heard her. I felt as if a wave had broken over me and I was lying on the beach stunned and gasping for air.

I suddenly realized what Beg had meant when she told me that I must try to stop being so afraid. Why had she not made it more clear? Or had she? Had I been so overwhelmed by my grief and failure that I had not been able to understand what she was saying?

Now the whole truth burst on me with devastating clarity. It was my fault not Shad's. I realized how much I had relied on it being his fault and how I had come to this appointment with the righteous hope that I would be justified.

Oh God, poor Shad! How angry I had been at him. And it was all my fault and for such a stupid reason. My God, if only I had realized, if only. . . . Maybe I could have done something with this cruel magic of mine and I would have had a child and Shad would never have left and. . . . Maybe I would have been less angry and then he would have stayed. . . . I was such a coward. It had been pure cowardice that had caused everything—all this grief and pain. Oh God. I was such a hopeless nothing of a woman, such a failure, such a waste of flesh and blood.

Out in the street again, I walked. I walked and walked. I felt as if everything inside me, every thought and feeling had been scooped out and I was just an empty shell. I could not think. I would not think because that would bring the screaming at the back of my mind to the surface.

Eventually I found myself standing on the Rostock bridge looking down at the cold black Novksy river. I had no thought of killing myself. I had no thoughts at all. I just watched that black water and the little shards of ice flowing underneath and wished I could flow away with it.

Someone touched me on the arm.

"Is it so bad?" said a voice gently. Nikoli Terzu was standing beside me.

"It would not work anyway," he said. "It is hard for a mage to kill himself. At the moment of drowning your magic would take over and rise you up again."

I shook my head. My throat was too thick to speak.

"What did the healer say? Did she tell you you were barren?"

"She told me I wasn't," I choked, and then I could not stop the tears any longer.

"Come," said Nikoli, "I have a carriage. Come."

*   *   *

It was much later, but we were still in Nikoli's carriage, driving around and around the Imperial Deer Park. The short winter day was drawing to a close but it was cosy inside the carriage. Magical flames flickering in tall glasses gave off a pleasant rosy light. We had fur blankets wrapped around our legs. Nikoli poured me another glass of sweet red wine which he warmed with a little magic.

"How did you know where to find me?" I asked, finally able to muster enough interest in life to ask the question.

"I was at a meeting in the White College," he said smoothly. "My servant saw you going into the College of Healers and saw you come out again. He realized that something was wrong and came and told me. I shall reward that man in gold."

He stared into his wine for a moment. "I am a fool for saying this since it is so much against my interests, but if you are not barren, you can go back to Moria. You can take back your rightful place as Lady of Ruinac again."

"No. The man I was married to has found someone else."

"Well, he must give her up. If you are not barren your divorce is not legal and neither is his second marriage. He cannot take your land and titles from you for such a reason."

I stared at him. It took me a moment to work out what it was that he didn't understand about the situation.

"It's not like that," I said. "We are . . . I am still Lady of Ruinac. We were not married because of lands. We were quite humble people when we met. It was only the liberation of Moria that brought us such prominence, you see. We were married because we wanted to be married."

"A love match?" he said, with a slightly wondering tone. Such things were considered a little low class among the Aramayan aristocracy.

"I am really little more than a peasant and so is he," I said. "And if he has found himself another woman whom he can love better, I don't want to force him to take me back. I have no legal right to anyway. We were not even married in the eyes of the Aumazite church. We were married by his people, the Klementari. An agreement and a return of rings is all that is required to signify the end of a Klementari marriage. So there's no point in my going back. Our marriage truly is over. Anyway, I might as well be barren. I am a coward. I doubt if I could overcome my fear."

I put my face in my hands. I had no more tears left but it did not lessen the grief. He touched my shoulder tentatively, for all the world as if I had not been weeping on his chest for the last hour.

"It is a fearful thing to lose a child," he said quietly.

I shrugged. All I could see now was how much I had needed for it to be Shad's fault. And how that feeling, so unjustified, had destroyed everything. I felt grey despair.

"Perhaps I should go back to Pepita's," I said.

"As you wish."

I felt the frisson of magic as he gave wordless instructions to the driver. Nikoli seemed to have an endless supply of clean white handkerchiefs. He took out another one and began fussing about, patting my face and tidying my hair. His slim brown fingers were deft and light.

"You will tell the countess of this, won't you?"

"I suppose," I said. "She has problems of her own."

"If you do not, I shall," he said. "You must not try to bear your grief alone."

"I will be fine," I said bleakly.

He was silent for a moment and then he said,

"If there is no reason for you to go back to Ruinac, perhaps you will consider staying in Aramaya and making a new life among those who are disposed to value you for the wonderful things you have done. There are people here already who care very much for you."

And he kissed me, briefly and softly on the lips.

I NOW SAW that for at least a year the certainty that Shad would leave me because we were childless had twined itself like some dank weed around all my thoughts, twisting them out of recognition. Thinking thus I had been angry at him, especially since often I felt that my childlessness was his fault. The shock of the healer's diagnosis cleared my mind. I saw that this bitterness and the underlying fear must have pushed Shad away from me and toward Edaine. How terrible it must have been for him.

Had I any real reason for expecting him to leave? It was fear that had made me act in such a destructive way, that had made all my fears true. If I had not been so afraid and obsessed with his leaving, perhaps Shad would have stayed. If I had not been so afraid, perhaps in time we would have had our child.

I felt as if I had wantonly destroyed my marriage. Shad had truly been right to leave me and I had no business longing for him after the way I had behaved. For several days I locked myself in my room and Kitten put it out that I was ill. This brought dozens of bouquets of flowers and other presents to the house, which if anything only increased my feelings of shame.

Finally, however, I returned to my social round, if only because Kitten literally dressed me and dragged me out with her. It was the right thing to do. With things to interest and distract me, I was able to return to a kind of superficial normality. Underneath I felt like something within me had broken.

It snowed on and off for a couple of weeks, but finally it snowed for several days in a row and the snow stayed. People began to say that winter had really begun. The only place I had seen snow before was the small snowdrifts in the Red Mountains. At first I thought Akieva's snow charming. It made the grey winter streets and leafless trees into a sparkling white confection, all pure and clean looking. Every time I went past a window I had to stop and admire it. Sadly the snow did not stay pretty for long under the heavy Akievan traffic. It quickly turned into dirty slush and the places where drunks or dogs made water against walls or treetrunks were nastily visible.

I discovered that sleighing was not a blood sport when Prince Nikoli took me out driving in his sleigh, a horse-drawn vehicle that rested on runners and was capable of going at tremendous speeds.

He was a good driver and we spent a wonderful afternoon dashing around the Imperial Deer Park. Out here the snow was at its unspoiled best and several times we saw animals; little tree creepers in their white winter coats and deer fleeing away through the trees.

In the midafternoon we stopped under some trees where one of the prince's servants was waiting with a lit brazier and a hamper of food and drink. We stayed warmly wrapped up in the sleigh while he served us. I was a little surprised that Nikoli had brought the servant all the way out here since he could warm himself and his wine without a brazier or a servant. It seemed, however, that this was the way things were done in Aramaya, for the servant told Nikoli of the other servants who were waiting in other parts of the park for other noble mages. I suspected Nikoli enjoyed having someone to command. How could I blame him? Part of me enjoyed these small moments of splendor too.

"Oh this is wonderful. The snow is so beautiful away from the city."

"It is beautiful. I have a small cottage in the woods outside the city half a day's drive away. Perhaps you will come there with me someday."

"That sounds lovely," I cried and then something about the way he looked at me made me wonder what exactly I was agreeing to.

"Perhaps sometime when Kitten is free."

"Of course," he said with a slight smile. I felt foolish then for reading too much into his words and yet it was hard to shake the suspicion that he was courting me. He had continued to be just as much my friend after the College of Healers as before. In fact if anything he was more friendly. He bought me books and sent me flowers and hothouse fruits. I suspected if I had been an Aramayan woman I would have been in no doubt of the situation. But perhaps not. What goes on between men and women is always very complicated and here it was made more so because I did not really know how I wanted to respond. I only knew I felt very lucky that he had found me after my interview at the Healers College. I didn't even think to wonder then how much of a part luck had really played in it.

To cover my confusion, I asked if he had had any luck finding out about the Deserovs.

"Yes, I have. It's fortunate that you asked me to look into it. Pytor Deserov seems to be prepared to go to enormous lengths to persuade your friend to leave Akieva. I was astonished."

"Is he planning to have us assassinated then?"

"Oh no nothing so serious yet. He was planning to threaten to expose you as a barren and divorced woman, if you and the countess did not leave Akieva soon."

"Damn," I said. "What will happen if it all comes out? I mean, I am a divorced woman. People must wonder why I am here without my husband."

"Not at all. In Aramaya married couples frequently spend

little time together. And you are still wearing a ring. There's no reason why anyone should know you are divorced. And there is no need to worry about Deserov either. My master went to him and pointed out that to harm you could damage the interests of our whole country. Deserov is studying patience now."

"Of the whole country? God and Angels, Nikoli!" I wanted to say I was hardly that important but it seemed ungrateful. "It's very kind of him to go to the trouble."

"It's not kindness. It's good policy. What I said to you when we first met is not just flattery, Dion. You are a tremendous help to the demon hunters. And people are delighted with you. Coming to Aramaya has been one of the most fortunate things you could have done. Truly, I think that people would still admire you if it came out you were divorced, but you cannot be too careful. The Aramayan public can be very cruel sometimes."

This was a depressing topic. It made me remember how much I had lost. Nikoli squeezed my hand. "Anyway, Deserov should know better than to try and attack you."

"Perhaps he only meant to threaten us."

"Perhaps. Although I must admit I am astonished by the strength of his reaction to his cousin. It seems beyond all sense. Why does he fear her so much?"

"Kitten says he simply likes to have his own way."

"It's possible I suppose. That can make people unreasonable."

"Do you think you could find out any more about Deserov?" I asked.

"I already have it in hand," he said. "I want to be sure it is not more than frustrated willfulness before I leave the subject alone."

"Thank you Nikoli," I said.

"I want only to be of service to you," he said.

He leaned close to me and kissed me then and when I did not pull away, he kissed me again deeply and slowly and with his arms around me this time. I found I enjoyed it.

We sat in the sleigh wrapped in furs and kissed for some time, feasting sensuously on each other's lips and skin. It was slow and delicious and I felt heat rising in me. It had been so long since I had felt simple desire for a man.

"Perhaps one day soon you will come to my winter cottage with me," he said softly against my lips.

"Perhaps I will," I said.

"Do you know, gentlemen, I have a great desire to go to the country," said Kitten a few days later to the company who were taking refreshments in our box at the Compass Rose.

"My dear Countess," said Nikoli. "The emperor is rumored to be returning to Akieva any day. Surely you do not wish to miss the start of the winter Season."

"He is rumored, but he does not come. Anyway I was not thinking of very deep in the country," she said. "It's just that I was remembering my childhood in the Central Highlands and wishing I could see them again. It is always beautiful at this time of the year."

"Sweet Tanza, Countess, are you a Central Highlands girl?" said Count Boris Dzigan. "Which part do you come from? Near Ostrava? By Aumaz's teeth, my dear lady, I have a favorite house there, a little hunting lodge. I can't leave Akieva myself at the moment, otherwise I would certainly set up a party. No, but this is ridiculous. You shall have your visit to the country. I beg you to go anyway. Nikoli could be host for you, couldn't you Nikoli? I'm sure you're not doing anything much at the moment. Are you my boy?"

"Not a thing," said Nikoli with a wry grin.

"Then you must take these ladies up to Ostrava. The countess is right. It is beautiful up there at the moment."

"Why are we going to the Central Highlands?" I asked Kitten later.

"Shree Tarko is there and now that all the Deserovs are in Akieva, we can go there without fear of being interrupted. I am determined to see my old home just once."

"Kitten, is that wise? Should we push the Deserovs any further?"

"That's the beauty of getting Count Dzigan to offer us

his house. They won't know. Two well-bred women staying at a public inn would excite comment in a district but two women staying at a private house are quite unremarkable. Dear Count Boris. I wonder if he knows?" She smiled teasingly at me. "And it would be even better if we used false names. I wonder what we could tell Nikoli. . . ."

"There is no need to tell him anything," I said crossly. Sometimes Aramayans annoyed me the way they had to go about everything in this roundabout way. "He knows all about you and the Deserovs."

"How disappointing. Still perhaps we should make up something anyway. He will be let down if we don't try."

"Kitten!"

"Oh have you no love of intrigue, Dion?" Kitten pouted merrily. "You'll never make an Aramayan."

"Did you mean for us to go with Prince Nikoli? It was a masterly piece of work if you did."

"You are all my puppets!" she cried with an extravagant gesture. "Actually I didn't plan for it. It was just an extra piece of sugar. Isn't it excellent? Such a charming and attentive man." She patted my cheek with her fan and went away, laughing at the face I pulled.

Nikoli arranged the whole thing. Count Boris's house near Ostrava was a long day's drive from Akieva. The three of us traveled in his large covered sleigh, though since it was a beautiful day we mostly traveled with the top down. We were cozily tucked under fur rugs and Nikoli and I took turns in making the floor of the carriage warm. It was such a long way that we stopped only to change horses; traveling with mages means that you can have hot food and drink without an inn.

The landscape was wonderful with white snow, stands of evergreen trees, and rugged mountains that grew closer and closer. The little villages we passed were no longer wretched and dusty but snug and cozy-looking under their blankets of snow. Everyone was in high spirits.

It was well after dark when we arrived at Count Boris's. The big house itself had been closed for the winter but a cozy little guest house in the grounds had been opened for us and servants made us welcome. Propriety dictated that Nikoli stay at the inn in the nearby town and so he left us for the night. Kitten and I went walking in the snow in the darkness.

Several times we heard a howling in the distance.

"Wolves," said Kitten. "You see that dark mass against the sky. That's the Ivory Mountains. You would think there would be no wolves so close to Akieva, but the Ivory Mountains are full of wild secret valleys where they hide."

That night instead of dreaming about Shad or Alinya, I dreamt of wild wolves playing like happy dogs on the moonlit snow. Some of that joyous freedom stayed with me into the next day.

That day, Kitten and I donned enormous fur coats and Nikoli and his coachman drove us to a small nearby wood. Kitten and I got out and walked through the dark, silent evergreens until suddenly we came upon a cleared area. Shree Tarko stood before us, a beautiful old grey house with a steeply sloping red roof and faded white shutters. As we had expected, it was completely shut up. The sky above was a pale grey and something about the snowy field before the house and the dark forest all around it suddenly made me feel as if nothing else existed. It was a restful feeling.

We walked slowly round the house. Kitten's eyes became dreamy with reminiscence. Wanting to give her time alone with her memories, I suggested that I sit on the verandah of the house, keeping magical watch. She agreed and disappeared around the back, but she quickly returned.

"Can you get me into the house?" she said.

I would have had scruples about breaking into anyone else's house, but I felt no compunction at all about those selfish Deserovs. Why, they hardly ever came here and yet they kept it from Kitten.

"The windows are warded," I said. "I'm strong enough to get you in without setting them off, but not without making it obvious that the wardings have been tampered with."

"When I lived here we used to leave one door unwarded

so that the servants could see to the place while we were away. It was this door around the back."

I followed her round to a rather insignificant looking cellar door. Sure enough it was not warded, merely sturdily bolted. The bolts were easy to undo using magic.

We climbed up into the house. It was cold and smelled of mildew and everywhere the furniture was covered with white sheets. To me it was just a house, but Kitten was delighted. She ran around looking under the sheets and exclaiming at everything. When she went upstairs, again I thought I should leave her alone. I sat on the stairs and listened to her wandering about on the floor above. I was warm and comfortable in my furs. I felt a certain contentment knowing that Kitten was happy and that I was helping her be so along with a certain relaxation at being in this dark quiet house. Even all closed up, it had a nice atmosphere. Instead of thinking about Shad as usual, I found myself thinking of Nikoli and the funny things he had told us on the journey up here. What a kind and generous man he was. I knew I did not love him, but I liked him. He was the kind of man I thought I could love given enough time to forget the past.

I was certainly physically attracted to him. Remembering the time we had kissed in his sleigh made my skin tingle. My physical relationship with Shad had been soured by anger and I had begun to think I was dead below the waist. Part of me was simply happy for the proof that this was not so. But it would be wrong of me to follow desire, when I knew perfectly well that my heart was still set on Shad.

"Ah, my old home is as perfect as ever," sighed Kitten as she came down the stairs. "Look what I found. Still behind the loose board in the attic where I used to hide it."

She opened her hand and showed me a little doll made from a wooden clothes peg. A face had been crudely but cleverly carved on the top of the peg and two little wooden arms had been attached to the sides with a pin. She had the most exquisitely made little dress on.

"My nurse Annushka made it for me. Dear Annushka.

Oh well. I suppose she is dead by now." She brushed a tear from her eyes. "She was like a mother to me."

I put my arm around her.

"I'm happy enough," she said "It's just melancholy to see it all again. Come on, let's go. The dark will be coming soon and the prince will be waiting for us."

After we had locked the house, she put her arm through mine and we crunched back toward the wood. Just as we entered it Kitten turned, pulled down her hood and took a last longing look at the house. Her fair hair gleamed in the pale light.

"I should have brought an Arkady apparatus," I said at last. "Then you could always have had this."

"Don't say that," she said with a twinkle. "I might make you come back."

Suddenly someone shouted. A figure came plowing out of the woods nearby.

I reached out to seize Kitten's arm, but she had already turned toward the figure.

"Come on Kitten!" I cried.

"No! Wait!" she said.

"Katya! Madame Katya," the figure cried. To my surprise it was a woman, although I could see the figure of a man hovering in the shadow of the trees.

"Nikita!" cried Kitten suddenly, running toward her. "Nikita, is it really you?"

"Madame Katya," said the other as she came up. "Madame Katya. It is you!"

The two women embraced and then suddenly the other woman pulled away and dropped to her knees before Kitten and kissed her hand. This Nikita wore peasant costume and had a round pleasant face that went with her solid figure.

"Madame Katya. Forgive my forwardness, but it's so good to see you."

"Oh Niki, Niki. Not so formal—I'm not your mistress now. Get up. You'll catch your death." Kitten dragged the woman to her feet.

"Oh, Madame. The others will be delighted to hear you

are alive. Are you well? Are you happy? Where have you been?"

"Oh Niki, no. You mustn't tell anyone. Prince Vassily wouldn't like my being here. I'd get into terrible trouble."

"Then you have come without his permission. He hasn't taken you back?"

"No, that will never happen. I have no business being here, but I wanted so much to see it."

"Of course you did Madame. Who's to blame you? I'll keep your secret. Of course I will. Though there is one person I would like to tell, if I may Madame. Old Annushka. She will be so happy to know you are well."

"Annushka! Annushka is still alive? But how is she? Where is she?"

"She's living with her nephew Yuri. He's a gloomy sort of fellow, but a good enough heart. She is comfortable. And well. Annushka must have been tanned by Aumaz I think. She is still just as brown and tough as ever. And will probably last forever. She still milks fourteen cows every day even though she must be at least sixty summers. Oh she will be so happy when I tell her."

"Fourteen cows! This Yuri must be a man of substance. And how about the others . . ."

She took the other woman's arm and together they walked on exchanging news. I followed. I was uncomfortably aware of the man behind us following silently through the bushes. He was staying in cover and I only knew he was there because I felt him with magic. It did not take much thought to realize why he was so shy. Nikita was obviously a serf of the estate and for all her knowledge of High Aramayan, her clothes indicated that she was no longer a house servant. The only likely reason she and her companion would have for being in the woods this winter afternoon was for poaching. She must have trusted Kitten a great deal to have revealed herself like that.

Shortly before the edge of the forest, Nikita left us, though not before Kitten had given her all our money and asked her to give half of it to Annushka.

"With pleasure Madame," she said. "Oh she will be so

pleased just to hear of you again. Good-bye and Aumaz bless you Madame. And don't worry. I shall keep my tongue between my teeth."

Kitten smiled as Nikita plowed away through the snow.

"Annushka is alive. How wonderful. I must send her some more money when I get back to Akieva. Perhaps she would like to come and live with me, perhaps . . ."

"Are you sure that woman won't say anything?"

"No, I trust Nikita entirely. Don't worry. She has no liking for Vassily and Pyotr. She'll do all she must to protect me from them just as she always did. That was an entirely lucky meeting."

Neither of us knew then how truly she spoke.

A strange yet delightful light-heartedness possessed me that night. It seemed as if the three of us were in a world of our own, where neither past nor future mattered. The housekeeper had cooked us a wonderful meal and we drank sparkling wine chilled in the snow. The three of us talked and laughed uproariously.

All though dinner Nikoli teased us by tickling our hands with a magic touch. He had such wonderful control. I could not have done anything as small as that. Every now and then I felt the magical touch on my cheek. I would look at Nikoli accusingly and he would give me a look of mock innocence which struck me as exquisitely humorous.

Nikoli's coachman played the stringed instrument known as the yertsa and it turned out the houseman did too. The two of them played while Kitten and Nikoli danced sprightly Aramayan folk dances. Then Nikoli called for something slower and dragged me from my seat. We danced around the room held in each other's arms. Suddenly I felt magic all around me and looking around saw that we were now dancing above the ground, skimming lightly and gracefully in the air. Kitten lifted her glass to us and I felt so wonderful that I made tiny gleaming stars appear in the air and rain down around us. The players stopped for a moment and cheered before going back to their instruments and we danced around and around till the room spun and I was breathless. Finally we came to earth.

"The countess has gone," said Nikoli and it was true she had slipped away while we were dancing. Listening with magic I could hear her at the other end of the house washing her face for bed.

Nikoli smiled at me, his eyes full of sly questions. "Shall we send these fellows away and have another drink?"

I hesitated only for a moment. My head was light with the wine and I felt reckless and restless.

Nikoli's smile was so charming. He was such a handsome man with his warm brown skin and his wonderful dark eyes. He poured more of the delicious wine. His graceful hands caressed the stem of his glass. I felt as if he had caressed my flesh. Suddenly my skin was tingling for his touch.

Suddenly shy I got up and went to the window.

"What a beautiful night it is. The moon on the snow. It looks like silver."

"Yes," said Nikoli softly.

I felt a whisper of magic like a touch—like the touch of a finger stroking softly down the back of my neck. It sent the most wonderful feelings down my spine, making me shiver with pleasure.

"Nikoli, stop that," I said, turning to him.

He got up from the table and came over to stand beside me.

"Do you really want me to stop it?" he said softly. I could see that he knew how delightful it was.

Again the magic brushed my cheek in an infinitely soft caress. It moved to my lips and lingered on them like a longing finger.

The feel of it made my stomach flip-flop with delight.

"Nikoli!" I said, mildly admonishing to cover my shyness. "You can be getting no pleasure from this. Doesn't magic deaden strong feelings in you as in everyone else?"

"It gives me pleasure to give you pleasure," he breathed softly. He took my hand and kissed it. His soft lips lingered on the skin.

"Oh Nikoli," I said. I kissed him then and put my arms

around his lean body and felt his strong arms around me. We kissed and kissed with greater and greater hunger, arms tightly round each other, fingers digging urgently into flesh, desire rising too hotly to be denied.

When I awoke in the morning a part of me said that it must never happen again. Another part of me asked why not.

We left Count Boris's house that morning—to stay any longer would have been to invite discovery. All the way home Nikoli held my hand under the fur rugs for all the world as if we had been village sweethearts. Now I was really separated from Shad. I was frightened by the step I had taken, but Nikoli's hand beneath the furs was warm and comforting.

That evening when we arrived home we were greeted with the news that the Imperial court had returned to Akieva, marking the official beginning of the winter Season. The Korosovs too had returned to their townhouse. So it begins, I thought. I was glad to have some real purpose at last.

The following morning Kitten and I went down to look at the Korosov house, hoping that we might also obtain a view of Dally and perhaps get a chance to speak with her. It was in the finest part of town where long rows of elegant white houses faced onto squares with fenced gardens in the center of them. Kitten had obtained the key to the garden opposite the Korosov house, so we promenaded up and down the street before the house a couple of times and then sat in the square pretending to belong there.

It was a clear day and the sun looked charming on the newly fallen snow, but no sane Morian would have been outside in such freezing cold. The square was full of Aramayans however, elegant women strolling in pairs like us and children taking the air with their entourages of servants. For once I hardly noticed the dear little mites holding the hands of their nurses. I was too intent on watching for Dally.

All morning we walked and sat in that square, watching. A few people called at the house but were not admitted, which indicated, according to Kitten, that the Korosovs were not "at home" to visitors although apparently they were in the house. Once a liveried man servant came along the street and called at a number of houses including the Korosovs.

"Invitations to court," said Kitten knowledgeably. "Many people will be made happy by the receipt of such an invitation today."

We were not made happy until around noon. A carriage bearing the Korosov crest came round to the front of the house. Kitten and I got up off our bench and walked over to the nearby pavement. Thus when the door of the house opened we were strolling casually down the street toward the carriage.

Lady Natasha Korosov and a well-dressed maid came out onto the stairs followed by a tall, dark, sharp-faced woman in plain blue mage's robes.

"Bezra Haziz," whispered Kitten in my ear. At that moment Lady Natasha turned and looked straight at us. It was Dally! It had to be her!

I felt so sure of it I almost called out. But though I had the feeling she recognized us, she did not acknowledge us. Instead she looked back quickly over her shoulder at Madame Bezra. The tall dark-eyed woman was scanning the street in the other direction much as a guard would.

The unspoken warning froze the cry of recognition on my lips. Kitten and I reached the carriage just as Lady Natasha was about to be handed into it by a waiting footman. Again she looked at me and this time she gave me the tiniest of nods. The she looked away quite casually and climbed into the carriage. Bezra Haziz followed her.

"Do you think it was Dally?" asked Kitten as the carriage drew away.

"She knew us. I'm sure of it. It must have been Dally."

"Well she must already have heard you were in town," said Kitten. "She didn't seem very surprised to see you."

We returned to Pepita's house to find Nikoli Terzu waiting for us. He had come to take us for kesh and cake at one of the kesh houses overlooking the Novsky. My heart sank a little, which seemed very unfair to the poor man. Here was a complication. All my life I had been too prone to give in to physical desire and it only complicated matters. Now it would be even more difficult to keep him unaware of Dally.

"But you hate walking in the cold," he said when I told him we had been out walking.

"It's not so bad," I said. "Such a lovely day. I am determined to learn to like it."

"Look, look Dion!" cried Kitten. She and Pepita came rushing down the stairs in a flurry of silken skirts. Kitten was holding up a piece of embossed card. "We have been invited to a reception at the Palace. We are going to meet the emperor!"

I didn't know whether to laugh or groan. I would become more visible than ever. But the emperor! It would be really something to meet the man at the center of the world.

Pepita and Kitten were beside themselves with pleasure. They danced around and cheered as if they had won some great victory.

"Me invited to court," said Kitten. "Won't Arina Deserov just scream!" She kissed the invitation. "But oh, Peppa dear, what am I going to wear?"

"There's the court dress from the second act of Lady Flavia's Gift. It would furbish up very nicely."

"Appear at court in a theatrical costume? Oh I couldn't. Could I? How piquant. Yes, let's do that. But how about Dion? You're the lead in this play, Dion. It's you he really wants to see. What have you got to wear?"

"There's my second best mage's uniform," I said.

Pepita, Nikoli, and Kitten all looked at me.

"It's silk," I said defensively. "Surely that will do."

The three of them burst out laughing. Evidently not.

I did not see Dally at all in the next two days for I was too busy preparing for my court appearance. At least, I was busy if you could call standing like a scarecrow and being prodded with pins and being asked my opinion of pieces of brocade for which I cared nothing, being busy.

Apparently one had to appear at court in the traditional

dress of the Northern Barbarian dynasty to which the emperor's family belonged. It must have been a mere parody of traditional dress however, for it would have been impossible for the Northern Barbarians to perform the feats of horsemanship for which they were famous in the long robes that the men wore.

Likewise unsuited to riding was the long flowing robe for women worn over several richly brocaded petticoats, stiffened with bone so that they stuck out and made a cone shape. My robe was mage's blue and cut low at the neck. I protested at such exposure, but apparently it was important so that the emperor's magical bodyguard could lock an iron necklace around my neck before I entered the presence. I'm not sure why Kitten's neckline was even lower than mine. She assured me that the reason was entirely practical and that it was absolutely accidental that it displayed her fine cleavage to its best advantage.

My hair was to be piled up, with a tiara-shaped golden headdress upon it and a white muslin veil behind. The whole costume made you look like a walking cone. It was quite difficult to walk in without making the petticoats flounce up and look stupid. In fact I had to practice walking up and down with one of the petticoats on over my dress for hours to achieve the right gait.

It was not easy to have such a dress made in two days, especially when most of the city was preparing for the court reception, but luckily the dressmakers at the Compass Rose Theater were just as skilled as the fashionable couturiers and put together a very creditable costume for me. Every day Nikoli visited me, although I did not make any effort to be alone with him. It worried me that I still thought more of Shad than I did of him. He very kindly read to me while I stood having pins stuck in me and walked me up and down in my petticoat giving me advice. He did not seem to mind my holding him at arm's length. Was it possible that he too regretted becoming more involved? Once, however, I felt the tender touch of magic stroke the back of my neck. Turning to look in his eyes, I saw that he was simply giving me space. The thought touched me. I hardly felt worthy of such consideration.

The reception would be enormous and I hoped that in the crush I'd be able have a few moments' speech with Dally and find out if she was well or if she needed help. Now that I had seen her I was very impatient to make contact with her. For this reason, when Nikoli offered to take us to the reception in his carriage I refused, even though I could see he was hurt by it.

The Winter Palace with its huge golden dome was as magnificent from the street as it was from the river. The royal palaces of both Moria and Gallia would have fit into this huge building ten times over. As we presented our invitation just inside the entranceway, a member of the magical bodyguard stepped forward, took an iron necklet and wristlets from a red cushion and, with great ceremony, locked them around my neck and wrists. The feel of the iron made me uncomfortable and panicky. I have always hated the chill touch of it. But it was necessary. Mages can work iron from the outside, though it is unpleasant for them, but when it is placed around their necks it disrupts their ability to perform magic, making them just like other people. No mage is allowed in the presence of the Emperor of Aramaya without wearing an iron necklet.

Following the other guests we walked through long hallways of exquisitely polished wood, crowded with statues and paintings and guarded by an army of footmen, until at last we came to a huge set of doors. Beyond them an enormous room with a high ceiling glittered with chandeliers.

Everybody queued at the door before being announced by the Master of Protocol and walking down the length of the immense room to the throne at the other end. It was so far away that the emperor was little more than a silvery blob on the golden throne.

The throne hall was filled with a silent crowd of people standing along the walls, all richly dressed in velvets and brocade court dresses. It looked as if the procession of people down the throne room had been going on for hours. My heart sank looking at them all. Would I be able to find Dally in all this crowd?

But as we approached the dais I saw her standing near the front with Bezra Haziz and a stout middled-aged man with a stern but flaccid face, short grey military hair, and cold eyes. My mind was so full of them that I did not notice the emperor until we reached the dais.

The single throne was a mound of gold worked in whirls and patterns. Its hectic-looking mass made the young man who sat upon it wearing a plain silver silk robe stand out even more. Emperor Zamarton the Fifth of Aramaya. His dark hair was uncovered and only the great ruby surrounded by a gold sunburst around his neck proclaimed his office.

For all his northern ancestry he had much the same coloring as Nikoli. He was eighteen and had been emperor for almost a year. Eighteen is young to take on such responsibilities—yet he did not look bowed down. He looked around the room with vivid interest as if this were not just a ritual moment but a fascinating activity laid on for his enjoyment. He had a skinny, half-grown look. There was a hint of acne on his cheeks and chin. Below his robe I could see his feet sticking out. They were enormous, far too big for the rest of him. Like a puppy, he was all out of proportion. He reminded me almost painfully of my beloved nephew Martin at his age. If he grew as Martin had, in a couple of years he would be a tall, well-proportioned, clear-skinned man.

"Lady Dion," the emperor cried enthusiastically even before I had risen from my curtsy. "How wonderful to meet you. We have read of your exploits on the Peninsula."

He made as if to rise from his throne and to come down the stairs at me but then as if remembering where he was, he subsided back. An elderly gentlemen standing beside the throne looked noticeably relieved. He must be the emperor's chief adviser, Count Strezleki. The emperor noticed his adviser's relief: his eyes twinkled and he gave his elderly keeper a particularly angelic smile.

"Lady Dion we hope you will be able to honor us with a private audience very soon. I would very much like to hear more of your activities."

"The honor would be all mine, Imperial Highness," I said.

He nodded politely to Kitten and then we were ushered away to a place in the crowd.

For what seemed like another half a day we stood there in the crowd watching one person after another being presented to the emperor. I understood enough of what was going on to realize that the emperor had paid me an enormous compliment. He hardly spoke to anyone else, restricting himself instead to a gracious nod and smile. Apparently this ceremony signified the opening of the court and of the winter Season in Akieva. The word *season* was apparently taken from the term *hunting season*—at such ceremonies as these young men were presented at court and were then considered formally available by those families looking for a husband for their daughters. Girls were presented more rarely; it was the custom in many families not to present their daughters until they had been safely married or, in the most conservative families, until they had produced a male heir.

"Does the emperor get reintroduced to every one of his subjects every year?" I whispered to Kitten.

"Of course not," said Kitten. "But every Aramayan of note is introduced to his emperor at least once in his life and attendance at court is a sign of loyalty. Now be quiet. And stop twitching."

It was all very well for her to say this, but I had a terrible itch in the middle of my back and couldn't seem to scratch it under my heavy clothes. Personally I didn't know how people who lived at court managed the uncomfortable clothes or standing all the time. My legs and back began to ache and the chill of the marble floor seeped through my thin shoes and spread up my legs. I understood now why most of the Imperial palace was made of wood—it was much warmer in these dreadful Aramayan winters.

As new people came to the front of the room, the rest of us moved slowly toward the back. At least it kept the blood circulating. I watched Dally over on the other side of the room with frustration. Would this ever be over?

Kitten and I had agreed that she would keep Nikoli busy

while I tried to get to Dally. The sky outside had begun to darken by the time he was announced and the ceremony ended shortly afterward. Trust Nikoli to have the sense to arrive close to the end. Everyone in the room swept their lowest curtsies and bows and the emperor, followed at a discreet distance by his train of advisers, stepped from the dais and left the room.

The moment the door closed behind them a sigh ran through the room and there was a hubbub of noise as each person turned to his neighbor, no doubt exclaiming in relief.

It fascinates me the way people claim to love their rulers and yet they surround them with so much irksome ritual that it becomes a burden to be in their presence. I'm sure there is some profound truth about the nature of love to be drawn from this.

As waiters began to bring out glasses of wine and little cheese and meat pies, Kitten and I separated, she to head for Prince Nikoli with a spurious story of losing me in the crowds and me for the last place I had seen Dally.

Getting through the crowd resembled fighting your way through a thick hedge—a thick hedge, moreover, that kept grabbing your arm to tell you how pleased it was to see you and how much it admired your work. I had just managed to avoid the Dean of the White College and was beginning to think the whole thing hopeless, when a voice behind me cried, "The Demonslayer of Gallia! How much I have longed to meet you!"

I turned and saw Dally coming toward me with a cheeky grin on her face, hand outstretched. There was something in that hand. I put out my own to meet hers. Then suddenly there was a stout body between Dally and me and a pasty hand gripped her outstretched one. Was that paper I heard scrunching?

Count Taras Korosov patted the hand he held. "Now, now, my dear, you must not be forward. You have not been introduced."

Dally's face fell. For a moment her eyes pleaded with me and then she cast them discreetly down and did not look at me again. Bezra Haziz appeared at her side and began whispering something in her ear.

"My dear Lady Dion," said Count Taras, bowing low. "I beg of you to forgive my ward's bad manners."

"There's nothing to forgive," I said. "I would be happy . . ."

"Pray excuse us," continued Count Taras bowing. Dally swept a curtsy to me without looking up.

"It has been a great honor," she murmured. They drew away through the crowd and I stood looking after them, thinking that I should follow them, but having an uncomfortable feeling that it would do Dally more harm than good.

"They are very protective of her," said a voice beside me. I looked up and saw Prince Nikoli standing there. "As well they should be. If she holds the emperor's fancy, she will be a jewel beyond price."

Kitten had come to my other side. She gave me a quick apologetic look. Apparently Nikoli had been too much for her.

"Do you know that young lady?" asked Nikoli.

"No, why should I?"

"Nobody knows where she came from but it sometimes seems to me that there is something similar about the way you both speak Aramayan. Perhaps a trace of a Morian accent."

"Oh my God. Quickly this way," said Kitten. "There's Pyotr Deserov, coming toward us. Oh Dion, let's go. This place is crawling with Deserovs. And they're all furious to see me here."

I had no idea if the Deserovs were there or not but I was extremely keen to take Kitten's cue and escape Nikoli's too perceptive gaze.

"Yes let's," I said. "If you will excuse us Prince, I hope to see you later."

We pushed away through the crowd fending off well-wishers. I hoped Nikoli was not too hurt and cursed myself for getting so involved with him. Yet would things have been less complicated if I had not slept with Nikoli? Not really. I wasn't sure when it had started to happen but he was now a warm presence in my life and one that I would have missed very much if he had not been there. If only he had not been a demon hunter.

Suddenly Kitten gave a little gasp. I looked round and saw a shocked look on her face. Dally and her two keepers were nearby, heading for the door even faster than we were. Dally leaned heavily on the tall mage's arm. I guessed that she had said something to Kitten as she passed but I was forced to wait until we had made it to our carriage before I could find out what it was.

"She said "Hello Kitten Avignon," as she passed us. But how could she have known? Dally's never seen me before."

There was a look of vague horror in Kitten's green eyes.

"You're always telling me everyone knows who you are. Couldn't that be how she knew? Perhaps she's heard of you as she'd heard of me."

"A young unmarried girl? I suppose it's possible. I don't know. There was something in the way she said it. . . . It chilled me."

We both knew what was worrying her. Dally had never met Kitten but Bedazzer knew her well. His master Norval had used him to torture and rape her all those years ago in Gallia. I put my arm around her.

"Bedazzer could not possibly be at the emperor's court even in Dally's form," I said. "They search all people close to the emperor to see if they are demons incarnate in this world. And she could not practice necromancy here in Akieva either. They guard against that. Any association they may still have must be taking place somewhere else."

If only I had had some contact with Bedazzer—some idea if he was indeed involved in all of this.

"Of course. You're right," Kitten said, but she remained shaken. I did my best to turn her thoughts to more cheerful subjects. I felt wretched to have brought Bedazzer back into her life even as a mere memory.

Later when Kitten was quietly asleep, I wrote to Nikoli apologizing for being so brisk. I should have apologized to Shad a bit more often. I would not make the same mistake again.

The following morning I received a note telling me that there had been nothing to forgive and asking me to accept a handsome red-bound copy of Antra's *Demonologies*. He always knew what I liked.

A day later a richly dressed servant brought an invitation to a private dinner from the emperor. Both Kitten and I were asked.

"I am glad he has invited Kitten," I said to Nikoli when he came to escort me to a telescope viewing. "But I do wonder why, if it is to be a scientific gathering. Do you think he has heard of her reputation for learning?"

"May I speak bluntly?" said Nikoli. "I suspect he is curious to see the notorious Katerina Deserov or . . . what did they call her in Gallia . . . Kitten Avignon. Her turning to the honey sisterhood caused a wondrous scandal here but her beauty and charm is almost as legendary to some Akievans as your power. And few who have met her have been disappointed in that beauty and charm. There is a certain romance about a truly great courtesan."

"So it *is* widely known who she is," I said, thinking of Dally yesterday. I would be glad to tell Kitten that. Perhaps it would soothe her a little.

"Yes, it is. But it is not generally spoken of."

That figured. It was the Aramayan way.

Lens grinding was a great hobby among the Aramayan nobility and there was great competition to see who could make the biggest and the best. Count Stefan Golitsyn was the current winner in these stakes. Through the window of his residence we could see a church steeple a considerable distance away while the same steeple was just a blur in the nearby telescope of his friendly rival Lord Anton Stolypin. As with most of these scientific gatherings, the viewing itself was secondary to the partaking of refreshments and the gossiping about who was building or designing or writing what. (And who wasn't speaking to whom as a result of this building, designing or writing.) I had been long enough in Aramaya to be sure of having plenty of acquaintances other than Nikoli to talk to at an event like this. The crowd was mostly nonmages who had a passion for science with a scattering of mages. There were even several other women there.

One of those women was Bezra Haziz. I tried not to stare at her. Should I try to get into conversation? The dilemma was quickly solved for me. Most Aramayans wait for a formal introduction, but Haziz simply came over and introduced herself.

"We are both women and both mages," she said. "I felt you would not mind if I spoke to you. I did not know who you were yesterday. Now I am not surprised that my pupil was so excited to meet you."

Was there a double meaning behind those words? Did she know I was Dally's aunt? It was impossible to read anything in her cold dark eyes. Her face was lean and sharp and so was her tall body. Her grey hair was tied loosely in a bun. Her skin was the bronze color of many southern Aramayans.

She would not be a gentle teacher. In fact I could not see her as a teacher at all. She had the gaunt hawklike look of some queen of a older and more savage time; the kind of legendary queen who orders assassinations and sets her children fighting among themselves that she might keep power. She did not seem someone who craved power, rather someone who already had it and knew how to get more. This woman was a mere governess? I did not believe it for a moment.

"You teach Lady Natasha Korosov?" I asked, and she said calmly that she did and led the conversation onto women's education. I wondered what allies such a woman might call on in a magical battle. I was certain she was more cunning than me. For this reason I was unwilling to show too great an interest in Lady Natasha.

She was not shy about trying to get information from me, however. She asked me if my surname was common and then if my family was large. I replied dishonestly that yes, Holyhands was a very common Morian name, due to our widespread veneration of St. Belkis of the Holy Healing Hands and that no, I was an only child. If she was going to make a connection between Dally and myself I was not going to help her.

Of course if Haziz knew of Dally's necromantic activities,

she could have made a link between us through Bedazzer, so it was lucky that I had suppressed the names of the demons concerned in my reports of dealings with them. It would have been extremely suspicious for her to have asked for those names on such short acquaintance.

While we were talking something blue on her wrist caught my eye.

She saw me notice.

"You are admiring my tattoo?" she asked. She showed me it. It was the shape of a small crocodile.

"A tattoo?" I asked, surprised that any woman would have such a thing.

"It is the symbol of the River Cult," she said. "All children born in Marzorna are tattooed with such a mark. No doubt you think it very uncivilized."

"Not at all," I said politely to keep the conversation going. "Are none of the Marzornites Aumazites then?"

"None," she said. "The Marzornites worship nature in the form of Het the river if they are desert dwellers like me or Aliceander the crocodile goddess if they are marsh folk. Aumazite missionary work has been largely unsuccessful in Marzorna. Aliceander, particularly, is a savage god. Fortunately the Aramayan Empire is tolerant. It is ironic, is it not, that a civilized rational mage like myself should carry always the mark of such superstition?"

I did not know how to answer this diplomatically, so I said, "I have heard of nature worship cults before. Some people draw great magical power from such worship. Is it so in Marzorna?"

She looked at me strangely and then she said, "It is true I have seen things done in Marzorna I never saw anywhere else. But most mages refuse to believe nature magic is real."

"The more I know of magic the less I feel I really know. There are many strange things out there in the world," I said.

"Some say that nature worship and the worship of pre-Aumazite gods is based on real beings who once existed," said Haziz with a curious look in her eyes. "Beings who might even still exist out there on the fringes of the known world. What do you think?"

"I suppose it is possible that people used to regard great mages as gods."

"Or demons," said Haziz. "But I wonder what kind of being nature magic might throw up. Perhaps an area of great natural power might create some kind of spirit."

"Are you speaking from experience?" I asked, curious about her manner.

"Not at all," she said blithely. "Merely speculating. The marshes of Marzorna are a mysterious place, that is all.

I suddenly had the feeling she was baiting me, trying to make me feel that she knew something I didn't. I changed the subject back to women's education.

This part of the conversation came back to me later that day when Kitten told me that there was someone else watching the Korosov house.

"Simonetti tells me they are a group of young Marzornites."

Marzornites! Was this what Dally was involved in? Was this whole thing something to do with Marzorna? With this crocodile cult?

I told Kitten of my conversation with Haziz.

"This is beginning to look complex," she said. "Marzornites have no love for the Aramayan Emperor. I wish to God we could get a word with your young Dally alone."

"A thing I would pray for every night, if I prayed. Perhaps I will be able to speak to her at this private dinner of the emperor's tonight."

"Perhaps. Although I never knew anybody to have a private conversation in the Winter Palace. And she is so very well guarded. Ah well, all we can do is keep trying."

"You have another suggestion, don't you?"

"We could try and get into the house to see her. She has her own bedroom."

"Is that possible?" I said.

"Of course. Don't I make the impossible possible? Isn't my name Katerina Deserov?" she said grandly.

"Only sometimes," I pointed out wryly.

ACCORDING TO KITTEN, the emperor's private dinner was extremely informal. When I learned this I felt very sorry for the emperor. How stiflingly formal his life must usually be. Everyone wore court attire and magnificently liveried servants processed between the table and the door with the devout zealousness of priests at a religious ceremony. Probably the informality was expressed in the way the emperor lounged on a small oak throne chased with silver instead of his big golden throne and wore his favorite uniform instead of court dress. We were allowed to sit in his presence, but Kitten had warned me to eat before I arrived for there were limits to "informality." When the emperor put his knife and fork down, no one else was allowed to eat either. Since the emperor was a young man more interested in science than food, little actual dining was done. The chef must have been very discouraged by the amount of food that returned to the kitchen untouched.

Kitten and I were seated on either side of the emperor. He spoke mostly to me, but I noticed that he shot the odd fascinated glance at Kitten, who was deep in conversation with the Imperial Watchmaker. Had Nikoli been right then?

I thought it rather appealing that this very intellectual emperor could still be interested in backstairs gossip.

My impression of him as an enthusiastic pup was confirmed by the questions he plied me with. Though he was very interested in the world of demons, he was even more interested in the techniques Shad and I had used to revitalize the dead area around Ruinac and how we had planned our new city. I found myself wishing Shad had been there to help me explain everything, especially when the emperor asked me if I would write a report about Ruinac for him. It had been Shad who had performed the long, painstaking experiments with different plants and different ways of enriching our soil and he who made the practical plans for the laying out of streets and drains.

Count Strezleki, the Imperial Watchmaker, the Imperial Astronomer, the head of the Imperial Mages, and one or two other such favorites were present at the dinner. As I had hoped, Lady Natasha Korosov was also there, sitting at the other end of the table among the ladies-in-waiting who surrounded the emperor's mother, Princess Feodosia. Only her guardian, Count Taras Korosov, was there to chaperone her that night. She spent most of her time looking shyly down at her plate although her face lit up delightedly whenever the emperor spoke to her.

After dinner and a very brief sip of kesh in an elegant drawing room, the emperor led the way up a spiral staircase to a small room just below the golden dome of the palace where a series of telescopes had been set up for viewing the night sky.

"How delightful!" exclaimed Kitten. "Will we be able to see the Jewelbox through this telescope? I should very much like to see it again."

"I did not know you enjoyed astronomy, Countess," said the emperor. He blushed a little as he spoke and she gave him her warmest smile, which made him blush even more.

"I am interested in all aspects of the New Learning, High One," she said. "I would be very grateful to know what advances have been made in astronomy since I was last in Aramaya."

After that the emperor simply had to show her all the workings of the telescope and how to focus it on the various objects in the sky. Kitten effortlessly held his entire concentration, causing him to completely forget Lady Natasha.

Well fancy that, I thought. Kitten was setting herself to charm the emperor. I shot a surreptitious glance at Count Taras and saw that he was displeased. On the other hand, for a fleeting moment a look of amusement crossed Lady Natasha's face before she dropped her eyes again. The look reassured me for otherwise I could recognize nothing of the forceful Dally I had known back in Moria in the shy, mousy Lady Natasha. Dally would have been about nineteen years old. Lady Natasha's shyness made her seem much younger.

She neither looked at me or approached me all evening. It was as if she did not dare under the watchful eyes of Count Taras. What had Dally got herself into? I was more and more certain that she needed rescue, but there was no opportunity for me to speak with her even though I positioned myself close to her as we climbed up and down the stairs to the observatory.

Having descended from the observatory, we were allowed to sit and finish our kesh and sweet wine. Kitten had revealed just the right amount of knowledge of watchmaking to keep both the emperor and the Imperial Watchmaker engrossed in explaining things to her. This obviously infuriated Count Taras, for suddenly, after making a few inquiries to me about Gallia, he said very loudly, "And tell me about this Kitten Avignon, Madam. I cannot imagine a true prince having such a vulgar creature as a courtesan at his court. Stories tell of her great beauty and charm but surely it is only courtly falsehood. Surely she was a crude creature with raddled skin and coarse manners."

The emperor could not help himself. His eyes flew to Kitten's face. Everyone else in the room froze to sudden silence.

"On the contrary," I said. "She was indeed the most gracious and beautiful of creatures."

"Now, now, Lady Dion," said Kitten gently from across the room. "Do not go telling fibs to Count Taras. How can you expect him to believe them? I'm sure he knows a great deal more about courtesans than either of us."

A smile lit up the emperor's eyes and for a moment I thought he was going to cry "Well done." Count Taras bowed politely toward Kitten like a fencer acknowledging a hit, but his mouth was thin with displeasure. To be a great lover was admired in Aramayan society, but to know a great deal of courtesans implied that one was too unattractive to appeal to decent women.

"What were you doing?" I asked Kitten on the way home. "One does not charm emperors merely to pass the time."

"He seemed quite a nice young man for an emperor," she said rearranging her brocade skirts casually. "It would be a bitter shame if he fell into the hands of something like Bedazzer, especially if I have the means to stop it."

Her voice had a cold ruthless edge to it. It was the tone of a soldier, not the honeyed tone of a courtesan.

"It may not be Bedazzer we are up against," I said.

I felt her relax and when she spoke again it was in a more normal voice.

"Nonetheless, that Taras Korosov is up to something and Dally is a part of it," she said. "Control of the emperor is the most likely prize. Any plan Korosov is in is worth thwarting. He was never a nice man and I doubt he's become one now. But you saw how hard it was to speak to Lady Natasha tonight. I really think you should consider my plan of breaking into their house."

"It's a fine plan, but isn't it too early to be considering it? We may get other chances."

"If we are going to consider the plan as possible then we must start preparing now."

"What sort of preparing?" I asked.

I found out soon enough.

The Korosov house was well guarded from magic. If we were to break in, then we must do it by more conventional means. So that evening, instead of sitting quietly in my room with a hot milk drink and a good book, I found myself in the freezing cold night, attempting to scale the back of Pepita

Sandorez's house on a rope. Attempting was the best description: a life of magery does not fit you for feats of physical strength.

"Hmm," said Simonetti, viewing my efforts. "I don't think we will be breaking into Korosov's house this week. You had better go inside and have a hot bath and a rubdown from the wife. Otherwise you'll be in agony tomorrow."

Otherwise? Otherwise!!! I was in agony the following day even after the rubdown. I had to use a magic soothing on myself before I could walk.

Nikoli in his usual perceptive way asked me if I had fallen over and I agreed that I had, after which he was embarrassingly tender. When Kitten left us alone he wanted to kiss me. Although I had decided that I should not get more deeply involved with him, it was so nice to feel his lips and his arm around me and to lean my head against his strong shoulder. He smelled of some sharp clean scent and his hands were so wise and gentle. Despite my best intentions we wound up making love on the chaise in the closed up dining room.

Afterward Nikoli sighed. "You Morians are so indecorous. Will I ever actually get to a bed with you?"

"I don't recall you saying no," I said roundly and we both laughed. Laughter was good. It smoothed over my uneasiness.

Later over luncheon, Nikoli told us of the gossip that was flying all around town concerning how Kitten had charmed the emperor the previous night and how the little Korosov's nose was out of joint over it.

I wondered how the Deserovs would take this and did not have long to find out. Before luncheon was over, four men arrived with papers from the Prekazy and began to search Pepita's house from top to bottom using a method calculated to cause the most possible destruction. Pepita and Kitten both followed them around the house rescuing vases and protesting angrily, but it was Nikoli who made the real difference. He sent a message to the White College and a short time later Count Igor Strugatsky came thundering in at the front door shouting that such an honored mage as the

Demonslayer of Gallia could not be subjected to such harassment. He was followed shortly after by a tall stooping man in black who proved to be the Chief Demonslayer. His sinisterly well chosen words added to Count Igor's thunderings quickly drove the Prekazy men from the house.

"And you can tell Prince Deserov that he would do better to pay more attention to some of the emperor's other fancies," shouted Kitten after them.

While I was climbing up the back of Wilby and Pepita's house, the two Prekazy informers needed to be kept ignorant of our activities. Suza gave Jan the kitchen hand a sleeping potion and sat by to see he did not wake.

Kitten, who did not need to practice climbing, said, "I shall take care of Misha," and disappeared into the house. It was important that I learn to climb this wall, for I would not be able to use magic to get into the Korosov house and if I slipped and used it to rescue myself the whole attempt would be given away. Nonetheless, I had the feeling that half the point of my wall climbing was to give the three of them the pleasure of deceiving the Prekazy.

A few days later I found out how Kitten was keeping Misha busy.

Early one morning I saw him going surreptitiously into her room and worried that he might be doing something sinister. I went quietly to the door and put my hand on it. I used magic to look through the wood into the room and saw that Kitten was still there. She was wearing her softest finest bedgown and as I watched she went over to Misha and kissed him deeply. Horribly embarrassed I withdrew quickly, but I taxed Kitten with it later.

"You must not do this," I said. "You are not a courtesan anymore and Dally is not worth such unpleasantness."

She laughed and flicked my cheek. "What makes you so sure it's unpleasant? Don't worry. He's a tasty man and very proficient in bed."

"But he's also a Prekazy informer. How can you enjoy sleeping with him?"

"Actually I find it adds a certain stimulus. Oh don't look

so worried, my love. I'm not doing anything I don't want to. If I didn't fancy him I'd give him a sleeping potion like Jan."

I begged and cajoled her, but she would not be persuaded. I had hoped she might take a lover in Akieva, but I was slightly horrified by this. It seemed bizarre to have an affair with a servant who was also an enemy when she had several very nice suitors more than willing to share her bed and escort her to the theater.

Although he was a very fine looking man. But he did not look like a fool. I hoped Kitten knew what she was doing. I could hardly keep a closer watch on her now.

Once your muscles stop hurting there is something very satisfying about physical achievement. I began to understand why Kitten enjoyed all the riding and swordfighting that she did. By the end of the week I could haul myself up the wall without falling.

This was a good thing since all our attempts to talk with Lady Natasha Korosov had been a complete failure. Kitten, the Simonettis, and I all took our turn at following her and Madame Bezra round the town, but even though Suza Simonetti managed to speak to her long enough to ask her if she was Dally Holyhands, none of us got any words out of her. I began to wonder if she needed help after all. Perhaps she wanted us to just go away. This thought worried me even more as it suggested that she must then be up to some activity she knew I would disapprove of. I could not leave her alone without knowing the truth.

Ten days after the Imperial reception to proclaim the opening of the winter Season, we decided to make an attempt to get into the Korosov house.

"But first," said Kitten, "there's something we must do."

As well as posing as our servants, and despite the presence of government spies, Suza, Captain Simonetti, and assorted hired helpers had been watching the Korosov house since we had been in Akieva. This was how they had become aware that the house was also being watched by others. Suza tracked them to their lodgings. She fell easily into conversation with the washerwoman, their landlady, and discovered that our fellow watchers were a gentleman of Marzorna called Ahmed El-Lamak and his two servants.

"And very nice well behaved gentlemen they are too, despite what they say about Marzorna-folk," the washerwoman had said.

"And what do they say about Marzorna-folk?" I asked Kitten after Suza had given us her report. "That they are godless heretics?"

"Oh, nothing so trivial," said Kitten. "Though I suppose it is a type of heresy. They simply show a strange reluctance to be part of the great civilizing Aramayan empire and this is taken as a sign of deep perversion."

Since my conversation with Bezra Haziz I had looked into the Marzornite crocodile cult. We mages of the Aramayan tradition drew power from what was within ourselves. The Marzornites however, drew on the life force of nature much like the Klementari at home in Moria did. Because it drew on such a wide source, nature magic could be extremely powerful. Unlike the Klementari, who worshipped the earth itself, the Marzornites, especially the marsh folk, believed in a fertility goddess who was supposed to be an aspect of the river Het and whose symbol was the crocodile. It was rumored that those marsh folk who had strong magical powers formed a religious army dedicated to her, but not much else was known about the cult. It seemed the marsh was very inhospitable to outsiders, especially mages.

I had learned a great deal more about Marzorna itself.

It was one of a handful of "independent" states on the borders between the Great Aramayan and Soprian Empires. They were buffer states, states who owed their continued independence to the fact that the two unfriendly Empires were reluctant to have a mutual border.

But this didn't stop the Empires from trying to influence the internal policies of their buffer states. Marzorna was led by a Sultan who was "advised" by an Aramayan resident. The resident was currently Aramayan, but eventually there would be an uprising and the leaders of that uprising would invite the Soprians to help them and the new ruler would have a Soprian resident to "advise" him. Similar changes had happened three times in the last one hundred years and there was no reason to think it would not happen again.

Though Aramaya and Sopria often swapped harsh words over Marzorna, they never really went to war over it. But it was important to each "advising" power to seem to be in control. In reality nobody could control Marzorna, not even its native rulers.

The country lay where the mighty river Het formed an enormous river delta before draining into the Sunlit Sea. Half was cruel desert and the other half was an enormous marsh—an impenetrable forest of reeds. The people who lived in that marsh—however many that was—did exactly as they pleased. What they pleased to do as often as not was to harass the troops of whatever power was currently "advising" the Sultan at his desert capital of Shebaz. A posting to Marzorna was one of the most dangerous in the Aramayan Empire; usually it was a punishment as it had been for Count Taras Korosov.

"Since the Marzornites tend to hate whoever is their Resident and Count Taras was Resident of Marzorna until the late emperor's death it seems unlikely that these young men are friends of his," said Kitten. "Which means they could be friends for us. They might even be able to give us some idea of what is going on with your niece."

"So how do we get to talk to this Ahmed El-Lamak? I suppose we are going to send Simonetti round to kidnap him or some other such adventuresome activity."

Kitten laughed. "I was thinking we might be very un-Aramayan about this and start with a simple invitation to visit."

Monsieur Ahmed El-Lamak was a man in his early twenties with huge dark eyes fringed with long lashes. He was slim and lightly built, but I did not think he was a weakling. His calm, capable manner reminded me of the Simonettis. No doubt like them he could be relied upon to extract himself from any given situation with a minimum of fuss and a maximum of effectiveness.

Certainly he knew exactly who I was. It was the only piece of knowledge he revealed, however. Though we asked him why he was interested in the house of Taras Korosov, he would not tell us and when I mentioned that I was looking for my niece Syndal Holyhands, whom I believed to be part of the count's household, there was no sign of recognition in El-Lamak's eyes. He merely nodded thoughtfully and then said that his masters would prefer him not to reveal his business.

"It has been a great honor to meet the Demonslayer," he said as he bowed over my hand before he left. "I thank you for your interest and regret I am unable to help you. Good day, ladies."

The whole interview left me feeling frustrated and foolish. However, Kitten said, "That tree may yet bear fruit." and went calmly away to talk over the details of our break-in with Simonetti. For all her delight in fine clothes and good conversation, it was these moments of adventure that my friend relished the most.

Kitten and the Simonettis' forward planning was impressive. Shortly before Count Korosov had arrived back in Akieva, the chimneys of his town house had been swept. Simonetti had bribed the chimney sweep to break a catch on one of the attic windows against the possibility that we might later need to get in. It was a well placed window looking onto a narrow alleyway that ran along the side of the house. Bars and magical wardings protected the first three floors, so the attic was our only real chance for a discreet entrance. The chimney sweep had given us a good map of the house and we had bribed a maid to tell us who slept in which room. Finding our way to Dally seemed straightforward under these conditions.

Thus it was that in the dark of the moon a couple of nights later, I found myself using my newfound skill of rope-climbing up the four floors of the Korosov house and being pulled in at the window of a small attic box room by Kitten. Without magic to keep me warm it was freezing.

Both of us wore breeches for easier movement. Kitten was

armed with a club which she stuck into her belt and she carried a small pack on her back. We each carried extra ropes. It was not beyond possibility that when we left we might have to take Dally with us.

Kitten lit two candles and passed one to me before moving softly to the door, opening it gently, and peering out. Then she motioned me to follow her. My hands were trembling. I reminded myself that Dally might need me and that nothing worse than recognition and embarrassment would probably happen to us.

Being a mage and a man with a personal mage, Count Taras could afford to set up extra wardings and we had no way of knowing that he wouldn't. We had to move very slowly because I could only rely on my innate sense for magic. If I had actually used magic, I would have set off every warding in the house and we would certainly be discovered. Evidently, however, Count Taras was relying on the fact that this quarter of Akieva was very safe. During our long tense creeping down the servants' narrow staircase and out into the grandly furnished areas of the house, we came across nothing more alarming than the odd creaking board.

Finally we reached Dally's room. There was a light under the door. After listening at it for a short time Kitten opened the door gently and we went in.

Dally was lying awake on the bed staring at the ceiling. The first thing I noticed was the iron necklace that showed above the neck of her nightgown. As we entered the room she turned slowly toward us. Her eyes glittered oddly in the light of our candle.

I went toward her, my hand outstretched.

"Dally, I want to help . . ."

Suddenly she sat up and let out a piercing scream.

I rushed to the bed and gripped her by the shoulders.

"Dally, please, it's me, Dion. I don't want to hurt you. Let me help you."

She simply kept on screaming and screaming, a terrifying sound, and yet between screams her eyes and face were completely calm. It was as if she was simply making a noise, letting off an alarm that had no relation to her own feelings.

"Dally," I shouted.

Kitten dragged me away from the bed. I could hear shouting outside in the corridor and suddenly the room was suffused with bright light. Wardings came up all round the wall. Their wailing drowned out Dally's screams.

It was too late for discretion now. I turned and, using magic, smashed the glass and bars at the window. Catching Kitten about the waist I leaped out through it. My last sight of Dally was of her sitting neatly up in the bed. She had stopped screaming, but there was a bleak expression of despair on her face.

Outside there was no friendly darkness to fade into. The whole Korosov house was glowing with a brilliant white light. Simonetti was there and then we were all running, running headlong toward dark streets, feet slipping on icy cobblestones. There were people behind us. Even when we finally reached a dark alleyway, it was no protection from magic. I could feel it like a huge glowing eye behind me, searching. Someone was looking for us in the Bowl of Seeing. I kept on running. The only hope was to put distance between me and the house. Using magic to get away would only have made me stand out more. Suddenly a man appeared at the alleyway corner and caught Kitten and me by the arm.

"Nikoli!"

"Get in here," he said, pushing us into the open door of a carriage. He bundled the protesting Captain Simonetti in after us, jumped in himself, and pulled the door shut as the carriage jerked into motion.

"Quickly," he said throwing a fur blanket over our knees. "They may stop us."

In a scramble of flying material, Kitten and I seized our cloaks from Simonetti and draped them around our shoulders, hiding our male clothing. We pulled the cloths that we had used to cover our hair from our heads. Simonetti dropped to the floor and lay there prone at our feet and we covered him with the blanket. Not a moment too soon.

The carriage stopped and the door was opened. Nikoli did an admirable impression of a haughtily surprised gentleman.

"My good fellow. What is going on here?"

"Good evening, Highness," said a man. There were two of them, dark figures standing in the doorway. We could see their breath steaming against the white light of the glowing house behind them.

"I feel sure you are going to explain this unmannerly intrusion," said Nikoli.

"A break-in, Highness," said the man. "Couple of fellows at Count Korosov's place. Usin' magic they were."

"The cheek of the fellows," said Nikoli. "And the cheek of you too. Do I look like I've got housebreakers in my coach?"

He hammered on the ceiling of the coach and shouted for the driver to drive on. But the man at the doorway was made of sterner stuff.

"Your name, Highness, if I could please have it."

"I should have you whipped for your impertinence, fellow. I am Prince Nikoli Terzu and these are my cousins, Ladies Daria and Galina Terzu. Are you content now? Then perhaps you will close the door behind you and stop letting in the cold."

"I do hope your cousins are both in town," said Kitten as we drove away.

"Huh," said Nikoli. "Do you think I am an amateur? I have been to the Opera with them this very night. Mind you I don't claim to have your gifts at misrepresentation. I do hope that now I've been kind enough to be of service that you are going to finally tell me what your interest in Lady Natasha Korosov is."

"Of course I have been watching you," said Nikoli. "Do you think it was an accident that day after you went to the Healing College, Dion? My servant was following you."

The calm way he spoke took some of the shock out of his words, but nonetheless the surprise was unpleasant. It seemed so . . . underhanded.

We were sitting in Nikoli's study drinking hot spiced wine.

He had taken us to his house despite our protests that we wanted to go home. As I had long suspected, Nikoli was like a velvet brick—pleasant but entirely unyielding.

Kitten looked annoyed at this talk of spies. So did Simonetti. "Your people must be bloody good," he said. "I never saw them."

"They are," said Nikoli simply. He turned to me. "Do you still believe Lady Natasha to be your niece, Dion?"

"I don't know what to think. Why did she scream if she was Dally? And why did she scream like that? It was as if she was some kind of automaton. She was wearing an iron necklace even though she was not at court. Do you think perhaps Haziz and Korosov have enslaved her in some way? Some way I don't know of?"

"In all the years I've been a demon hunter I've never seen a way of turning someone into a slave without making them a mindless puppet. Perhaps he holds some threat over her."

"Yes, the necklace makes me wonder about that. No mage likes wearing it. But that is why we broke into the house. Why should she betray us when she had the opportunity to speak secretly with us? When I first came she seemed very anxious to speak with me but ever since that first meeting . . ."

"There must be some complication we don't know about," said Kitten. "Perhaps she was afraid they knew we were there. We should try again."

"Perhaps she is not your niece," said Nikoli. "Perhaps this is some kind of devious trap to get control of you, Dion. You are the Demonslayer. If a necromancer could manacle you and tap you . . ."

Necromancers had a way of drawing on the power of other mages known as tapping. As a mage of unusually strong power, I represented quite a prize to the necromancer intent on using this method. But if Count Taras or his associates were intent on making use of me in that way surely there were much simpler ways to capture me. Dally had been in his hands well before I had come to Aramaya, before Shad had even left me. How could he have known I would see the Arkady Illusion and react as I had?

"I don't think I am the target of this business," I said. "I doubt it has anything to do with me. Such a scheme would be elaborate beyond belief."

"But you will keep it in mind and not go charging into strange houses again, I hope," said Nikoli. "Or if you will not think of the danger, think of the scandal that would have been caused had you been caught. You are the Demonslayer of Gallia. You cannot be seen using your power unlawfully."

These Aramayans. All they ever thought about was how things looked.

"I must speak with my niece," I cried in frustration. "That is all I want."

"Why? Because you suspect her of being involved in necromancy?" said Nikoli sharply.

I tried not to look dismayed—tried to cover the moment with protest. "She was wearing an iron necklace. That says to me she is not willingly involved with whatever is going on."

"She does not seem unwilling to charm the emperor," said Nikoli.

"Do you believe she is involved in necromancy?" Kitten asked Nikoli.

"We believe Count Taras to be," said Nikoli. "For many years he has been an indiscreet dabbler on the fringes. Haziz is the brains in that crew. Her presence indicates that his involvement with the Secret Colleges has become more serious."

"If you have been watching him, you must know something about Lady Natasha and where she came from," said Kitten. Her eyes were narrowed.

"Lady Natasha comes from Marzorna but she is patently not a Marzornite. It is impossible for the demon hunters to watch everyone they suspect of necromancy. We have only been watching Korosov since his ward began to win the favor of the emperor. Before that the Prekazy were responsible for watching him and I'm afraid their agents in Marzorna are . . . inefficient."

This conversation was going nowhere.

"Nikoli, everything you say about the danger of scandal

is true yet I must speak to my niece," I cried. "You must see that. We must find out what is going on. For the emperor's sake, if not for hers."

"Yes," he said. He reached over and took my hand. "But please, you must allow me to handle this. I have the resources of the demon hunters to call on."

I stared at him. I did not want to surrender Dally to demon hunters, even one as reasonable as Nikoli.

"I promise I shall send for you the moment I know anything," he said. "Will you promise me not to undertake any more of these potentially embarrassing plans?"

I looked at Kitten. She raised an eyebrow in an expression that said *might as well. We have nothing to lose.*

I was not so sure I agreed with her.

"I wonder if I might speak to you alone for a minute, Prince Nikoli," I said.

"What is it that the others can't hear?" he asked me after they had gone.

I was uncomfortable. I knew I was about to try and exploit Nikoli's softness for me, but I was not sure how far I was prepared to go. I liked Nikoli. I didn't want to make use of him.

"You've been a good friend to me, Nikoli."

"I had hoped I was more than that," he said.

His words made my guilt even worse.

"Kitten told me I should have asked you to help us a long time ago, but I hesitated because you are a demon hunter."

"So you do suspect that your niece had dabbled in necromancy," he said with his usual uncomfortable perceptiveness. Damn him and damn me for revealing too much.

"I suspected as much, when I found out what you were doing," he continued. "I suppose you will ask me out of affection for you to turn a blind eye to Dally's crimes."

"I would never ask that," I said. "It's true that there were signs that she was dabbling in necromancy back in Moria. But she was young and lonely and ignorant and perhaps she has done nothing very wrong. Perhaps she turned away from it later. This is not unheard of in Aramaya, surely. And she was wearing an iron necklace. Surely that means she is under some duress."

"I agree that it is a hopeful sign."

"Then you will not judge her too harshly?"

"Too rigidly you mean? Where do you want me to draw the line? How many murders before it is too many?"

His words made me feel ashamed.

"You know I'm not asking you to overlook that," I said softly, not looking him in the eye.

"I'm relieved." There was silence.

Then he said softly. "I do understand you. You are afraid for your niece. I would feel so about Alexi or any of my boys. But I think you hate necromancy as much as me. If Dally has knowingly committed crimes, you would not really want to see her go free, would you?"

"No," I said, praying that it would not come to that. Though how much hope did I have that it would not? He sighed and came over to me. He put his hands around my face and turned it up to look into my eyes. His eyes were gentle and calm.

"Dion, I would do anything to protect you from hurt. But I will not let a necromancer go free even for you. We must have that clear between us."

The declaration touched me.

"I understand entirely," I said, because I did. I did not know what I would do if I found that Dally had been slaughtering people to feed her demon. Even though she was my niece and her dying mother had asked me to look after her, such actions had to be stopped. And punished.

He leaned his head against mine. "I wanted only to help you and now I see this has complicated everything between us." He sighed. "I could bear you being still in love with your ex-husband, but not that you might be keeping me sweet for the sake of your niece."

"Then I shall not," I said.

"Do you promise?"

"I promise."

He kissed me then, a gentle lingering kiss. His lips felt

good on mine and there was such a warm kind feeling between us. Here was a man I could certainly come to love.

But the feeling faded once I was out in the carriage with the others and I remembered that he had had me watched.

"Don't you trust him?" said Kitten. "I believe him when he tells you he will be easier on necromancy than the Morians would be. You have no need to fear him there."

"But it depends on what Dally has done. Don't you see? I may simply have led the demon hunters to her. If she is burned at the stake it will be my fault."

"We could keep on with our own plans," said Kitten, though there was doubt in her voice.

"We have given him our word, we will not," I said. "And it seems almost inevitable that he will find out if we don't keep our word." As I said this I recognized that there was a part of me so confounded by Dally's behavior that I was inclined to let Nikoli take over the whole business. I began to wonder if I had come to rely on him too much. But he was so extremely capable.

"True," said Simonetti. "We must find out who his spy is; that is our first priority Madam."

"I already have an idea about that," said Kitten grimly.

It was almost dawn when we got home and all further discussion was postponed. Alone in my room, I threw my cloak down on the bed and sat down beside it, rubbing my face in my hands. Confused and anxious thoughts raged round inside me. I wondered if I would need magic to help me sleep tonight.

There was movement behind me as a curtain pulled back from the window. I leapt up and whirled around, ready to fight. A dark figure stood there.

"Please Lady, do not harm me. It is Ahmed El-Lamak. I mean you no ill."

He moved slowly forward until I could see him in the candlelight. I let myself relax but only outwardly. What did I know of this El-Lamak person, apart from the fact that he didn't like to answer questions? I asked him one anyway.

"What are you doing here? How did you get in?"

"I saw what you did tonight. I wanted to talk to you so I slipped in at the servants' entrance when everyone was leaving the party tonight. Why are you so interested in Syndal Holyhands?"

He looked tense. Now I would get something out of him.

"I have told you. I am her aunt. I want to see that she is safe and well," I asked. "I thought you had no interest in Dally."

He was silent for a moment.

"I have met this Syndal," he said carefully. "She gave the impression that seeing her Aunt Dion was one of the things she dreaded most and I know why she dreaded it. And now this Dion comes to Akieva and is close friends with one of Aramaya's most efficient demon hunters. Have you come to punish Dally, Lady? To have her burned at the stake for the things that happened back in Moria."

My heart sank. I could see now exactly how it must look to Dally. Was that why she screamed?

"Oh damn," I muttered.

I had thought of the fact that Dally might have done some very wrong things, I had even considered the fact that she might have become a necromancer, but I had never thought that she might actually regard me as the enemy.

I remembered the last time I saw her when the great Cathedral of Ruinac came crashing down around our heads. Dally tried to blackmail me into telling her the demon Smazor's true name. She wanted a demon she could control as she could not control Bedazzer. Exhausted and shocked, I lost my temper with her. "Better dead than a demonmaster," I had shouted and then I had lost my grip on the Cathedral and the stones had rained down on us. No wonder she mistrusted me. She couldn't know how much I regretted what had happened and how many excuses I was prepared to make for her.

"She is my blood kin. I only wanted to see if she was safe. Until tonight's fiasco the demon hunter didn't know of our connection," I said. I hoped he did not know enough about mages to hear what I was not saying. "We, our family, thought her dead and are glad to learn otherwise."

"And the demon hunter?"

I thought of Nikoli. I wished now that we had not had our conversation about necromancy. I wished he had not kissed me, that he was not my friend and lover. I might still have to betray his trust.

"Yes, he may be a problem now. If only she hadn't screamed! Why did she scream?"

"I don't know," he said, "but she does it when I approach her too. That is why we have not tried to take her ourselves." He signed and I sensed him relaxing. "I do not understand it. Before Taras Korosov captured her, we were in love."

"Sit down and tell me what we can do to help each other," I said.

My research had given the impression that the Marzornite desert aristocracy welcomed the foreign advisers and Marzornite resistance stemmed from the marsh and was rooted in the naive and uncivilized belief that Marzorna could rid herself of foreign conquerors. But then what I had read had been Aramayan.

Ahmed told a different story. He was the younger son of a Marzornite desert nobleman and the role of such younger sons was to harass the troops of whoever was advising the sultan at the time. "Many single grains of sand together bury the city," as he put it. According to him, most of Marzorna was involved in the resistance against the foreigners simply as a matter of principle. The marshes were a useful place for everybody to hide and the marsh folk allowed the desert dwellers to do so in the interests of weakening foreign rule.

It was on a mission to Karanagrad to buy weapons that Ahmed met Dally. She was working as a mage/bodyguard for Ivan Popov, the man who ran the criminal underworld of Karanagrad.

"She was hating the things that he asked her to do, but you understand—she was a marked woman. He had caught her practicing necromancy when she was still too young to know anything else. He had contacts all over Aramaya and Sopria and as a mage she was his most prized possession. It would have been difficult for her to escape him."

"So she does practice necromancy."

"She did when she was a lost little girl in the slums of Karanagrad," said Ahmed. "But she has put all that behind her now. Popov had her trained in safer magic. He didn't want the demon hunters on his trail."

With Ahmed's help Dally escaped Popov and the marshes of Marzorna offered her safe hiding from even him. Here she began to aid Ahmed and his men in their resistance to the Aramayans.

"She was taken captive in a raid on the Aramayan tax treasury. I don't know what happened. They were waiting for us. They were waiting for Dally. When she was taken we didn't expect to see her again. We couldn't believe our luck when we discovered that she was Count Taras's new foster daughter."

"Then Lady Natasha is Dally," I said.

"What else could she be? A golem? A shapeshifting mage? A bound demon? All these things might be possible in Marzorna but not here in Akieva in the web of protection that surrounds our "beloved" emperor. And yet. . . . My Dally would never willing help Korosov. I cannot believe that. He must have her under some kind of duress."

I remembered the iron necklace. Then I remembered Dally. She had shown a certain insane gallantry in avenging her mother. Might she not now be working to free Marzorna with the same insane gallantry. Working right at the top.

I suggested this to Ahmed.

"Why would Korosov be aiding her? Or Haziz? They have no reason to wish for change. I do not know what is happening with Dally, but I know that to find out I must speak with her. Just as you wish to."

He was proposing an alliance.

"What do you suggest?" I said.

"For many months, we have been watching for an opportunity to kidnap Dally," said Ahmed. "We have a plan and a hiding place set up. But she is too well guarded by mages for us. You could overcome her guards."

"That's insane!" cried Kitten when I told her the following morning. "You cannot kidnap the emperor's cousin's foster-daughter in the middle of Akieva and hope to get away with it. What did you say to him?"

"I said I would think about it. It seemed like exactly the kind of thing that I promised Nikoli I would not get involved with. And yet it would give me a chance to speak to her. I could not just say no."

"You know such an audacious plan might actually succeed," said Suza Simonetti, who had been calmly pouring out the kesh. "Nonmagical security is very lax here in Akieva."

Kitten looked at her and all kinds of possibilities dawned in her eyes.

"I suppose there's no harm in our considering the plan," she said.

For the next fortnight we considered. None of us tried to approach Dally for fear of further consequences. Nonetheless we kept her under observation. No doubt they had tightened their defenses but otherwise nothing seemed to have changed in the Korosov household. There was no sign that Dally had been punished or that the count was aware who had broken in. Kitten and I were invited twice more to small gatherings at the palace, but I got no opportunities to speak to Dally. Although both times Kitten monopolized the emperor's attention, he gave little indication of wanting to be on a more intimate footing with her. In the regimental mess halls, the officers often bet on who would win the emperor's attention and Lady Natasha Korosov was still the favorite candidate. The emperor had recently bought the famous Gorki clock with its dancing metal bears just to present to her.

"He has no taste, to prefer that insipid Lady Natasha to you," I told Kitten one day when we were taking kesh at one of Akieva's many elegant cake and kesh houses. To be honest I was amazed.

"On the contrary, he is a young man outgrowing his older

advisers and becoming ready to take up the reigns of power for himself. A shy young woman who looks up to him as wise and brave must certainly have more appeal than a confident older woman who might well become bossy. Part of me wishes it was not so. Part of me is relieved not to have to play the courtesan again. But we will find out what is what with this Natasha Korosov before too long."

"Have you discovered how Prince Nikoli found out about us yet?" I said.

"Simonetti has not found any new informers," she said tartly, "but he has discovered that friend Misha is not from the Prekazy, but a colonel in the city watch."

"So he is the one reporting to Prince Nikoli? But how did he find out what we were doing?"

"Yes," said Kitten. "That is the annoying question. I suppose I should have realized he was clever enough to know we were up to something, but how he found out what it was I really don't know."

She put down her cup with an irritated gesture. Was it my imagination or was she really angry? Yet I had seen Misha going into her room that very morning. She had not broken with him.

"I thought I was successfully keeping him distracted. I must be slipping in my old age," she said, and changed the subject.

Though I met Ahmed a couple of times at kesh houses, it was only to tell him to be patient. I felt uneasy about breaking faith with Nikoli. Ahmed begged me to consider his plan and it was a good plan. He and his servants had a canal boat on the river Novsky where they planned to take Dally immediately once they kidnapped her and they had hired a lonely house on a nearby branch of the river where they planned to keep her if they could not gain her cooperation.

Ahmed continually assured me that Dally was not a necromancer. Certainly he had never heard of Bedazzer. In my heart of hearts I was still reserving judgment on this, but I did learn something else interesting from him.

"If Dally had been a necromancer the marshes would have

been much safer for her and perhaps Korosov would never have taken her. The Crocodile Men dislike foreign mages in the marshes, but they happily tolerate necromancers."

"What do you mean?" I asked. "What are Crocodile Men?"

"They are the army of priests and mages who worship Aliceander the Crocodile. They are a strange bunch. People say they are shapeshifters. I only know that one came to our camp when I first brought Dally into the marsh and told me that she was not to go beyond the Dahaz Water margin, on the very fringes of the marsh. We did as we were told. I know better than to annoy the Crocodile Men. It is said that there is a necromantic fortress deep in the marsh and that they take payment from the necromancers in return for leaving it alone."

I was startled. "But nobody wants a necromantic fortress nearby. What about the marsh folk?"

Necromancers needed living humans to fuel their spells and usually they preyed on the surrounding countryside.

"I don't know. Strange things go on in the marsh and it is a persistent rumor. And somebody in the marsh buys many slaves, though there is no land to be worked there."

How horrible. Poor slaves.

"And I have seen that some mages die in the marshes and have their bodies dumped in the Shebaz town square as a warning and others return to Shebaz safely after several weeks," continued Ahmed. "Where are they all that time? Think about it. The marshes are the perfect place for such a fortress. But if it is indeed so, if Dally were a necromancer they would accept her, not ban her from the marshes. So you need have no qualms about rescuing her, Lady Dion."

Ahmed would have been dismayed to learn that such assurances just made me less willing to join him. If there was no chance of Dally being involved in necromancy, and from the way he spoke of her there was not, then I was quite content to let Nikoli Terzu and his demon hunters deal with the problem.

But as soon as we had resolved this problem of Dally, I

must speak to Nikoli about investigating this rumored fortress in Marzorna. That could not be allowed to go on.

Nikoli and I had become closer after our conversation about necromancy. I was uneasy about his spying on me, but I had decided that it was just part of his Aramayaness. It was hard to remain annoyed at him when he was so kind and attentive and I was touched that my revelations about my niece seemed to endear me to him rather than disgust him. I also thought less about Shad when we were together. We went everywhere together, to the theater and to scientific meetings and he called often at my house. We were discreet about our affair, but no doubt there was talk. But it was not very scandalized talk. Nothing was known of my divorce, and it did not matter that people thought I was still married to my husband. In fact it gave me greater freedom. Few Aramayans married for love, and once a woman had produced heirs for her husband, no one questioned it if she found comfort elsewhere. If the Lord of Ruinac minded me having an affair, then he should not have let me come to Akieva on my own. That was the Aramayan way of thinking.

Nikoli would take me riding in his sleigh to his little cottage in the woods just outside Akieva. We would stay all day, dancing and flying through the branches of the pine trees, running magically with the deer in the forest and making love on the little divan. Sometimes I felt guilty. Here was I three months separated from Shad and already I had a new lover. Other times I felt triumphant. See how easily I had found myself another man! And oh, the new awakening. For over two years every time Shad had taken me in his arms I had longed anxiously to become pregnant this time—that was when I was not lying next to him in the darkness stewing in anger that I was not. Oh, the ease to touch a man and to be touched and to think only of pleasure and the softness of skin. If there was not the openness or communion that had been between me and Shad even sometimes at the end, well I felt certain it would come with time.

Sometimes I would awaken in Nikoli's arms to feel magic all around and to hear him muttering words under his breath.

"You were cold my darling," he would say softly. "Just a little magic to warm you up."

I would indeed feel wonderfully warm and relaxed and I would curl comfortably up against him. It never even occurred to me to question his explanation.

But if everyone else was waiting, Dally had suddenly become very active. Once as I was climbing out of a carriage in a crowded street, a street sweeper quickly handed me an envelope, before slipping away into the crowd. The envelope held a torn off piece of paper containing the Korosov crest, a handful of sand and some dried grass. Another time when I was leaving the theater after I had spent an evening staring thoughtfully at Dally in the box opposite, a street urchin came up and gave me a piece of black woollen fabric "from Lady Natasha Korosov."

I could make nothing of either of these little gifts. The sand and the grass had no significance for me and as for the cloth, I thought that Dally had been wearing blue not black when I had last seen her. Perhaps she only meant to keep my interest alive with these gifts. If so it was effective.

The only thing I was really unhappy about was that I could not get Nikoli to tell me what he planned to do about Dally. He told me he had several schemes running but they had yet to come to fruition.

"He is probably waiting for an opportunity just like us," said Kitten. "He cannot just arrest her for questioning. She has the emperor's favor and must be treated carefully."

I hoped that was all he was being evasive about. Sometimes I wondered if I should help Ahmed El-Lamak in his plan. I would have preferred a chance to size up the situation before the legal system got involved. Were the chances of getting caught so very high? Nikoli had said he would be tolerant, but I had experienced Bedazzer's wiles. I knew I would be much more forgiving toward Dally. And could I trust Nikoli to call me when he finally got his hands on Dally? Even though I was so intimate with him, I did not feel sure of him. He had a clever devious mind and I had begun to realize just how little I knew about his activities as a demon hunter or indeed anything of what he did when we were apart.

One day while I walked with Kitten along Akieva's elegant main shopping street, a young woman in servant's dress bumped into me. While I was still exclaiming my apologies and surreptitiously checking my purse, she pressed something into my hand and hurried away.

It was a white silk rose.

A white rose. The edges of its petals were faintly colored with pink. Pink. What did that remind me of?

Kitten stared at the rose and suddenly she gasped.

"Dion, do you remember? Andre Gregorov!"

I did. My God! White roses tinged with pink. They were the first present Andre had ever given me.

Bedazzer. The sand and the grass. He had first kissed me on a beach and first made love to me on grass. On a dark woollen cloak. I had thought those things were messages from Dally, but they were messages from or about Bedazzer! Dally could never have known about these things unless Bedazzer had told her. I had told nobody but Kitten about the roses and the rest only Bedazzer knew. He was somewhere in this. And if Bedazzer was in this, what would the demon hunters do if they found out? Dally must surely burn!

The following day, I told Ahmed El-Lamak I would help him to kidnap Lady Natasha.

It was another freezing night close to the Midwinter Festival, the coldest and darkest time of the year. We waited in a quiet street near the Korosov house. Taras Korosov always passed down this street on his way home from the Winter Palace. Now it had been blocked by a broken-down cart in the middle of the road. Two horses stood patiently before it. Only the very observant would have noticed that they were not actually properly harnessed to the cart and that Simonetti, who was bending over to fix the wheel, was taking an extraordinarily long time about it.

Ahmed, Hakim, Kitten, and I crouched behind a snowdrift at the side of the road. I had not known what cold was till I came to Aramaya and discovered snow. When I muttered this to Kitten, Ahmed laughed softly in agreement and said yes it was just our luck to be forced to do this in an Akievan winter.

I wore a voluminous cloak and the robes of a male mage and Kitten too wore men's clothes. We all three of us had cloths bound round our heads in the manner of Marzornites in case we were seen. Our faces were darkened in the manner of street criminals.

It was dark even in this wealthy part of town. Though Akievan houses set lit torches at their front doors, they can easily be put out by falling snow or a few well-placed snowballs. Most of the wealthy hired torchbearers if they went on foot or bought little mage lights if they went by carriage.

Suddenly Kitten nudged me. A signal light had flared at the other end of one of the streets leading to our hiding place. We drew back further into our cover and a minute later a carriage twinkling with mage lights slowed as it turned into the street. Seeing Simonetti's cart blocking the way, it came to a stop.

Luckily for us Lord Korosov relied on magic to keep him safe and only had the minimum four guards.

"Hey serf," shouted the coachman. "What the hell do you think you're doing?"

"Broken wheel," said Simonetti doing his best country bumpkin impression. "I could move it if you'd give me a hand."

The coachman swore. There was a thumping on the roof of the carriage and one of the guards got down from his perch on the side to speak into the window.

There was a thud. The coachman felled by Simonetti's thrown cudgel slumped in the driver's seat and suddenly everything was movement and noise. Ahmed hit the man at the carriage window hard on the head and shouting and thudding came from the roof of the carriage as Kitten and Hakim subdued the guards at the back.

Keeping an eye on the one remaining front guard, I dashed across the cobblestones. Even as I grabbed for the carriage door, there was a flash of light and runes blazed forth all over the carriage, emitting high pitched screaming. The door of the carriage lurched in my grasp as the horses began to squeal and plunge.

I wrenched it open and smashed through the strong wardings that shimmered in the doorway. There was a roar and a ball of magic fire came sizzling out at me. I was already protected against such an attack. I bowed my head and pushed myself up into the carriage against the surging force.

Suddenly the fire cleared. I was inside the carriage. There was a huddled shape in the far corner. Dally! It was obscured quickly as the dark form of Count Taras flung himself at me. He wasn't bothering with magic. The force of his bulky body smashed into me, but my magical protections held. He was thrown back with equal force. Someone darted past me and seized the huddled figure in the corner. Dally began to scream as she was dragged toward the door.

"No," shouted Count Taras. He turned to strike at the other figure. I threw a magical blow and he collapsed on the floor.

"Quick," shouted Simonetti. He had the screaming and struggling Dally over his shoulder. Out on the street again now, I reached out and touched her on the temple to still her. I felt the power go out of me, but still she screamed and struggled. But I had used magic. Why hadn't . . .

There was the sound of horses as Kitten and Ahmed took off.

"Shut her up damn you," shouted Simonetti as we ran toward the corner of the street.

"I can't . . . I . . ."

Simonetti turned and thrust something into my hand.

"Here."

I stuffed the cloth into her screaming mouth. Still she screamed, though muffled now. We reached the corner.

Our carriage was waiting just down the street. We ran toward it, our feet shushing and slipping in the snow. I pulled open the door and Simonetti shoved the wriggling woman inside.

Then suddenly there was a burst of magic and the street blazed with mage light.

"Suza go!" shouted Simonetti. I turned to see black figures standing all around. Demon hunters! Lots of them! My God! This was a trap? But how?

"Suza," shouted Simonetti.

The figure on the box of the carriage turned. It was a man.

Simonetti lunged for him. "Where is she?" he shouted.

There was a thud and he collapsed to the ground.

Nikoli stood there behind him.

"What are you doing?" I cried.

"I arrest you for the kidnapping of Natasha Korosov," he said loudly. Then in a softer voice. "Please get into the carriage quietly. I won't be able to keep your identity a secret if you struggle."

"This is all my doing," I said. "My servants were only following orders. Please don't hurt them."

His face was deadly serious. I had betrayed him. We both knew it.

"Very well. Now come along."

"How could you?" he shouted later. We were in a drab little room in some grey building belonging to the demon hunters. "You promised not to do anything like this. You promised me."

There was an edge of exasperation to Nikoli's anger that made me feel like a small child. Somehow my guilt did not make it any better.

"I'm sorry Nikoli. I just had to find out."

"What?" he shouted. "I cannot believe you are trying to protect a necromancer."

"She's . . . I wouldn't . . . She's not a necromancer."

I couldn't think of any answer to this that didn't give me away.

"Dion please don't lie. You are very bad at it. Are you going to tell me why you wanted so badly to see Dally before the demon hunters did?"

I hesitated, but it was better he not know. Perhaps he

wouldn't find out. Maybe there was nothing to find. Maybe I had overreacted. Small hope, but still hope.

"No" I said. "I've already told you. If you won't believe me, there's nothing I can say."

"Damn you Dion. After all this time why can't you trust me?"

"I'm sorry Nikoli."

"Sorry?" he said with emphasis. "Well now I've got to go and clean up this terrible mess and try to keep the name of the Demonslayer of Gallia in the clear."

He got up and went to the door.

"What about my servants?" I said. "Simonetti and his wife, are they safe and well?"

"They are well enough. I have had healers tend to them."

"Have you taken anyone else?"

"The countess and your Marzornite friends have got away for the moment if that's what you want to know. It's only a matter of time."

"What are you going to do with Dally now. Are you going to question her? Can I see her?"

"You ask me that after what you've done? You've got some damn cheek!"

He put his hand on the door handle. "Stay here till I come back. Do you think you can trust me that far? There are wardings and guards in this place and things will only get much worse if you try to escape. Oh honestly Dion. To try and kidnap the emperor's favorite. Of all the reckless, stupid things to do."

He went out closing the door briskly behind him.

Something about those last words did not ring true. I began to suspect that he was going to forgive me. At first I was relieved that I had not lost his friendship and that he was going to protect me from the mess, but as I sat in the room I began to wonder if in fact his anger was as strong as he had first made out. Had I really caused so much trouble? If he'd been so concerned about covering things up why had he brought the Korosovs here instead of simply taking them home? He had done nothing to gain access to Dally himself, but now he was getting a chance to question the emperor's untouchable favorite. In fact I had done him a favor.

I could not help feeling annoyed that he should try and make me feel guilty in this way. Then I remembered that I had made him a promise not to do anything on my own. I felt guilty all over again.

Though was it as simple as all that? When had he found out? Surely he'd had time to stop the plot before it had got so far.

When Nikoli returned he came with servants who brought warm water, towels, a woman's blue mage robes for me to change into, and some sweet mint tea. I calmly washed my face and went behind a screen and changed my robe, but when the servants left, I attacked.

"If we are asking about trust Nikoli, it occurs to me that forty demon hunters don't just materialize on a street corner at a moment's notice. Or was I unlucky enough to interrupt the regimental ball? You've continued watching me, haven't you?"

He smiled coolly. "It's true. I sensed when you gave me your word earlier it was . . . provisional. I've had you followed ever since so when you left to kidnap Dally, I heard about it. Obviously you discovered something that changed your mind about keeping your promise. I wish you would tell me what it was."

He touched my cheek.

Now I wanted to apologize, but I wasn't going to, I mustn't. He was just being manipulative.

"If you knew what was going to happen you could have stopped me if you'd wanted to," I said.

"Yes. I could have arrested you before you began the kidnapping," he said.

"But in rescuing Lady Natasha you now have an excellent chance to detain and question her, don't you? So have you?"

Suddenly he smiled. It was a tired smile that did not really reach his eyes but it was a smile.

"You are not without cunning are you, my little Morian?" he said. "It was an insane plan, but it did seem to contain the seeds of opportunity."

"So you have questioned her."

"Not yet. I sent for a demon huntress. Yes, such creatures do exist. One must keep in mind that Lady Natasha Korosov may one day be one of the emperor's wives. She cannot be interviewed and examined by a man. I have just been instructing Madame Elena."

He made a courtly gesture with his hand like one welcoming a guest to his house.

"Perhaps you would care to watch the interrogation."

The interrogation room was a high-ceilinged room with a very fine lattice running along one side of it. Behind that lattice was a darkened room where several people could sit quietly and have a good view of the interrogated person's face without being seen.

For over an hour we watched Madame Elena question Dally. We learned nothing new, or rather we learned new things but none of them had the ring of truth. The whole story of Lady Natasha's supposed life came out: how she was the illegitimate daughter of Count Taras and a woman of Moria, who had been living in one of Aramaya's coastal provinces, how she had been adopted by the count while he was Viceroy of Marzorna, how the emperor was her ideal of what a man and an emperor should be. When asked if she was Syndal Holyhands, she said, "I am Lady Natasha Korosov." When asked why she had sent me sand and black cloth and a white rose, she answered again, "I am Lady Natasha Korosov."

She was oddly calm. She did not look scared or amused or even surprised by any of the questions. Impressive coolness especially in such a young and supposedly shy woman. If there was anything she did not want to answer she simply repeated her name as if she were an automaton that did not know any other way to act. Once she lifted her eyes to the lattice behind which we sat. She gazed so directly at me that I drew back.

After an hour Madame Elena left the room and we met with her in the corridor. She was convinced that Dally was hiding something important. But could we dare to mindsearch such a high noble without permission? Nikoli decided that it must be done and that he would bear the responsibility. I cannot say I envied him at that moment.

We went back into our observation gallery and a few minutes later Madame Elena entered the interrogation room. There was a woman healer with her.

She explained to Dally that she was going to mindsearch her and that there would be a little pain but that the healer would soothe her when the search was finished. Dally did not react at all. She simply sat with downcast eyes and let herself be organized into the proper position as if she were a doll. Was this passive creature really my niece and the woman Ahmed had spoken of?

Madame Elena put her hands on Dally's temples and I felt the frisson of her magic as she began the search. She was sitting with her back to us turned a little to the side so that we could see Dally's face again. It was calm. Dally gave no sign of any pain.

Then suddenly Madame Elena let out a cry. Dally, too, squeaked and slumped forward. She almost hit the floor, but at the last minute Elena caught her and pushed her back on to her chair. Nikoli and I sprang from our seats.

In a moment we were in the interrogation room. Dally was still unconscious. The healer had her on the table trying to revive her. Nikoli and I pushed past her. I felt Dally's pulse and checked under her eyelids.

"What happened!" cried Nikoli.

"She just fainted," said the healer.

"Madame Elena? What . . . ? She's gone. Elena! Where are you?"

The door of the interrogation room was locked. With a burst of power, Nikoli broke it open and charged into the hallway. I heard the alarm wardings start screaming and the confusion of guards in pursuit.

Dally. What was wrong with her? She was breathing fine and her eyes were open now but there was no awareness in them. A terrible fear filled me at the sight of those empty eyes. They reminded me of something. . . . For a few moments I could do nothing but shake her and call her name.

"Madame!" cried the healer. "Madame stop. You are doing no good. Come. The girl is not dead. We must examine her calmly."

"What happened when she fainted?"

"Lady Natasha just suddenly slumped forward. And it was like Madame Elena had received a shock of power. She was so stunned she almost let the girl drop."

"And before that . . ."

"At first she couldn't seem to get into the girl's mind. It was odd. I've worked with Madame Elena before. She never has such trouble."

A mindsearch. Maybe that would give some clue. Quickly I fastened my thumbs to Dally's temples.

"Slowly," said the healer. "She can still feel pain."

I pushed my mind tentatively down into hers. Down and down. I couldn't . . . find it. There was no consciousness there. Just . . . nothing. I looked and looked just as Elena had. It wasn't that there was nothing in her mind. There was instinct and simple reactions to pain. But that was all. It was like the mind of an animal. Or worse, because animals often have simple personalities and a shallow layer of memory and what was in Dally's head did not even have that. It was as if she no longer had a being.

Suddenly I remembered the women at Lord Shugorsky's manor house. Their minds had been empty just like this. What had they done to them? What had been done to Dally?

"Is Count Taras being kept here?" I asked.

"Yes. I was watching him till Madame Elena called me. His Highness the Prince ordered that he be kept asleep until we were finished with Lady Natasha."

"But you could wake him up."

She nodded.

"Let's go! Take me to him."

She shifted uneasily from foot to foot. "Lady, we had better wait for Prince Nikoli. He would not like us to question Count Taras without him. Count Taras is the emperor's cousin. We must think of the reputation of the regiment."

Dammit!

I wanted to shout at her that he was a necromancer who

had done something very dire to my niece and perhaps to Madame Elena too, but it would have done no good. I bit back my words.

"Very well. You stay here with D . . . Natasha. I'll see if I can go and find the prince."

I was not sure what I intended to do. Since Nikoli had not come back, he must have his hands full and I had no intention of waiting for him. I had to find out once and for all what had happened to Dally.

But as I came out of the room, I heard a great noise in another part of the building. There was the nerve jangling feel of magic everywhere and a faint stink of smoke. I ran down a couple of corridors till I came to the long entrance hall. It was full of smoke and the wall around the front door was black. The hall was full of people and as I came in two stretchers were borne past me. Nikoli was standing against the wall. He had his hand over his face. At first I did not notice this, so intent was I on my mission. I went up to him and took his arm.

"Nikoli we have to talk to Count Taras."

He turned. The look on his face was dreadful. A wasteland of pain.

"Nikoli what's wrong?"

"She burned them!" was all he could choke out.

At the top of the entrance hall, Nikoli had finally caught sight of Madame Elena just as she was about to go out the front door.

Using the Voice of Command he had called out to her to stop and the two young guards at the entrance had moved to intercept her. Both of them had been boys Nikoli had trained. Instead of simply stunning them, Elena threw out an enormous fire bolt.

"She looked at me," said Nikoli when he had got control of his voice. "She turned and looked right into my eyes and then she turned back and she burned. . . . She knew I knew them. It pleased her. I know it did. How can I know that? What kind of creature . . . ?"

I was beginning to have a very bad feeling about this.

Most necromancers liked to cause pain. Had Dally somehow transferred her being into Madame Elena's body?

"We have to speak to Count Taras," I repeated.

Count Taras had been brought in unconscious. He had not been drugged but was simply being held in a kind of suspended animation. The demon hunters were cunning. When Taras woke up they would have been able to claim that he had been unconscious all that time. In case he awoke early, they had even put a locked iron necklace on him identical to the one he wore at court.

Nikoli no longer seemed to care much about Taras's feelings. He broke the sleep spell and had the healer bring the count back to consciousness. Almost before Korosov was awake, Nikoli began.

"You niece is dead," he told the befuddled count.

"Dead. My . . . Natasha is dead!"

"We mindsearched her," said Nikoli. "Something . . ."

"You what . . . Sweet Tanza. You fools! Do you realize what you've done? My God, it's out. It's free. You must stop the person who did it."

"Why?" snapped Nikoli.

But Prince Taras's sense of self preservation had surfaced. "What is this? What have you done? I am the emperor's cousin. I demand you set me free immediately. I will complain to the emperor."

"You will not complain to the emperor," said Nikoli icily. "Nobody but my people know where you are. And you shall stay here until you tell me what I want to know. Or I will mindsearch you. Now what has been let loose on our poor city?"

Count Taras refused to answer, no doubt counting on the fact that Nikoli could not keep him there long. Unfortunately for him, he didn't realize that Nikoli was angry enough to violate the person of the emperor's cousin with a mindsearch.

While Nikoli pressed his hand to the temples of the protesting Taras, I watched him closely, all defensive spells at the ready in case what had happened to Elena also happened to Nikoli and I was forced to bring him down. But nothing unusual happened. Except that we finally found out what we had wanted to know for so long.

Count Taras had been involved with the secret colleges since he was a very young man. He liked the way necromancy enhanced his power, but it was difficult to exercise it easily. Its main attraction was the weird and bloody excitement of communicating with the demon plane, which he regarded as little worse than a blood sport like hunting or cockfighting. Like other such noble men, he merely dabbled. He was at heart a timid person, afraid of his own pain and not overly addicted to the pain of others.

In his mid-thirties Taras became involved in a scandal over the illegal selling of military commissions and as punishment he was made Resident of Marzorna. It was here he truly became involved with necromancy. Ahmed had been right. There was a necromantic fortress in the marsh and Korosov talked of "paying the crocodile" to leave them alone.

The necromancers in the marshes were pleased to have one of their own as Resident and wanted him to protect and nurture their fortress. Count Taras was determined to be rewarded for this role and thus he progressed to the stage of making his first pact with the demon plane.

In Marzorna he came into contact with Bezra Haziz. Haziz was a powerful and ruthless mage skilled in both ordinary and demon magic. She was brilliant at thinking out new spells and methods and an expert in demonology. She was supposed to know more about them than anyone living. It was rumored that she had once been to the demon plane and survived.

The secret colleges' greatest problem with demons was the difficulty in controlling them. You could draw power from the demon plane, and usually you could control this, but if you were strong enough and lucky enough you could bring the demons through into this world to do your bidding. This gave you immense power. Only a few had tried this however. It took a person of psychotic courage to use an enslaved demon on this plane. They were immensely cunning, seeking always to cause the deaths of those who enslaved them so that they could run free in this world and consume its teeming life. You had to instruct them in every small detail if you did not want to have a convenient fatal "accident."

The fact that this immense power was too dangerous to use was an endless frustration to necromancers and a problem that Bezra Haziz had set herself to solve. Through years of work, of scouring old manuscripts and testing out old legends, Haziz had come up with a limited way of using demons safely.

Lady Natasha Korosov was the result.

At this point of Korosov's story, Nikoli cleared the room. He asked me to take notes on a fresh sheet of paper.

"We will protect these words with wardings," he said. "We cannot let this knowledge become too widely known."

Haziz's technique was stunning. It seemed to disagree with everything I had ever learned about demons. The theory of it was that some demons had a being, what we humans might call a soul or spirit, which was separate from their physical existence. As with humans, the spirit needed some kind of physical housing to survive. Only the most powerful demons had developed this being. Most were still mindless shuffling masses of hunger. It was only those with beings who could communicate with the human plane.

Among necromancers, who knew the most about demons, the idea that demons had beings was not a new one. There was even evidence that attempts had been made to bring a demon's sprit through into this world separately from its body before. But only Bezra Haziz had successfully put a demon's being inside a human body.

With excitement I remembered the two young girls at Shugorsky's manor. Aramayan mages are great copiers of each other. Could it be that some other necromancer had been trying to copy Haziz's technique?

Dally had fallen into Haziz's hands at a lucky time. She had already tried bringing Smazor's being through but the body she had prepared for his reception had exploded and Smazor's being had dissipated. Neither she nor anybody else had ever been able to summon him again. It looked as if Haziz had destroyed him. She was certain she knew what had gone wrong, but the secret colleges were unwilling to lose more of the limited number of demons they could make contact with.

Like all prisoners, Dally was to be sacrificed to demons. She could not resist calling on Bedazzer to save her and Haziz caught her in the act and found out about the existence of a useful demon not known to the secret colleges. Demons are always happy to betray other demons. It was not hard for her to find one who would give her Bedazzer's true secret name for the pleasure of seeing him enslaved.

It represented the perfect opportunity.

Haziz used the convenient Dally as the fleshy vessel in which Bedazzer's spirit was contained. And contained he was. He had no connection at all with his physical substance on the demon plane, and this robbed him of all magical power and also gave him no opportunity to bring that body through into this world should he successfully kill his mentor. His motive for doing so was thus considerably lessened. And though he hungered, being insubstantial, he did not have the same needs as a demon whose body had been bought into this world. He would not fade or become unreliable if he was not fed. His physical powers were limited to those of the body he was in, and if that body wore an iron necklace as Dally did he could not even use her magical powers. If he destroyed that body, his being too would die.

So this was the answer to that strange hungry darkness in my mirror all that time ago at Dubrovny, I thought triumphantly. I had been right. It was one of those mindless dark demons Smazor had spoken of. Very likely it was what was left of Bedazzer—the gross physical mass of him that remained after his being had been extracted by Haziz. It must have been drawn to my mirror by some instinct, but had been too mindless to make any kind of contact with me.

The masters of the secret colleges of necromancy had been disappointed with Haziz's creation. What was the point of a demon slave that could not bring down mountains and destroy armies?

But Taras Korosov was an experienced courtier. He instantly saw a use for Haziz's experiment. The creature that had been Dally still had a demon mind. It could still see into the minds of humans, read their innermost thoughts, and sense those thoughts over a distance. It still had the same powers of charm and beguilement that demons had always had. And most important of all for Korosov's purpose, hidden within a human body and with no connection to its own plane, there was no way for Bedazzer's being to be detected beyond a mindsearch. All the demon-watching magic used to protect the Aramayan emperor was useless against it.

And it was in the body of an attractive young woman. Count Taras knew the potential of an attractive female body.

So he took the body that had once been Dally Holyhands, and calling it Natasha Korosov, brought it to the court to beguile the young emperor as Bedazzer had once beguiled me. Its spirit was ordered not to speak to strange mages or to tell anyone the truth about itself just as if it had been a complete slave demon. That was why Dally would not speak to me after our first meeting at the Imperial reception.

But Bedazzer had still outsmarted them. He must have been desperate to get out of Dally's powerless body. Here he was surrounded by food with no way of feeding on it. He had manipulated me into kidnapping Dally. Probably he had known every one of my doubts and anxieties concerning her. Had we been sucessful I would have been the one to mindsearch him. Then he would have had my powers to exercise as he now exercised Elena's. Nikoli's arrest had saved me.

"And Dally's being?" I asked Korosov. "What happened to the girl's original being?"

"The girl's being was drawn out into a iron phial. . . . It is well known that humans with two beings become unstab . . . Oh Aumaz, what will become of me now . . . I shall be burned . . ."

"The being, Korosov. Where is it?" asked Nikoli, turning him back to the desired train of thought.

But all Korosov cared about was his own skin. He didn't know what had happened to the iron phial and didn't much care.

The thought of someone's being being trapped in a iron phial was horrifying. Would Dally be conscious? If so would she even know where she was? Or would she just be in some terrible dark limbo?

"We need to get someone to the Korosov house," I cried. "We need to search for it."

"Don't worry," said Nikoli, "It's been taken care of."

A team of demon hunters had raced to the Korosov house, but Madame Bezra Haziz had already gone. By the time we arrived the house was being thoroughly searched. Nikoli ordered people here and there, sending them to search the city and warning them to be very careful of both Haziz and Madame Elena.

"At least Haziz knows this Bedazzer's true name," he said to me between orders. "She will have some control over him. If he has not already overcome her. Oh my God, the creature may be able to jump from body to body. What a nightmare!"

At that moment a hush fell in the room and the tall quietly spoken man who had come to my house to chase off the Prekazy entered. I still did not know his name. Everyone addressed him politely as Monsieur. Later I learned he was the emperor's uncle.

"It was a plot against the emperor," Nikoli told him without waiting to be asked.

Monsieur nodded in the direction of a private room and Nikoli followed after him.

I turned to one of the demon hunters who was still left in the house.

"Did Madame Bezra leave anything behind?"

He nodded. "She left very speedily."

"Can I see her room? Was there an iron phial among her things?"

He opened a box on a nearby table and took something out. It was a small egg-shaped container made of iron.

I resisted the temptation to shake the phial. I could hardly bear to imagine how it must be for Dally. Would she survive the experience? Trapped, shut in a tiny space with nothing to think about or do, no one to speak to, probably no idea of where she was or why or if the experience would ever end. A nightmare, a living hell. Would she have gone crazy from hopelessness?

It was vital that we get her out of this iron phial as soon as possible, but I didn't want to unravel the problem alone. I had only the vaguest idea of how to go about it. I must question Korosov again and I wanted other learned opinions before I committed myself to a course of action. If I opened the phial without getting the spells right, there was a good chance that Dally's being would simply dissolve. Nikoli was the best person I knew of to help me.

But when Nikoli and Monsieur finished their meeting I was horrified to discover that Nikoli was being sent immediately to report to the emperor.

"No," I cried. "You must help me first. I've got to get Dally out of this phial."

Nikoli patted my hand and told me it would have to wait.

"No," I shouted. "Can't you see? It must be hell for her in there. For God's sake Nikoli help me. I don't want to do this alone. At least let me speak with Korosov again."

Nikoli looked deeply embarrassed by this naked show of emotion, but Monsieur said calmly.

"Prince Nikoli must make his report. The emperor must be informed. But I agree that your niece must be freed as soon as possible. I shall aid you, Demonslayer. If you would be so good as to stop shouting."

In the end Monsieur and Prince Gagarin from the College of White Magic both helped me. Luckily Count Taras had been present at the ritual when Haziz drew Dally's being out of her body and now out of fear for his safety he was extremely cooperative in describing to us all he knew of it. Logically all we needed to do was to perform the ritual backward. But if we did one thing wrong that could well be the end of Dally.

We spent a long time arguing over the order of runes and calculating the possible permutations of each step of the ritual before we finally began.

Because the phial was iron, I had no way of knowing if Dally was even inside it, but it had been the only iron phial at Korosov's house. I prayed that it might be the right one. Fearfully I said the words and followed the ritual and at the last moment cracked the phial open over Dally's mouth. I saw something white hover there for a moment before it was gone. For a horrible moment I thought that it had been lost, but then Dally began to groan and move her head from side to side. That was not the end of the suspense. How could anyone have survived six months in that tiny phial and not gone insane?

We had left the iron necklet on Dally because a madwoman with magical powers was too horrible a prospect to think of. For a few terrible moments I thought my fears were justified. Dally opened her eyes, curled up in a ball and began to scream. Not the automatic screams that she had screamed that time in her bedroom, but terrible gutwrenching screams of pain and anguish and fury. Screams that described what it must have been like in the phial.

"Dally, don't!" I cried. "It's all right. You're free. You're safe. It's me, Dion, your aunt."

She was rolling around clawing at the bed. I tried to catch her in my arms and comfort her, but the moment I touched her she started clawing at me. Unsteadily using her hands like a small child's, she pulled herself up on me till she was in a sitting position. As she did the screaming changed into a howl and then into a slow dangerous growl. I saw that she was not crazy, but simply fighting mad. She was the daughter of a woman who had dragged herself home hundreds of miles after being tortured and fed on by demons. She herself, when only fourteen, had traveled back that route with only a demon for company to wreak pitiless revenge on her mother's killers. I should never have doubted she could survive such mere captivity.

I<small>T WAS NOT</small> until midday the next day that I left the demon hunter headquarters.

I could not leave Dally; despite all her bravado, I could see that the captivity had left a terrible dark shadow on her. She would not sleep, for she was afraid of waking up in that timeless nothing place inside the phial again. She became frightened of the darkness in the room and the fact that there were no windows and she questioned whether I was really was her aunt. She staggered round the room periodically throwing herself against the door and shouting and cursing in the mumbling, bumbling voice of a drunkard. The curses became clearer as she slowly regained control of her body again.

"Where is that Haziz cow?" she kept screaming. "I'll kill her."

I did my best to soothe her. I had her moved to a room with a window and then I, or rather Monsieur, whose commanding voice seemed to calm her, made her lie down and rest and get used to being in her body again. I sat beside her for a long time stroking her hair and her arms and telling her of Moria and her cousins. Every now and then I rubbed calming waves of magic into her skin. In the early hours of the morning I fell into a sleep of exhaustion. It had been a day and a night since I had set out to kidnap Natasha Korosov.

When I awoke it was the middle of the next morning. Dally was sitting by the window eating some breakfast. She was beginning to get control of her movements and though she ate clumsily, she did not spill much. The moment she saw I was awake she asked if I could have her iron necklace taken off.

"We shall have to ask Monsieur," I said. I was not really sure I wanted her to be able to use her powers yet.

She looked disgusted at this and expressed the opinion that I had always been a spineless worm.

I was relieved rather than offended by this remark. I had been worried that her mind had been damaged by its time in the iron phial. The normal Dally did not cling to my hand and beg me not to leave her again. The normal Dally had a very poor opinion of me and no qualms about expressing it.

"I'm glad to see you back to your old self," I said. "I must go home now. If you don't mind?"

"Why should I mind?" she scowled, though I could see from the movement of her hands that she was frightened.

"I shall send a healer to sit with you," I said. "And I will ask Monsieur about your request. I shall not leave you until you are recovered, Dally. Your mother asked me to look after you before she died."

"And a wonderful job you've been doing so far, I don't think."

This was actually a pretty fair criticism.

"Well, I shall do better from now on," I said calmly. I wasn't as afraid of her as I been five years ago. That made it easier to bear her abuse. "But now I must go home. Your friend Ahmed El-Lamak will be waiting for news of you."

"Ahmed!" she cried. Joy softened her expression.

"Yes he has been laboring this six months to rescue you and I'm not sure he knows yet if he has succeeded."

"Give him my love," said Dally softly as I left the room.

★   ★   ★

A clerk ordered a carrying chair to convey me home. Despite the sleep I was bone weary and my thoughts were worried and not very coherent. I worried about what had happened to Bezra Haziz and if Bedazzer was still contained in Madame Elena's body and if Kitten and Ahmed were safe and I must make sure someone was sent to Lord Shugorsky's house to see if they could find iron phials containing the beings of the two young girls we had found there and . . .

I leaned back in the chair and fell into a kind of fretful daze. I was still swamped with worried thoughts when I ran up the steps of Pepita's house.

"Is the countess here?" I asked Misha as he opened the door.

"Yes, my lady. And there is a gentleman insisting on seeing you."

There was a seat in Pepita's hallway where people often sat to remove their overshoes. There was someone sitting on it now. Someone who jumped up the minute I opened the door. A small, well-made man with dark curling hair and gold rings in his ears.

"Dion!" said Shad, coming toward me with outstretched arms.

For a moment my traitor heart turned over. I was filled with such joy to see him. I wanted to throw myself on his chest and feel his strong arms around me. Only for a moment.

"He is your estranged husband," a voice in my head reminded me. "He doesn't love you anymore."

Someone should poison those little voices in your head.

"Dion," said Shad again. He stopped, obviously groping for words.

Then he burst out suddenly.

"Dion, please don't just leave me like this. We've got to talk about it!"

For a moment I goggled at him.

"But . . . but you left me!"

A look of bewilderment came onto Shad's face.

"What?" he said softly.

*   *   *

"But I never sent any letter," he said, kneeling beside me and taking my hand. We were in the drawing room. I was sitting on Pepita's overstuffed chaise. "You have to believe me. Edaine must have done it."

This was not as impossible as it sounded. Shad had never been very good at writing. He still printed his letters in a round childish hand—the sort of writing that was easy to forge.

Such a malicious thing to have done, but knowing Edaine, I could well believe it.

"But there was your ring," I said. I looked at the hand on mine. There was a gold wedding ring on it. "I thought you'd left me."

"Oh my darling I love you. I never sent you my ring. This ring has never left my finger. Ask anyone. I've never wanted to end our marriage. It's just . . . we fought so much. I thought if we were apart a little time, it might help us to cool down. When I came home and discovered that you'd gone and that you were safely with Kitten, I assumed you thought the same. But I never wanted us to part. I came as soon as the Storm Season was over. It's been hell since I got your letter. Life would be horrible without you."

"Oh Shad. It's been horrible for me too."

I was crying. It was so wonderful—the feel of his arms and his lips soft on my cheeks, the downy skin on the back of his neck. . . . I still loved him so much and it seemed he still loved me.

"What made her do such a terrible thing? Did she forge the ring?"

I lifted my head from his shoulder and looked up at his face just in time to see an uneasy look. A guilty look. I didn't want to see that. I didn't want to suspect anything. No!

I looked away quickly. There was a silence.

I wanted to know. I must know. Otherwise I would always suspect.

"Why, Shad?" I asked.

"It must have been my fault. I was so furious when I arrived at the gathering and of course she was there and she was so sympathetic. I said things. She must have thought. . . . I'm sorry Dion. I apologize. It was disloyal of me, I know."

"But the ring?"

"I love you Dion. I promise you that I never thought of Edaine except as a pleasant person."

I let him put his arms around me and kiss me. It felt so good. But there was something else. He had never been able to hide things from me. The part of me that had to know and the part that didn't want to know warred with each other. It took a few moments for that treacherous part that had to know to win.

"The ring," I said. "That ring she sent me was a forgery, was it?"

"It must have been," he said. "Because look, here is my ring. It never left my finger."

"But how did she know what had been engraved inside it?"

"Oh for God's sake Dion. Please. Stop this. I've come all these miles to find you. Doesn't that mean anything to you?"

"Yes," I said embracing him. "Oh yes, it does."

"I love you. I've never cared a snap for Edaine. Why won't you believe me?"

He leaned forward and put his head in his hands.

"Shad," I cried. "Sweet Tanza! I'm sorry. I'll try not to be jealous anymore."

He signed and his body went limp and dispirited.

"I've never been able to lie to you Dion. I can't lie to you now. Just remember that that surely means something. I do love you. I never meant to leave you."

He took my hand and with a grim look on his face began to speak.

"When I got to the Gathering I was still very angry and full of despair. Sometimes it seemed that it didn't matter how much I loved you. We couldn't seem to be together without fighting. Anyway, I had some drinks and I took more hazia than I should have. In the morning I woke up in Edaine's tent. In her bed. I don't remember exactly what happened. But I have a bad feeling something did. Edaine certainly seemed to think something had. She was all full of triumph and ready to set up house together."

His admission came like a blow. I should never have pushed him to make it.

"I lost my ring that night," he said. "Maybe Edaine took it off. Maybe I took it off. It would have been the decent thing to do. Anyway later she denied that she had it. But she must have sent you the letter that night after I was asleep. She hated you Dion. She shone with triumph. And then she was so angry at me. Oh God, and I never realized. If only I'd known. I got Symon to help me make another ring, because I was afraid of what would happen if you found I'd lost it. I'm so sorry Dion. I would give anything to undo what happened. Oh, Dion, please don't cry like that."

I couldn't help crying. I had been so happy and now I felt like I'd lost him all over again. Infidelity had always seemed to mean the end of a relationship.

He got up and began to pace the room. I didn't want him to. I wanted him to hold me and persuade me that I could forgive him and forget the whole thing and that it really didn't matter.

"I'm sorry," I choked, trying to explain. "It just hurts."

"Well now you know how I feel," he shouted suddenly. "Three months apart and you already have another man."

Nikoli. Oh God! I'd forgotten about Nikoli. Shad had found out. My guilty face must have told him he was right, but at least the shock stopped my crying.

Anger had overwhelmed Shad now. I remembered that he got angry more easily if he was feeling guilty.

"I was easy to replace, wasn't I? I arrive in Akieva and start asking for you and the first thing I hear is that you've got some high class mage as a lover. Some prince. I suppose he's every thing I'm not. Three months! And you have the gall to be self-righteous."

"I wasn't being self-righteous," I cried. "But I thought you'd left me. I thought you had a new wife. I thought I was free."

"Do you want to be free then?"

"No. That's not what I mean! But what I did was not the same thing."

"I was drunk and lonely. What I did didn't mean anything. And I told Edaine as much as soon as I was awake," he shouted.

"I thought you'd left me," I screamed at him.

"What the hell is going on?" said a voice from the doorway.

Pepita Sandorez stood there. Her eyes were sparkling dangerously. Both Misha and Kitten stood watchfully behind her.

"I was under the impression this was supposed to be some sort of reconciliation. So will you kindly explain why instead I have brawling in my drawing room?"

A cold feeling of despair filled me. It had all started so well and now once again we were fighting. I looked at Shad and he looked at his feet. What were we going to do? If only Shad had come a few weeks ago. . . . If only Edaine had never sent that letter. . . . If only I had never sent him to the Gathering alone. And yet what kind of a life did we have together in Ruinac? Always fighting like we were fighting now.

"I am sorry Dion. I should not have let myself get angry. I would like to talk things over if we could. Perhaps now is not the right time. We have both become upset."

"Yes," I said. "I will try to calm down. I'm sorry too, Shad."

"Perhaps I should let you get some rest," he said. "The Countess says you have been away two nights with Dally. You must be tired. I shall return to my inn. I am staying at Dukov's. Will you send for me when you are more ready? Good. I'm sorry that we argued. I have come to Akieva to ask you to come back to Ruinac and live with me again and I still hope that you will forgive me and do so. Here." He took my hand and pressed something into it. "Here is your ring. Keep it. I don't want it back unless it comes on your finger."

He went.

*   *   *

"You mean you mistook someone else's handwriting for your own husband's!" cried Pepita incredulously after I had told them what Shad had said.

"Well he never learned to write properly," I said, knowing full well how foolish I sounded. "His printing is easy to forge. I've done it myself. It was the ring I believed. I didn't think he would ever have parted with that ring. If only I'd confronted him when I first got the letter. I should have known that he would have come to me face to face if he'd wanted a divorce. It was just . . . I couldn't give him a child and Edaine could and I . . . oh, Kitten, I've made such a mess of things."

"Oh Dion," said Kitten in exasperation, though she squeezed my hand kindly. "That child you can't have is like a millstone around your neck. What are you going to do?"

I looked at the ring. He had slept with Edaine. How did I know he was telling the truth about what had happened? More to the point, we had already started fighting again.

"I have no idea," I said. I stared at my hands.

"I'm not surprised," said Pepita. "If I heard such a story in a play I would not believe a word of it. But I hope you will not think me unsympathetic if I say that at the moment I am much more worried about whether we are to be arrested."

To be honest I was relieved to change to another subject. I told them everything that had happened at the demon hunters' headquarters.

"The poor child," cried Pepita. "My God, do you mean this Bedazzer thing can jump from body to body at will? How ghastly."

"Do you think that's what has happened to Haziz?" asked Kitten.

"Haziz still knows his true name. There's a good chance that she has got control of him again. She may just be running for cover. The demon hunters will want her burned after this little episode, if only to stop her from spreading her knowledge of how it's done."

"But what if Bedazzer *is* out there on the loose?" cried

Kitten. "What if he's killed her? Are you going to go after him?"

"I will have to, won't I?"

"You could destroy him now," said Kitten softly. "He would never trouble you again."

The thought disturbed rather than pleased me, and that realization disturbed me even more. Bedazzer was the ultimate predator, cunning, ruthless, endlessly hungry and he had kept me in fear for years. And yet . . . there was a magnificence about him, a reckless, merciless, exhilarating magnificence like that of all predators. It was that exhilaration that had first drawn me into Bedazzer's sphere.

I shook myself. If I did not destroy Bedazzer, his evil cunning would simply destroy someone else and then someone after that. Demons were not creatures to admire, but creatures to simply fear.

"I will have to destroy him if I can," I said, telling myself that as much as I told Kitten.

Suddenly Wilby Sandorez rushed in.

"My dears, be ready. The Prekazy are at the door."

The two drably dressed men at the door were neither Prekazy nor demon hunters however. They were from a third group, the city watch. And they had not come to arrest us both for kidnapping. They wished me to help with their inquiries into the disappearance of Lady Natasha Korosov. May I be preserved from ever becoming involved in the Aramayan legal system again. Just working out who is responsible for what is too complicated and frightening for a mere outlander.

I was taken in a closed carriage to a tall grey building near the Winter Palace and here I sat in a small waiting room for a long time. I knew this was just a tactic to make me nervous and so I tried not to be, but I was tired and worried. The Aramayans had great respect for the privacy of important people and I hoped for this reason that they would not mindsearch me. If they did, the whole truth about our kidnapping of Lady Natasha would come out and so would Nikoli's coverup. Although our kidnapping had been instru-

mental in revealing Lady Natasha as a demon and in saving
the emperor from a plot to dominate him, the very fact that
we had contemplated and carried out such a plan and Nikoli
had attempted to hide it showed a lack of respect for the
emperor and his family that would have shocked most
Aramayans.

I was under no illusions. It was very likely that the emperor was extremely angry at me. When someone you love
is unmasked as a false traitor, you do not thank the one who
unmasked them. I did not wish to add more fuel to his fire
by revealing our plot.

Finally a group of mages came to get me and I was taken
to a small dark room without windows. Here they sat me in
a chair, blindfolded me, and left. A few minutes later a man
came in and began to question me. He had the most un-
speakably oily insinuating voice and, though they were
harmless enough at first, slowly the questions he asked become more and more humiliating.

He wanted to know all the details about my relations with
Prince Nikoli. Were we lovers? For how long? Had I ever
made love to Bedazzer in the form of Andre Gregorov?
What were my physical relations with my husband Shad
Forest, the Lord of Ruinac?

I was a 27-year-old married woman and I did not consider
myself a prude, but these questions seemed unnecessarily
intrusive to me. Even though I was not manacled and could
easily protect myself against this oily voiced man, the situation with the blindfold and the questions was vaguely sexu-
ally threatening. When he began to ask me the details of my
affair with Nikoli, how often we had made love and in what
positions, it became too much. Some things you do not discuss with strangers.

"Why must I answer this?" I cried angrily.

"If you are not prepared to cooperate we shall be forced
to mindsearch you," said Oily Voice. Suddenly I realized I
was trapped. If I refused a mindsearch and answered these
humiliating questions they would know I had something to
hide.

"Then you must mindsearch me," I snapped recklessly at

the man. "I do not think these questions are relevant and I will not answer them."

"Very well," said the voice.

I pulled off the blindfold just in time to see the figure of Oily Voice disappearing out through the lighted doorway. It was pitch dark in the room. I lit a mage light on my hand and sat there waiting and working through the ritual that calms the mind. I had a horrible feeling of having failed my friends. Now the city watch would find out everything.

Instead of mindsearching me, however, the group of mages returned and took me to a cold whitewashed room that looked exactly like the demon hunters' interrogation room, even down to the lattice over one side of it. The moment I entered I knew there was someone sitting behind that lattice.

A politely disbelieving man with a pleasant voice now questioned me, first about what had happened with Lady Natasha Korosov at the demon hunter's house, and then about my niece Dally. I did my best to gloss over her relationship with Bedazzer, but it was difficult under the questioning to entirely disguise it. I did my best to play up my niece's loneliness and lack of experience and sensible guidance, but I was just beginning to feel worried when there was a knock at the door and a man came in with a note. My interrogator read the note and a look of surprise appeared on his carefully controlled features.

He got up and left the room. The moment the door was closed, someone began to speak from behind the lattice.

I recognized the voice of the emperor immediately but since he had taken so much trouble to hide his identity, I figured I had better not show my recognition. As he began to ask his questions I understood much better why I was here. He was trying to determine whether there was anything left of the shy young girl he had loved in Dally. I was brutally honest. Lady Natasha Korosov had been entirely a creation of Bedazzer and the sooner he realized that the better.

When he asked me about Bedazzer, without waiting for more questions, I told him all about my relationship with Andre Gregorov who had been Bedazzer in human form. I told him how Bedazzer had read my mind and become the very person who would most attract me and how he manipulated me into loving him so much that some element of that tenderness still remained in me. I told him of how for long years I had blamed myself for loving him, of how I had felt secretly evil and unclean and of how with time and with the love of a kind and understanding husband, I had come to realize how wrong I had been to feel that. As I talked I remembered what a wonderful husband Shad had been and how happy we had been together in those first years before Alinya. I had grown enormously in confidence when he had encouraged and supported me as Lady of Ruinac and as a teacher of magic. His love had made Bedazzer so irrelevant that now when I looked back on how upset I had been over it, I could barely imagine why.

From behind the lattice work came the quiet, choking sounds of a man weeping. My heart turned over for the poor young emperor. What a way to learn about love. I hoped it would not blight his life. This was the natural consequence of the presence of Bedazzer. How very wrong I had been to regret the destroying of such magnificence! His magnificence was the magnificence of a heavy foot among a nest of ants. To be a cruel destroyer was his very nature. He could be nothing else. I must finish him if I could.

Outside the early winter night was coming down. It had been snowing heavily and the drifts had not yet been brushed away. The city watchhouse was in a cul de sac just off a busy street. I slogged down to the main street to see if I could find a hire chair or carriage to take me home.

"Dion," cried a voice, and someone bundled in a fur coat came shushing toward me. It was Shad. He was carrying a fur coat which he threw around me.

"Kitten told me the watch had taken you. Are you all right? Did they mindsearch you?"

I was so tired, I forgot about our argument and let him put his arm though mine and take my weight on it.

"Are you warm enough?" he said. "God this country has appalling weather. How do they stand it?"

"It's horrible, isn't it?" I said. "You get used to it though. We need a carriage."

"I've got one waiting. Come on."

The carriage was waiting but the horses were unhitched and being walked up and down in the street to keep warm. We climbed inside while they hitched up the horses. It was out of the wind and Shad had bought as many rugs as you would expect a Peninsula man faced by an Aramayan winter to bring. He piled the rugs over my legs and also introduced me to Marco, a Gallian mage he had met on the boat who had agreed to be his translator in Aramaya.

Trust the ever-resourceful Shad to have found a guide. Most educated Peninsula folk learned High Aramayan, for it was the language of learning. Shad was a woodcutter's son, however, and only spoke the languages of people he had met. Unlike many men, he did not trouble about his inadequacies, but simply found another way to overcome them. He was good at picking up languages and, if I knew him, by now he would have learned to speak Aramayan quite well and was simply keeping Marco with him because they had struck up a friendship. Despite my husband's warm heart however, he had no compunction about dispatching Marco (wrapped in one of the fur rugs) to sit on the box with the coachman so that we could talk privately.

Unlike most people he knew all about Dally's past. I had no hesitation in telling him what had happened, even down to my conversation with the emperor. I had never had any difficulty telling him things. Perhaps that had been half the problem between us. In a close relationship some negative feelings may be better left unexpressed. Shad had always put people's safety above any difficult feelings he might have had for them. He listened sympathetically to all I had to say.

Until I said, "I could almost wish you had not involved yourself in this. The emperor may still become angry at us."

He said, "If there is trouble then I must be there with you. I'm still your husband."

And suddenly the memory of Edaine loomed into the carriage between us. I felt myself stiffen and he must have felt it too for he suddenly hissed, "I have things to forget too."

"I thought you had left me."

"It did not take you long to forget me."

"At least . . ." I bit the words back. This was hopeless. Here we were fighting again.

We sat in bleak silence until the carriage drew up outside Pepita's house. I did not want to leave him on this bitter note.

"Thank you for being so kind to me," I said.

He took my hand.

"Dion I have always loved you and I think I always will. I beg you to forget what happened."

"I am trying," I said. "I promise. You must forget too. I promise you it was all a mistake."

But I couldn't really describe my relationship with Nikoli as nothing more than a mistake to be forgotten. Poor Nikoli. What was I going to do?

Nikoli was at the house early the next morning. I had never seen him so emotional.

"Has he come to take you away?" he cried. "Will you go?"

I had no idea how to answer these questions.

"I don't know," I cried. "I'm sorry Nikoli. I really don't know. The first thing we did when he arrived was fight."

"Why has he come? Tell me what happened!"

I did my best to tell him calmly what Shad had said and how the return of the ring had been a misunderstanding. Nikoli listened unsympathetically, interrupting frequently with "so he says," and "that's his story, is it?" until finally he cried. "Surely you don't believe this fabric of lies? It's laughable. His mistress has rejected him and he's come crawling back to you. Can't you see that?"

"Nikoli, I . . ." I had considered this possibility and rejected it as unlikely. I could have suspected Shad of falling in love with another women, but I would have trusted my life to his honesty.

Nikoli caught me in his arms.

"Dion, don't go back to him. He doesn't deserve you. He'll only hurt you again."

The anguish in his voice was overwhelming.

"Nikoli, I can't decide anything without a lot of thought and discussion. Please. Don't worry."

I pulled him down on the chaise beside me, put his head on my shoulder and cradled him in my arms.

"Don't go back to him," he said softly. "We have so much together. We share magery. We are colleagues as well as lovers. You cannot have that with him. And he can't give you children. But I can. Maybe I already have. Maybe my seed is already growing inside of you."

He touched my belly gently and at that touch a memory came to me of his rubbing my stomach while I slept among the furs in his arms.

"Nikoli! Have you been trying to make me pregnant?"

"Yes."

"But . . . why?"

"You wanted it so much. I thought it would make you happy."

"Well yes I did, but . . . shouldn't we have talked about it first? Or waited until we knew each other better? I mean if I was going to have a child I'd rather be married to its father."

He sat up and looked at me in astonishment.

"Married. But I'm already married. I thought you knew that."

"You're married?" I was horrified. I was having an affair with a married man! Aumaz! After all my anguish over Edaine, here I was doing the same thing to some other poor woman.

"But you can't . . ."

"All Aramayans are married. But it doesn't matter. Nobody minds."

He looked so innocently astonished that I wanted to hit him.

"How could you? Damn you Nikoli, how could you?"

"But what's the matter? Nobody cares about that."

I couldn't face him anymore. Or myself. I ran from the room.

Kitten was coming down the stairs.

"What's the matter?"

"Nothing!" I cried pushing past her. "Everything. Oh my God, how could he?"

"Dion don't," cried Nikoli behind me.

Then suddenly he was on the stairs above me catching my arms, eyes pleading.

"Dion, listen to me!"

"No," I cried. "How can we go on after this? Just go away. I hate myself." I could feel his magic trying to catch hold of me but I pushed it aside and ran.

"Don't do this," he cried after me. "You can't do this to me."

Safely in my room, I threw myself on the bed, face in hands. My God what a mess. I felt so unclean. Damn him. How could I have been so stupid? I had assumed because he courted me that he was free to do so.

After a time Kitten knocked on the door.

She came in and sat down on the bed beside me.

"My God, Dion, I don't know what to say."

Something in her voice brought back what I had lost.

"Is he gone then?" I asked bleakly.

"He's downstairs. I told him I'd talk to you."

"Oh Nikoli," I groaned. "Why didn't he tell me? Did you know he was married?"

"All Aramayan nobles over twenty are married. If I had thought about it, I would have assumed you knew or that it didn't matter to you. You've loosened up a lot since I first knew you."

"But I draw the line at sleeping with other women's husbands."

"Maybe you are wise. But listen . . . Nikoli says he and his wife have lived separately ever since their third child was born."

"You mean he's a father too. But he never . . ."

"They are with their mother on their country estates. He gets on so badly with his wife that he doesn't go there. I'm sure he is telling the truth. I can't make him see that it is different for you. But does it have to be?"

I understood what she was saying but I still felt unclean.

"If only he'd told me first, I could have made a decision instead of finding out like this."

"Yes. He seems to be one who forgets such things. Is it true he could give you a child?"

"It might be," I said. "He is not as powerful as me, but he is powerful. That's another thing he tried to do without telling me."

"But think how happy you would have been if he had succeeded."

She was right. I would have been. I almost wished he had succeeded before I had found out about his wife.

"But I can't have a child with a married man. Can I?"

"A child is a child. Your mother didn't need a husband. Do you?"

But no matter how tempting the idea of using Nikoli to get a child was, it also horrified me. He was a person with feelings, not to be deceived in such a way. Even if I could do such a thing, I would still have to get over my unease at his being married.

I could not just turn my back on Nikoli. When I had recovered, I went down to speak with him. I felt so ashamed about our relationship, I found it very difficult to walk into the room.

He was very stiff and formal.

"I suppose this is good-bye," he said. "No doubt you will be going back to Moria with your husband as is proper. I had thought you had no respect for empty forms, but I see now I was wrong."

Suddenly I felt terribly sorry for him. If he did not get on with his wife, why should he be punished for that? I knew how that was. I did not get on with Shad.

"I am not going home to Moria now," I said. "I don't know if I will go back to Shad. Every conversation we have had since he came here has ended in an argument. Can you base a marriage on that?"

"I could not," he said bitterly. "Our arguing hurt our children too much. You would find the same thing. But you will not see sense. You still love him and you will believe his lies and go back to him and be miserable together. I can see it already."

"Oh Nikoli," I said. I felt like I was standing in the ruin of some beloved place. "I have been so happy here with you."

"Not happy enough, it seems," he snapped. He shut the door after him with a snap.

Part of me felt angry at having my good intentions spurned so. So much for love that disappeared so quickly. And what business did he have to be angry anyway? He had deceived me. But had he avoided questions about his private life or had I simply not asked them? We were two people from different cultures. I saw now how little I understood him.

I saw either Nikoli or Shad, and sometimes both, every day for the following week. Sometimes I felt my love for Shad still strongly alive. But was it love or some sick self-destructive dependency? Every time I decided I should go home with him, Shad and I would have an argument.

For instance, I tried to tell him what the College of Healers had said and that it was my fault that we were childless and he got very angry and said that he was sick of my always looking for blame. We were childless and probably always would be and everything would be better if I just learned to accept it as he had and stopped overreacting as if it was the end of the world. Having decided to watch my tongue more, I tried not to get angry for as long as I could, but the remark about overreacting was too much. I shouted that it was a very ordinary human thing to want to have children and anyway I wouldn't have cared so much if he hadn't made so much of it. Then as usual things descended into sniping personal remarks and I wondered why I had ever thought I could live with him again. I could see us spending the future lying silently in bed side by side hating each other. That was no kind of marriage. Especially now we were both unsure of each other's fidelity.

At such times I would find myself yearning for the happy times I had spent with Nikoli. I had come to the conclusion that I had overreacted to his marriage and that I should not feel guilty for our affair. Outside sources confirmed that he had told the truth about his relations with his wife. He saw his children every spring when they visited his family and was by all accounts a devoted father. But I did not talk about any of this with him. He had completely withdrawn from me. He was charming and polite but if I tried to talk about anything personal he would change the subject or firmly tell me that it was a private matter. Only occasionally did the mask slip enough for me to see that he feared that I would leave him and did not want to be hurt by it. How I wished he would be more demanding or more loving. Then I would have felt I had some reason for staying with him. Yet for some perverse reason, his reserve made me care for him more because I felt I had hurt him. Possibly he knew I would react so.

Could I leave my husband of five years for a man I hardly knew, who was, moreover, married to someone else? I liked and admired Nikoli, but was this enough for the kind of relationship he wanted? Perhaps he could give me a child, but then maybe he couldn't either. There was so much I didn't know about him. He had had me watched, he had manipulated me over Dally, he had tried to make me pregnant without telling me. All these facts worried me. Would Nikoli ever have confessed had he been unfaithful to me? I had a feeling that this was not the way he worked.

"You will not have any peace from them while you keep them both on a string like this," said Kitten. But I did not know what decision to make. Or which possibility of happiness to surrender.

A PART FROM MY plowing my personal life into a morass,
a great many things happened that week.

I awoke one morning to hear shouting from Kitten's bedroom and when I emerged I discovered that she had dis-
missed Misha the majordomo, or rather insisted Pepita do
so. Pepita was dismayed to lose such an important servant
but Kitten was adamant.

"He was spying on you and Shad and passing the information on to Nikoli," she said angrily when I asked her
about it later. "There are limits, I tell you, and he has
crossed them. And I don't care if he is a tasty fellow," she
snapped at Pepita who sighed and removed herself from
the room.

I saw Misha later going through the hallway. At the door
he stood and looked back up the stairs for a moment, with
his jaw set as if he had things to say and was tempted to
run up the stairs and say them. Then Simonetti ushered him
firmly out.

"Are you certain he was spying on us?" I asked Kitten.

"Unfortunately, I am," she said. She was in a depressed
mood and remained so for several days. Obviously she had

grown very attached to Misha. I tried to confront Nikoli with Misha's spying but he simply denied it.

We discovered the whereabouts of Haziz when Ahmed, who had been worryingly absent for a couple of days, returned. When Simonetti and I had not turned up at the canal boat, he had gone to the Korosov house where he had arrived just in time to see Haziz and Madame Elena driving off in a carriage. Reassured by Dally's absence from the party, he had followed the two women until he was certain that they were heading for Marzorna. The news filled us all with relief. At least Haziz still had control of Bedazzer. There was less chance that he might get free to lay waste to the country.

When I told Monsieur, the Chief Demon Hunter, of this, he announced that he was going to put together an expedition to clean out the Marzornite necromantic fortress and asked me to accompany it. It was not going to be easy. Because of Marzornite hostility to Aramayan mages, just getting to the fortress might be a long slow fight. Monsieur asked my opinion on how strong a force we would need. I told him that if Marzornite nature magic was as strong as Klementari magic, it would have to be very big indeed. As the days went by I managed to persuade him that it was important that Dally should accompany us and that until then she should be released into my custody.

I went to see her every day. She remained locked up at the demon hunters' headquarters but she was comfortable. She had regained complete control of her body but she was still restless and anxious. Where is Bedazzer now? she would ask every day. What is being done to capture him? The news that Haziz was heading for the fortress at Marzorna combined with letters from Ahmed calmed her a little.

But when I told her of our plan to invade the Marzornite marshes, she was her old blunt self.

"I think it's a rotten plan. Completely stupid. You'll give Haziz weeks, maybe months of warning and she'll take Bedazzer and disappear. Oh, you are hopeless Aunt."

"You have a better plan?" I inquired coldly. "Perhaps you

think I can take on the whole Marzorna marshes by myself. If that's the case, I'm afraid you overestimate me."

"Well if you had any guts you'd already have gone to do it. Don't be so dense Aunt. You don't need to go at this head on. You could slip into the marshes by yourself and probably go completely unnoticed by the Crocodile Men. All you would need to do is outfight Bedazzer, and you've done that before."

I was stung by her words. There was a grain of truth in them.

"Well you might believe in throwing your life away with gallant and ill-planned schemes, but I don't," I retorted sharply. "How would I find this secret fortress without using magic for a start? Count Korosov had no idea of the way there."

"I might have known you'd just make excuses," she said in disgust and refused to talk to me again that day.

I was sorry for this because as my annoyance cooled I could see her suggestion might work. I did not say anything to Monsieur because I suspected he would try and stop it, but that night I told Ahmed what Dally had said. He became thoughtful and said that it might be possible to hire one of the marsh folk to act as a guide.

"I will send to my followers in the marsh to tell them to find one," he said. "But I do not want to leave Akieva until Dally is released. Do you think that will much longer?"

"It depends on how she behaves," I said. "If she tries to escape then the demon hunters will become suspicious of her and keep her imprisoned longer."

"Lady Dion, this is Dally we are talking about. She will not do such a foolish thing."

Obviously our experiences of my niece were entirely different.

But Dally had matured since I had known her in Moria. She bore her captivity patiently and did nothing to endanger her standing with the demon hunters. Apart for this one exchange she did not favor me with her low opinion of my character either. Instead we talked quite amiably on soothing neutral topics like our family at home. She still slept badly but she did not seem ready to talk of her time in the phial. Though I let her know that I was willing to listen, I did not press her. I did not ask her about her relationship with Bedazzer, either. She told me enough to make it clear to me that she was no necromancer.

Then late one evening six days after I had rescued Dally, the strangest thing of all happened. Nikoli had been to see me that night and we had talked about the coming invasion of the Marzorna marshes and other impersonal things. He did not stay late, because it was snowing outside and looked to be getting worse. Afterward I was tired. But as I climbed the stairs to bed, there was a tremendous pounding on the door. When it was opened, two people stumbled into the hall. One of them was Shad and he was carrying a third person in his arms.

"Dion! Come quickly!" shouted Shad as he put his burden down. He had taken his fur coat off to wrap around it. When I ran down to him I saw the coat contained a shivering woman. She looked vaguely familiar. From the look of her, she was already well into a fever, probably pneumonia, for she was very inadequately dressed for the weather.

"How is she?" said the other person, who I saw was a much older woman with a brown weatherbeaten face.

"I cannot tell yet, but she is very ill. But you are freezing too. You must get warm. Go into the drawing room. There is a fire there. Shad take her. You, doorman, go get blankets and something hot to drink."

At that moment Kitten appeared. "What is all the noise? . . . Oh my God! Annushka! Annushka, is it really you?"

She flung her arms around the weatherbeaten old woman and the two embraced in a transport of delight. Now I recognized the sick woman as Nikita, the woman we had seen at Shree Tarko. But that was not important at the moment.

"We must get her to bed quickly," I cried.

"No," cried Annuska suddenly. "We left Shree Tarko yesterday morning. They will have missed us by now and the Prekazy. . . . Your cousin will expect us to come here, Madame Kitten."

"You are serfs," said Pepita, more as a statement than a question. "Ivan, order the carriage. I have friends who will hide you."

"No Pepita, we can hide them at the house where we were going to take Dally," cried Kitten. "Ahmed is there and will look after them."

Everything dissolved into a hustle and bustle. I did not pay much attention to what was going on. If the sick woman was to go out into the night, I must do some healing work on her. I warmed her and began to draw the infection into her arm so that I would be able to suck it out. The moment I needed my healer's tools, Shad was there handing them to me. We had worked together like this before and while I sucked the infection out of Nikita's arm through a pipette, Shad coaxed her to drink a little warm tea.

Then Nikita was wrapped in a blanket and Wilby and Annushka carried her out into the sled. I went to get my coat, but Kitten stopped me.

"You must stay here, Dion."

"But Nikita needs more care."

"I know. I will send for a healer when we get there. But if the Prekazy are going to come, one of us must be here. Pyotr Deserov will get very suspicious if we are both away."

I saw her reasoning. "Very well, but keep Nikita warm."

"I will," she said. She kissed my cheek.

"Thank you Dion. If they come, tell them that I am having a late supper with someone. Make it sound salacious. They'll have no trouble believing that."

Then the door closed on her and the swirling snow outside.

I suddenly noticed that Shad was shivering. His coat had gone with the two women. I drew him into the warm drawing room calling behind me for a hot drink.

"What happened? Where did you find those two?" I asked.

"I stumbled across them in an alley nearby. They came to Akieva in a dairy sled yesterday and just after they arrived they were attacked and their coats stolen. Today they walked across Akieva. They were lost. They wanted the house of

Katerina Deserov, but it was difficult for them to find people who knew. I couldn't leave them, especially when I saw how far gone the young one was. That Annushka is a game old thing. I think she just about carried the young one across Akieva. Anyway I was going to make them go to a nunnery but Annuska asked me where Kitten Deserov was and luckily I knew. They couldn't have gone to a nunnery if they were escaped slaves. Can you imagine this country? I mean slavery. And everyone told me Akieva was so advanced."

"Yes, I was shocked too. Such progress and combined with such misery."

It was nice to talk like this but there was something else bothering me.

"What were you doing out there though?" I asked him.

He tensed.

"I was watching outside to see if he went home," he said slowly. "When he left, I left. He does the same when I visit you, you know. I don't blame him. I'm not going to give you up easily either."

I was cut to the heart by his words.

"Oh Shad I didn't mean for it to happen like this,"

"I know sweetheart. It's just a big mess."

I put my arms round him and squeezed him tight. His wonderful strong arms came around me. I wished we could just melt together, letting all the complications dissolve away.

"I want to come home with you Shad, but we argue so much. Perhaps it's not meant to be."

"Don't say that," he whispered softly against my hair. "There has to be some way we can go on together. There must be."

The door opened and the servant came in with hot tea, causing us to jump apart guiltily. The ridiculousness of married people acting so guiltily made us both laugh.

Then as the servant was laying out the cups there came another pounding on the door. This time it was four men from the Prekazy. They had orders to search the house for runaway serfs and they did so, roughly and thoroughly. I followed them around with the female household staff rescuing bits of crockery from them, while Pepita stood at the top of the stairway, her favorite vase clasped to her bosom, looking for all the world like the martyred St. Estrella and disclaiming in her loudest voice that she was a poor persecuted wretch. Shad was horrified and protested at the men until their leader turned to him and said,

"You live here? No? Well go home then. Or do you want us to take you in for obstructing officers in their duty?"

"Shad maybe you'd better go," I said, seeing that Shad was quite prepared to be arrested in my defense. "We will be safe enough. I'll see you tomorrow afternoon." I kissed his cheek.

"Very well," he said uneasily.

"Oh Pepita, we have been a great trouble to you," I said to Pepita after the men had gone and we were cleaning up. "I shall buy you some new plates."

" 'Tis a mere nothing," said Pepita. "True, I was a little annoyed when Katty made me dismiss Misha, but as for annoying the Prekazy, my dear child, it's an honor and a privilege."

Despite the search I felt very happy. Shad and I had made a breakthrough that night, albeit a small one. Perhaps things would be better now.

I awoke very early the following morning to find Kitten standing at the end of my bed. Even half asleep I could tell something important had happened.

"You know why Annushka came here?" she said. "She wanted to tell me that two years ago the healer who pronounced me barren was convicted of making false declarations of barrenness. Apparently she had been taking money from families to help them get rid of unwanted wives. Annushka had always thought that there had been something wrong with the way Vassily and Pyotr had gone about putting me aside. Last night after the healer had cared for Nikita, I asked her to examine me. There is a created blockage there. If I had a small operation I would be as fertile as any other woman."

"You could have a child!" I cried.

"I could get Shree Tarko back. No, more than that. I could force Vassily to put aside his current wife and have his children declared illegitimate. There is a great deal of anger against families who use such methods."

There was a savage look on her face.

"Would you?" I whispered, suddenly afraid of that look.

After a moment she relaxed and the horrible look went away.

"Of course not. But no wonder Pyotr wanted me away from Akieva. Think what a disaster it would have been had I found out. And Vassily knew Annushka was suspicious. She was beginning to fear for her life and her nephew told her to run. Isn't it amazing? To think that I might never have met Norval or you or gone to Sopria or the Peninsula."

"My God, Kitten. What are you going to do? Are you going to punish them?"

"I have no idea what to do," she said. "I feel as if the world has turned inside out." A wry smile came over her face. "Perhaps I should thank them. Think of it. I might still be Vassily's wife. What a lucky escape!"

It promised to be a good day. The sun was sparkling on the snow. I was getting somewhere with Shad. The Deserovs' hostility toward Kitten now made some sense. I set out for the demon hunters' headquarters in Pepita Sandorez's winter carriage, for the previous day Monsieur had finally agreed to release Dally into my custody. I wondered if he would have agreed so easily if he knew how tempted I was to take Dally and leave Akieva.

All through the past week as I worried about Shad and Nikoli I had been uncomfortably aware that somewhere miles away much more important matters were taking place. Bedazzer was out there, no longer so securely trapped inside a body weaving his wiles against Haziz and the necromancers of the marsh. Apart from the havoc he might wreak jumping from body to body, what if he managed to open a gateway between our world and his? Then he would be free to ravage this world for all its life force. My old home at Ruinac was at the site of the last great demon outbreak. In the few hours that demon had been free, a third of all Moria had been laid waste and half of its population killed. If Bedazzer was going to get free I wanted to be close enough to stop him quickly. The distinct, ugly possibility that he might be able to ravage all the land between Marzorna and Akieva before I even knew he was loose was horrible.

With Dally released my only reason for staying in Akieva would be Shad—and Nikoli. Although I knew I would be reluctant to leave Akieva with that situation still unresolved, I also knew I could never live with myself if I failed to stop Bedazzer because I was too busy deciding between two men.

But the situation was closer to resolution than I realized. When I brought Dally down to the carriage that morning, a man wearing a huge hooded fur coat was standing beside it. I did not recognize him until he turned to face me.

"Prince Deserov," I said. "Dally, this is Prince Pyotr Deserov of the Prekazy."

She looked at me apprehensively, but I was fairly sure he was not interested in her. As far as I knew, the Deserovs were not yet aware that Kitten knew their secret. Now I was going to find out for certain.

"Ah Lady Dion. What a charming coincidence. I wonder if I might have a word in private. In your carriage perhaps."

All three of us climbed into the carriage. I was not going to leave Dally standing unwatched in the cold.

"I have an order here which I would like to show you," said Prince Deserov, passing over a piece of thick paper. It was an Arrest and Deportation Order for one Shad Forrest, Lord of Ruinac.

"But who . . . why?"

"Your husband has been deemed an undesirable foreigner. He shall disappear tonight and be deported to Moria in chains. The order is signed by one of Prince Nikoli Terzu's clerks, but the prince is the one who had the power to order it," he said.

"Nikoli did this? Oh Aumaz! How could he?"

"Yes, a remarkably crude plot. One entirely unworthy of Prince Terzu. Lady Dion, do not be hasty. It is the duty of the Prekazy to execute such orders, but the arrest can be delayed at my discretion. And I would do it for a friend."

It was blackmail, pure and simple. I wanted to tell him

that Kitten knew his dirty little secret and it was too late to bother, but I could see quite clearly that that would not serve me.

"What do you want me to do?"

"Leave Akieva. Both of you. I'm sure you can persuade my cousin."

I felt a certain exaltation. He did not know it was too late. But I must play my part carefully if I was to ensure Shad's safety.

"I am engaged to help the demon hunters in Marzorna. I have given my word," I told him.

"My dear Lady Dion. I am not an unreasonable man. What could be better than your going to Marzorna early for reconnaissance? And taking my cousin. Just don't return afterward."

"Very well," I said. "But how shall I know my husband is safe after I have left? Give me the order."

He folded the paper and put it back inside his coat.

"Later. When you are gone. But if it is anxiety for his safety that prevents you from going, you should take him with you. Or if you are not on good enough terms, he should seek sanctuary with the Morian Ambassador." He smiled unpleasantly. "The publicity of such an arrest should ensure his survival should we be forced to carry it out."

He got out of the carriage and I ordered the groom to put the horses back into the harness. I hardly thought about Prince Pyotr or the pleasing fact that he was doing all this too late. I was too furious at Nikoli. I could have fireballed the whole Headquarters and then some.

That underhanded bastard! How dare he! No doubt he would have some little plan to do with a ring and maybe a letter that was supposed to make me believe my husband had left me again. Then he would probably let me come crawling back to him. Well if he thought that was going to work he had another thing coming.

"What was that about Aunt?" asked Dally.

"It was about Prince Nikoli Terzu being a slimy underhand . . . Dammit, that's it. I'm going to see him now. Come on Dally."

I took her wrist and pulled her from the carriage. With Dally trailing behind me (for I did not entirely trust her) I stormed back into the building and straight up to Nikoli's office. I pushed past his protesting secretary, charged into his room and slammed my hand down on his desk. Nikoli's astonishment only made me more furious.

"If Shad Forest disappears, I will never speak to you again," I shouted. And then without waiting for an answer, I turned on my heel.

On the way back downstairs I noticed Dally was grinning.

"What's so funny?" I snapped.

"My, my, Aunt. You certainly told him."

My first impulse was to send to Shad and warn him of his danger, but I conquered that impulse. Pyotr Deserov could gain nothing by arresting Shad now. But if we were to leave Aramaya I would definitely make sure Shad left with us. I did not trust Deserov an inch.

I felt the need to consult Kitten, however. Half-formed plans needed to be turned into action. I was almost grateful to that nasty Prince Pyotr. Not only had he spurred me on to leave Akieva, but he had robbed me of the choices that had so confounded me. I was angry enough at Nikoli to have few qualms about leaving him behind, and I had to take Shad away from Akieva now, even if it meant we fought all the way to the marshes.

By the early afternoon when Shad arrived to see me, the house was busy with preparations.

"We have to leave Akieva at once," I told him as he came in the front door.

He hardly seemed to hear me. "I have to talk to you," he said, agitatedly pulling me into the drawing room.

"Your fancyman, that prince, came to see me," he said as the door closed behind us. "He said you wanted me to go home."

What was this? Damn Nikoli.

"Well he lied as Edaine lied," I said. I tried to take Shad's arm to soothe him, but he shrugged me off. "Don't let him upset you Shad. Just forget it. We've got something more im . . ."

"He told me . . . he told me you were carrying his child," he cried.

"What? Why on earth . . . ? It's not true."

"But he could give you a child, couldn't he? Not like me. You've always blamed me that we had no other child after Alinya, haven't you?"

I denied it as I had denied it every other time Shad had said this. Only this time I meant what I said. Too late. He was too upset to even listen.

"The prince. . . . He said that if I was a mage, I could have got you with child. Is that true? It is, isn't it? I always suspected it and so did you. That's why you went so cold on me. You regretted ever marrying me, didn't you?"

"No, Shad!" I cried, horrified.

"And now you've found a man who can give you a child, you're going to leave me for him, aren't you?"

"No. Please. Calm down. Listen to me."

"Aren't you?" he shouted.

"No. No, I'm not."

"Prove it then. Show me. Pack your bags immediately and come home with me."

"Damn it, Shad. We can't. I've got to . . ."

I was going to say there was Bedazzer to finish off, but I didn't get the chance. It was horrible—like shouting through glass at someone looking the other way.

"You need time to think about it, do you? Stop lying to me Dion. What were you going to do? Come home and try and fool me the child was mine. Well I've worked it out now, so it's not going to work."

"Shad, for God's sake listen to me . . ."

"You don't want a husband. You want a stud bull. This child thing has become the Holy Quest of your life, hasn't it? Because it's the only thing you can't magic up. But I never thought you'd go this far, Dion Holyhands. An affair with a married man just for the sake of his seed. It sickens me. You sicken me."

He turned and stormed out of the room. I ran after him.

"Shad," I cried. "Don't go."

He was out in the hallway storming toward the front door. I raced after him and caught his arm.

"Shad listen to me. You must come with us," I cried. "It isn't safe here."

"Just leave me alone," he shouted

Desperation filled me. I felt as if the Prekazy were waiting out on the very doorstep to arrest him. How was I going to stop him. As he reached for the door, I flung sleep at him. In all the time I had known him I had never used magic against him. It was only as he lay unconscious in my arms that I realized what I had done.

"Dion!" cried Kitten, running down the stairs. "What happened?"

I laid him down gently on the carpet at her feet.

"He wouldn't listen, damn him. Why wouldn't he listen? Oh Kitten! He will never forgive me for this."

The journey to Marzorna started badly and only got worse. Oh, the journey itself went well enough. We made good time and had no accidents and few delays. But the atmosphere between the members of the party—or, to be more accurate, between other members of the party and me—became uglier and uglier.

I had expected Shad to be angry with me. I had held him asleep until we were well out of Akieva for just that reason. He showed no signs of forgiving me for kidnapping him. I felt so miserably guilty about the situation that I could not bring myself to even approach him.

"What have you done to Uncle Shad?" said Dally, after a couple of days. "He used to be such a cheery man."

Tersely I told her about the kidnapping.

"Well, what a grouch," she said. "You saved his life. You should tell him so."

Yes indeed Dally was her usual abrasive self. It was all very well for her to say what was obviously true, but she missed the more subtle side. Shad was entirely right to be angry at me for breaking our unspoken pact that I should never use my superior magical skills against him. It was, if possible, an even greater betrayal than my affair with Nikoli had been.

Yet perhaps Dally did understand something of the situation.

As I got up to leave the room she said, "You know you don't need a husband, Aunt. My mother never did. Nor did Grandma."

It made me wonder if I loved Shad or if I was simply afraid of being alone. Dally's mother had been an unhappy woman with a drinking problem. She was no example to follow. But my own mother had never bothered tying herself to any of our fathers and she had enjoyed her life much more than I currently was. But then my mother had had all the children she had wanted—seven of us. She had had magic too and could have stopped herself conceiving, but she had wanted us. Just as I wanted a child.

If only I could have one. Everything would be all right then. But if secret fear was preventing me, I could not see how I would ever overcome it. I had never been courageous and I could see the hope that the fear might fade corroding my life even more than the fear was. Every month hope would be destroyed. Every month the fear of disappointment would prevent what I hoped for from happening. It would be a trap. Much wiser to accept myself as barren.

I found myself regretting leaving Nikoli. I could understand what it must be like trapped in an unhappy marriage and I felt sorry for him. What he had done was underhanded, but understandable in terms of love. In fact sometimes in maudlin moments of loneliness, I saw it as something of a compliment. As my anger faded I remembered what a kind friend he had been. That was more than the sullenly silent Shad was now. And who knew—if we had both tried perhaps we would have been able to have children together. Was this my real source of regret over Nikoli?

Perhaps . . . perhaps Kitten could have a child now. And I could help her bring it up. It wouldn't be as good as a child of my own, but it would be something to love and care for. Some stake in the future. Yes, it was a wonderful idea.

As we progressed south and the landscape changed slowly

from snowy to soddenly rainy, I became more and more consumed with this wonderful daydream. So consumed, in fact, that one night I revealed my idea to Kitten.

She took it remarkably badly.

"I refuse to be treated as just another source of children for you," she had shouted as the argument had got more heated. "I'm more than just a womb."

And "I'd never let you near any child of mine. Your obsessiveness would smother it."

After that things had been said on both sides that would have been far better left unsaid.

"Why do you always want other people to do things for you? The problem is your own cowardice," she shouted finally before the door slammed behind her. After that she moved out of the cabin we shared. Fortunately there were few other travelers and no shortage of cabins. Traveling at this bleak time of year was expensive since all riverboats had to carry travel mages to keep the canals free of ice.

We made the argument up, but things remained cold between us. We continued to have separate cabins. Kitten started dressing as a man so that there could be no expectation otherwise.

On the sixth day of our journey, we reached Hasaka Ferry, a junction between two canals. A shabby inn smelling of salt fish was the only building there. For as far as the eye could see grey brown marsh and mud flat stretched out on all sides of it. We had several hours to wait before the next riverboat, so we hired a private sitting room at the inn. It was an unpleasant day. A bitter wind howled in from the mud flats, moaning under the eaves and making the inn sign creak eerily. Small squalls of rain came out of the dark grey sky and peppered the muddy street outside. Even with a roaring fire the room was chill. Everyone's spirits were dampened by the miserable surroundings. Kitten and Shad sat by the fire drinking kesh and exchanging infrequent remarks.

By then Ahmed was the only person in our party I cared to speak to. Dally's poor opinion of me mattered too much on days like today when I shared it. She and Ahmed were playing a game of cards which I did not join in. I knew it was mean of me, but Dally and Ahmed's happiness together were hard to bear when my own private life was collapsing in a heap around me.

Boredom and depression finally drove me outside. It was freezing, but I kept myself warm with magic. I wandered up and down the muddy little track before the inn and its outbuildings. The bleak surroundings matched my mood. I would never have a child. It was fair of Kitten to accuse me of being fearful, but I honestly did not think I could ever overcome that fear. Alinya's death still haunted my dreams. Had my desire for a child become an obsession? When two people you trust accuse you of the same failing, it's time to seriously consider the matter. Was I so obsessed that I was beginning to see those I loved as no more than a means of getting babies? Had I treated Shad as a stud bull? Was my continuing attraction to Nikoli only due to the hope of children? My heart still turned over every time I saw a small child and I felt a longing for my dear, dead Alinya, but many women longed to have children. Was I really carrying these feelings to unreasonable lengths? Would I, as Kitten had accused, ruin the life of any child I mothered with excessive, obsessive love? How could she say such a terrible thing? What if it was true?

The dikes surrounding the inn were firmer and much easier to walk on than the track. I climbed up on them. From up here the wind was fierce. Night had fallen. Several rain squalls—clouds of tiny droplets—were swept into my face by the wild wind. I stood at the top of the dike, letting the cleansing rain and cold whip into me. I felt all old worn ideas being torn away. It was impossible to feel anything but exhilaration in such a wind. I don't know how long I stood there, but suddenly I heard someone shouting behind me.

I looked down and saw Shad waving at me.

"The boat's here," he shouted. I clambered down the dike toward him.

"For God's sake, Dion, have the sense to come in out of the rain," he said loudly as he took my elbow irritably and began pulling me toward the lights of the inn. "Don't think standing out here is going to make me feel sorry for you, because it isn't."

What a petty thing to say. Anger filled me. I snatched my arm out of his hand.

"As if I'd bother," I snapped, "You stupid man. You're not even smart enough to realize that I saved your life back there." Ungrateful sod! I left him standing behind me and climbed onto the boat feeling the warming fire of anger course though me, but it had drained away by the time I reached my cabin.

I had a large five-bed cabin all to myself. There was a lighted brazier in the corner, but it was still very cold. Exhausted, I sat down next to the brazier and leaned my head against the wall. I felt as if anger and cold had washed me clean—clean and bare. I stared at the burning coals. Water dripped out of my soaking clothes and formed a puddle on the floor.

A few minutes later Shad opened the door and came in.

"I brought you a cup of tea," he said, holding out a mug.

A cup of tea. All our married life together, every morning without fail he had brought me a cup of tea. I knew it was a peace offering, but I no longer felt up to doing more than saying, "Thanks."

He put it on a stool beside me. He did not go. When I looked around he was leaning against the door frame, his arms crossed against his chest, staring at the floor. I knew that this was an opportunity, that I should say something to him, but I had no idea what that something should be. Perhaps it was the same for him.

Perhaps it was better to be quiet.

There was a slight shudder as the boat began to move.

"I should get out of these wet clothes," I said.

"Yes," he said. "It's late."

He picked up my bed roll and began laying it out on the bare mattress of the bunk.

"Thank you," I said. Slowly I pulled off my clothes and hung them on hooks and stools around the brazier. Even my underwear was soaked. I took this off too and wrung some of the water out of my hair. I was acting as I had acted with Shad all our married life, and it was only when I turned and saw the heat of desire in his eyes that I remembered I was also standing naked before a man.

For a moment we stood there just looking at each other. Something melted inside me under the heat of his gaze and everything outside the space between us seemed to dissolve away.

I went over and slid my hand onto his neck, beneath the collar of his shirt.

"I'm sorry," I said. "Sorry for everything."

His hard arms came around me, crushing me against him. The silk smooth sheen of his leather coat against my flesh, the faint scent of woodsmoke on his skin, the delicious feel of his fingers on my bare back. Oh, the blinding pleasure of it. I wanted to sink my teeth into his shoulder and pull him down on top of me.

"Oh Dion, it's my fault. I should be sorry. I was so afraid I was going to lose you. Oh forgive me, forgive me."

His words were getting tangled up in our kisses.

"No more words," I whispered. "They don't work."

"Yes," he said.

Afterward we lay in the darkness holding each other. I was too afraid to say anything lest it destroy the truce between us. I think he was too.

At last he said, "In a few days we will be setting out for the marshes of Marzorna. Dally tells me it will be very dangerous for you to enter that region."

"Yes," I said. "Not as dangerous as entering Moria under the witchfinders though. It is not so large. I can take to the air and get out without too much difficulty. It is Dally you should be worrying about."

"I would be happier if you would stay in Shebaz and let Ahmed and me find the fortress. Then we could send for you."

"I couldn't do that. It would take twice as long and if Bedazzer got free you would need me. In fact I had thought to ask you if you would stay in Shebaz. There is no necessity for you to risk your life."

"Oh God," he cried suddenly. "Why did I ever think you would stay with me? I have nothing to offer you. I can't protect you, I can't give you children. You would be better off with Nikoli."

I was astonished at this outburst.

"What are you talking about? I never needed protection. I never wanted it. And as for children, that's entirely my fault. It has nothing to do with you."

"No," he said. "Nothing you do has anything to do with me. I'm irrelevant in your life. That's what I discovered in Akieva. Don't you see?"

"How can you even think that after what just happened between us? I love you. I want to be with you." I put my arms around him. "After all this time and all that has gone wrong, here we still are together."

He held me tight, pressed his face into my shoulder.

"Then you have no idea of going back to Nikoli Terzu after this," he said.

This was no time to be too precise.

"Since the Arrest order, my heart turned against him," I said. It was almost the truth. "How can you be with a man who acts so dishonorably? No, I have no idea of going back."

"I should have done the same, had I had the chance. I tried to lie to you over Edaine."

"And you didn't succeed, did you? I don't think you have dishonor in you, Shad."

"Love can be a very dark emotion," he said simply.

After a while he said, "Will you be able to forget him, when you know he can give you a child?"

"He couldn't," I said shortly, knowing that despite my longings this was probably the truth. But why must Shad ask like this?

"Ever since Alinya died I have been so afraid you would leave me. I felt so much that I failed you. I know I acted unreasonably in Aramaya, but it seemed to me that all I feared was coming true."

His words cut me. Of course that was how he had felt

and I had been too wrapped up in exactly the same feelings to realize it.

"Don't you think I feared the same things with Edaine," I cried sitting up. "Why do you think I ran away in the first place? Oh I hate this. We are fighting again. Why did you have to bring this up?"

"Dion," he said softly. "This is an imperfect world. People who love each other sometimes fight." He drew me down beside him again. "And these are things we must talk about if we are ever to have any peace together."

"Well, you have no reason to worry about Nikoli. Anyway, don't you think it's worse for me? You could have a child with any normal woman."

"And I already know that's not what I want. Otherwise I would have stayed with Edaine. I always wanted to have a child, but I can accept it if I do not. I think you want it much more than me."

"Yes . . . beyond all reason."

"I didn't . . ."

"Oh, I know you didn't say that, but Kitten did. And it's true. The desire for a baby is like a gaping hole inside me. But you don't have to worry that I'll leave you. I would have to overcome my magic to become pregnant and I doubt there is anyone in the world who could do that."

"Oh my love," he said, softly folding me in his arms.

Marzorua

AFTER THE SNOWS of Akieva, the best thing about Marz-orna was the golden sun. Even though it was winter the sun was hot enough to warm you through.

At last after days of traveling, we were going into the marshes. The mud brick houses of the Marzornite capital Shebaz had disappeared from view and now the country was covered with fields, little copses of palm trees, and beyond that the huge dunes and sandstone escarpments of the deep desert. It was only irrigation from the river that made it possible for the Marzornites to grow food at all, and river-trade that brought any kind of wealth into the country. In a land where water was so scarce, no wonder people wor-shipped the river. Even I could see that the magnificent and mighty River Het deserved worship.

All around us the rich brown expanse of river was dotted with triangular-sailed native boats. We were traveling in a native ferry, built much like those other boats but twice as big and with two sails. It was driven by the wind and by the river's considerable current.

The ferry's deck was crowded with bundles of cargo and cages of squawking or quacking birds. It was good to be out of the country where serfdom prevailed. In Shebaz people looked you in the eye without fear of being beaten. Here on the boat the people kept separate from us but not because they were afraid. Most of the passengers who crouched between the cargo were marsh folk. Everyone in Marzorna wore long flowing robes but the marsh folk also wore a kind of headdress that covered everything except their eyes and hands and made it difficult to tell which sex they were. Such robes must be a dangerous impediment to swimming if you fell into the river, but when I said this to Ahmed he told me that they only wore such garments outside the marsh to protect themselves from curious outsiders.

"They doubt the true allegiance of we desert folk to our mother Het," he said, touching his chest over his heart at the name. "Thus they hide themselves from us. It is unfair criticism from those who put the Crocodile before the Mother."

Were they all in collusion with necromancy? Ahmed had given me to understand that people did not dare disobey the Crocodile Men, so quite probably they were victims as much as anyone else. But these sinister mud-colored robes, surely designed to hide a multitude of sins, made it very hard not to be suspicious of them.

There were children among the Marzornites, but I was making an effort not to notice children anymore. It's best not to dwell on what you cannot have. I was aware that a small part of me also hoped that if I stopped thinking about the problem, I might still manage to conceive. I accepted that that hopeful part would just have to learn from experience.

Today, however, I found it easy to forget those children, for my mind was full of Bedazzer. So full in fact that I wondered if it was not in some way his doing, though I was fairly certain it could not be. I would see him soon. And this time I would get the chance to finally be free of him. Did demons fear dissolution in the same way as human beings? Did demons feel fear? I suspected they did. In a sense they were feelings incarnate, those cruel animal feelings which humans had as well but which we tried to civilize with love, honor, self-sacrifice, and the other qualities which made up our humanity. How hideous he must find his captivity with Haziz—starving in a lush landscape of food. Feeling life force that he could not consume all around him, stripped as he was of all his glorious power. Ridiculous that I should feel empathy with such a terrible creature, but I knew my heart was still influenced by the love I had felt for him as Andre. It was a dangerous illusion that I could only guard against by being aware of it. Yet he had been part of my life for almost ten years, however rarely I thought of him consciously.

Now he waited for me in the marsh. He would be more desperate than he had ever been before, for when I had bested him before there had never been any danger of his being destroyed. Now if I killed his being he would no longer exist, except as that dark hungry mindless thing that had appeared in my mirror. What would be the outcome of our meeting? Was it possible that he might finally be too cunning for me? Or that his savage certainty would overcome my secret reluctance? Our meeting might lead to disaster. I must make certain it was not so.

I wondered if he knew I was coming. I had a feeling he did. Had he told Haziz? It was quite possible he had not—that to keep her ignorant of our arrival might serve his cunning purposes.

We were counting on that (unwise though it was to count on anything with a demon) and so we had all adopted small disguises.

Shad and I had changed our names and adopted the guise of well-bred travelers with Ahmed acting as our native guide.

"So you are going to continue to masquerade as my aunt's husband," Dally had said when we had discussed it, a piece of cruel teasing I could cheerfully have strangled her for.

But Shad merely smiled and bowed. "It's a masquerade I'm beginning to get a taste for," he said. "And hopefully your aunt will grow to enjoy it too."

He grinned at me in such a sly manner that I found myself blushing like a fool.

"My, my," said Dally, impressed despite herself. "You are a smooth fellow."

"Naturally," said Shad. "Do you think that with her opportunities your aunt would settle for less?"

It was a remark which would have led to battle in the bad old days, but somehow our reconciliation that night on the riverboat had resolved things between us so much that I merely took it as a playful compliment. Shad and I were getting along amazingly well. I dared to hope it would last.

Dally crouched beside me under a canopy at the back of the boat wearing the flowing robes of a marsh woman. She had dyed her skin the bronze color of the Marzornites using kesh berries.

"You will be safe because nobody knows you're here," said Dally. "But there are people who will recognize me. Therefore I must adopt a different persona." Hers was by far the most dangerous masquerade.

Kitten still wore her man's clothes and claimed to be my brother. Although Ahmed and Shad had disliked such a risky disguise, it made sense. Kitten was a striking woman and Bezra Haziz might well be on the lookout for two women of our description in the vicinity of Shebaz. Kitten had always enjoyed the freedom of action dressing as a man gave her. I suspect she was also glad that no one was likely to offer her money for a tumble in the sail closet. She was extremely good at the impersonation and had the walk and mannerisms down pat. If she was rather an effeminate man, she was no more so than many other Aramayan aristocrats. She was down on the deck now, swapping hearty remarks with the Aramayan boat captain and she had fooled the innkeeper in Shebaz so thoroughly that he had spent the previous evening regaling her with the details of his voracious and probably entirely imaginary sex life over a bottle of wine.

"Do men ever tell you these things?" I asked Shad after Kitten had told us the details.

"Well, occasionally," said Shad, who had looked a little embarrassed by the whole story. "I just never felt right about telling you. Honor among men, you know."

Kitten told everyone we met that we were traveling into

the marshes to do a study of the customs of the marsh folk. She was busily plying the captain for stories of the marsh dwellers, while Shad, who fell easily in with the spirit of such things, bought several little crocodile-shaped beads from other passengers.

As we traveled, clusters of reeds began to appear along the banks and small, reedy islands dotted the water. The river widened till it became a great plain of brown water. Here we stopped at a bustling little town called Jeru. Almost all the non-marsh folk got off and a great many more figures shrouded in muddy brown robes got in. Ahmed came up and told me that this was my last chance to get off the boat. It might well be safer for me to stay out of the marshes till they decided what to do. I refused. I was not going to delegate such an important task to other people. I knew how to disguise my magery during the day and I had brought an iron necklet to wear at night so that I could prevent myself from betraying my nature while I slept.

I was not terribly worried about the possibility of being harmed in the marshes. Though they covered over half of Marzorna, they were not so very enormous. I figured I could escape from any attackers using the brute magic of flight. I was more concerned about the others.

Shortly after leaving Jeru, the marsh began. The number of reedy islands and reed beds increased until most of the great wide river disappeared and we found ourselves sailing down a deep channel between impenetrable walls of reeds. The whole world had became the brown water, the brilliantly green reeds, and the bright blue sky like a close-fitting lid on top. Occasionally a palm tree broke through the reeds. There were none of the sounds of life—the shouting of people, the quacking of ducks, the mooing of stock—that we had heard before we had entered the marsh. Only the papery shushing of the reeds and the creaking of the boat filled the gentle air. The marsh smelled of rotting vegetation and mud, like the smell of leaves beneath a tree. The captain who had been so hearty earlier became silent and Kitten came back and sat down beside us.

"What a closed-in world," she said.

We stopped several times at little jetties or dry banks sticking out of the reeds. There seemed to be no roads to or from them, just walls of reeds all around. At each stopping place canoes laden with produce and manned by shrouded figures that looked like lumps of river mud were clustered about the jetty. The canoes were made of plaited reeds tied together in long sinuous shapes. There would be an outbreak of chattering and hubbub as people scrambled in and out of them and handed bundles of ducks or chickens about. Then the ferry would move off, causing the canoes to dance in its wake like fragile green sticks. The whispering silence of the reeds would close in all around.

At last in the midafternoon, we came to what passed for a town here. Behind a large jetty was a wide muddy area where the reeds had been trampled down. A cluster of little conical huts made of plaited reeds stood in the clearing and a group of brown shrouded marsh folk crouched on the jetty.

"This is Matti, where we get out," said Hakim, Ahmed's servant.

All the other passengers got out here too, for it was as far into the marsh as the boat came. After a great deal of fussing and struggling we found ourselves standing on the jetty surrounded by piles of boxes and bundles, the paraphernalia of rich foreigners traveling in uncivilized parts. The boxes and bundles actually contained trade goods and weapons, but they made a convincing show.

As soon as the boat was unloaded, the crew began to get out the oars. They were keen to leave. The captain came up and said urgently to Shad,

"At least let us take your wife back with us. Surely you can see this is no place for an Aramayan woman. There is no accommodation."

He dropped his voice. "And these people are pagan savages. Strange things happen here at night."

"I say, I hope so," said Kitten. "There will be plenty of material for my monograph on the marsh folk, if it does."

"I thank you for your concern Captain," said Shad politely, "but I am well able to protect my own wife." He gave me the tiniest of wry glances as he said it. "And we are well supplied with native guides.

Ahmed bowed at the captain who obviously thought native guides, good or otherwise, were no consolation. But though he was unconvinced, he had business awaiting him all along the river and a strong desire to get out of the marsh before night. Eventually he climbed onto the ferry and it rowed slowly away.

While we had been talking with the captain all the marsh folk had disappeared in their canoes into the reeds. By the time the ferry was gone, the village looked completely deserted. I could not see anyone in the dark interiors of the reed huts though I had an uneasy feeling of being watched.

The quietness was eerie.

I had thought once we got in among the reeds that the whole of that secret country would somehow be open to us but of course it was not. Paddling in small native canoes at water level along narrow channels, the marsh seemed even more closed-in. But it was no longer quiet and still. The place teemed with life. Ducks swam past quacking self-importantly, the water rippled with the movements of insects, hundreds of birds seemed to trill and rustle in the reeds, and a glistening wet water rat disappeared off a bank with a plop. As we glided through the sunlit waters I saw lizards sunning themselves on rotting logs. A tall white heronlike bird stalked the frogs that hopped like damp green jewels among the creeping plants that twined through the reeds. The dank smell of decaying vegetation was everywhere and yet from that decay burst this living green world.

"It's beautiful," I said.

Dally looked at me as if I was mad. "If you say so. I've spent months hiding out on the edge of this marsh and even there it's eerie. Like a maze with eyes. I like it even less in here."

"I hope my men have found a guide for us," said Ahmed from the other boat. "Otherwise it may take us months to find this fortress."

"If we do not get lost, or eaten by crocodiles," said Ahmed's servant Hakim gloomily.

We spent the night on an island. It was not so much dry land as a type of platform or raft made of plaited reeds. According to Hakim the river level changed several times during the year and the island was able to rise and fall with it. It felt quite solid and stable even though you felt like you were walking on cushions. On the island were a couple of barrel-shaped huts also made of plaited reeds. Two elderly women greeted us with cold kesh, a surprisingly refreshing drink. They were the first marsh folk we had seen unswathed in robes. I was interested to see that they looked much the same as the drylanders, for all that their culture was so different. They wore the usual native costume, a simple long shirt and loose trousers and a cloth wrapped around their heads against the sun. It was not modest, but it was eminently practical.

One of the old women, Shari, was Ahmed's old nursemaid, so she could be relied upon not to gossip about his business. Shad, Kitten, and I changed into native dress and hid our Aramayan clothes in her hut. Although we would never look like marsh folk, native garb ensured us a measure of anonymity.

Ahmed and Hakim went off in a canoe to make contact with some of their men. The rest of us sat peacefully on the island. Golden evening sunlight filtered through the reeds and reflected warmly on the dark water. Slowly the edges of the sky turned pink. It was still wonderfully warm, if a little humid. Dally sat on the other side of the island dangling a fishing line in the water. She avoided speaking since that would only make it clearer that she was not a marsh dweller. The rest of us sat silently together. We were all aware that anyone could be watching us, unseen in the reeds. We drank more kesh and watched several small boats come past carrying goats.

"There is water meadow nearby. People graze animals," said Shari, who spoke some Aramayan. She told us not to dangle our legs in the water. This was the land of the crocodile.

"Do they take many people?" said Kitten peering into the water.

"Not us people," said Shari. "We are faithful worshippers. She protect us from them. But she not protect foreigner like you. Must take care."

"Do they really never take the marsh folk?" I asked, wondering that crocodiles could be so selective.

"Occasionally the crocodile take marsh folk," said Shari now. "Only when she is displeased with that person. She never take our children. She is giver of children."

She went on to tell us that if a woman craved a child she went with her man and slept in one of the secret places in the marsh and if they were true believers Aliceander the God would come to them in a dream and make them fruitful.

True believers, I thought cynically. That gives them a way out if it doesn't work. God forbid that childlessness be blamed on the God. Then I looked up and saw both Shad and Kitten were looking at me. Realizing why, I glared at them. I didn't need any further reproaches.

"Such children are called Children of the Crocodile," continued Shari. "They are strong mages or heroes. God bless animals of the marsh too so that marsh folk never go hungry."

I had seen crocodiles lazing on the banks of the Het and in Shebaz. They looked like savage killing machines, with their thick repulsive scales and reptilian eyes, horrible when compared with the kindly Aumaz and his son Tansa of the religion I'd been brought up in. How could anyone worship such a nasty beast?

"Does she not frighten you?" I asked.

"Person should be afraid of God. It is proper so," Shari said simply.

Funny that she called her God, for I had a definite impression that this Aliceander was female as fertility goddesses usually were. Perhaps it was just a language problem.

With the coming of twilight the marshes were full of mosquitos. Shari gave us a salve that kept them away and lit little lumps of incense made of herbs and magic in several bowls. She brought us cheese, bread, and some kind of deliciously crunchy leafy vegetable.

The temperature dropped but not unpleasantly. A chorus of frogs began to sing among the reeds. The darkness was much more noisy than the day had been. We sat around the dim light of the mosquito bowl.

"Is it true that crocodiles can sense magic?" I asked Shari. "If so, why do they not attack your little bowls?"

"Foreign magic bring crocodiles," she said. "They attack foreign tax gatherers when they use magic in marshes."

There was something chilling about this. Did such brutal creatures really have such a selective magic sense?

"Ahmed is taking a long time," said Shad.

"Perhaps he stay where he is tonight," said Shari. "It better not to travel far after dark. Crocodile Men roam abroad."

I looked over at Dally. She nodded reassuringly.

"Maybe we go sleep now," said Shari.

We crawled into the huts and lay down on reed mats with goat skins to cover us. It was a surprisingly comfortable bed. Shad and I lay chastely side by side, but in the darkness he reached out and squeezed my hand. I watched a little clay crocodile that hung in the doorway as it swung with the movement of the island and fell asleep with the whispering of the reeds in my ears.

The following morning before dawn, Hakkim and Ahmed returned with several other men. Most of them were drylanders like Ahmed, but one was a marsh man called Kemal. The drylanders were a little wary of Kemal and I soon found out why. After they had spent a great deal of time looking for a guide and getting no response from the marsh folk, suddenly Kemal had come to their camp and offered to guide us to the necromantic fortress.

"It may be a sign that the marsh folk want to do away with the necromantic fortress after all," said Ahmed softly.

"Or it may mean they plan to do away with us," said Kitten shortly.

"Somehow, I think not," said Ahmed.

Kitten shrugged. "I hope you're right. But we must keep a eye on him."

I watched Kemal surreptitiously. He was a middle-aged man with clever secretive eyes. He was wearing much the same clothes and belt pouch as everyone else, but something about him screamed "mage." He seemed like one who acted, not one who merely guided others. At least the Klementari had taught me to feel nature magic. If he was indeed a Marzornite mage, I would be able to tell when he was working magic.

As dawn was showing pink over the reeds and turning the black water into dark silk, we climbed into small reed canoes and set off.

"The water looks so refreshing," I said to Ahmed. "I wish I could swim."

"It is not safe here," said Kemal from a nearby boat. "But I will tell the Lady when it is safe if she wishes."

He smiled at me knowingly. He spoke very good Aramayan for a marsh dweller. Once again I felt certain that he was a mage. I had an uncomfortable feeling he knew I was too.

"Thank you," I said politely to him. I resolved to be on my guard. We could only wait and see.

We did not travel entirely by boat, but walked for some time along muddy dikes that ran through fields of tall reeds and past occasional lush grassy meadows.

The signs of the crocodile cult were everywhere. Huge stones had been carved and painted with sharp-toothed animal figures. Once we came upon a pole with a crocodile skull at the top of it. The jaws were decorated with ribbons and little strings of bones and a dead heron had been staked to the crossbar, its wings outstretched as if it were on a rack. Bedraggled white feathers still hung from its decaying flesh.

"Nature is a mother who sometimes tries to kill her children," said Shad softly as he looked at the shrine. "This cult seems much more savage than the beliefs of the Klementari."

"Yet the marsh folk seem very contented and prosperous," said Kitten. "They and their children look very healthy."

"Savage and creative," said Shad. He put his hand on the pole as if drawing some force from it. "The two bind together like strands in a rope."

"You are a wise man," said Kemal.

Shad turned away from the shrine quickly. "I have studied nature cults for many years," he said dismissively. But his eyes were shining. I knew that look. It was the one he got at Klementari ceremonies.

I could not blame him. Beyond all reason I liked the marsh with its fresh green walls of secretive reeds and blue sky streaked with humid grey clouds. Tiny birds warbled in the reed beds and sometimes huge white herons with long trailing legs would break startlingly from cover with a harsh cry and an explosion of wings.

"This place is so alive," breathed Shad in my ear.

Yes, that was why I liked it. If I opened my magical senses I could feel the life force teeming through it. In fact the marsh was more alive than any place I had ever been before. The more I sensed it, the more attuned I became until I almost broke into a song of praise. It was a wonderful feeling. No wonder the Marzornites could keep great regiments of Aramayan mages out of the marshes. Harnessed, such power would be enormous.

We stopped at midday. After eating, the men lay down to sleep in the shade of the reeds as was the custom in the heat of the day and Dally, who had been a silent presence all day, lay down among them. Shad withdrew into the reeds and I saw him sitting there with his eyes closed as if breathing in some wonderful scent.

Restless with the feeling of the marsh's life force, I wandered down the hillock to the water's edge. I found a little hollow among the reeds and curled up in it, watching the water gently lapping on the muddy bank. I felt twice as alive as I had been before. A little time later Kitten came down to the bank. I wondered if she was as affected by the marsh

as Shad and I were. I did not call out to her in case I broke
some kind of spell.

She stood on the bank looking around and after a time
she began humming and poking about with her toe. Suddenly she took off her shoes, jumped right into the mud and
started squelching about in it with obvious pleasure.

"What are you doing?" I said

"Oh there you are! This is wonderful mud. It's so nice
and . . . gooey!"

"You're crazy."

"But I'm happy. Oooooh, I just love it when it runs between your toes like that."

I crawled out of my hollow.

"I bet it's full of disgusting slimy things."

"Huh," she said. "You're just jealous because I've got
mud and you haven't."

It was nice looking mud, clean and silty and sprinkled
with little sparkling flecks of mica. I took off my shoes and
put a foot in. The cool mud oozed between my toes in a
way that used to reduce me to ecstasy when I was a child.
It was just the right consistency, soft yet powdery.

Kitten squelched over to me and took my hand.

"I'm sorry for what I said back on the boat. For all of it.
I overreacted."

"I'm sorry too." I said. "I guess I have become obsessed
with having a child. I still want one so much."

"Oh Dion. That's entirely understandable. Only if you
can't. . . . You have so much of life left before you. You
must not ruin it with wanting what you cannot have. Other
things are also good."

"I know. I'm trying to accept it."

"Promise?"

"Promise."

We hugged. I felt overwhelmingly happy and relieved. Yet
in the back of my mind I still felt longing. Would I really
never have a child to share such happiness with?

Kitten began to sing a song about mud. I recognized it
as a song I had learned as a child. Soon we were squelching
around and singing softly so that the others would not catch

us being so foolish. At the end of every verse we bumped hips and cried, "Hey!"

"You have to twinkle your fingers like this," said Kitten holding her hands up in the air. "That's what Annushka used to do."

Then suddenly I felt something huge and magical slither across my senses. I cried out and seized Kitten, hauled her back up onto the dry ground and partway up the hill. It was lucky I was still wearing my iron necklace, for I tried to cast a spell to protect us both and might have given myself away to hostile forces in the marsh had the iron not stopped me. Nothing came out of the water and trying to use my own magic had blocked whatever it was I had sensed from the marsh.

The others were suddenly gathered around us.

"What was that?" asked Shad, whose face was white with shock.

"I felt something," I cried. "Something out there. Something magical."

The men looked uneasy except for Kemal who said, "Of course you did."

He went forward over the mud bank fumbling in his pouch. He stopped, clasped his hands together under his chin in a kind of ritual gesture, spoke a few words, bowed and threw something small and red into the water. The moment the little red thing hit the water, I felt the fear lifting. Somehow I knew it was safe to go back down to the water's edge and wash the mud off my feet.

"The spirit of the marsh dwells among the reeds," said Kemal. "That is what you felt even with your foreign senses. She stirs sometimes in her sleep and must be propitiated by a true believer."

He showed me his little bag full of red beads carved into the shape of crocodiles and reed heads which he carried for just such moments. The spirit of the marsh. The magic had felt big enough to be the whole marsh. It was hard to believe that little red beads could placate something so huge.

Shad caught his arm.

"The spirit of the marsh. But how can that be? It was alive. It had being."

Kemal looked at him for a moment and then he made a sign before Shad's face. It was a ritual sign, not a magic one.

"Just what I said," he told Shad, turning away dismissively. "You have simply felt the spirit of the Crocodile."

"Earth and Air, Dion," said Shad to me quietly. "I never felt anything like that. It knew itself. I am sure of that."

"Should we be afraid?" I said.

"I'm not sure. It was curious, not angry."

But I was afraid. I surreptitiously removed my iron necklace. Being helpless had suddenly started to make me nervous.

All the rest of the day I kept a weather eye out for crocodiles in the water or on the banks. None came, but several times later that day I saw hooded figures crouching among the reeds. I would not have paid much attention to them, except that they shimmered with nature magic. Even more worrying was the fact that Shad did not seem to see them. Once I saw a hooded figure lying prone on an opposite bank. It slid headfirst into the water so suddenly that I jumped.

I turned quickly and saw Kemal was watching me. I should have expected it.

"There are people hiding in the reeds," I said.

"Do not be afraid," he said calmly. "They will not hurt us."

I did not feel him magic me, but he must have for suddenly I felt reassured and there was nothing at all reassuring about those crouched figures.

Nothing happened to us that night even though I slept badly for expecting something. The following day, as we were walking along yet another muddy path, Kemal stopped us.

"Crouch down," he said. He crept forward to where the path turned through the reeds and peered down it for a time. Then he waved his hands for us to come forward. As we passed the turn of the path we came out onto another waterway. A large boat, almost the size of the ferry we had come down on, was tied up to the bank. Its sail flapped limply in the breeze. Its decks were slick with some kind of dark fluid. Blood!

The river was empty. There was no sign of any bodies. Hakim and Ahmed disappeared into the reeds to find the canoes that should be hidden there. When they found them the canoes were spattered with blood and we all helped to sluice them out.

We felt apprehensive about going out onto the water, but the river was peaceful and Kemal said it was safe. As we pulled away from the bank I turned to look back and that was when I saw the front of the empty boat's sail.

The Aramayan words "Death to all necromancers" was written across it in blood.

"Who did this?" I cried to Kemal.

"The Crocodile Men probably. They have decided they want the necromancers out of the marsh."

"What?" cried Ahmed. "Why didn't you tell us this earlier?"

Kemal shrugged calmly. "I am with you, aren't I?" he said. "Do you think I would be here against their will? Let us go now. They will not like it if we tarry here."

The reeds whispered more loudly for a moment as if in a sudden wind.

"May I ask you about the Crocodile Men?" I said to Kemal when we stopped at midday.

"You may ask, though I will not answer everything," he said. "The Crocodile Men are the mages that serve the God."

"Aliceander?" I asked, confused again by the male name for something that was so strongly female in my mind.

"Who else? It was She you felt yesterday in the marsh,"

As we walked through the whispering reeds he told me the story of the marsh folk's creation; of how in the beginning there was the marsh, dankly fertile with decay and of how one day the Crocodile Aliceander found two eggs in a

pile of rotting reeds. She took them into her mouth but did
not eat them. Instead she held them there in that warm wet
red place and cared tenderly for them until they hatched
into the first man and the first woman and were able to
swim for themselves. He told me several other stories of
Aliceander but that was the one that stuck most in my mind.

"Why have the Crocodile Men turned against necromancy?" I asked finally, made bold by his willingness to talk.
"They tolerated it well enough in the past."

"Because it pleases Aliceander to drive them out, just as
it pleased her to tolerate them in the past. That is all a
mortal needs know of a God's actions."

We stopped that night at a floating village—another platform of plaited reeds but much larger this time. Kemal said
the villagers might be persuaded to help us if we could work
out a way to attack the fortress.

"It is only a few canals away. You have been asking me
about its magical defenses, Ahmed," said Kemal with a sideways glance at me. "This close I can cast a small spell to
show them."

It was the kind of magic many nature worshippers could
do and gave no indication of whether or not Kemal was a
real mage. He leaned over the edge of the reed island and
scattered a handful of reed fluff on the water. Instantly a
picture of the fortress appeared, reflected with wonderful
clarity. The whole building glowed with necromantic wardings. Kemal gave us views of the fortress from all sides. We
could see no weak point in the magical protection. My heart
sank. I was almost certain I could not get through such
strong defenses.

"How do they power such spells? They must surely use
human beings as fodder for the demons to get such strength
into them. Do they not prey on the marsh folk?"

"The Crocodile would not have it so," said Kemal calmly.
"No, they grow their own. There is an enormous village
within the walls."

"But they would use up all the people," I said.

"It is a village of breeding couples," said Kemal. "They

are mindblasted prisoners who produce babes which can then be sacrificed to the demons in return for power."

Our whole party stared at him in horrified silence.

"But that's horrible," cried Shad. "Those poor little babes."

Kemal shrugged and turned away.

"It has always been so. At least they are not marsh folk."

His story and his response to it left a chill behind. I had begun to trust Kemal, but now I reconsidered.

I slept lightly again that night and sometime toward the center of the night I had a vivid dream. I dreamed I was lying on my reed mat looking out at the moonlight and a voice came from outside.

"Little mage. Little mage," it said. "Come out here. I have something to show you. Look in the water."

It was the voice of the dark and beautiful Andre and it filled me with a sensuous, lazy longing like the memory of lost love. I tried to move toward it and found myself paralyzed. I started awake in fright.

I was lying on my reed mat looking out at the moonlight beyond the hut. I sat up and looked around. Kitten and Shad were sleeping nearby. I pinched myself. I was awake. Something was missing. The voice!

Andre! But Andre was Bedazzer. Sometimes he had called to me in dreams, but only when there was a mirror to see me through. There were no mirrors here.

"Look in the water," he had said.

I got up and went outside.

The cool light of the moon reflected silver on the water as if it were a huge mirror. Tentatively I went to the edge of the island where Kemal had performed his Bowl of Seeing spell. I was not sure if I wanted to answer any calling from Bedazzer and yet . . . it might be useful to find out what he wanted.

I knelt down by the silvery water and waited. Almost immediately the shape began to appear on the surface. A magical projection. As the features slowly formed, I saw it was a woman's face, Madame Elena's.

I gasped.

"Little mage," said a voice. "You must not trust . . ."

Suddenly something hit me hard in the back and before I could think any more I was in the water flailing about, choking, blinded, unable to find the air.

I tried to reach out with my magic but . . . that damn necklace again. I was choking. Something huge brushed against my leg in the water. Then hands grabbed me and pulled and I was out in the blessed air again and being dragged up the island.

Suddenly a terrific roar cracked the silence and I saw something that looked like a log lunging at me through the water. Panicking, I seized the reeds and half threw myself, half crawled onto them, clambering over the person who was dragging me, tumbling, rolling, grabbing at the iron necklace on my neck and pulling.

The log lunged up onto the island and scrabbled at the edge with its claws. It let out another huge roar. Its crocodile mouth was all fangs, bone white and blood red and the stench of carrion looming over me. Then there was a blast of magic. The crocodile closed its mouth with a snap, gave a grunt and slid back into the water.

"You fool," shouted Kemal. I realized that we were clinging to each other. "What were you thinking of? You do not lean out over the water like that and you a foreigner. Of course a crocodile will take you, fool. Now I have offended Her and must make restitution."

A hubbub of people surrounded me, blocking out his scolding. Goat skins were brought and wrapped round me. I was patted dry. Yet as my terror drained away, I remembered that blow to the back. Someone had pushed me in. As Shad and Kitten helped me back to my hut, I looked up and saw Kemal watching me in calm silence and realized that now I would never know what Bedazzer had wanted to say to me.

I was freezing. Kitten piled the goat skins on top of me. Shad came and huddled against me. His warmth was welcome against my chilled back.

"What on earth happened out there, Dion?" he said softly.

"He pushed me in."

"What!" cried Kitten.

A shadow glided out of the back of the hut. It was Dally. She must have been waiting there.

"She's right," she said softly. "I saw him." She knelt beside me and rubbed my shoulder. "Oh you are shivering," she scolded. "Why are you such a fool, Aunt? Why didn't you watch your back?"

"Why didn't you, if you were so clever?" I snapped.

"But what were you both doing?" asked Shad.

"I had a dream about Bedazzer. I needed some air," said Dally

"It wasn't a dream," I said, teeth still chattering. "He was calling us. He was trying to communicate something."

I told them what had happened.

"You think Bedazzer is really still inside Madame Elena?" asked Dally.

"Who can say? I saw what he wanted to show me."

"You are both missing the point," said Kitten. "Bedazzer cannot hurt you just by communicating, but what about Kemal? Did he call up the crocodile? Did he try to kill Dion? We must keep a close watch on him and you must not be alone with him, Dion."

"I don't think he wanted to kill her," said Dally. "He pushed her in and pulled her straight out. He wanted to frighten her."

"Or maybe he wanted to stop me speaking with Bedazzer," I said.

The following morning we rowed out to see the necromantic fortress. Shortly after leaving the village we came to an area where the reeds had all died. There was no sign of birds or animals. Everything was suddenly silent, except for the sound of the dry grey stalks clattering together in the wind. They looked like the bars on a cage.

"What has happened here?" asked Shad. "This is horrible."

"A blight came out of the fortress during one of their evil experiments," said Kemal. "This part of our marsh has died. We cannot say when it will live again. It angered the Crocodile."

I could feel the absence of life. It reminded me of the land around Ruinac which had been destroyed by a demon. An experiment. I remembered Count Taras and his description of how Bezra Haziz had destroyed Smazor. Was a demon so destructive that even its insubstantial being could cause such damage? No wonder the Crocodile Men had turned against the necromancers. But why had they befriended death mages in the first place?

After paddling for a time we climbed out and crawled through the crunching brown stalks over a high muddy bank. There, to my surprise, was the fortress. It was very low for a fortress—only a couple of stories high. No wonder it could not be seen from a distance. It covered most of the small island it stood on. There would be room within those walls for the village Kemal had spoken of. But it was impossible to see it from here, because the walls were as high as the central tower and very strong looking.

"It is believed to go down into the ground for some way," said Kemal. "There are gratings all around it to let air in to the lower stories. And see that pipe. . . . There are a series of them and sometimes water comes out of them. Those lower stories must get very damp. The pipes are probably the outlet for some kind of pump. They are far too small to be crawled up without magic and now they are protected by strong wardings."

"And the gratings?" asked Kitten.

"They too are guarded from magical and physical attack. None of them are loose."

The fortress was closed up and there was no sign of anyone coming or going in the day we spent lying in the reeds watching it. Not surprising if the marsh folk had turned against the necromancers.

"Do they have good food stocks?" asked Kitten.

"Very good," said Kemal. "They could probably last six months or more like this."

The only movement near the fortress was among the crocodiles sunning themselves on the shores around it. There seemed to be an enormous number of them. Sometimes they slithered into the swirling water and swam away only to be replaced by others. Sometimes they just lay there with their wide gaping mouths open showing horrible arrays of yellowed teeth.

"Does the Crocodile God send them there?" I asked Kemal, who was crouching beside me.

"Perhaps," he said shortly. "Perhaps they simply come for the carrion. There is always plenty."

Later as we sat on the bank sharing a jug of cold kesh before returning to the village for the night, we discussed our prospects. Glumly.

"So much for dealing with Bedazzer without the Aramayans," I said. "We could never get into that fortress alone. We simply do not have the power."

"Well our journey is not entirely wasted," said Kitten. "At least we've done a useful reconnaissance for the demon hunters."

"Demon hunters," said Ahmed. "You can't imagine the complications that's going to cause."

"I can guess," said Kitten. "But I don't see how we can take that place alone. Come on. There's no point sitting here on this mud bank any longer."

"I shall not come with you," said Kemal. "There is someone I must meet with tonight. I shall return tomorrow."

We left him standing among the dead reeds and got into the canoes.

Since the previous night Shad had been sticking close to my side. He and Dally came in the same canoe with me, and they elected to paddle. They were not as fast as Ahmed and Hakim and we fell behind.

I sat in the prow of the canoe. Although I was enjoying the sun, I was wary. My experience with Kemal last night had prompted me to remove my iron necklace today.

"I wish we could use magic," said Dally, paddling away. "It would . . ."

"Sweet Tanza look at that!" cried Shad.

I turned at his cry and saw Kemal coming down the long waterway toward us. He glided over the surface of the water like a man skating on ice. His face was solemn. He did not react to us at all. The eerie sight captured our attention so that we did not take much notice when the canoe stopped with a thump against a mud bank.

There was a slight sucking sound. The sound made me turn fast enough to see something suddenly shoot up from the mud bank.

A tall dark figure lunged at me. Before I could react, it caught me in muddy arms and began to drag me out of the canoe.

Dally screamed and so did I. I thrust out a burst of power to push it away. There was a blast of ignition and mud exploded everywhere, but the arms around my body did not loosen. Shad and Dally were shouting. Again I blasted it with power and again and again. Mud spurted. I felt someone pulling at my feet, hands that clutched and then were gone.

I kicked and struggled and my hands thrust deep into and through mud, pulling pointless handfuls of it away. The thing was mud. All mud. I was up in the air above the canoe now and with a horrible squelching sucking sound, the figure was oozing back down into the mud bank. I struggled in its arms and threw out yet another blast of power but the mud was sucking me under. Behind me I heard Dally scream. The last thing I saw was the thing's pitiless eyes. Cold yellow reptile eyes with pupils like slits. I tried to gouge them as we went down but suddenly the mud came up over my face. Everything was black and thick and I was drowning in mud—thick, choking, slimy mud.

12

I HAD A dream. I dreamed of a mother with a child at her breast. I was the mother feeling the exquisite pleasure of the babe suckling me, but I was also the babe, lying warm and safe with the thick milk coursing down my throat, coursing down all over me.

I woke slowly and unwillingly from the luscious dream. I was curled up on something soft and warm. I rolled lazily.

Then a hard white light hit my eyelids, shattering the dream.

My mouth was full of mud. I choked and sat up quickly, spitting the mud out. I was covered in it.

Where on earth was I? To one side of me a series of wide steps rose up into a colonnade of grey stone arches. No building. Just a single line of graceful arches framing portions of blue sky.

I was lying on a warm mud bank, just below the bottom step. I remembered the mud figure dragging me down, remembered drowning in the brown sludge. I jumped up quickly and half-climbed, half-crawled up the hard stone steps, leaving the treacherous mud behind.

The climb was long and steep and my lungs felt full of

grit. I had to stop halfway up and lie down, exhausted, breath rasping in my throat. I coughed up black slime. Afterward I felt better. I looked back down the stairs at the muddy trail I had left and the place I had crawled from.

Below me at the bottom of the stairs was a murky pool, black as a piece of night. Across the other side of the pool were tall reeds crowned with feathery heads, rising up from the water like a sheer wall. The square pool was enclosed by the stair and the arches on two sides and by the reeds on the opposite two sides. Only the mud bank I had been lying on disrupted the terrible symmetry. I had an uneasy feeling that the bank was not permanent—that it moved with the will of whatever inhabited it.

Where are Shad and Dally? I thought suddenly with alarm. I must find them.

I turned and fright almost stopped my heart. A figure stood on the steps above me.

Where had that come from? Surely no one had been there before. Whoever it was was standing against the sun. I had to look sideways at it. I tried to be calm. I did not think it was Kemal. It looked like a woman. A very beautiful woman, though I was not sure how I knew that. She seemed to be wearing a long robe.

I sat back on my haunches and squinted up at her.

"Hello," I said tentatively. "Where am I?"

The figure turned with sinuous grace and moved out of the sun. I cried out in shock. Oh God! It was not a robe she was wearing, it was a tail, a huge lizard's tail. She turned her face to me. Cold yellow eyes with slit pupils stared down into mine from a face that had human features and yet was by no means human.

With the fear, magic began to flow through me. I summoned it to protect me.

"You dare!" shrieked a voice. She swept out an arm and magic flung me flat on my back against those stairs.

She was on top of me then. Arms on either side of me, fierce green face staring down into mine. That huge, cold magic lay like a stone on my chest. I tried to heave it off, but I could not. I tried again and again. I felt like I was scrabbling at the lid of a coffin, shut tight above me.

"I can't breathe," I gasped. "Let go."

The force pressing down on my chest burst away suddenly, but she still had my arms pinned to my sides.

She let out a hiss of breath.

"Fool. . . . Why did you come here?"

Her reptilian glare bored into me.

"Who are you?" I said. I was not going to tell this creature anything without knowing what she was. Was she some kind of necromantic being? I tried to reach out to sense her, but it was useless. She was simply too strong. It was like trying to sense the core of the sun.

With another hiss of breath the woman relaxed.

"You are a foolish mortal," she said in a tone of amused contempt. "And only a mortal. How did you get such power without tapping the other world?"

Then in an eye-blink she was gone. I was free. I sat up and looked quickly around, expecting a blow.

She stood behind me in one of the arches. For a moment I glimpsed two brown-shrouded figures behind her and then they were gone. How had she got up there so fast? And where were those others now?

I could see her clearly now. She was slender and enormously tall. Her skin was like that of a snake, all soft green-brown scales. Her skull was elegant—fine-boned and smooth-skinned except for a crest of dark green like a close-fitting cap on her head. She was breathtaking, shimmering with magic. In fact she shimmered with so much magic I was not sure there was any other substance in her.

"Who are you?" I asked again.

She walked down the steps toward me with a lazy swinging stride. Her tail dragged behind her on the ground like the train of an Aramayan countess. Here walks beauty, that stride said and it was right. Even to my human eyes this creature was delicate, graceful, and so beautiful. I was amazed at how beautiful she seemed, even though I was terrified.

"I am Aliceander. Aliceander the Crocodile," she said.

"Tell me who you are and what you are doing in my domain." She leaned down and said softly to my face, "And then I might let you live."

I pressed my trembling hands to the hot stone steps and tried not to cringe away from her. She was enormously stronger than me, whatever she was. Was she necromancy? She felt like Klementari magic, nature magic . . . like that huge cold magic I had felt moving in the marsh. Yes! That had been her! The spirit of the marsh. The Crocodile. The thing that all those marsh folk worshiped. Not some imaginary deity but an actual being here before me!

"My name is Dion Holyhands." Fear and wonder made me stammer. "I meant no harm coming here. I want to get into the fortress, the necromancer's fortress. There is someone there I am searching for."

"The abomination!" She spat out the word with such savagery that I thought she was going to bite me. But instead she stuck out a hand.

There were black claws on the end of each finger.

She put the claw on my cheek and drew it down ever so gently. I cannot describe how delicious the touch was. She must have been using magic on me, though I could not feel it. How otherwise can terror have a delicious touch?

"You seek the unnatural creature that those necromancers have brought across from the world of destroyers, don't you?"

She could only mean the world of demons and Bedazzer.

"Yes," I said breathlessly.

"But you cannot get into the fortress," she said. "The wardings are too strong."

"No. But my friends . . . Shad and Dally. What have you done with them?"

"She is here," said Aliceander simply.

She gestured and I saw that Dally was lying curled up on the mud bank at the bottom of the stairs just as I had been. Perhaps she was even dreaming of mothers and babies as I had.

"She dreams of her heart's desire," said Aliceander disconcertingly.

Suddenly I was terrified.

"And Shad, where is he? What have you done with him?"

"Nothing," she said. "He was of no use to me."

"Is he safe?"

"I do not harm my worshipers."

Her claw on my cheek turned my face back to hers.

"You cannot get into the fortress, can you? The wardings are too strong and your friends are not even mages."

"Perhaps," I said. I was angry that she would not tell me more of where Shad was. I hoped he was unharmed.

She looked at me. Her lips curved in amusement.

"No," I said. "I don't think we can."

"I shall help you," she said.

"Why?" I said without even thinking.

"Stupid mortal!" she roared. She reached out and her claws bit into my throat. "You don't ask questions of Gods."

The cold magic came down like mud. I struggled against it, trying to break through, but I was as helpless as a child.

She stared down into my eyes with her cold arrogant glare.

"I could kill you," she said. "I should kill you for your impiousness. But you could be useful to me."

"I beg pardon," I said. If I lulled her I might get a chance to get away. Despite my fear I felt excitement too. It was her glamor, the mysterious wonder of her. A creature that was neither human nor demon, but seemed to be made of pure nature magic. A creature that should not even have existed in this world. Suppose she could help me get into the fortress. . . . What an ally!

"Yes, that is right," she said softly. "Give yourself in service to the God."

Suddenly the thought of what our alliance might really mean came to me. The hair shivered on the back my neck. The Crocodile Men had taken payment to leave the necromancers alone. She had taken that payment. She'd been a friend of necromancy. Maybe she still was.

"Do you mean to give me to the necromancers?" I whispered fearfully.

She bent over me. "Still you ask questions, little mortal."
That beautiful reptile face was amused again. "Will you
never learn? You can feel my magic, I see that. Aliceander
sees that you are a very worthy tool. You will join with her
in breaking down the wardings. Then my crocodiles will
flood inside and you and I will destroy the abomination and
its masters."

"And will you destroy the fortress then?" I asked. She
had not exactly answered my question. I still wondered what
came after I helped her.

"You are such a fool!" hissed the Crocodile. "I know you
arrogant mages. You see no God greater than yourselves
and you will not admit one even when a God comes and
claws you in the face. Be grateful that such foolishness
amuses Aliceander, for you would not want to offend her."
She leaned closer to me. "Would you?"

"No," I gasped. Her eyes were like probes. I felt as if they
were exploring the insides of my skull. Did I really want to
aid such a creature—a creature who must have tolerated
necromancy in the past? This weird inhuman creature who
should not have existed under any system of magic I understood. I was almost certain I could not trust her. Yet the
chance to get into the fortress and destory Bedazzer. . . .
Or was this some convoluted demon plot?

"I can give you what you desire most in the world," said
Aliceander softly. She put her clawed hand on my belly. "I
am the giver of life. The life of the marsh. You will trust
me and help me and in return I shall not kill you as is your
due, but give you a child for your belly."

She was changing. Breasts swelled on her flat chest and
in the triangle beneath her belly she suddenly had a man's
penis and testicles.

She laughed at my surprise.

"I am a God," she said. "Not fixed by your mortal rules."
As I watched, all her sexual characteristics, male and female,
disappeared, shrinking back smoothly into her body. In a
moment her scaled torso was smooth and sleek again.

She spread clawlike hands over my cheeks and leaned

forward and kissed my mouth. A cold kiss but delightful. The mixture of delight and revulsion I felt amazed me.

"Tonight my Crocodile Men will come and we shall go to the fortress. You will prove yourself worthy of my gift then."

She turned and seemed to walk into the sunlight, up through the arches where the shrouded figures awaited her.

"For now, rest. My people will bring you food. Awaken your niece."

And suddenly she was gone.

"What if she does give us to the necromancers?" said Dally.

"Should we refuse to help her?" I said.

"Can we? She will kill us, won't she? Can't she? She is stronger than you, Aunt."

"But she might not be stronger than the two of us," I said.

"You don't really believe that, do you?"

"No. But is it logical that she would give us to the necromancers?"

"Would she be logical? She gives me the shivers. What manner of creature is she?"

"She uses nature magic. In fact I wonder if she is not a personification of that magic."

"Can nature magic take form and walk around like that?"

"It would be interesting to find out."

"Interesting? Interesting! The whole idea is horrible. You are a dreamer, Aunt. Has it occurred to you that she might just be one of Haziz's earlier experiments taking a convenient form? We are captives of this awful creature who is more powerful than both of us put together and all you can do is call her interesting."

"Well there seems no point in getting upset about our situation," I said mildly and then stopped, amazed at my own calm. Maybe I was braver than I thought. But I knew it wasn't courage. I felt the same wonder over Aliceander as I did over the life force in the marsh. I knew she was untrustworthy, but she felt completely different from the demons I had known. If only I could be sure that Shad was safe.

"I do not kill my worshipers," she had said.

Did that mean he was safe somewhere? I had to believe it did. Oh, I was a fool, blinded by her glamor. She had sheltered the necromancers all this time. Why? For money? That hardly seemed believable. What do Gods need with money?

Dally sat down and put her head in her hands.

After a moment she said, "You know, Aunt, while I was lying asleep on that bank, I could hear and see everything she said to you. I wanted to shout at you to fight her, but I could not even move. It was like being back in the phial. So helpless."

I put my hand on her shoulder and quite suddenly she leaned against me as if wanting closeness.

"You remember that time all those years ago when I asked you for Smazor's secret name," she said. "And you told me I was better dead than a demonmaster. Well when I was locked up in the phial I promised myself I would tell you this, but somehow . . . I was too proud, I guess. Anyway, you were right about demons. I came to recognize that they couldn't be used for any good purpose. And if I hadn't been tempted to call on Bedazzer when Haziz and Korosov had me in prison I'd never have been inside that phial."

She shuddered again. I put my arm around her

"No," I said, "but you probably wouldn't be alive now either. Haziz would have fed you to her demons."

"Dear old Aunt," said Dally gruffly. "You know you're really not a bad sort at all." She pulled away from me and looked down at her hands, embarrassed.

"I'm gratified you think so," I said. But I was touched.

"When I left the great Cathedral I didn't know what to do. I was afraid of you, I guess. Bedazzer kept whispering in my ear that you would kill me if you got the chance."

"Oh Dally. I never would have."

"I know that now. . . . He is a deceiver like all his kind. I kept a stone hand from one of those statues in the Cathedral, do you remember?"

How could I forget. Darmen Stalker the demonmaster had filled his Cathedral with statues that the demons could animate in this world. They could draw life force through them as well, if they could get hold of anything alive. I was still amazed that I had been six days in that Cathedral without being drained by one of those hungry destroyers.

"Bedazzer could animate the hand at will," she continued. "I carried it with me. I was so lonely and he was my only friend. He rescued me several times in the beginning. There were people who sought to rape or rob a girl traveling alone. If I pressed the hand to their flesh, Bedazzer fed on them and killed them. And saved me. But I was never very easy with him. Some part of me must have believed you after all. And twice he tricked me into killing innocent people. I robbed a couple of drunken sailors in Olbia. He told me he'd just make them unconscious, but when he'd finished both of them were dead. That was how I got money for the passage to Aramaya and how I escaped the witchfinders who came looking for me."

"You don't have to tell me this."

She was not listening to me, caught up as she was in her unpleasant memories.

"I met Marianne on the boat to Aramaya. She was an old woman traveling alone. She had a weak heart. She wanted to see Karanagrad before she died. Oh she was a lovely woman. She was so kind to me and I was happy caring for her. Then later when she was dying in Karanagrad, I begged Bedazzer to save her for me. He told me to lay the hand on her chest and to cut my finger for some blood. He had the gall to tell me afterward that she had been too weak to take the treatment, but I knew that he had sucked out her life force. I knew it. I'd killed her. Poor, dear, Marianne."

Her voice broke on a sob. I tried to put my arm around her again, but she shrugged me off.

"After that the demon hunters came, because, as you know, using a demon in that way is necromantic magic and they watch for it. I got away and I destroyed the hand and although I did things later for Popov that I'm not proud of,

I'd learned my lesson. I'd learned the hard way that you were right."

What could I say to this confession? Her remorse was obvious. We sat there in silence and I patted Dally's back as comfortingly as I could. I did not feel it was very adequate consolation but so little consolation ever is.

"Eat something," I said at last. "Then we should try and sleep. You will need your strength whatever happens to-night. We must fight together at our best. We may be able to take the necromancers even if we cannot best Her."

A shrouded figure with scaly brown hands had brought us a plate of food. Dally ate some bread and cheese. I noticed she left the meat. I did not blame her. I did not want to eat the Crocodile's meat either.

"Think, Dally. Isn't this Aliceander at war with the necromancers now? Surely that is cause for hope."

"If even she cannot get into the fortress without help, that does not argue that we have much chance of besting the necromancers."

"No, it does not mean that at all," I said, suprised that she didn't know this. But then her education had been un-usual. "Magic in defense is much stronger than magic in attack. They could keep her out and still be weaker than she. We shall just have to wait and see. Imagine if she is telling the truth. We will destroy Bedazzer."

"Yes," said Dally trying to sound enthusiastic. She nib-bled gingerly at the bread and cheese. I watched her eat. I was certainly a fool to find anything exciting about Alicean-der and yet. . . . Suddenly all our talk of demons came back to me. Demons fed on life force, but so did nature magic. Aliceander was a being of nature magic. Did she too feed on life force? Had the necromancers fed her on those poor babes as they had the demons? Had this been her price? I went cold at the very thought of it.

"Tell me, Aunt," said Dally suddenly. "If everything goes as she says it will, would you really take a child from that creature?"

"Oh God, no!" I cried without even thinking about it.

Some strange and sinister thing growing inside me? The very thought filled me with squirming horror.

"Are you sure, Aunt?"

"Certain," I said and I realized to my surprise that I had reached the end of my search. There was a limit to how far I would go for a child. And suddenly I could see clearly how this longing had begun. It had begun with Shad and my love for him. With a desire to express that love in making something special together—to have a physical manifestation of love. And perhaps to have something in case our love ended as I had always feared it would, even in the very beginning. I had wanted Shad's child. When had that changed? Had it changed?

Once again I longed to know of Shad and if he was safe. But the only way to find out now was to get through this.

"We shall have to do better at fighting together, Aunt." Dally broke in on my thoughts. "That business at the mud bank was a fiasco."

"Mmmm. Yes we must. Here. We must try and tune ourselves better to each other. Take my hand, Dally. Relax. Open yourself to me."

"Relax," said Aliceander's voice in the darkness. "Open yourself to the God." Her claws dug into my flesh.

A full white moon hung overhead. The air was thick with sweet-smelling smoke. The drums pounded a rhythm as the Crocodile Men drummed themselves into a battle frenzy. All around us dark figures leaped and shouted in the firelight until they collapsed, writhing on the ground, to slide finally headfirst off the bank. The moonlit water was full of long shapes silently snaking and twining.

I relaxed as best I could and immediately the cold magic burst through all my barriers, overwhelming me. Resisting the urge to push it away, I let my own magic flow with it, not blended so much as moving side by side, slow and smooth like a layer of honey spread over bread. Bones and muscles begin to stretch and groan as my face lengthened to a snout and my body began to flatten into something harder and longer and much, much crueler.

13

ODIES, TAILS, SNOUTS, and claws thrashed all around me. My hard new skin loved the cold wetness and the rough contact of other hides. I could see in this brown world—see the mud and the reeds and the dark crocodile bodies so surprisingly graceful in the water around me. I could see the little silvery movement of fish beneath, a sight which made my teeth ache with the desire to chomp down. Using my paws, I thrust my compact killer's body down to the marsh bottom. My claws dug deliciously into the ooze.

But Aliceander called and her call could not be denied. This new body felt her brutal beauty strongly. All the magic in my being was focused on her. I could sense her cold, implacable nature, but still I was too human to truly know her, mysterious creature that she was.

As I joined the sinuous horde, a small part of me still whimpered with terror at suffocating, at being lost, at being attacked by those dark crocodiles. I kept close to the side of the shining Aliceander and when she rose to breathe I rose too. I could not be sure where Dally was—I could not feel her through the beacon of Aliceander's power, but I thought she was the crocodile who stuck close to my side.

Snaking together through the water, we came to a stone wall slimed with river weed. It was so deep and dark here that even with my new vision I could not see the bottom. The crocodiles swam along the curve of the wall. At one point it bulged outward as something like a buttress jutted from it, running down into the darkness beneath.

The crocodiles rose to the surface to breathe and then dove, plunging down into the blackness, till even Aliceander was just rough skin felt in darkness. Yet still I had no doubt about her call and followed without faltering.

We dove until the bottom mud oozed beneath my snout. Together we slithered through that slime. Stone scraped over my back and then we were swimming upward. Above us was a small circle of light which got bigger and bigger as we got closer. We were inside some kind of shaft. It was getting lighter. I could see that we were circled by manmade stone walls. We were inside the buttress. I hoped for air at the top. My lungs were beginning to ache. Above, the circle of light widened and widened till I could dimly see the lip of the hole.

Then, almost at the top, we suddenly thudded against an invisible barrier. Blue runes flashed out. Panic filled me. I must have air. My chest was screaming for air. I must draw in some air! But where from? I struggled. The magic within me tried to draw air though the walls but they were crawling with blue runes and spells.

Had Aliceander brought me here to kill me? Had she . . . ?

The Crocodile turned and dug her claw sharply into my chest. Suddenly my lungs relaxed, full of the most crystal-pure air. I calmed my magic, gathered it together, felt it twining with Aliceander's cold power. Aliceander, Dally, and I rose through the water, magic blending and moving together like wonderful music and the warding burst before us in a great booming release and the tingling of shattered magic.

"Onward, onward," urged the silent call of Aliceander. The crocodiles streamed through the broken warding in a frenzy.

Beyond was a ramp, a steep belly-dragging climb on slippery stone up toward a dark room lit by a few smoky torches. The slope was thick with crocodiles swarming, writhing, thrashing their tails as they clawed heedlessly up, past and over each other to the top of the ramp and out into the room beyond. My crocodile body was hard to manage out of the water and the noncrocodile me dreaded sliding back into the dark shaft. For a time I could only lie still, clinging to the ramp under the sharp scaly horde.

From beyond the lip of the ramp terrible screams broke through the deep grunts and bellows of the crocodiles. Something long and thin came hurtling through the air and down onto the ramp. A nearby crocodile lurched upward and grabbed it in its jaws. I only realized it was a human arm when I saw the hand dangling limply out between the reptile's teeth before the crocodile chomped it down.

By the time I reached the top, a magical battle had begun. Balls of magic fire burst nearby as I dragged myself over the lip of the hole. The floor shook. The air was full of the smell of singeing crocodile flesh. There was answering green fire from the chamber floor.

I wanted to join in but . . . Curse this clumsy body! This close to the ground and with only crocodile eyes, I could not work out where the fireballs were coming from. All I could see were the lower walls of a huge chamber and a rain of fireballs dropping from above.

The chill gaze of Aliceander's magical force was turned away from me, although I sensed it nearby. Here was the opportunity to change my form. Fast as I could I scrabbled away from the squirming mass of crocodiles and the blasts of fire. There was some kind of stone thing before me. I slithered behind it and hunched there. Muscles groaning and bones shrieking, I forced myself slowly back through the change, feeling the magic that had come from Aliceander flaking away like dry mud.

It would have been easier to change more quickly, but a quick change is so painful that it is hard to concentrate on your surroundings. I was afraid of the other crocodiles whose killing frenzy filled the chamber and who might easily mistake me for prey. Meanwhile the fireballs rained down, shaking the chamber with their detonation and hitting my stone barrier.

As the blurring of change-pain cleared, the first thing I noticed on the wall above me was a huge mirror covered in black runes. The scratched glass indicated that it was used for magic regularly. The stone barrier I lay behind was an altar and I lay between it and the mirror, while behind me was the chamber where crocodiles were still crawling out of the hole in the floor. In the misty depths of the mirror I could see exactly what was going on back there. From a gallery running around the top of this huge chamber, ten or so defending mages rained down fireballs. The stairs leading up to the gallery teemed with a green-brown mass of crocodiles slowly working their way upward against the destructive blasts of magic.

There were other mirrors all around the chamber wall, each with a stone altar before it. What luck! We were in the fortress's torture chamber, the place where people were sacrificed to demons and their life force ransomed in return for the demon's magic. That ramp in the floor must be where they disposed of the bodies. This was the center of the fortress, the place that powered it, and we were in a unique position to cripple that power.

Without a second thought I threw out a blast of power that shattered the mirror before me.

The reaction was instantaneous. Even before the glass had stopped showering through the air, every fireball in the room was focused on my hiding place. The storm of fire was so powerful that it destroyed the stone table. I ran for my life, covering myself with power, running along the line of mirrors.

To hold that tremendous storm off by myself would have made it impossible to do anything else. However I knew that they would not dare throw such force at the mirrors for fear of breaking them. As I threw myself behind another stone altar with another mirror behind me, the fireballs lessened abruptly. But they could see my reflection in that mirror and the bursts of magical fire were now delivered with more precision, pounding away at the stone of my hiding place. I did not bother returning their magical fire. Instead I stuck my head round the side of the altar whenever I had the chance and threw wild blasts of shattering power at the other mirrors around the room. Three times I filled the air with broken glass, but the force of the mages' fire was strong. From what I could see in my mirror, half the mages were now fighting the crocodiles while the other half sent blasts my way. This meant that the teeming horde of crocodiles was gradually climbing higher toward that gallery.

Smash! A mirror nearby shattered. I hadn't shattered it. Either the crocodiles had caught on to smashing the mirrors or . . . Dally! Dally was safe and with any luck seeing through human eyes again.

Suddenly a huge face appeared in the mirror behind me. Bedazzer. Bedazzer as himself all fangs and talons and huge snout.

Screaming.

"You stupid bitch! Are you insane? To aid that evil thing, that creature! She will destroy you! She will feast on your life force like she has on others."

Suddenly the whole room boomed. Bits of stone and glass filled the air. I hit the floor, half stunned with the impact. When I pulled my hands away from my face again, Bedazzer was gone. Aliceander was standing over me.

"I did not say you could destroy the mirrors," she roared. She looked even more monstrous than Bedazzer as she reached down and gripped me around the throat.

"I . . ." I almost told her I hadn't. Dally must have. Or more likely the necromancers. Was this a sign they were abandoning the fortress? Then the astonishing nature of the reprimand struck me.

"Why not? It's the only way to stop . . ."

"Why not? You ask me why not?"

Still gripping me by the throat, she lifted me high into the air. Her talons dug into my flesh. It hurt so much. I tried to pull myself out of her grasp, but she held on and shook me about.

"Arrogant mage. To question a God."

She pulled me closer to her. Her face was ferocious.

"I tire of you. No more of your arrogance. You have served your purpose."

Suddenly a fireball enveloped us. I saw it looming over her shoulder just in time to protect myself. Aliceander didn't. As the roaring flames engulfed us, she let go with a yowl and I tumbled to the floor at her feet. Some instinct of self-presevation prompted me to fling myself away from her as hard as I could go. As I crawled blindly across the floor, something gripped my hand. Then, somehow, I was out of the fireball, my hand in Dally's, running across the chamber toward the mass of crocodiles. They turned toward us like a roaring wave.

"Jump," I shouted to Dally, gripping her around the waist as I heaved us both into the air. The crocodiles lunged up at us. We leaped above that terrible green tide with only inches to spare. The air crackled with magic as we leaped through it, but we made it onto the gallery. We dragged our stunned bodies up, ready to fight. Only to discover that the gallery was empty.

At the end, where the stair had led down to the torture chamber, there was only empty space, the stone wall around it smoking slightly. At the other end was a closed door. Without another thought, Dally and I made for the door, spurred on by the blasts of magical fire that followed us and the terrible yowling scream that came from Aliceander below.

The hallway beyond the door was empty too.

"Do you think they've run?" I cried.

"Could be," shouted Dally running away down the passage. "Come on. I think I know the way."

The fortress was full of magic. Bright blue runes thrummed on the walls and the air crackled with it. We heard shuddering blasts of power coming from above, proving that at least someone was still here. But once, as we ran past a place were the wall had collapsed, I caught a glimpse of the night sky above and saw balls of blue fire shooting away from the fortress. Escaping necromancers.

"Quickly, Dally! They're getting away!"

"Up here," cried Dally, turning up a stair. "This is where they took me to put Bedazzer in me. I'm sure of it."

We sprinted up the winding staircase two steps at a time. At the top was another big room and another mirror. Blue runes stood out around it. A gateway! An open gateway! The floor was slick with blood. There were bodies lying everywhere. I ran anxiously toward the gateway and saw that not all the runes were glowing. Thank God! It was not fully open.

"Aunt! Here!" shouted Dally. She was standing over by the altar stone. Two trussed up bodies wriggled on it.

One was Madame Elena. The other was Bezra Haziz. Both of them wore the iron manacles which stopped them from using their magical powers.

Elena was screaming hysterically.

"Help me!" shouted Haziz. "That thing's coming. Those bastards left me here for her vengeance. We have to get him out of here. She mustn't have him. You've got to help me open a gateway. Quickly. You can do it without sacrifices. I know you can. Come on. Untie me. Quickly woman, we have to do something. If she gets him, there'll be all hell to pay."

Dally and I just stared.

Which one was Bedazzer? Was he still in Madame Elena who was screaming hysterically, or Haziz who was calm and cool? Logically it would be the calm Haziz, but also logically Bedazzer would conceal himself for as long as possible and that meant acting whatever part needed to be played. I wasn't about to make any quick decisions. I would not set either of them free.

"God! Aunt, what'll we do?" said Dally.

There was no time for finesse. I could hear the growling and shrieking of Crocodile Men nearby.

"We have to get out of here. And take them with us. Undo their feet."

"Are you insane?" shrieked Haziz. "We have to open that gateway. It's our only hope. If she gets hold of him she'll consume him. Then she'll be able to draw on his power. She'll be three times as dangerous."

Perhaps Aliceander could draw on Bedazzer's power like that. Who knew what she could do? Perhaps Haziz was simply trying to save a valuable demon from destruction. Or perhaps she was Bedazzer trying to fool me into opening a way for his body into this world. None of these reasons were good enough to make me open a gate. I turned and shattered the mirror. Both Haziz and Elena let out terrible shrieks.

Ignoring Haziz's furious shouting and her attempts to kick and bite me, I pulled the bonds off her ankles and dragged her up onto her feet. Dally, who was blessedly quick, followed suit with Elena.

"I'll take these two," I cried to Dally. "Can you get yourself out of here?"

"I think so."

I seized both struggling women under my arms and with a surge of power threw myself at a smashed window on the other side of the room. Up and up and through and out into the night sky and . . .

Suddenly the air seemed to turn to mud. Thick, invisible mud. I could not break free, was stuck fast in it. My magic could not get a grip on it. I felt myself sliding back.

I turned in midair and saw her.

Aliceander the Crocodile was standing on the floor beneath the window. From the palm of her hand came shining golden rays of power, power that spread over me like a net and caught me up. She threw back her head and laughed a sharp-toothed laugh. Then she began dragging me back like a fisherman drags the fish.

I pulled away as hard as I could, but the slow dragging was inexorable. She was stronger than me and she had the whole marsh to draw on. I slid and slid, resisting all the way, down, down toward the window.

"I will have it," screamed Aliceander with wild triumph. "I will have it and then I will have you, arrogant cow mage."

I had to stop myself. In desperation I flung myself from side to side searching for a weak point, but I could not break out of the net.

But I could . . .

I threw myself downward just as I was about to slide over the windowsill.

The wall was strong. I clung to the window frame, pushing myself down. The magical net dragged and stopped. My body was jammed hard against the wall, with just my head and shoulders above the windowframe. I braced myself with magic against that wonderful strong wall, feeling the runes that held it together, strong runes, thrumming against my belly. I hung on for dear life.

Aliceander yowled. We must have looked infuriatingly close, Haziz, Elena, and me, our heads sticking ridiculously in at the window. Furiously she howled and dragged and dragged at me. The force of the net dug agonizingly into me, but still I held on, stuck fast.

Elena was still shrieking hysterically in my ear and Haziz was cursing in the other one.

"What can I do Aunt?" cried Dally, appearing beside me.

"Get away," I cried. "Get help. I think I've got a chance here."

I was lying but I wanted her out of this.

"You can let me go," shouted Haziz. "For God's sake. Let me go and I can help you. The three of us might have some chance. Quickly now."

Aliceander shouted at the Crocodile Men and several of them began to climb up the wall toward us.

"I will have you," she screamed. "I will have you all."

Dally knocked them off with a blow of magic but more started to climb.

"We have to risk it!" she cried in my ear.

She was right. It was worth the risk. We were all in this together. If Bedazzer was in Haziz, he would surely wait till we got free before he tried anything. I reached over and using the force of magic broke the iron collar off Haziz's neck. I did the same with Elena.

"Together," said Dally. "Come on! Pull!"

With a mighty heave the four of us pulled. I felt the force strain. It loosened and broke. We thrust ourselves backward as hard as we could go. I felt Dally and Elena's magic and Haziz's even stronger magic surging all around me. We shot away from the wall and plunged through the air. As we plunged, I felt Haziz turn against my arm, saw her lean toward me, mouth open, felt the surge of her magic change direction, saw something white inside her mouth . . .

"No," I screamed. Terrified, unthinking, I struck at Haziz with all my force and she, screaming, suddenly fell away. She righted herself with magic, seemed to lunge away sideways with a sly glance and then sudden horror filled her face. Golden tendrils of power gripped her.

"No, No!" she screamed and it was Bedazzer's demon yowl this time. "Save me! Save me, little mage!"

She plummeted back through the window, caught in Aliceander's force. Aliceander seized her in her claws with a triumphant howl.

"Die, Abomination!" she shrieked. And she put her hands into Haziz's chest and ripped her open like an old shirt, thrusting her face savagely into the cavity.

Did I really see her swallowing white mist? I know I heard a final terrible howl from Bedazzer as Aliceander lifted her bloody face to the sky. Then he was gone. Completely gone. Aliceander slumped to the ground and began to crawl drunkenly away. The Crocodile Men gathered around her.

And so Bedazzer finally left me.

Elena laughed and screamed hysterically against my shoulder. Dally plucked at me.

"Come on, Aunt! Let's go while we still can."

I took her hand and as fast as we could we raced up into the dark sky above the marsh.

There seemed no point in disguising our magic now and using it helped us find the others. They were very close, hiding in the reeds near the tower and we had to turn back in our tracks to reach them. Shad was safe. The others had found him floating unconscious in our canoe. They had figured our disappearance had something to do with the fortress and they had returned to see if they could rescue us.

Of the fearful journey back afterward I will say little. It was all very well for me to use magic to find the direction of Shebaz and to push the boats along as fast as I could, but the marsh was a maze and every path seemed to end in a dike or canal going the wrong way. And Madame Elena, who had shared her body with a demon's spirit for many days, was in a terrible state and needed all Dally's and my skill to prevent her from slipping into madness and taking her own life. Thank God for Shad's superior woodcraft. He had a fair memory of the route Kemal had used to bring us to the fortress. Even then it was horribly slow and every moment I expected Aliceander to explode out of a mud bank shrieking her fury.

But there was no sign of her and the marsh folk we met were kind and helpful. I could not help remembering how she had collapsed after swallowing Bedazzer. Perhaps she was too harmed by him to be capable of coming after us.

Still, I was glad when on the morning of the second day we saw the towers of Shebaz and even more glad when I saw the huge riverboats bearing the insignia of the demon hunters, riding at anchor in the river.

Once again I was bringing my friends into shore using magic and once again Nikoli was waiting there for me, though this time he had several regiments of real demon hunters behind him. And beside him stood a tall, distingished-looking man with military bearing.

"Misha," shouted Kitten, and when we pulled up to the dock she leaped out and threw herself into his arms in a most un-Aramayan manner.

14

IT WAS EARLY morning in Shebaz. The sun was a red ball through the grey river mist. The water looked refreshing, but I could not look at it without thinking of crocodiles. And yet I had seen no crocodiles in Shebaz at all. It was as if they had all withdrawn west down the river, to where She lay in the marsh, dangerous but mysteriously silent. Up here on the escarpment where the temple of Het stood there were few people about. And yet someone called my name. I turned and saw Nikoli coming toward me.

I did not know how to respond. He had been cool and distant to me ever since we had been in Shebaz. Nobody would ever have guessed we had once been lovers.

Yet now he came straight up to me and took my hand.

"You are really going back to Ruinac with him?" he asked precipitously.

"Yes. I'm so sorry."

He stood there for a moment head bowed, holding my hand tightly in his.

"You are the only woman I ever met that I could really share things with," he said softly as if he were making a disreputable admission. "Does that mean nothing to you? He's not a mage like we are."

"Our sharing meant a great deal to me," I said. "I shall miss it. I wish we could remain friends."

"I don't think I have a big enough heart for that," Nikoli said. He stared away down the river. It was too painful for us to meet each other's eyes.

"I understand," I said, because I did. It's self-indulgent to expect someone to love you, even as much as a friend does, after you have rejected them. Still the bitterness in his voice saddened me. He had been caught in the middle. I wished we were not having this conversation. I wished we had met when I had been truly free. We would have made something special together. But I knew that though Nikoli and I shared magecraft, Shad and I agreed on what constituted right and wrong and on what was honorable and valuable, and this was a much more important thing to share.

"I will be leaving Shebaz tomorrow," he said. "There is no work for the demon hunters here and Madame Elena needs better care. I shall escort her back to Akieva."

He lifted my hand to his lips and kissed it quickly.

"I will never forget you, Dion," he said, and then he turned and was gone.

"I will remember you too," I called after his tall dark figure.

I felt wretched, burdened down with guilt and sorrow. Surely Nikoli deserved happiness as much as anyone else after the lonely life he had led with a wife who hated him and children he saw only in spring. But as I turned and went back along the temple terrace, there was relief too. Things had been resolved and I felt certain now that I was on the right path.

I did not blame Nikoli for going away so quickly. Our party had resolved itself into a series of couples which could only have made things worse for him. Shad and I, Kitten and Misha. Since he had come to Shebaz I had had a chance to get to know Misha, or Colonel Michael Dukov of the city watch as he was properly known. I was impressed with how much he reminded me of Kitten. Adventurers, both of them.

Would he be her last lover or a brief passion? I think not even Kitten knew the answer to that, but I was certain she would enjoy whatever happened with her usual zest for living.

And Dally and Ahmed were as devoted as ever. I gave their union an Aunt's blessing, though I would never dare to tell Dally that. They would be unwise to return to the marshes now that Dally had so offended Aliceander. This meant that their days of harassing the Aramayans were probably over, for which I was secretly glad. Ahmed talked of returning to his father's tents in the deep desert. I hoped it would be an exciting enough life for them.

But I was not thinking of them now as I wandered in the fresh morning air, looking at the faces carved on the temple pillars. I was thinking of Aliceander. I had told the demon hunters simply that I had been kidnapped by the Crocodile Men. Had I been wise to disguise her part in this? I was certain now that Aliceander had given the necromancers sanctuary in return for some of the life force that had been released to feed their demons. Should I not have encouraged the demon hunters to come with me into the marsh and destroy her? It was probably the right thing to do. After all, you must kill a cattle dog when it gets a taste for the blood of the cattle.

And yet was it as simple as that? Were the marsh folk victims of an evil God? I did not think so. I was almost certain that Aliceander had swallowed Bedazzer to protect the marsh and her worshipers. Letting loose Smazor's being had put a blight on the whole area around the fortress and Bedazzer would have been just as destructive, and she must have known perfectly well how swallowing it would affect her. I heard later that it was a bad season in the marsh that year. The animals and humans were not fertile and the reeds produced few seed heads.

No, evil as her pact was, Aliceander had protected the marsh folk faithfully for generations. I could not really believe her to be wicked. She knew enough to hate Bedazzer. She was a creator as well as a destroyer and she must naturally abominate a being who could only destroy. Though I wondered often if I was right, I chose to do nothing.

Her evil was nothing compared to Bedazzer's. He had been a shadow in the background for most of my adult life. I was certain he was destroyed. My certainty surprised me, for I had not seen him for several years before coming to the marsh. But perhaps I had always sensed him there lurking malignantly inside mirrors, waiting for me. I was relieved he was gone, but in a way he had been part of the terror and wonder of magic and now that too was diminished.

For three nights in Shebaz I had the same dream.

I dreamed that Kemal came to me; Kemal of the knowing eyes. Stretching his hands out through the whispering green reeds, he said, "Here is Her gift for you."

In his hand was a big green lily leaf and lying on it was a tiny baby no bigger than my finger. It glowed warm and red, more beautiful than any jewel. I longed, oh, how I longed, to take it in my hands and clasp it to my chest where I knew it would melt and become one with me.

For the first two days I had been tormented by that dream. I had felt again all the emptiness and anguish of Alinya's death.

Am I a fool to refuse my only opportunity of ever having a child? I thought.

Yet I could not bear the thought of any seed of Aliceander's growing within me, even though I tried and tried to master my revulsion. I knew that even if she meant her offer she would exact some terrible price in return for the gift.

On the third day Shad and I talked about the future. We resolved to put our longing for a child behind us as best we could and let nature take whatever course it chose. As for the lands in Ruinac over which we had worked so hard, we agreed to offer to train my nephew Derrum as our heir. He was a serious, painstaking lad who would make a good lord and, more to the point, he was the only child in my family who had no magical powers.

Afterward I fell into a restless sleep and Kemal was waiting there again, gliding through the reeds with his huge green leaf and beautiful gift. Sometimes in that half-world between sleep and life you can change dreams. Summoning a tremendous effort, I closed the leaf over the jewel of life within and pushed Kemal's hands away. As I did so I saw a long glowing red cord leading from the child back into the reeds. I pulled away quickly lest I tangle myself in it and woke, with a start, to find myself lying on the bed beside Shad, dripping with perspiration.

"Dion," he said tentatively. "What happened? You never glowed with green light in your sleep before."

I walked back through the quiet streets of Shebaz to the house where I was staying and climbed the series of ladders to my room. It was dark and hot in the room and I pushed open the shutters. Sun fell on the bed where Shad lay. The light fell across his lean hairy chest and he stirred.

"That sun is wonderful," he said, rolling over with a long sensuous stretch and smiling at me. The skin round his eyes crinkled delightfully when he smiled.

"Have you been out?" he asked.

"It was such a lovely morning," I said. "I saw Nikoli. He is leaving tomorrow."

His face took on a vulnerable look.

"Are you sorry?" he said softly.

"Only for Nikoli," I said. "Not for me."

I went over and put my arms around him and felt his arms closing to hold me.

I would probably never have a child and sometimes I would be bitter and sad about it. But there would be other sources of happiness. That seemed certain.